C0-APP-691

Behind the Slickrock Curtain

A Project Petrichor Environmental Thriller

Jonathan P. Thompson

***

Lost Souls press

Published in the United States by
Lost Souls Press
Colorado
www.lostsoulspress.com

ISBN: 978-1-7346553-08

Cover design, interior design, and artwork by
Jonathan P. Thompson

"The ideal subject of totalitarian rule is not the convinced Nazi or the convinced Communist, but people for whom the distinction between fact and fiction and the distinction between true and false no longer exist."
— Hannah Arendt, *The Origins of Totalitarianism*

"Truth isn't truth."
— Rudy Giuliani, August 2018

Dedicated to the memory of
Lisa "Juniper" Matlock
1968-2019

PART ONE

Sacrifice for the Sun

Sometime in the 1990s, on the night of the winter solstice.

The old car creaked and bobbed along the two-track road over an undulating sea of stone, the wailing of Ennio Morricone's Spaghetti Western tunes slicing through the silence. The old Rambler American station wagon rolled to a stop, the engine fluttered off, the headlights went dark. The motor ticked and gurgled, and as the heat escaped from the steel cocoon of the car, the breath of the two occupants enveloped their heads. Starlight touched the stone, a satellite glided silently across the sky, and the blinking red and white beacons of a jet plane carrying its human load from Los Angeles to Chicago scraped through the moonless night.

The man in the passenger seat, long with long features, his dirty-blonde hair jutting out from a black wool hat, spoke: "Malcolm, I …"

"I know, it's a big leap, Peter," Malcolm said as he flexed his gloved fists anxiously. "And I know we've been talking about this forever, but this is it. I've got a line on a building, an old fruit warehouse out toward Bayfield, and get this, I even found a printing press. Hand-cranked. We can print out a broadside — a radical newspaper that gets the truth out there, at last. I figure we call it the Animas Art Collective. Or maybe the Durango Art and Culture Collective? Except I want it to be political, too, you know? I want to change the way people think and do things. To be a catalyst for a paradigm shift. Or is just calling it a 'collective' enough?"

"Calling it a collective is probably just enough to get our asses kicked, if that's what you mean. You shouldn't have drank that huge coffee from the gas station, Malcolm. You're talking like your head's about to explode."

"It is about to explode. I'm about to explode. We gotta do this thing before

..."

"Before what?"

"Before our hometown gets too gentrified. A real estate office opened up in the old hardware store on Main. Pretty soon there won't be anything left downtown except land pimps and t-shirt shops and faux fancy restaurants. It's outta hand. And if we don't do this, then someone else will, only it will be a watered down version made for mass consumption by retirees and fitness freaks."

"Say we do it, Malcolm. Say we move into an old barn and we rope in all three other artists in Durango into joining our little commune ..."

"Collective, dude. Not a commune. This isn't some hippy bullshit."

"Collective. Then how do we fund the thing?"

"We sell our art, our books. We get grants. I don't know. We sell my cookies. They're famous among a certain Durango demographic."

"Middle-aged divorcees, you mean? The ones who like you because you're semi-literate and you're not old enough to have a bunch of baggage, yet? The ones who think you might be good in the sack because you like Rilke?"

"They like my cookies, you asshole. They go apeshit for them. And they're smart. I bet Alice Smith would even join our collective."

"I'm sure she would. And next thing you'd know you'd be boinking your eleventh-grade English teacher."

"What kind of slut do you take me for? Look, I even mentioned it to Yvonne Martin. She liked the idea. Said she was too old to be a member of any such thing, but that she'd donate a painting."

"You talked to Yvonne?" Something caught in Peter's voice. Jealousy? Anxiety? Yvonne Martin was the pre-eminent painter of the region, and Peter had emulated her with his own art. She was, in some ways, the spark behind the idea of the Collective, even if she didn't know it.

"She comes into the bakery a lot. It's not like we had a big heart-to-heart or anything. Relax. Also, members would have to pay some kind of membership fee or something, right? I'd have to keep working in the bakery at first, and you'd have to keep your job for a while."

"Dude, I'm a short-order cook at Lori's Family Dining."

"Exactly. A local institution."

"The official tagline is 'legs and eggs.' Where's the culture in that, Malcolm?"

"Hey, is that one waitress, Donna, is she still working there?"

"Jesus, dude. And that's another thing: How long will it be till you meet someone and fall in love and forget about this whole pipe dream once again? How much of this is just you trying to distract yourself from Maggie dumping you, anyway?"

"It's not like that. I promise I won't fall for anyone who's not in the Collective. Okay?"

"And what about these books that you keep talking about? Who's going to write them? A printing press only can do so much."

"Exactomundo, bro. I already wrote one." Brautigan craned around and reached into the back seat and dug out a cardboard box, of the kind that holds a ream of copier paper or a manuscript. Two big rubber bands circled the box, the lid covered with intricate ball-point-pen doodles. As Brautigan lifted it he marveled at the impossible heft of the stack of paper, and of the words. "Voila."

"Wow. What is it?"

"My first novel. It's sort of a postmodern coming of age, midlife crisis thing," Malcolm mumbled. "About an old uranium miner and two brothers and one's dying and the other's morally bankrupt because he lost his connection to place, and maybe the brothers are actually two sides of the same person, and, well, you get the picture."

"Hmmm," said Peter, inspecting the box. "Hildebrandt's Hideout. Good name. Publisher?"

"Yeah, I've got a publisher: The Durango Arts Collective."

"Okay. Well, I'm fucking freezing. Let's get on with what we came out here for, shall we?"

Peter had insisted that they make the four-hour drive out into this land of loneliness, despite the bone-numbing cold, to perform their biannual ritual to mark the apex of the sun's elliptic. Peter also had some news to share, but Brautigan had hijacked the occasion to ramble on about his collective. The more Malcolm talked, the more hesitant Peter was to say what he needed to say.

"On with the Sacrifice," Malcolm said, before tugging on the handle and swinging the heavy door open, splinters of cold shooting up his nostrils. The tailgate's hinges squealed. Malcolm reached into the disorderly pile of gear and sleeping bags and pulled out a bottle of wine that his girlfriend Maggie's parents, make that ex-girlfriend, had bought on their trip to France, and that they had gifted to the young couple, who vowed to save it for their fifth anniversary. It was a 1982 Montrachet, of which Brautigan knew nothing except that it was expensive, and so he had surreptitiously pilfered it in the breakup. Now it would be Brautigan's sacrifice, for the sun.

If they don't sacrifice something on the solstice, the earth won't reverse its seasonal tilt, and the sun will continue sliding down the horizon until it disappears altogether, derailing the cycle of the seasons, and throwing the universe out of balance. A guy named Greg Whitman had invented the ritual and passed it down to his young acolytes. Whitman was a contrarian, anarchist, mapper of stars, artist, a misanthrope, and an erogynist. He'd wandered off from his rusty old single wide trailer sitting on the edge of a bean field west of Cortez a year earlier, on the solstice, in fact. To where, no one knows. Peter and Brautigan had both virtually worshipped the guy, but Peter's personality and manic energy were far more Whitman-esque than his friend's, and Peter had slipped into the void Whitman had left. He spouted aphorisms, which, in the Instagram age, would have become instantly viral memes: "Fuck 'em if they can't take a joke! Fuck 'em if they can!" "We're all moths striving for the light! Some of us dive into the flame, some of us spend our whole life banging our head against the window."

Peter was fearless, impulsive, in constant motion, always diving into a new art project, prone to violent swings in mood — definitely a member of the charred-wings club. Malcolm, not so much. Normally, Malcolm was the one injecting a sobering dose of reality into Peter's flights of fancy, which made tonight's dynamic seem odd.

"Malcolm," Peter blurted with a forced casualness as he threw a backpack over his shoulder. "I, umm, I've got to tell you something."

"Shoot."

"I'm going to New York."

"Yeah? Sweet. What for? For art?"

"Well, yes, as a matter of fact. I got a fellowship out there and ..."

"Cool. That's really awesome, Peter. For what, a few months? That's perfect, actually. It will give me a chance to wrap up some of the logistics around the Collective and then when you come back, we can fire it up."

"I'm not coming back."

Malcolm stopped, turned, looked out into the night.

"I'm moving out there. I've got a room rented and everything. Malcolm? I'm sorry. I was trying to tell you, but you wouldn't shut up."

"Fuck you, man. Fuck you. I can't fucking believe this." Malcolm balled up his fists, clenched his teeth, took a step back and toppled against the side of the car. He wanted to puke, but somehow the cold air kept the bile inside. He tried desperately to hold back the tears. With his goofy Peruvian knit hat with ear flaps and his duct-taped-together down jacket and his trembling lips, he looked especially pathetic — and especially lonely. "Don't you see, Peter? You don't have to move. That's what the Collective is all about. You don't *have* to go to New York or San Francisco. You can stay."

"I can't stay, Malcolm."

"What the fuck did I do? First Maggie dumps me and now you? Now you're dumping me, too? Peter?"

"Jesus, dude, I'm not dumping anyone. Admit it, if you were still with Maggie you wouldn't be talking about the Collective. You wouldn't even be out here right now."

"Bullshit. Fuck, Peter. Fuck, fuck, fuck. I'm happy for you. But, damnit, I was counting on your help. There's no way, now."

"That's not true. You've got Dale and his movies, Jennifer and her writing, Sarah and her art, Bruce and his photography, Michael, Ivan. It'll be fine. You don't need me."

"I do need you, and you know it. And you know what this makes me? This makes me the guy who couldn't leave. It makes me the one who remains after everyone else scurries off for opportunity and success and glory in New York and California and everywhere else. Thanks a lot."

"Then come with me. You can get a job somewhere, at a newspaper or a publishing place, and we can find a cheap hovel to rent and make it work. I could use your help."

"I don't think so."

"Why not?"

"Because I can't, Peter. I can't forsake the homeland. I can't leave it to the rednecks, the illiterates, the gentrifiers, the corporate land-rapers."

"It will always be here, this place. No offense, but it doesn't need you."

"Yeah, but *I* need *it*. Can you imagine me in New York? So go. No hard feelings. Maybe I'll come visit you in N-Y-C. Sleep on your couch for a while."

"Sure, okay. Now come on. Let's just do this." Peter pulled a cardboard tube out of his backpack, popped the plastic cap off, and removed a rolled up, thick piece of paper. Malcolm recognized the painting, and let out a nervous chuckle. Peter had painted it over several months' time, and entered it in a prestigious national contest and won. Collectors wanted to pay good money for it, but Peter refused to sell. He was oddly shy about showing it off in Durango — Malcolm had seen it just once, and briefly at that. He was pretty sure that Peter's parents hadn't seen it at all. It was a sort of landscape, but also a portrait, of a woman who seemed to be made of sandstone juxtaposed against a dark and tempestuous sky. The woman was tangled up in a spiral of fishing line, or a spider web, that emanated from what looked like an eyeball atop an oil derrick. The line sliced her apart and scattered her. It was strange and creepy and beautiful and oddly familiar to Malcolm, as if he had dreamed the exact same scene. But, then, that's what art is, right, the manifestation of dreams? Peter called it *I love, I think, therefore I am.*

Malcolm grinned — a nervous tic of his. "You're not …?"

Peter trembled, his face placid but determined. He would not back down, and Malcolm knew better than to bother trying.

"It's just a painting," Peter said, looking out at the darkness, punctured by pinpricks of light: a little cluster of houses on the Rez, perhaps, or a car making its way up from Kayenta. "Much bigger sacrifices will be made."

"Ain't that the truth." Brautigan's emotional metabolism burned hot, and he had already moved through the pain of abandonment into the giddiness that always follows, the feeling of weightlessness that rises from inevitable loss. He wiped his snotty nose on his glove and walked around the car and pulled a corkscrew out of the glove box and used it to open the bottle of wine.

"I thought that was your sacrifice?"

"Not anymore. This is for drinking," Malcolm said, setting the bottle down on the hood and picking up the cardboard box with his manuscript inside. "This one's for sacrificing."

"Oh come on, Malcolm. Don't be melodramatic. You can still do your collective. Still print your books."

"Nahh. It's a stupid idea, anyway. And this novel? I made the mistake of letting my dad read it. He basically accused me of plagiarizing the whole damned thing."

"He didn't mean it. He was drunk. You should know better. Have your mom read it. She's the one who bought you the typewriter, isn't she? She's the one who you got the creative gene from, too. Don't be so fucking patriarchal."

"You don't even know what that means." Brautigan took a swig out of the bottle, closed his eyes, relished the flavor, then handed the bottle to his friend. "Come on."

They felt and heard the end of the world before they saw it, the stratified walls of the gorge, doubling back on itself like a giant umbilical cord, and far below a sliver of the the San Juan River, a dim shimmer in the starlight. Malcolm picked up his box and motioned for Peter to hand him the lighter. Peter pulled off his glove, reached into a pocket, pulled out a yellow lighter, held it for a moment.

"You sure?"

"Yeah. It's just words, after all."

Peter handed Malcolm the lighter. Malcolm flicked the flint. Flicked it again. Sparks but no flame. He turned so his body blocked the wind. Flicked it again. Nothing. "Well, shit."

"Just throw it off the edge. It's biodegradable."

Malcolm nodded. He held the box like he would a frisbee, took a step back, and flung it into the void. But instead of gliding out into the emptiness like a frisbee, it fell in a precipitous arc, landing with a thud on the bench just twenty feet below.

"Damnit! I gotta go down there and throw it right this time. Give me your flashlight."

"Forget it, Malcolm. It's probably all mixed in with all the other garbage. It's like the fucking Mexican Hat dump down there and if you go digging around you'll get syphilis."

"Syphilis?"

"Hepatitis. Whatever. It's better this way. It could have hit someone and killed them if it really went off the edge."

"Yeah, good point. I can see the headlines now: *Death by two-hundred-thousand words*. What a way to go. You're just out enjoying the desert moonlight and *wham*."

Peter picked up his painting, held it in one hand, the dud lighter in the other, and waited for a gust of wind to pass. He looked at Malcolm, his lips moved but his voice was silent, as if he were trying to say something but was unable. He turned his back to the breeze and bent his tall figure over the painting, sparked the lighter, and a flame leapt up on the first try, illuminating his face. He pushed the fire against the lower corner of the painting. Blue and orange flame licked its way into the woman and the storm. Smoldering embers lifted themselves up into the cold and the darkness and floated away like fireflies, melding with the stars. Peter's face glowed in the light from the conflagration, and then the paper, the paint, the figures were gone.

Malcolm held up the bottle to the emptiness and took a swig. Then he turned and walked away from the edge and stopped at the deepest water pocket around. He crouched down and flipped on his headlamp, releasing a blinding light onto the bottom of the pothole. Thin patches of ice and crystallized snow appeared atop fine gray dirt, laced with black.

It looked as dead as any patch of dirt in the desert. But just under the surface was life, suspended, a cornucopia of critters just waiting to be born. In a few months' time, thunderheads would rush like spaceships over Monument Valley, and the San Juan, and then here, over Cedar Mesa, where they'd dump their loads, filling up the tinajas in the sandstone with deep, cool water. Life would bloom in the mud, almost instantly, as if it were carried down from the heavens inside each drop of rain. The cool desert water would swell with organisms that had defied both time and logic by lying dormant in the dusty pothole bed, awaiting the signal to self-resurrect: tiny brine shrimp wriggling through the water, alien-like blobs known as ostracods, and much larger tadpole shrimp, one of the oldest species on earth, a prehistoric creature that precisely mirrors fossils left by its ancestors during the Jurassic era. The pool is a time machine made of earth and stone, activated by adding water, a precise memory of this place when it was covered by a shallow, inland sea some ninety million years ago.

Brautigan lay a large blanket over the dirt to protect the sleeping creatures and the two men put their pads and bags down on the blanket. They sat and wrapped themselves up in the pothole, sheltered from the wind. A fire would have been nice, would have offered a little warmth. But that would surely cook the critters and, besides, the two friends had adopted Whitman's doctrine, which says campfires are like televisions, mind-sucks that pull our attention away from the stars, the night, the things that count.

Brautigan filled up his camping mug with wine, and then Peter's. He took a big sip, the custardy, spicy, woodsy, vanilla richness a surprise. "Damn," he said. "I never knew wine could taste like that."

Peter took a drink and nodded. "How much did that cost?"

"Don't know," said Malcolm, knowing even then that he'd always associate the taste of good, white Burgundy with heartache and loss. "Maggie's parents bought it for us. I imagine it wasn't cheap."

"I'm sorry man."

"Sorry?"

"About Maggie. And about New York."

"I know."

The silence lingered. They leaned against one another and watched the stars and sipped wine and shivered until, at last, slumber arrived.

Missing

Ten days before the Summer Solstice, present day, Durango, Colorado.

"That weasel-toed slimeball," Eliza Santos muttered aloud as she coasted into her conspicuously half-empty driveway on her one-speed Hathaway cruiser bike. "He's still not back."

The weasel-toed slimeball, in this particular instance, was her husband, Peter Simons. And he was one of those elusive creatures because he was now officially twenty-four hours overdue from what was supposed to be a few days of alone-time in Utah's canyon country. Standing in the driveway, sweat dripping down the side of her face, Santos habitually reached up to worry her long braid, only to find it, like her husband, missing. She had cut her long, black hair a week earlier, and now wore a disheveled pixie cut to which she was still unaccustomed. She mussed her hair with her hand, and looked up and down the street to make sure she hadn't missed Peter's old and rundown truck. Maybe he'd parked in front of that new house going up, the fancy one a few houses away, just to piss the owners off.

No truck. Just a tidy row of mid-century box-houses with Subarus in the driveway, punctured by that million-dollar wall of glass, gleaming in the afternoon sun, soaking up the early June heat like a solar oven. Why are the wealthy so stupid, she wondered, even as she asked why it was that a shiny black Cadillac Escalade was sitting in front of the Halls' house, its windows opaque with tint. The Halls weren't exactly Cadillac folks, nor did the gargantuan vehicle fit here in Tupperware Flats, a sort of suburb to historic Durango, Colorado — if a town of fifteen-thousand could have a suburb, that is.

If someone happened to be sitting behind the mirrored windshield of the Escalade, and happened to be watching Eliza Santos, they would have seen,

10

even from that distance, her jaw muscles flex as she clenched her teeth. The observer might have seen it as a sign of concern. In fact, Eliza wasn't all that worried about Peter. He'd done this sort of thing before, and in all likelihood was just wandering around in some canyon, following one of his whims, oblivious to the fact that his real life was waiting for him. After all, Peter was Peter, a man for whom time and deadlines and commitments were mere abstractions. He would come back, walk into the front door, and raise his hand in greeting as if nothing were wrong.

Mostly she was frustrated and angry that he could be so selfish, and, even worse, that she now had to deal with this shit, adding yet another item to her overloaded plate. She already had a precocious, teenaged daughter with whom to contend. The illustrious city council — composed of a land developer, a personal fitness trainer, and three real estate agents, two of whom were former professional athletes — had voted the previous night to cut the public library's budget and put the money saved into a new mountain bike park. Eliza was the director of the library, meaning she would have to hand out pink slips, decide which books not to buy, and walk around and shut off lights to lower the electricity bill. Meanwhile, her aging parents, who still lived in her hometown of Santa Fe, were a mess: Her mother seemed to be slipping into a haze of dementia while her father drank himself into a dementia of his own making, even as he made the moves on her mother's caretakers and spent his days writing a book that he titled: *Magic Money: The Shaman's guide to personal finance.*

Now she had a missing husband, and would have to decide whether to call out a search party. If she did, and Peter was just being Peter, then she'd end up looking stupid and probably would have to pay the tab for the unnecessary search. If she didn't, and Peter turned up dead, then she'd have some explaining to do to her daughter, along with years of therapy for which she'd have to pay.

She flipped the kickstand on the bike, left it out in the driveway, and walked inside in a futile attempt to escape from the searing heat. She tried Peter's number. It went straight to voicemail. She walked into the bedroom and turned on the swamp cooler and peeled off her work jeans and shirt and bra, and threw on shorts and a t-shirt. She went to the kitchen, opened the refrigerator, pulled out the bottle of white wine, poured herself a glass, gulped half of it down, refilled, and headed back into the living room where she sat down on the couch and found the number for the San Juan County, Utah, sheriff's office, which was already programmed into her phone for this very reason. She knew herself well enough to know that if she didn't call it would nag at her like a pebble in a shoe, slowly wearing its way under her skin.

She pushed the little green "call" icon, anachronistically shaped like an old-school telephone handset. Melanie Shumway, dispatcher and gossip-hound, answered after less than one ring, marking the moment — 4:34 p.m. on Monday, June 11 — at which Peter officially went missing. It was ten days prior to the Summer Solstice, and two days after a fast-moving fire burned through drought-infested forests of the Jemez Mountains in New Mexico before engulfing a facility at the Los Alamos National Laboratories. When the fire was extinguished, several pounds of sensitive, "strategic material" had gone missing, just like Peter.

"Ummm, hi, I'm calling because, well, my husband's gone. Gone missing, I mean."

"Gone missing, eh? Have you ever considered how stupid that term is? I mean, you can go shopping. You can go hiking. But can you really go missing? What does that even mean, anyway? It's as if a person were my car keys or sunglasses, you know?"

"Excuse me?" She paused, as if waiting for an explanation of Shumway's odd behavior. It did not come. "You see, he was supposed to be back yesterday afternoon and he's still out there somewhere?"

"Okay, honey, I'm just trying to make conversation. Where was he last seen?"

"I don't really know," Eliza said, wincing at Shumway's use of the passive voice. "*I* last saw him on Friday around noon before he left. His name's Peter. Peter Simons. He went hiking over there somewhere and he hasn't come back. I just wanted to know if …"

"If we've pulled a rotten carcass out of a canyon?"

"What?"

"I'm kidding," a sharp cackle burst from the phone's speaker. "Of course we didn't. But we did find his truck. Just yesterday Deputy Lyman slapped an abandoned-vehicle ticket on a 1987 Toyota four-by-four pickup registered to a mister Simons. It was sitting in Parley Redd's Mercantile parking lot for at least two days. That's illegal, you know? It's like leaving your luggage in the airport. A big no-no. His truck's red, right? With one of them KEEP UTAH WILD bumper stickers on there?"

"Yeah, that's his truck, alright." Eliza sighed. She had repeatedly pleaded with Peter to take that damned sticker off his truck, to stop wearing his politics on his sleeve or, for that matter, the bumper of his car, particularly in Utah.

"Would you like to file a missing person's report?"

"No, no, not yet. Thank you," she said, already regretting the phone call. "Maybe you could just keep an eye out?"

12

"You bet. And don't worry, I'm sure he's okay."

"You think so?"

"Sure. If he were dead, someone would have smelled him by now."

Before Eliza could respond her phone beeped, signaling that the call had ended. She thought about calling back, about making some sort of formal complaint about the woman's brusqueness, but didn't know what it would accomplish. Better to stay on Shumway's good side. In a small town people like her held an inordinate amount of power.

Besides, the dispatcher had asked a good question: Where was Peter last seen? She sat back, took another swig of wine, and logged into her and Peter's bank account. He had used his credit card three times on the previous Friday, first at the Durango post office, where he spent five bucks, apparently to buy stamps or send a package, then at the Walgreens pharmacy, where he spent $300 for God-knows-what, and then at the Sonic Drive-in on South Broadway in Cortez, Colorado. Walgreens would not give out any information about its pharmacy customers. Not knowing what else to do, Santos called Sonic, and spoke to one disembodied voice after another, trying to find the person who waited on Peter so she could glean from them a fragment of information about her husband's whereabouts or state of mind. She tried to picture the face behind each voice — this one a mascara-smeared high schooler who lived with her mom in a ragged hotel room, this one a middle-aged man who had worked in the mines or the oil patch or the bean fields, and this is what it has come to, damnit.

Finally, Lindey Hurley, a seventeen-year-old carhop got on the phone. Yep, she remembered Peter, could never forget the guy who had left a five-dollar tip and fit the description of Simons — tall, good-looking for an old guy, driving a beat-up, rice-burner truck with a Replacements sticker on the cab's back window. Hurley loved the Replacements.

Santos sputtered in surprise a little at that, and had she not been engaged in such an important query, might have counseled the young woman on her music selection. She also might have pleaded with her to stay away from boys until she got to college, to avoid letting some testosterone-addled hottie with a nice smile and good abs derail her dreams. "So, was he in a hurry? Did he have anyone with him? Was he distraught?"

"He ordered a banana shake *and* a Sonic Boom," Hurley answered. As if that were everything.

At precisely the moment that Hurley said, "Boom," someone knocked loudly on the front door. Eliza thanked Lindey, hung up the phone, and unconsciously tugged at the hem of her shorts in a futile attempt to get them to cover a little bit more of her thigh. She opened the door to find a man and a woman standing on the little porch, both wearing sunglasses and bluetooth earpieces, tactical pants, and black jackets with deep orange trim, despite the stifling heat. The two resembled those huge wasps that flew around in the desert and laid eggs in paralyzed spiders. They held up ID badges, and the woman, her dark hair pulled tightly back into a ponytail, said they were agents from Clearwater Incorporated, working under the auspices of the Department of Homeland Security, and they needed to ask her a few questions about her husband, Peter.

Eliza took a step back into the cool of her home, as much out of shock as to escape the stench of the cologne one or both of the agents were wearing. She did not invite them inside.

The woman agent asked if Eliza knew Peter's whereabouts, if she had noticed anything unusual in his behavior lately, or if he had been associating with anyone new or suspicious. "What was he looking for in Utah?"

"Looking for?" She honestly didn't understand what was being asked. As for unusual behavior, well, they apparently didn't know Peter, lest they'd know that that was a stupid question. She decided not to bring up Peter's recent suspicion that medical drones were spying on his thoughts, or his belief that a massive weather-control project was underway in the San Juan Mountains. "He's an artist. Now unless you have a warrant or something I'd like you to leave now."

Eliza slammed the door and locked it, then watched the two wasps walk up the street to the black Escalade parked in front of the Halls' house. She noticed the shadows that each of them cast, and the way the sun hung high in the sky. Summer Solstice would be here soon, and with it Peter's habitual need to sacrifice something. She couldn't handle this alone. She needed help. And she could think of just one person who might be able to offer it. But before she called him, she needed to go out and buy another bottle of wine.

Malcolm

The long June day's last sunlight shone harshly through the west-facing windows of the small apartment, on the southwest corner of an old brick building on the south edge of downtown Tucson. The diminutive air conditioner shoved into the window battled noisily against the sun's heat. The machine was losing.

Against one bare white wall, a table made of plywood atop two sawhorses held a laptop computer. In a hard, simple IKEA chair, a man sat hunched over the laptop's keyboard, his fingers moving deftly across keys worn to the point of being unreadable. Pause. Type. Wipe the sweat off his palms on his shorts. Pause. Type. Pause. Type. Sit up straight and flex shoulder blades. Type. Pause.

Brautigan had chosen this apartment after his former wife, Melissa, booted him out of their former abode. It was cheap, and he thought that living in the little, old apartment complex would offer some sort of instant community: wine-soaked dinner parties and barbecues in the parking lot and borrowing a cup of sugar from the neighbor, that sort of thing. It would provide an antidote for the misery he'd been feeling since finding out, via Facebook, that Melissa was not just sleeping with Chad Trudeau, sustainable real estate developer extraordinaire and darling of the wealthy, white environmentalists of Tucson, but that she was also in love with him and no longer had any use for Malcolm or their marriage.

After moving in, however, he'd found little in the way of community, save for the landlord, Emilio, who was an agronomist and the leader of an Ayahuasca ring. He was a small man, wiry, built to move up the steep slopes of the Andes, his long black hair flecked with gray. He was always asking Malcolm — whom Emilio called "Fucking Guy" — to write something, a letter asking for funding for research on a new strain of quinoa, or huitlacoche, or extracting the alkaloids from sacred datura. And then there was Natalya, an

15

attractive and mysterious woman with an entire flock of angry, loud cockatiels and a creepy looking mannequin clothed in paisley-patterned gold lamé. Natalya once told Brautigan that she had run away from a lucrative engineering career to join a circus, where she served as resident psychic, palm reader, and general seer, before moving to Tucson to manage the erotica section of a used-book store.

It wasn't exactly a potluck kind of crowd, and even if it were, Malcolm wouldn't be able to prepare any of his signature dishes — i.e. his famous chocolate chip cookies — because his apartment wasn't equipped with an oven. The rental agency had touted its *"sans le four"* apartments as part of a new trend emerging alongside rising global temperatures. It was simply too hot to bake anything, so why waste space and time and energy by installing an oven? Oh, yes, and that will add a hundred bucks to your monthly rent.

Anyway, Brautigan already had plenty on his plate, so to speak. He was, after all, a media mogul of sorts, busy overseeing and cranking out content for his digital magazine, *Alt-News*®. Writing under the byline Juan Lopez-Shapiro, Brautigan churned out at least two articles per day, accompanied by carefully curated content from around the web. His notoriety was growing — 50,000 Twitter followers and counting, a robust Facebook page, and a Reddit topic page dedicated entirely to the expanding *Alt-News* universe — along with revenues and the pressure to keep a steady stream of words flowing onto the digital page. An editor at *Mother Jones* had recently wrote: "If there were a fake Pulitzer for fake news, it would surely go to Juan Lopez-Shapiro and *Alt-News*. It is the most insidious propaganda organization in America today."

For an alt-truth organization, it just doesn't get any better than that.

Really, the fake news label was a bit unfair. Lopez-Shapiro never *fabricated* news, he simply explored the various possibilities behind the "real" news spewed by the mainstream media. For each of the three to four articles per day that he wrote, Lopez-Shapiro a.k.a. Malcolm Brautigan followed a similar formula. He always began with a legitimate news story, preferably one that hadn't gotten a lot of attention, and that was brief enough to leave room for, say, embellishment.

For his fourth piece of that sweltering June day, for example, he chose as his seed a short article on page six of that day's *Tucson Tribune*, headlined, "Vandals strike Ronald J. Drumpf Memorial Border Wall -- again." It was a short story, explaining that for the fourth time in as many weeks, someone had sabotaged equipment that was used to re-construct the giant barrier on the US-Mexico border that had been blown down in a massive windstorm the summer before (and which had killed three dozen members of the so-called Border National Guard, an ultra-right-wing, heavily armed group of incels that was holding a reunion next to the wall when the windstorm struck). Worse, the vandals had cut through the supposedly impenetrable wall with what appeared to be a battery-powered saw from the Mexican equivalent of Home Depot. The damage was fairly minor -- some sugar in a front-end loader's gas tank, survey stakes pulled and burned, and a human-sized hole in the wall. It was ripe for the Lopez-Shapiro treatment.

Next, he rewrote the story, massaging the facts just a bit, to give it a little more punch. "Inside sources tell *Alt-News* that Antifa agents are the likely culprits behind a series of attacks on the new border wall, and that these are just 'dress rehearsals' for a much bigger, deadlier action," he wrote. "Documents unearthed recently show that the Obama administration's lax policies allowed hundreds or even thousands of Antifa terrorists to penetrate the US border and embed themselves in American communities where they are now posing as 'refugees' while they engage in radical leftism, anarchy, veganism, throwing soup cans at police, and otherwise wrecking American Heritage. First Man and Secretary of Defense Jared Kuckner said that a US nuclear submarine has positioned itself off the coast of Antifastan and is prepared to take action if Antifa leaders don't stop messing with the wall."

It wasn't a lie. Not really. It was more like speculative journalism. Maybe the vandals *were* just George Hayduke-wannabes, or migrants, or narco-traffickers, but they might also be terrorists looking for a way to sneak a dirty bomb into Houston. It was a technique that could be applied to almost any topic, from climate change, to gun control, to the most novel strain of coronavirus, to wearing face masks, to the protests erupting in nearly every city and every town in the nation. Some might accuse him of pushing conspiracy theories or peddling fake news. He preferred to think that he was sparking readers' imaginations.

He did a final copyedit, looking for opportunities to drop in the keywords that would trigger algorithms and break down the collective immune defenses against disinformation, thereby clearing the way for the story to go viral: *prayer rugs, funded by Soros, voting fraud, border crisis, thugs on a plane, climate change hoax, class warfare, Deep State, Hillary's emails, out-of-work coal miners, Clinton Foundation.* He published the piece on *Alt-News* and wrote up a series of ten tweets and Facebook posts, each with different, provocative hashtags: #TheNewGreatWall, #TacoTerrorists, #NukeAntifastan, #RememberDrumpf. He scheduled them to post every hour through the night, so they'd catch people as they checked their feeds while in the bar, or after having sex, or during sex. He looked at his clock. It had taken him twenty-seven minutes and forty-two seconds, start to finish.

Another hard day's work behind him, he got up and opened the freezer, reveling in the cold, viscous air as it poured out onto his face. He grabbed the blue-tinged bottle of gin, ice cubes, a glass, and the shaker, and mixed himself a very dry martini. He shook, poured, watched the frost on the glass turn to chilly dew, then carved a pungent spiral of lemon peel and dropped it in. Wanting to savor that first sip out on the stoop, he shut off the air conditioner, carefully walked across the room, and opened the front door, letting in a hot breath of air. He turned off the lights and sat on the step in the semi-darkness.

The sounds of the city flitted through the night: sirens, a dog barking in the distance, the gentle roar of traffic, the thump-thump of a souped-up woofer. Beneath it all, thousands of air conditioners hummed laboriously as they battled against the ever-oppressive night heat. Electrons shivered invisibly in the wires that sliced across the starless bruise of the night sky, feeding off of the web-like machine that churned away day after day, burning through ancient swamps and sea creatures to generate steam to turn the turbines to create an electromagnetic field to excite the electrons to send the kilowatts through miles upon miles of wires to power our televisions, our phones, our laptops, our lights, the monstrous pumps that push the water up from the Colorado River to "recharge" the dwindling aquifers around here, and to cool our abodes to habitable temperatures, all the while prodding the power plants to crank out more juice, and spew more carbon, slowly turning the urban heat island into a global one.

"Hey there," came a woman's husky voice from the darkness.

Brautigan looked up, startled to see his neighbor, Natalya, standing on the sidewalk a few feet away. Natalya and Brautigan met every Wednesday evening to play backgammon and talk, always in her cluttered apartment. He couldn't remember the last time he had seen her out in the world.

"You know," she said. "When I first came here, to the city, after my stint with the circus, I missed the darkness more than I missed the coolness."

"That's probably because back then the temperature sometimes dropped below ninety, even in concrete-land. There was still a little coolness left."

"I suppose so. I can't even remember what it felt like. Coolness, I mean."

"Or rain? Snow? A sky that isn't smoky? Sometimes I would give just about anything to go back in time, to the days when there was still a real monsoon, when the clouds would pile up at the end of a late-July day, the temperature would plummet twenty degrees, the wind would whip the trees back and forth, and sheets of rain would pour from the cobalt sky."

"Yes, I would like that very much," Natalya said. "And to inhale the petrichor once again."

Natalya was an enigma. One minute she might look thirty-two, the next sixty-two. Her hair's style, and color, changed weekly. She could talk for hours about her former life without saying anything tangible. Brautigan had begun to doubt the veracity of her anecdotes, mostly because her storytelling techniques were remarkably similar to Juan Lopez-Shapiro's. She liberally peppered her stories with specific minutiae, such as the color of her ex-lover's trapeze outfit, or his sexual proclivities, yet she was elusive when it came to more meaningful details. She wouldn't say what kind of engineer she was, where she was from, or when she had come to Tucson or why. One time she said that the scar on her cheek was the result of a trapeze accident, yet another time she blamed it on a circus tiger lashing out after a lifetime of abuse. Lopez-Shapiro used this sort of intentional vagueness to trip up the fact-checking organizations that had cropped up following the first Drumpf's election. Brautigan's repeated attempts to verify or refute her story proved fruitless.

Brautigan was pretty sure that Natalya was not her name, that she had never been an engineer, and that she was yet another middle-aged, middle-American, middle-class person who had woken up one morning to find her life to be terminally mediocre, so she fled her corporate job and her boring life to come West. Perhaps she was drawn to the Desert Orgasm in Sedona, or some New Age cult. Maybe she just wanted to reinvent herself, which she apparently had done with some success.

Brautigan didn't blame her for concocting an alternate past. After all, who didn't have a collection of different identities? To his *Alt-News* readers Malcolm was Juan Lopez-Shapiro, sometimes Michael Baines, and even once, when he felt the need to have a female byline, Hillary Haxton. But to his family and friends and Natalya he was Malcolm Brautigan, freelance editor of internal newsletters for various corporations.

Natalya, whose hair color that night was silver with purple streaks -- an inversion of the sky colors at the moment — sat down on the step next to Brautigan. She was close enough that he could smell her scent, lavender to match her blouse, with a hint of citrus and maybe vetiver. She eyed the martini in his hand, then reached over and slid her finger up its side.

"Promise me something," she said, her voice soft.

"Anything," Brautigan said, the gin loosening up his limbs and his inhibitions.

"When you do go back to the time of rain and snow, and when you do experience the aroma that fills the air when the first drops of rain hit the sandstone and the sage, think of me."

"The petrichor, you mean? I promise, on one condition: Tell me the name of that circus you ran away with."

"It was run by a family from Bulgaria. The Borislavas. Circus Borislava."

"Ahh, yes," Brautigan said, marveling at the way the skin around her eyes crinkled as she smiled. "Hey, let me make you one. A drink, I mean. You'd save me from drinking alone."

"I'd better not."

Before he could persist, Brautigan's phone squawked, a number with a western-Colorado area code showing up on the screen.

"Aren't you going to answer that?"

"No. It's the folks at OmnyBank. They want their money."

"You sure?"

"Sure enough. Who else would it be?"

"Maybe you should just pay your credit card bill."

"Screw that. Did you know that it would take four of my debt loads — *four of them* — to buy just one Patek whatchamacallit watch as a bonus for some junior executive? So no, I'm not going to pay, and I'm not going to feel guilty about it. Besides, I'm pretty sure Melissa racked up most of the bills, not me."

"Huh? I see."

"I know, I know, I'm not supposed to talk about Melissa. It's bad for my broken heart, blah, blah, blah."

"I wasn't going to say anything," she said, smiling, "but it's true."

Just as he was about to respond with a cringeworthy comment about her smile, a high-pitched buzz emanated from from above. Brautigan peered upward, while Natalya turned her head downward. It was a medical drone, making its evening rounds, checking the body temperature of anyone who was dumb enough to be outside in the heat, looking for signs of valley fever, COVID-21, hantavirus, or a resurgence of SARS-2020. President Drumpf II, known familiarly as The Ivanya, had ordered the CDC to blanket the nation with the drones following her father's death from COVID-19.

"How the hell do those things even work when it's a hundred degrees out?"

"You and I both know that they're not checking anyone's temperature," Natalya said, still looking at the sidewalk, her hands held up as if to shelter her head from the drone. "It's reading our thoughts, probing our memories."

Brautigan was skeptical, though he had recently read that such technology was in development. Researchers had purportedly figured out how to implant something into the hippocampus that could monitor activity in that part of the brain. By using the chip in tandem with memory-inducing pharmaceuticals, the researchers were able to jar memories loose in patients with brain injuries, amnesia, or dementia. They were essentially excavating lost memories and now, alarming privacy rights advocates, Russian scientists reportedly were working on how to read the memories, maybe even project them onto a monitor.

While his job may have been to stir up the public's paranoia, he didn't want to do the same on a personal level. "Enough with your conspiracy theories, Natalya. I'm mixing you a martini right now. Drink a few of these and you won't have any memories left to probe."

Natalya sighed as if genuinely considering it, and then, again, she demurred, standing up to go instead. "I'm afraid not, Malcolm. I must go. And remember, you can't hold your breath forever." And then she walked away, dissolving into the darkness.

"What the hell does that mean? Maybe tomorrow, then?" The loneliness seeped in, spreading through his chest like ink through fabric. He needed another drink. More than that, he needed food. More than that he needed to cook, and he needed someone for whom to cook. He went inside, cranked up the air-conditioner, put a pot of water on the stove, and set it to boil. He rooted through the cupboards listlessly before settling on the old reliable — linguine aglio e olio. He chopped garlic he had gotten from his farmer friend down at San Xavier, its pungent juices seeping into his hangnails with a sting, crumpled up one of Emilio's mouth-numbing dried chilis, and stirred it all into some olive oil. He tossed the pasta in the sauce, then topped it with zucchini shaved into transparent ribbons, a handful of fresh cherry tomatoes, and basil, and then doused it all in olive oil, lemon, and a little bit of salt.

He sat down on the couch with his food and opened the laptop at his side. Notifications popped up, indicating that his story was worming its way through cyberspace. The first retweet came from @DrumpfsterMG, followed closely by a flurry of other accounts with similar names, members of the network of automated users, bots that were created in "farms" in Albania, India, Macedonia. By the time he went to bed the story had over a thousand retweets. With each new "like," Brautigan's chest swelled, the endorphins kicking in as he relished the sensation of being a part of something bigger than him, even if it wasn't exactly real.

Still, something gnawed at him. He looked at his recent call-queue on his phone. The area code and prefix for the call he had not answered was from Durango, his hometown. Maybe it wasn't the credit card bastards after all. He Googled the number. It wasn't until he got to the third page of results that the name jumped out at him: Eliza Santos.

"Holy shit. What does *she* want?" He looked at the phone again, his finger hovering over the call button. Then he put it down, stood up, walked the few feet to his freezer, and mixed himself another martini. He hadn't heard from Eliza or Peter for ages, didn't even know if they were still in New York, or if Peter's painting career had continued its upward trajectory, and he didn't know if he cared. He took a sip, and then another, slipping from the euphoria of the two-drink buzz into a drunker and darker place.

The call was still on his mind when Malcolm awoke after a restless sleep. It stayed with him as he showered and threw on the coolest clothes possible, and walked the three blocks to the downtown coffee shop where he liked to work. Instinct urged him to move quickly, but it was June, in Tucson, and Brautigan had a perspiration problem, so he forced himself to go slowly, to breathe deliberately, to focus on keeping the sweat inside his body, rather than dripping down his face. It didn't work. By the time Malcolm pulled open the glass door and was hit by the chill air and rich smell of coffee roasting his back was drenched with sweat. He looked down to notice, with horror, that the perspiration also had drawn a pattern on the front of his shirt — two spots under his saggy pecs, a line in between, an oval emphasizing his middle-aged paunch.

He turned to flee, to run down the street to Starbucks where he could stroll up to the drive-thru with a minimum of human interaction. But Sophie, his favorite barista, had already seen him. Head down, he hurried to the bathroom and closed the door and turned on the fan and threw off his backpack and took off his shirt and hung it from a hook on the door so it would dry out. As he was yanking paper towels from the dispenser to soak up some of his back-sweat, he came up with another idea. He punched the button on the air-dryer and held his shirt under the blast of cool air — the city had banned hot air dispensers months earlier — until the dampness subsided, and then put his still-shirtless body underneath the stream of air in order to ease the perspiration. It worked so well that he unbuttoned his shorts and pulled the waistband of his underwear out to let the cool air blast-dry his sweaty crotch, as well.

It was just as his sweat glands eased up a bit, and he was congratulating himself for his face-saving, problem-solving genius, when the bathroom door, which he had neglected to lock, opened. A woman stood in the doorway, her face plastered with an odd combination of laughter and terror.

Brautigan jumped out of his crouch with alarm, his skull crashing into the air-dryer with a resounding thunk, his still-unbuttoned shorts falling down to his ankles. He looked at her. And she looked at him, her gaze wandering down his naked torso. When she reached his waistline, she snickered, scowled, then asked, in a tone that contained both scorn and humor, "What are you doing?"

"I… ummm… I have this thing with perspiration. A disease! Chronic, stage three diaphoresis and hyperhydrosis?" It wasn't a lie, exactly. He had used various medical websites to diagnose himself.

"Oh my God," replied the woman, who had long, pearl-colored hair, flawless makeup, form-hugging leggings, and a tank-top of similarly clingy material. "That sounds serious."

"Yeah. Really serious."

"I'm so sorry. So, so sorry." She backed out and slammed the door. Brautigan locked it and put his damp shirt back on and sat down on the toilet and breathed deeply until someone knocked. He wandered out, feigning nonchalance.

"Hey," he said to Sophie. She looked back expectantly but without any recognition or disgust or even pity. She must have missed the whole bathroom scene. "I'll take the usual."

Sophie looked back blankly.

"Sure, okay: a coffee, dark roast — French, Italian, whatever; room for cream; and a bagel with cream cheese."

"We don't do dark roast. It is so two-thousand-and-twelve. Medium?"

"Seriously? Okay. Medium, it is, then."

He paid, walked to the table where they normally keep the cream. There was no cream, or milk, or even that almond shit. Just a sign that read: "Save the coffee, kill the cream." He was about to get angry when it dawned on him that this was just more material for *Alt-News*. When he had a few minutes, he'd crank out a tirade against the coffee-elite and the War on Dairy. He sat down — medium roast, un-creamed coffee in hand — at the long "community" table, where the only communing going on was with placid screens.

Brautigan popped open his laptop to a blizzard of notifications. The border wall story was everywhere. He received a boob pic from @DeplorableLatina46. He clicked on the little heart button to signal his gratitude, even though he was fairly certain that @MerikaGretagan had sent him a photo of the same breasts a week earlier. But still no tweet or retweet from the president, either the dead one or the living one, which was the Holy Grail for Lopez-Shapiro and his ilk.

When Ronald Drumpf had expired, just weeks before the election, the attorney general and senate Republicans banded together to declare a national state of emergency, allowing them to install Drumpf's daughter, Ivanya, into the Oval Office and in her father's slot on the ballot. Military troops were sent to so-called anarchist jurisdictions — New York, Los Angeles, Chicago, Portland — on Election Day, to keep voters safe from soup-hurling Antifa, and electromagnetic pulses from unknown sources fried voting machines in Democratic strongholds. Ivanya won the election in a landslide. Protests broke out across the nation in response, and more troops — along with mercenaries working for private contractors — were sent in to keep the peace.

Amidst all of the brouhaha, @RealRonaldDrumpf's Twitter account continued tweeting without interruption after Drumpf I's death, during his funeral, and persists to this very day, as if his stubby little fingers were reflexively pounding on his phone in the gold-plated mausoleum constructed inside Mar-a-Lago. The tweets had the same syntax, the same misspellings, the same spittle-spewing tone as before. In the beginning everyone assumed that Ivanya or one of her aides had simply taken over the account, that she had inherited it along with everything else she had. But as soon as the election was over, @DeadRonaldDrumpf's tweets began targeting his daughter. He compared Ivanya's campaign, unfavorably, to his own, and insisted that his funeral drew much "yuuuuger" crowds than her inauguration. He attacked Ivanya and her siblings for being sniveling, entitled, weak, spineless disappointments. He insisted that he had not died of COVID-19 -- which was no more deadly than herpes — but from injecting bleach into his veins. He was livid about the World Health Organization converting the entire global fleet of cruise ships into floating quarantine colonies, an initiative endorsed by The Ivanya. He made crude, overtly sexual comments regarding his daughter's physical appearance, and insisted that since he was now dead, she was fair game. Most maddening to President Ivanya Drumpf was that the account gained millions of followers, dwarfing that of her own insipid Twitter feed, and had far more influence over her base than she did. She was enraged. Her husband created a task force whose sole purpose was to find out who or what was behind the phenomenon, but they got nowhere. Even Twitter was unable to silence the ghost account.

Lopez-Shapiro had been trying to get a retweet or some recognition from the living President Drumpf and then the dead one for ages. It still hadn't happened.

As far as the finances go, the presidential tweets — or lack thereof — were irrelevant. The GGF Foundation had deposited two-thousand clams into his PayPal account for his previous day's stories. Not bad for three hours of work. Officially, *Alt-News* was an independent news organization, which made its money off of advertising and individual donations. Most of the funding, however, really came from the GGF (God, Guns, Freedom) Foundation, a conservative think tank based somewhere in Utah. Brautigan had autonomy to choose, write, and edit his own stories, but occasionally Stan Hatch, the director of GGF, would send news tips, by which he meant assignments. Along with the day's payment, Hatch had sent him one such tip urging him to look into a "leftie smear campaign" against Interior Secretary Albert Fallon, who was under investigation for taking gifts from energy companies in return for shrinking Utah national monuments. Hatch wanted Brautigan's article to show that the smear campaign was being pushed by big-money environmental groups from California, who were in cahoots with the outdoor recreation industry.

Brautigan let out a heavy sigh. He was fine going after the big green organizations, but the fact that this played out in southeastern Utah and Brautigan's childhood backyard made him uncomfortable. He preferred utter detachment from his topics. He'd need more coffee before tackling this one.

"I like your necklace," he said to Sophie, as he stepped up to the counter for a second time, realizing as soon as it came out of his mouth that it might have been inappropriate and, along with the whole half-naked bathroom incident, might put him onto one of those internet creepy-guy lists.

"Thanks," she said.

"Umm… I'll have a flat white this time," he said, avoiding eye contact. "With real milk, if you have it. Make it a double. And one of those cookies."

As she poured the frothy milk slowly into the cup she happened to glance up toward the big plate glass windows facing the street. Her eyes widened. "Oh, no," she muttered. "They're back."

He turned around. Outside the huge glass windows a military-style MRAP truck blocked the street, and flak-jacketed, helmeted, black-clad humanoids yelled staccato commands, their assault rifles at the ready as they moved methodically across the pavement. Brautigan couldn't help but snicker at the lettering on the back of the stormtroopers' jackets: "CLEARWATER" in smaller print above "ICE." It was as if they had been sponsored by a raunchy beer from the early nineties. They were out early, amassing in the streets to attempt to squash the demonstrations that would surely come later in the day.

When he turned back toward Sophie her face was flushed and her eyes glassy with tears. "Damnit," she said. "The fascists. They'll beat the shit out of some brown kid and then gin up some fake tie to Antifa. Don't these idiots know what that word even means?"

"Well, actually, we don't really know what the situation is," Malcolm said in a tone that even to him felt patronizing. "Maybe Antifa *is* invading and these guys are supposed to be protecting us, so…"

For the first time that Malcolm could remember, Sophie looked at him as if she recognized him, as if he were not just another anonymous customer, and then she said, in a measured tone, "Who the hell are you, anyway?"

Instead of answering, he staggered backwards, bumping into a woman who was standing in line behind him. Beads of sweat trickled down his forehead. He stumbled back to his seat, and fell into it, only then noticing that he'd left his laptop open to the *Alt-News* Twitter feed. He slammed the computer shut, and headed for the door, trying to avoid Sophie's gaze. He stepped out onto the sidewalk, into the bright heat.

It was eerily quiet, as if he'd happened upon a modern dance performance, the only sounds the clip-clop of boot soles on pavement, the swishing of high-tech fabric rubbing against high-tech fabric. He tried to stay calm, and started to walk on his regular route towards his apartment. One of the cops saw him, and jerked the barrel of his rifle in Brautigan's direction: "Step back!"

He froze.

The cop's voice softened. "Go the other way. This sidewalk's closed. Nothing to see here."

Brautigan pivoted and walked quickly in the opposite direction, went around the block, then doubled back toward home. He turned into an alley, clinging to thin slivers of shade, but others had the same idea. He hopped over an amorphous lump of cardboard, blankets, trinkets, and then another and another. Somewhere under the debris were humans seeking shelter from the cruel sun. He had stumbled into a refugee camp, peopled by those who had been exiled from the nation of walls and windows, of health care and clean water, and of insulation and air conditioning. Landlords had stopped putting ovens in apartments due to the rising temperatures, but somehow they hadn't stopped putting people out on the street.

Brautigan retreated to the other side of the alley, feeling his internal temperature rise as he did so, aware that in an hour or so the sun would be beating down on the refugees. The heat would have its way with them. He stopped, turned around, and looked back just as an elderly man stuck his head out of the only real tent in the makeshift alley community.

Back before *Alt-News*, back before he'd lost his job, Brautigan was the health and environment reporter for the *Tucson Tribune*, the city's big daily. He pounded out stories about vanishing pygmy owls, the dwindling water table, and bulldozers scraping away the desert for yet another Tuscan-themed housing development. He wrote about climate change, about public transit, about renewable energy, about the saguaro's slow death, about the destruction wrought by the wall along the border, and about all of those who died trying to cross the border deep in the desert. He learned, then, in graphic and clinical detail, exactly what happens to the human body when it is subjected to such heat. The flesh actually begins to melt, suffering entropy in real time: organ dysfunction, renal insufficiency, disseminated intravascular coagulation, and acute respiratory distress syndrome — technical terms for being cooked alive. The residents of the little camp in the alley were equally vulnerable, regardless of the fact that they were in a city's downtown, surrounded by air-conditioned buildings and cars. Like the border crossers they, too, would roast, perhaps more slowly, but just as surely, and as with the migrants it would not be the heat that killed them, but the whole rotten system that criminalizes poverty and the desire for a better life. They'd be cooked due to insufficient funds, an increasingly common malady in these parts, even among those with homes. Just that morning three more people had died in the suburbs after the utility shut off their power because of an overdue bill.

At moments like these Brautigan's powers of detachment failed him, and the coals of outrage and despair flared up within. But what could he do? Write a story about it as if his words carried weight in this world? He scoffed silently, walked around the corner, and ducked into a little Mexican grocery store. He loaded up a shopping cart with bottles of water and Gatorade and energy bars. The guy behind the counter eyed him skeptically, but took his money, along with an extra twenty for a deposit on the cart. With a terrible racket Brautigan rolled the ponderous cart out into the street and down the alley and left it in the only spot of shade remaining, in front of the old man's tent. Then Brautigan resumed his slow and sweaty walk home.

Twenty minutes later, just as he was rounding the corner onto his street, his phone buzzed in his pocket. He answered without looking at the number.

"Yeah?"

"Malcolm?" A woman's voice. "Is this Malcolm Brautigan?"

"With whom am I speaking?"

"This is Eliza. Remember me? I need your help. Peter's gone —"

The phone went silent. Even Brautigan wasn't sure whether he'd ended the call or whether she had. As a wave of anxiety washed over him he hurried toward home.

Eliza

Eliza Santos held the phone tightly to the side of her head, wondering casually what ringtone Peter's friend and her ex-lover, Malcolm Brautigan, was hearing at that moment. She was a bit surprised when the voice, familiar but clouded with a digital hue, spoke into her ear:

"Yeah?"

"Malcolm? Is this Malcolm Brautigan?"

"With whom am I speaking?"

"This is Eliza. Remember me? I need your help. Peter's gone missing over in Utah and ... Malcolm? Hey, can you hear me? Are you there?"

Eliza pulled the device away from her ear and stared at the screen for a long time. Had Malcolm just hung up on her? Then a voice shook her out of her daze, coming not from the phone but from the doorway to her office. "Hey, you okay? You look kind of pale. Bad news?" It was Vin, her colleague, a part-time library employee. His real name was Vincent, but Eliza liked to call him Vin for reasons even she didn't know.

"Yeah, I'm fine. Hey, can you cover the desk for a few? I gotta step outside, get some fresh air."

She walked outside and found a bench in some shade. She texted her friend, Ann: "think I just did something really stupid." The ringtone (Neil Diamond's "Sweet Caroline") blurted from the phone seconds later. It was Ann.

"Please, Sweet Baby Jesus, please, tell me the stupid thing you did was humping that Vince guy, at last!"

"Shut up, Ann. No, that's not it."

"Ahhh. He's so damned hot, though, like Brad-Pitt-and-Mark-Ruffalo-had-a-kid hot. And he's sweet. And he's in love with you."

"He's dumb as a box of rocks and he's got Oedipus syndrome. I'm twenty years older than him."

"All the better!"

"And I'm married. Remember?"

"Hey, if your hubby can run off behind the sandstone venetian-blind then you should be able to frolic between Vincent's sheets."

"*Slickrock Curtain*. Behind the Slickrock Curtain."

"Whatever! Okay, okay, what's up?"

"I called Malcolm to ask him to come help find Peter. The call dropped before I could say anything, but still."

"Peter isn't back? That asshole."

"No, and I'm getting worried."

"You know what I think, don't you? Peter's got another family, and with them he's this super gregarious guy, the life of the party, plays baseball with the kids, and is a zero-angst graphic artist for a big corporation and makes enough money to fly his wife all over the world, and afford health care, and he has a huge penis and a tongue that won't quit."

"Oy vey, yeah, right, he's living the revenge life? Believe me, all he'd need to do is get off the spectrum for a day or two and it would be revenge life enough for him. Speaking of revenge, is *that* why I called Malcolm? I'm freaking out. Distract me."

"Okay. New business idea: Tea-infused vodka. And you call it naughty, but spell it N-A-U-G-H-T-E-A. Get it? It's not tea. And it's naughty. NaughTea." It was a nervous tic of theirs, brainstorming business ideas that would make them instant millions, freeing them from the middle-class working trap so they could live as Bohemians in Portugal.

"Pretty good, pretty good, but nothing compared to this: A shoe store that sells individual shoes."

"What does that mean?"

"You can buy just a left shoe, or just a right shoe. No pairs. Just single shoes. For amputees, or people who just lost their shoes or for people with two different sizes of feet, like me. We call it, UniShoe."

"Huh. I'll have to think about that."

"Think about it? Come on. It's never been done. The original OG."

"It's just OG, Eliza. If you add 'original' it becomes redundant. And it still doesn't work. Don't you ever talk to your kid?"

"Yes, I have, and it's like conversing with the Tasmanian devil."

"Well, my son only speaks an untranslatable dialect of Testosteronese. On that note, why'd you call Malcolm? Why not just file a missing persons report and let the cops deal?"

"He's Peter's oldest friend. Maybe he knows something?"

"Malcolm's also your ex-lover."

"Shouldn't there be some sort of statute of limitations on that term, like it runs out after five years, and then you just revert back to calling yourselves friends? It sounds so sleazy."

"You can't just un-fuck the guy. It doesn't work that way. Besides, you were together for, what? Five years?"

"We were in Silverton then. It shouldn't count."

"It sounds to me like you're really trying to rationalize away some latent feelings you have for your old flame. You did say once that your ultimate fantasy was to have Peter and Malcolm double-team you."

"I didn't say that! At least not out loud. And not when I was sober. I said that if you combined the two they'd make a great human being. They're good together and it sucks that their friendship faded away."

"Maybe if you hadn't married Malcolm's best friend ..."

"I didn't even meet Peter until years after Malcolm and I broke up. Okay? Haven't we been over this?"

"I know, I know. I'm kidding. Look, it's okay that you still have feelings for the guy. It would be weird if you didn't."

"That's not why I called him. I called because I need help and I guess I feel sorry for Malcolm, what with him losing his job, and his credibility, and his wife. Did Melissa ever marry the architect?"

"Who knows? I don't see why you can't ask Malcolm for help *and* get search and rescue out there."

"Well, it's just that ..." Eliza shuddered as she thought about the two security goons, reeking of Axe body spray, who had come to her door asking about her husband. If Peter was in trouble with the law, she sure as hell didn't want to lead the law right to him, did she? "I don't know. Maybe you're right." She paused, then changed the subject: "Oh, so get this, Ashley came to the library this morning, on her bike, dressed in the tightest spandex imaginable, with a plate full of brownies for Vin. But Vin can't eat them because of his diet."

"That guy doesn't need a diet. He's ripped."

"That's *why* he's ripped. He eats like a damned Neanderthal and Neanderthals didn't eat brownies. If I ever get into any of that, shoot me, please."

"Gladly. And then I'll marinate your dead body in Chunky Monkey ice cream to make up for everything you missed and then roast you on a spit. Vin and I will snack on your marbled flesh as we cavort in his cave on the furs of animals he chased down on foot."

"I'll let Vin know about your, um, plans."

"I gotta run. Just promise me that whatever you do, you won't sleep with Malcolm. That's a big no-no."

"The shithead hung up on me, so, no, I don't think a romantic liaison is in the cards."

It was probably inevitable that, after such a conversation, visions of Malcolm and Peter would come into Eliza's head. Since it was time for her lunch break, anyway, and since the bench she was sitting on was still in the shade, she decided to just sit back and close her eyes and let the memories run loose.

She still didn't know why she had left Malcolm so many years before. They'd had a decent relationship, the sex was good, they made one another laugh, and Brautigan was — for the most part — emotionally stable, which helped ground Eliza's impulsive Gemini nature. That was part of it, for sure: He was too damned stable, too intent on staying put and devoting his energy to the community of Silverton and his little journal, the *Dandelion Times*. He simply refused to entertain the possibility of leaving, ever. And so she up and bailed, loading her few belongings into her Toyota truck and fleeing to Santa Fe. She hadn't meant to break up with Malcolm, but after a few months of the long-distance thing the relationship just sort of eroded away, and while Malcolm was visiting on their fifth anniversary, she ended it, much to Malcolm's dismay.

In the months that followed Eliza embarked on a number of fleeting relationships, which brought her various degrees of satisfaction and, most importantly, dimmed the impulse to call Brautigan and ask him to come back. Those stretched into more lingering love affairs, less due to a meaningful bond than Eliza's own laziness. The longest fling lasted for three months, and it was with a woman. The sex was nice, but it all turned out to be too easy for Eliza, too obvious, too natural. She grew bored and drifted back into solitude.

Then, on a crisp October evening, when the sky was blue velvet scattered with stars, and the smell of piñon smoke and roasting green chiles saturated the air, Santos went to a party thrown by some artist friends of hers at their little adobe out on Agua Fria. Her friends were roughly her age, but they all seemed older, more together. She hated such events because everyone always asked, "What do you do?" And she would stare blankly back, imagining an honest answer: *Well, I make art. I ski solo into the Pecos Wilderness in the middle of raging blizzards, camp out among the bony aspen trees, and poach fresh powder all day long. I sit at the bar in Il Piatto, drinking a glass of wine and reading* One Hundred Years of Solitude *for the fifth time. I make more art. That's what I do.*

But that's not what they meant.

They wanted to know about her career, what she did for a living. For that, she tended bar at El Farol, catering to an older and older crowd of washed-out wanna-be artists, poets, and turquoise-bedecked white "gurus" who insisted they had fifteen percent Navajo or Apache or Cherokee blood, the type of sensitive, New Age guys who should probably be on the sex offender registry, if not for any specific crimes, then for their day-to-day demeanor. The tips were good and it paid the rent, but it didn't exactly carry a lot of weight in a crowd of sculptors, painters, film-makers, and poets, or the financial-services and real-estate folks who bankrolled them. So at parties she tended to stand around the bar and drink far too much and not talk to anyone. Which is exactly what she was doing that night when she heard a voice say her name and looked up to see a tall and lanky guy whose face was familiar but that she could not quite place.

"Peter Simons," he said, and then looked at her expectantly for the oddest, longest time. "Malcolm's friend," he finally said. "We met once in Silverton? Remember?"

"Oh, yeah, yeah," she lied. "Peter."

"The little sculptures you made. I'll never forget them. They were marvelous. Are you still doing art?"

She didn't remember Peter but she liked him. Peter, it turned out, was an artist, too. He had actually sold some of his work, and done a fellowship in New York and stayed there for a year or so afterwards, but it turned out to be too much. He moved back to Santa Fe, where the only work he could find was as a short-order cook down at the Cowgirl, putting him even lower than Eliza on the Santa Fe social-career ladder, so she felt comfortable chatting with him. Peter gave her a ride home that night, and, after babbling on about his paintings, he grew quiet and, in a stilted way that somehow came across as charming, asked her out to dinner.

On their first date Peter took charge, something to which Eliza was not accustomed. They ordered food to go from Bert's Burger Bowl, drove across the Rio Grande to a place atop a cliff below Los Alamos, ate it as they watched the sun's last light slide up the Sangre de Cristo Mountains, and then, after dark, he pulled a bunch of climbing gear out of his trunk, showed Eliza how to put the harness on and tie the right knots, and he lowered the two of them in tandem off a high overhanging cliff, so that they were dangling side-by-side in the darkness above the gurgling waters of the Rio Grande, where they kissed and groped and got as close to lovemaking as two can get while clothed and wearing climbing harnesses and defying gravity.

Within a year Santos was pregnant. She and Peter were married another six months after Adriana was born.

To Eliza's surprise, and maybe dismay, Brautigan took the news of Peter and Eliza getting together quite well. It probably helped that Brautigan, still in Silverton, was just falling in love with Melissa at the time. Brautigan and Melissa came to the wedding, which rekindled Malcolm's and Peter's friendship for a time. They went backpacking in Utah, met up in Durango, and Melissa and Brautigan came down for a weekend or two in Santa Fe, and they all went out drinking and eating and visiting museums together.

When Adriana was born, Eliza all but abandoned her art. Peter, meanwhile, went on a creative rampage, not only painting prolifically but gaining acclaim, too, while artistically outgrowing the Santa Fe scene. Eliza, being Eliza, was getting somewhat claustrophobic anyway, so they moved, almost on a whim, to Brooklyn, to a neighborhood where things were still affordable.

From a distance, Eliza continued to keep tabs on Malcolm via his *Tucson Tribune* stories and Facebook. Melissa called every once in a while to touch base and, Eliza suspected, to live a little vicariously through them. Brautigan wasn't the kind to pour out his feelings on social media, but when Melissa stopped calling and when the tenor of Malcolm's Facebook posts shifted, she could sense that something sad was afoot. Melissa's Facebook relationship status switched from "Married" to "It's Complicated" to "Single" to "In A Relationship," and Malcolm disappeared from the social media platform altogether. Eliza had wanted to reach out to him then, but it hadn't felt right, particularly since she and Peter were dealing with issues of their own. And when she suggested that Peter call Malcolm, Peter always put it off until he forgot about it. Then Brautigan lost his job at the newspaper and, from Santos' perspective, went missing altogether. When he answered her call on Thursday morning she was relieved to find that he still existed, but also anxious about inviting Brautigan back into her life, even if it was just to find Peter.

In Brooklyn, Santos had gone back to school to pursue a Master's in library science, something that she'd always dreamed of in an offhanded sort of way. It had been a good time for it. Peter was making enough money off his art to pay the bills, and he worked at home, so he could take care of Adriana while Eliza attended class. After she graduated she got a part-time job at the Brooklyn Public Library. It didn't pay much, but she was surrounded by books and by people, which were worth far more to her than money. Besides, she got first dibs on books that the library retired. She took them home by the dozen — ancient cookbooks that sang the praises of butter and lard, eighteenth century botanical studies of the northern Hudson River Valley, teenage mystery novels, an "etiquette for ladies" tome from the forties. At night, after Adriana fell asleep, Eliza delved back into her own art for the first time since Adriana was born, incorporating the ceramic figurines from her pre-Peter days into intricate dioramas made up of the old books and other found objects — a delicate egg shell, the tiny leg bone of a mouse, a bottle cap, a rusty piece of wire. She called them Time Machine I, Time Machine II, and so on, because they were intended to reveal the way objects, places, and people contain all that came before and that is still to come, and that if you're quiet enough, and attentive enough, you can sometimes glimpse all of that time in a single moment, in a single point, in a single place.

Her life was enrobed in an aura of bliss, for a little while. But she and Peter sat on opposite sides of a seesaw, and even as she was ascending, he plummeted into stagnancy. He came down with what their therapist-friend diagnosed as "a run of the mill case of imposter syndrome," and was constantly down on himself for his lack of originality, sure that someone was always about to expose him as a fraud. He continued to paint, but halfheartedly. He became short-tempered with Adriana, and no longer took her on long, meandering walks through the city, no longer sang her to sleep at night with Simon and Garfunkel or Lucinda Williams tunes. He lost the gift for gab that had drawn Eliza to him in the first place. He didn't sleep much and often got up in the middle of the night and took off, to where Eliza never knew, nor did she bother asking.

On a Thursday evening in August 2015, Eliza and Peter found themselves at the kitchen table, alone. Adriana, a precocious tween, was hanging out with friends, leaving little for the two to talk about. So they both gazed emptily at their phones.

"Holy shit," Peter said. "Check this out." On his screen was a video showing an emerald-green field slashed by what looked like a Tang-colored snake.

"What is that?" She asked.

"It's the Animas Valley above Durango. Some mine spilled into the river and turned it orange. It's nuts."

"Huh," she said. "Looks dramatic, but those mines leak nasty stuff into the river every day. You just can't see it, usually. This is only different because it's so colorful."

"That is really interesting."

"It's not that interesting."

"But don't you see, Eliza? It's the ultimate piece of land art. The spill, I mean. These guys from the EPA just made visible what always existed but that was unseen, and suddenly everyone's freaking out. Everyone suddenly cares about acid whatchamacallit. It's awesome. It's art. It's beautiful *and* it's sublime."

"I don't think they intended it that way. And even if they did, Burtynsky's already done it."

"No, no, no. Burtynsky takes pretty pictures of pollution," Peter said, standing up and pacing, more animated and verbal than he'd been in months. "He takes what is already visible and goes all high-def with it, makes it so dramatic that it becomes abstract, meaningless. It triggers aesthetic pleasure and moral despair, but no action, because Burtynsky's images are all so — inevitable. There is no before and after, it's just the destruction, as if it's always been so and as if there is no better way. This is different."

At the library the next day Eliza dug up some essays by two land artists, Robert Smithson of Spiral Jetty fame and Robert Morris. Both of them were interested in turning old mining and industrial sites and other environmental catastrophes into monumental works of art, but Smithson died before bringing his vision to fruition, and Morris was just too ambitious. Perhaps Peter could revive their efforts.

Much to her relief, he didn't. Instead, he went back to painting full-time, only with a palette that was quite heavy in Gold King orange. He started making money again, although it still wasn't enough to keep up with the rising rent in Brooklyn. As Adriana got older — and more expensive — they started talking about moving. After a bottle of wine they would sit out on the stoop and toss out destinations: Paris, Berlin, Hydra, both of them getting worked up about one place or the other. The prospect of moving, of gratifying Eliza's innate restlessness always made her horny, and they'd always end up making love frantically after these sessions, and they'd always wake up with a list of reasons the previous night's chosen destination wouldn't work, after all. Inertia therefore kept its grip on them, despite the financial challenges, and they stayed put for months.

Ronald J. Drumpf's victory in the election jarred them out of stasis. Eliza and Adriana cried for days, even as Peter remained sanguine. "It's just like the Gold King spill, the visible manifestation — in a garish orange form — of the pollutants that had been swirling around under the surface, backing up behind society's facade for years," he'd said, when Eliza confronted him over his lack of emotions following the election.

"Bullshit. The Russians hacked the voting machines, hacked the whole thing."

"Maybe they leaked the emails, maybe they generated some fake news memes on Facebook. But people believed all that crap because they wanted to believe it. Drumpf, or someone like him, has always been there like a draining mine. It was bound to come out sometime. In the end we'll just be left with the same old rotten system, only with different people in charge."

If Drumpf's election was analogous to the Gold King Mine Spill, then his presidency — like that of his daughter — turned out to be equivalent to the Bhopal disaster. Yet while Eliza and Adriana got angry, organized protests, wrote letters, traveled to Washington to march, even got tear-gassed outside the White House during a Black Lives Matter demonstration, Peter only grew more amused at the growing moral and political tire fire that the nation had become. He saw the Drumpf administration and all the wreckage it had wreaked as a giant piece of performance art, and his fascination with that side of it rendered him blind to the litany of human casualties it left in its wake.

Oddly enough the decay of their home country did not impel Peter and Eliza to go abroad. Rather, they felt compelled to go home, back to somewhere in the Southwestern United States, where Eliza felt like she could get a better footing for fighting against the rising tide of hate and white supremacy that emanated from the nation's capital, and where Peter could make his art without so much financial pressure. Eliza suggested going back to Santa Fe, maybe, or even Durango. Peter vetoed them, especially the latter, for reasons that weren't ever very clear, putting them once again at a standstill.

Then one evening in the spring the phone rang, finally snapping them out of the rut. It was Peter's mom, Sandra, calling to let them know that an old Durango artist, Yvonne Martin, a landscape painter whom Peter had admired and drawn inspiration from, had died of what appeared to be an intentional overdose of OxyContin and Maker's Mark.

"I could think of worse ways to go," Eliza said, instantly regretting her tactlessness. Peter took it in stride, and even though he was crying when he relayed the information to Eliza, he also seemed relieved.

"There's something else my mom said, some even bigger news."

"Bigger news?"

"She's moving. To Alabama. But she's hanging on to the house in Durango and says we can live there rent-free for as long as we want."

Hildebrandt Knows

Brautigan **walked the rest of the way home.** By the time he got there, sweat was dripping from his hair, his shirt was soaked, even his underwear was damp with perspiration. His aggravation with his own affliction was heightened when he saw two men, menacingly clean cut and wearing matching black suits, walk out of the parking lot of his apartment building. They both glared at him as they passed, and he glared back, wondering how in the hell they managed not to sweat while wearing all those clothes. To his relief they kept going, meaning they probably weren't from OmnyBank's collection agency.

Curiosity crept up the back of his neck about Eliza's call. Peter and Brautigan had grown up together and they were close friends through high school and into their twenties, but then the friendship faded, or evolved, depending on how one looked at it. He hadn't communicated with either Eliza or Peter for months, maybe even years. He grabbed his mail out of the box, walked into his apartment, clicked on the air conditioner, and shuffled through the mail: a letter from the collection agency regarding the OmnyBank credit card, and another letter from OmnyBank offering him a new credit card: capitalism.

But there was also a plain, white envelope, with "M.P. Brautigan" and his address printed on it in a typewriter-like typeface. There was no return address. The postmark was indecipherable. And it had a distinctive aroma to it. Just as he began to open it, his phone rang again. It was the same number as before. He answered.

"Malcolm?" she said.

"Yeah, yeah, sorry, I guess we got cut off before. It's been a while."

"Something's happened — "

"So, how's New York," he said, his voice a little too enthusiastic. "And

Peter's art?"

"Good. I mean, not good. Well, no, we're not in New York anymore. We moved to Durango. We've been here for a while."

"Durango?"

"Oh, long story," she said. "You didn't know? Aren't you on Facebook? We made a big deal about our move, you know."

"I'm not. But Durango? Really?"

"Right. Peter went missing."

"He went where?"

"He vanished. He went out to the canyons for a couple days. You know, behind the Slickrock Curtain, to recharge his batteries and all that. He should have been back by now. The sheriff's department found his truck, but that's it. And now I can't get through to them. Phones are down or something."

"I'm sure he's fine. He probably just found some canyon and started following it and lost track of time. Peter was never really good with schedules."

"Malcolm, I need your help. Can you please come help me look for him?"

"I don't know where he is."

"You know Peter, and you know this country as well as anyone. Please."

"Hey, I'd really like to help, but I've got work to do. I'm sorry Eliza. I just —. Look, if he doesn't wander out in a week or so, give me a call and I'll see what I can do."

"A week is too long. It will be too late then."

"Why? What happens in a week?"

"The solstice. And that thing you guys do. The sacrifice."

"Peter's still doing that? Who cares? Look. I'm busy. I've got a real job now and friends and my own life here and then you call up out of the blue and try to wreck it all. It's so typical of you, you know?"

"What does that mean?" Before Malcolm could answer the phone clicked, as if Eliza was tapping it against a hard surface, and then went silent.

As a journalist at the *Tucson Tribune*, Brautigan had specialized in wonk, policy, and untangling the byzantine bureaucracy that tries to steer the way the collective "we" treats the land and water and air they were gifted. He tilted toward nuance and the gray spaces, shied away from sensationalism and dichotomy. Meanwhile, the news industry as a whole was trending in the opposite direction. Readers needed stories that could be ingested in smaller and smaller bites, that could be taken in and comprehended during the glance between swipes. Headlines had to stand out in the firehose of information that assailed readers during every minute of every waking hour. Advertisers wanted clicks, page views, something called metrics.

Brautigan's editor, Laurel, was fifteen years his junior, had a master's degree in journalism, wore stylish thick-framed glasses, and had done a string of internships and staff gigs at *Buzzfeed*, *Vice*, and even the *New York Times*. She was brashly self-confident, and rightfully so, but also harsh, intimidating, tactless, and couldn't properly massage an aging writer's ego — or, more likely, she didn't want to. The higher ups pressured her daily to make the content more digestible, to compress it into marketable pellets. She often referred to Brautigan's stories as sawdust sandwiches, vitamin lasagne, or crunchy, which was not a compliment. "We're going to be emphasizing narrative storytelling from now on," Laurel told Brautigan a few weeks after she arrived. "No more wonky information dumps."

"Isn't our job to inform people?"

"Your naiveté would be cute, Malcolm, if only you were about twenty years younger — and cuter."

Laurel developed a Friday afternoon ritual that Brautigan came to dread. She'd walk out of her office near the end of the work day — possibly slightly buzzed on the bourbon she kept in her desk drawer — and call everyone in the newsroom to gather around. Then she would read the "doozy sentence of the week" in a dramatic way to the ever-shrinking news team. Usually she picked on a freelancer, or someone who wasn't there. It was rather funny, particularly when she did interpretive dance, until it wasn't.

On one of those Fridays, after Brautigan had turned in a six-thousand-word draft about a land exchange involving a parcel along the San Pedro River that provided habitat to an imperiled salamander, Laurel sauntered out of her office and called everyone around. "We've got a double doozy today, folks! Frank, give me some of that beatbox you're always doing at your desk. Yeah, yeah, perfect," she said, her bespectacled head bouncing up and down with the beat, as she broke into a white girl rap: "Okay, we've got the BLM, FLiPMA, NEPA, WOTUS and... Hey, can the beatbox, Frank, and give me a drumroll for the really sexy part: salamanders!"

Brautigan felt the heat of blush in his cheeks. He tried to shrink down into his seat, but his seat was one of those stupid exercise balls that Laurel had imposed on the staff, and you can't shrink into a bouncy ball. Sweat stains spread like ink through the fabric of his cerulean shirt. He forced a chuckle as if the story wasn't his.

"Look, everybody, the idea here is to write stuff that people want to read," Laurel said, glaring at Brautigan, inflicting him with a serious case of writer's block.

Once, he received a shaky, hand-written note from a retired professor praising his work. "The *Tucson Tribune* is lucky to have you," it said. "I'm a retired National Park Service biologist, and I really appreciate your stories and their comprehensiveness. Keep up the good work." The writer then went on to give a knowledgeable critique of Brautigan's most recent story on groundwater pumping's effects on flows in the San Pedro River. He taped the note on the wall behind his desk as a reminder that *someone* read his stories. For each note like this, however, there were dozens of troubling online comments, discomfiting not so much for the vile hatred that oozed from them, but because even most of the positive comments showed that the commenter had not read the story at all, or if they had, they had failed to comprehend it. It fortified a creeping suspicion that his work was inconsequential, that no matter how truthful, clear, compelling, accurate, or powerful his stories were, ultimately they would have no meaning in the world.

One night he expressed his insecurities to Laurel, hoping for some reassurance. Instead, she urged him to start tweeting and to be more active on social media in general. "You've got to build the Brautigan brand. You need an avatar, for starters. So get a decent headshot and have Phil over in art Photoshop out the wrinkles and those bags under your eyes, and when you think about stories, think about quotes or concepts that can be made into memes."

"Memes? Like on Facebook."

"Exactly. Simplify. Remember, you're dealing with the Republic of Philistine here."

Whether his readers were philistines or not, he developed obsessive compulsive disorder regarding the facts in his stories. He was terrified of getting something wrong, of adding an extra zero when talking about tons of mine tailings dumped in a river, or referring to megawatts when he should be talking about megawatt-hours. He often lay awake running through every word, every quote, every fact, wondering what he missed or whom he misquoted or whether the headline that some social media manager slapped on his story was too sensational. Most of his colleagues, at the *Tribune* and elsewhere, suffered from the same neuroses. It came with the territory. Their job was to get things right, to find the truth and communicate it, to be objective and fair and balanced and do no harm. Facts were the currency of the trade, and to get one wrong was to throw that currency away.

When Axios, a Manhattan hedge fund that itself was just a division of a corporate leviathan called OmnySyde Holdings, bought the *Tribune's* parent company, things got worse. All of the copyeditors and fact-checkers were canned the day after the sale. Brautigan was so anxious about suffering the same fate that his nervous tic of bouncing up and down on his exercise ball went into overdrive and on the downward bounce his weight proved too much for the rubber ball. A sharp and deafening report rang out as the sphere exploded, and Brautigan crashed into the floor ass-first with a sickening thud. He lay there for what seemed like hours, surrendering to the grimy office carpet that smelled vaguely like rotten banana peels, until Laurel called Brautigan into her office.

"You popped the ball, didn't you?"

"I was just sitting there and …"

She did not fire him. In fact, he got his old, squeaky desk chair back and a day off to tend to his sprained pinky. He even got a promotion, the more work for the same pay variety, and a new title: Health, Science, and Environment Reporter. He didn't complain and he didn't quit. He couldn't afford it. No one else was hiring, he'd be left without health insurance, and his wife Melissa was making even less as a paralegal at a social justice-oriented law firm.

As part of the merger, Laurel and, by extension, Malcolm, got a new boss by the name of Nick Sanders, who came over from the marketing department. Laurel was livid — the guy's only experience in journalism was a class at Arizona State — but she stuck around, and took out her frustrations on Brautigan, assigning him not one but three stories on the new prickly pear diet craze, each of which "performed" vastly better than any of his real stories. Write about how to get rid of belly fat, or about one upper-middle-class person getting shot on the "good" side of town, and the whole city hungers for the gory details; write about a dying world and no one gives a shit.

On one of those Saturday nights when he was in the office, trying to pound out copy for Sunday's edition, he got a Facebook message from someone whose name he didn't recognize, Jane Trudeau. It said: "How can you just let your wife sleep with my husband as if you don't care?"

Was this a trick? Some sort of spam to lure him in?

"Umm, sorry," he wrote back. "I think you got the wrong guy. Leave me alone or I'll block you."

"No, you're the right guy," she wrote back immediately. "Your wife is Melissa. And she's been fucking my husband, Chad, for months and now he says he's leaving me for her."

Brautigan turned then and calmly vomited into his little plastic trash can. Two days later Melissa moved out of their house and in with Chad Trudeau, tearing Brautigan's life, and his heart, asunder.

Brautigan waited for the phone to ring again. When it didn't, he closed his eyes and tried to meditate, tried to calm the rage that had popped up out of nowhere and that he had thrown at Eliza. After thirty seconds or so, he opened his eyes, took a few deep breaths, and finished tearing open the envelope from the mailbox and pulled out the sheet of paper. It was that old style paper that's vaguely transparent with a textured surface, the words in a typeface that indented the paper like a real, old school typewriter. He unfolded it and read:

When the diagnosis is dire,
and the waxy sun
dips between the Bears Ears,
old grudges will fade.
You will meet yourself
along the tangled lines of the spiral,
at the Bonanza that
only Hildebrandt knows.
The monster begets,
and the daughter seeks.
The planet burns
and shade is a luxury
Find Hideout.
Resurrect Petrichor.
Your memory will set me free.

Brautigan read it again, then again. If it was a poem, it was a shitty one. If it was a riddle, it was inscrutable, at least to Malcolm, save for a couple of terms: The Bears Ears referred to the landmark buttes in southeastern Utah, visible on the smoggy horizon from all over the Four Corners Country. Frank Hildebrandt was a Utah uranium tycoon who had briefly lived in Brautigan's childhood home a few years before his parents bought it. Hildebrandt's ghost knocked around on the family home's roof, terrifying young Brautigan nightly, and he became the universal boogeyman in the family's campfire stories.

And there was that smell again, coming from the paper. It was not pleasant — an unfortunate mix of Listerine, patchouli, Old Spice, and horse urine — but it was familiar, too, and triggered something, sent a flood of disjointed memories of youth onto Brautigan's mental movie screen. Brautigan peered at the postmark again, and once again was unable to decipher it. It looked like Albuquerque, which would mean that Joshua, who lived in Rio Rancho, was the most likely sender. The stilted poem seemed out of character for Malcolm's older brother, but it was probably his socially awkward way of mending the family ties. Things had kind of fallen apart after the previous Thanksgiving, when Joshua and their stepdad Sidney had drunkenly gone to blows over the quantum physics of turkey carving, a brawl that climaxed with the un-carved turkey sailing through a plate glass window.

Joshua was a physicist, and an intensely cerebral dude, so the riddle probably was layered with meanings that related to physics or string theory or quantum whatnot, things that Brautigan would never truly understand. Still the Hildebrandt reference, and the familiar odor emanating from the paper, was enough to spark Brautigan into thinking about home for the first time in months. He smelled it again. Then it came to him. It wasn't just one fragrance, but a combination of them, the exact scent that resulted from a pack of teenaged boys spraying themselves with perfume samplers at the local mall, circa 1985. He half-smiled, half-cringed at the memory.

He folded up the paper with the riddle on it and put it back in the envelope and into his messenger bag with his laptop. He looked around his apartment, at the dingy furniture, the unwashed dishes piled beside the sink, the junk mail, the empty wine bottles lined up along a wall, the detritus of loneliness. Maybe it *was* time to get away for a bit. He could do his work in Durango, or in Utah, or just about anywhere. Besides, there was no going back to his favorite caffeine joint after that morning's incident. He picked up his phone and punched the number from the most recent call.

"I'm in," he said, as soon as Santos picked up. "I'll leave tomorrow. No, screw it. I'll leave later today."

"Today?" Eliza said, her voice flat.

"What's wrong?"

"Nothing. That's just so soon. I need to kind of arrange things. Aren't you getting a late start?"

"Sure, yeah, you're right. Yeah. But, look, I'll stay in Holbrook tonight, at that Motel 6. I'll take my time and won't arrive in Durango till tomorrow evening. That should give you plenty of time."

"Is that the dump you and I stayed in once? The one that doubles as a porno-chainsaw-massacre movie set?"

"It is, and from what I remember, it was kinda hot."

"That was at least a century ago, and from what I remember there was something sticky all over the bathroom floor, a half-eaten can of SPAM in the refrigerator, and the shower head shot off and hit me in the head and gave me a concussion, probably allowing you to take advantage of me. Why don't you stay in Winslow at that one place. The fancy place?"

"La Posada?

"Yes. That's it."

"Great idea."

"I'll pay for it."

"No, you won't. I've got it."

"Really? I thought you lost your job at the *Tribune*? What are you doing for money these days, anyway?"

"Freelance stuff. Editing corporate newsletters, investor reports, that sort of thing."

"Newsletters? What corporations?"

"Oh, let's see, Synergex, Dynagen, uhhh," — looking down at the stack of mail on his table — "OmnyBank. All the big ones."

"OmnyBank? Gross."

"Gross?"

"Sorry. I'm impressed, I guess. So you'll be at La Posada tonight. Great. Maybe text me when you arrive? I need to keep track of you so you don't go missing, too."

In the aftermath of Melissa, Brautigan had thrown himself into his work with an enthusiasm that surprised even him. His motives were a little askance: He wanted to impress Laurel, on whom he'd always had a crush, as hopeless as it might be. It did make him a better employee. The "metrics" on his stories improved, Nick was happy, which took some pressure off Laurel, who showed her appreciation by not picking on Brautigan during the Friday afternoon roasting session.

When the email popped up on his screen, with the subject line "juicy tip," he almost deleted it, not because he suspected it was spam, but because it was from none other than Jane Trudeau, the ex-wife of the man who was sleeping with Malcolm's ex-wife, and he was still reeling from her previous message. He was a curious sort, however, and eventually opened it to find a photograph of some smug-looking middle-aged white guys standing on a boat. He recognized them immediately: Chad Trudeau — yes, that one — who was also a green developer who was building a celebrated mixed-use infill development in South Tucson, and who was the chairman of the board of Save Our Sonoran, or SOS, the tenacious and litigious local environmental group. Chad had his arm around Dirk Sampson, the CEO of RT Homes, a giant corporate developer who specialized in converting open desert into lush-lawned suburbs. Standing next to them, with a drink in his hand, was Gary Gimmel, the director of the sustainability center at the state university and member of the state land board. In explanation, Jane had written: "Spotted Owl Preserve isn't all it's cut out to be."

Spotted Owl Preserve was a massive "sustainable" development — a new town, really — that was going up on a huge swath of state land on the saguaro-studded slopes at the base of the Catalina Mountains. Initially Brautigan had been skeptical of the sustainability claims, but then Save Our Sonoran not only endorsed the project, but signed on as a partner. Brautigan had responded by writing a gushing article, highlighting the rainwater catchment systems, the super-efficient building requirements, the solar panels on every rooftop, the low-flow appliances. Nick was pleased, since for once Brautigan's story wasn't depressing. Now Brautigan worried that it wasn't accurate, either.

With the photo as a guide, and more info from Jane, he dug up an avarice-fueled scheme involving Sampson, Gimmel, and Trudeau, and sketchy loans, quid pro quos, outright bribes, and cocaine-fueled parties on Sampson's yacht. Still, when he sat down to write the story, he didn't play up any of that. Instead, he focused on what he thought mattered: the hundreds of saguaro cacti, the snakes, the lizards, the ocotillo, the fuzzy-looking chollas, the coyotes, the ring-tailed cats, the Mexican Spotted Owl. All of it toppled by bulldozers, their habitat paved over with "carbon neutral" concrete. It wasn't until several paragraphs into the story that he mentioned the slimy deal between Sampson, Gimmel, and Trudeau.

Brautigan finished the story and pushed "send." A few minutes later, Laurel walked by his desk on the way to Nick's office, raising her eyebrows as she did so. Two long hours later, Nick called him into his office, where he waited with the printout of his story. "Damn, Brautigan, this is some good stuff you dug up," he said. "Too bad you buried the lede. No one's going to stick around through all of this endangered species shit to get to the good stuff."

"What do you mean?"

"Here, I fixed it for you." He handed him the printout, splattered with red ink.

Green group sells soul in "sustainability" scandal
A Tribune Exclusive

Environmental activist group Save our Sonoran accepted bribes from corporate home developers and others in exchange for dropping its opposition to a massive "new urbanist" development at the base of the Catalina Foothills, according to documents obtained by the Tucson Tribune …

And so on. The prose was unrecognizable to Brautigan, and he winced at the repeated mention of "scandal," "corruption," and "hypocrisy," particularly since the spotlight was not on Trudeau or even Sampson, but the environmental group itself. It didn't seem fair, since most members probably were oblivious to the underhanded dealings going on, but he had to admit that it would be far more enticing to the philistines.

"We already ran it by legal," Laurel said. "We'll need everything documented."

"Documented?"

"Yeah, like copies of the emails between these guys laying out the whole scheme. You've got that, right?"

Actually, he didn't have it. In fact, a lot of the gory details had come from Jane Trudeau, who was not a rock-solid source. Suddenly he wasn't so sure about this whole thing. "Hey, Laurel, can I talk to you in private for a minute?"

"Sure, let's go to my office." Laurel was stern and serious until they got out of sight of Nick, then she started jumping up and down, a huge grin on her face. "I love you, Malcolm, I love you. This story. Holy shit. Nick's gaga over it, and rightly so. I will buy you not one, but two of those martinis you drink. Thank you. Now, send me the docs A-S-A-P so that we can put this thing to bed."

"Oh, gee, well, yeah, okay," Brautigan stammered, abandoning his intent to fess up and pull the story. He skulked back to his desk, opened new email accounts for Sampson, Gimmel, and Trudeau, and proceeded to create a plausible email chain that laid out all the transactions, then sent them to Laurel and Nick. The story ran the next day on the front page.

Brautigan was so anxious that he turned off his phone that night, locked the doors, and sat in the dark drinking red wine until he passed out. By morning he felt a little better, figuring the normal handful of people would read it, pass it off as Arizona business as usual, and move on. Instead, it went viral, particularly among the right wingers who saw it as validation of their suspicion that liberal developers and environmental groups were in cahoots and wrecking their livelihoods. The click-blizzard that ensued crashed the *Tucson Tribune*'s website. Brautigan had never experienced anything like it, that rush of knowing that so many people were reading his stuff, and that it was frothing them into a dangerous rage. Nick bought a round of drinks for what was left of the newsroom that Friday to celebrate record-breaking page-views for the story, and afterwards Laurel delivered on her martini promise, although it went no further, much to Brautigan's disappointment and, perhaps, relief.

Then on Monday it all came crashing down. The *Outcast*, the local alt-weekly, ran a blistering exposé of Brautigan's exposé by a reporter named Ted Denton, who was more or less on the same beat as Brautigan, only he had the liberty to inject a heck of a lot more snark into his pieces. The article revealed that

Melissa had left Brautigan for Chad Trudeau — giving Brautigan a strong motive for defaming Trudeau's character — and also revealed that Brautigan had faked the emails. .

Denton and the *Outcast* exacerbated Brautigan's shame with an accompanying puff-piece listing all the ways that Chad Trudeau had helped the community and robustly defending the sustainability credentials of Spotted Owl Preserve, omitting the fact that the development required the scraping of a huge swath of desert vegetation and the thousands of residents would make thirty-mile-long, fossil-fueled trips into town each day. It was totally out of character for Denton, whose tone usually was quite harsh when dealing with hypocrisy. An advertisement for Trudeau's condos plastered the entire back page of that week's edition of the Outcast, while an inside spread peddled lots at the Preserve.

Astoundingly, the *Tribune* did not fire Brautigan. The story was true, even if the emails were fabricated, and it and the ensuing scandal turned out to be good for business. Laurel, however, was disgusted with Brautigan, with the paper, with the direction in which journalism had gone, and she resigned a week later and took a job teaching mass communications at the university. Brautigan knew he couldn't stay, but he also lacked the courage to quit.

As a young man, Brautigan had secretly yearned for a cataclysm in his life so jarring that it would leave him little choice but to load up his backpack, sneak away in the night, and vanish into a deep and shady sandstone canyon where he would lay down on the wind- and water-softened stone and let the stream of cool air wash away the angst, the insecurities, the pain, and the noisy clutter of daily existence and allow him to forget the relentless ticking of the clock, to forget his dismal credit score, to forget the words, and finally to forget his own name.

This, surely, was the calamity he had craved, and yet instead of going missing, instead of retreating to the only real home he knew, Brautigan found himself stuck inside his own apartment, terrified of going out, scared to answer the phone or emails. When he finally emerged, his job was gone, as was his career and credibility.

Subsidence

Brautigan packed quickly, tossing camping gear into his car along with a handful of other necessities — some clothes, laptop, notebooks, running shoes, N-95 mask for smoke and hantavirus, and a bundle of surgical masks for other viruses. He dug through the closet and found the unopened box containing a survival kit that one of his advertisers, EndDays.com, had sent him in lieu of cash, and threw that in, too.

He walked around the building to Natalya's apartment to tell her he might not make their backgammon session for a while, but she didn't answer her door. Emilio wasn't home, either, so Brautigan wrote him a note and put it and the next month's rent in an envelope and slid it under his door. Then he tidied up the apartment a bit and loaded all the perishables in the fridge into a garbage bag. The walk across the parking lot to the dumpster left him on the edge of heat stroke. He locked up the apartment, took off his shirt so that it didn't get soaked with sweat, crawled gingerly into the 1985 Toyota Corona, the seat scorching his back and thighs, and pulled out of the parking lot of his apartment complex in the early afternoon. He was engulfed in both doubt and sweat by the time he was out on Oracle and chugging sans air conditioning through Tucson sprawl — strip malls and Starbucks and strip malls and Whole Foods. Finally, he made it out onto seventy-seven, past the cookie cutter developments and the last remaining trailer parks of Oro Valley, including the one where a subsidence crack — the result of too much groundwater pumping — had swallowed three single-wides and their occupants, a horse, and a sixty-six cherry red GTO a few months earlier. He pulled the spray bottle out of the cooler and blasted his face with it in a futile attempt to fend off the heat.

The motion of his steel, glass, and plastic cocoon on wheels took him not only through space, but also time. He found himself in the seventies, in the backseat of his parents' old station wagon as they descended out of the Pinal

Mountains to where they crossed a sharp line dividing winter from spring. His memories took the form of old snapshots, the colors both faded and gaudily intense at the same time: ugly brown sweater, mustard yellow slacks, washed-out turquoise sky, his dad's bushy mustache and sideburns as he drove and smoked, his mom leaning against the passenger door. Malcolm and Joshua hung their heads out the backseat window, both staring hard at the passing landscape in hopes of being the first to see a saguaro, and thus netting the grand prize — a Butterfinger, sickly sweet and chocolate-melty at the next gas station stop.

Brautigan was so caught up in his memories that he may have drifted a little over that solid white line, and didn't notice the hitchhiker until he had nearly made the poor guy into his hood ornament. "Aaaaah!" Brautigan yanked the wheel to the left, sending the vehicle into a sideway skid. Time slowed. His reflexes kicked in and he steered into the slide, and his car jerked to a relatively unscathed stop alongside the road. He gripped the steering wheel and stared forward, his heart pounding behind his eyes as he tried not to look in the rearview mirror for fear that he'd see a mangled body in the road.

The passenger-side door swung open and a booming voice spoke: "Yo, bro, thanks for the lift, but you shouldn't drive in the shoulder. You almost took me out back there." The hirsute man, shirtless, wearing cut-off jean shorts, tossed a guitar case on the backseat before plopping himself rather fuzzily into the passenger seat. "Hey, you wouldn't happen to be going up toward Superior? I have a gig there tonight."

"A gig?" Brautigan had a policy against picking up hitchhikers, not because he was afraid of being raped and killed, but because he didn't want to be forced to make conversation with a stranger. But then, he had almost run the guy down, so giving him a ride was the least he could do. "Don't I know you?"

"You've probably seen me play. I'm Mannfred Mannia."

"Man Fred who?"

"No, no: *Mannfred*. One word. As in the Mannfred Mann Earth Band. I'm a Mannfred Mann tributary."

"Tributary?"

"Yeah, like a solo version of a tribute band. The term's trademarked, by the way. You have a tape deck in this car? Awesome. I do all of my recordings on cassettes. You just can't beat the tonal quality, you know?"

Brautigan looked down at the old stereo. "Yeah, well, a lot of good it does me these days. My wife — er, ex-wife — sold my whole tape collection at a garage sale. Sucks."

"Well, shit. That ain't cool, man. That's like hawking your testicles at Dick's pawn shop. No wonder you ditched her." He pulled a cassette out of his little man-purse and inserted it into the stereo. "This thing isn't gonna eat my tape is it?"

Brautigan cranked the engine and started driving again, still trying to figure out how he knew the guy. From the speakers came the sound of acoustic guitar accompanying a solo singer, presumably Mannfred Mannia, wailing in a creaky voice: "… wrapped up like a douche another runner in the night." Brautigan looked at his newfound companion with raised eyebrows, but remained silent.

"Hey, see those huge piles of gray stuff over there," Mannfred said, pointing to a pair of symmetrical, perfectly flat-topped, monochrome mesas. "Mine tailings. Nasty shit. And they're just sitting out there on the banks of the Gila River, waiting for some sort of catastrophe. Breach one of those things and the tails would smother every bit of life in the river — or what's left of it — for miles and miles downstream, and the acidic soup within would poison the watershed for decades. But you already know that, don't you?"

"Uh huh," Brautigan said, wondering if the guy sitting next to him was the same person he'd picked up a few minutes earlier.

They were entering what's known as Arizona's copper mining triangle, where today's violence — the blasting, gouging, pummeling — remembers the horrors of the past, when General James Carleton, predecessor and inspiration to Herman Goering, brought the weight of the US military down onto the Apache people who had lived here for generations. Carleton scorched the earth, homes, and fields not just to move the Apache to reservations but, in his own words, to bring about their "extermination, to insure a lasting peace and security of life to those who go to the country in search of precious metals." He perpetrated ethnic cleansing not only to gain more *Lebensraum* for his white brethren, but also more *Bergbauraum*, space and security for the corporations to mine the hell out of the place.

"Hey, can you pull over up ahead. At the scenic viewpoint?"

Brautigan pulled off into a parking lot that could have accommodated Grand Canyon-sized crowds, but that was occupied by a single, pearl-colored, late-model Cadillac sedan. He cut the engine. The two men climbed out of the car, one excessively hairy the other excessively sweaty and hairy, both shirtless but too old and lumpy to be seen in public that way. An older man and woman, cuddled up on the sole picnic table in a public display of friskiness, saw the two men approaching them, disengaged, and quickly scurried back to their car and sped away. Brautigan and Mannfred walked over to the fence and leaned against it, trying and failing to take in the entirety of the yawning earth-wound known as the Ray Mine. Terraces lined the pit's edges like stairs, each one as wide as an interstate highway, and tiny-looking yellow dump trucks, each far larger than Brautigan's apartment, crawled along the terraces, carrying hundreds of tons of copper ore.

"Sublime," said Mannfred. "Truly sublime."

Brautigan wasn't quite sure what Mannfred meant, but he nodded sadly, anyway, gazing out at the various shades of ochre, red, yellow, and eerie blue, at the symmetry and order of it all. It was beautiful in a terrible sort of way, powerful and awe-inspiring and, Brautigan thought, inevitable. It doesn't matter who is in the governor's office, or the Oval Office, or Congress. It doesn't matter how many words Brautigan or anyone else writes chronicling the horror. The blasting will go on, the gaping pit will grow deeper and wider, the mechanized maggots will continue to ingest the planet's carcass. We will sacrifice the rivers and the fish for smarter phones, the ocotillo and saguaro for bigger houses, the owl and javelina for faster cars. We are the hungry ones, the insatiable species.

"They are doomed, and I am tired of being human," Mannfred said, barely loud enough to hear, "tired of being mad in a mad world." It was a line from a poem by Richard Shelton, Brautigan's favorite poet.

"And here I thought people didn't read poetry anymore."

Mannfred looked back and, without missing a beat: "It's not a poem, it's a meme. I saw it on Facebook."

Brautigan laughed, not sure which was a more apt symbol for the state of the world — the gaping pit before them or Richard Shelton as a Facebook meme. "Of course, you know that your phone came out of that fucking pit. And my car. And our laptops. And that guitar or whatever the hell it is you've got in that case."

"Okay, then let's give it back."

"What?"

"Give something back. To the earth. It's time, don't you think?"

"I'm not driving my car in there."

"Okay, then," Mannfred said, as he pulled out his iPhone. He looked at the screen, pushed some buttons, apparently checking his social media accounts one more time, then took a few steps back from the chain-link fence, wound up, cocked, and pitched that piece of glass and plastic, copper and circuitry over the fence. It sailed through the air, catching the afternoon sunlight as it spun end over end before dropping out of sight into the pit.

"Aren't you gonna need that?"

"Not really. Not anymore. I gotta landline, anyway."

"No shit? Damn. Well, thanks for taking one for the team."

They reluctantly climbed back into the car and rode in silence the rest of the way to the old mining town of Superior. Brautigan dropped Mannfred off in front of a rough-looking bar, evidence that gentrification had yet to subsume the mining culture.

"Just don't order a fucking Heineken," Brautigan said, "and definitely not a craft beer. These people will not tolerate that shit and will kick your ass. Oh, and sorry I almost ran you over back there."

"You bet. It was a pleasure riding with you. My name's Ted, by the way, Ted Denton."

Both men paused for a moment as if waiting for something to happen. Nothing happened.

"I'm Malcolm ... er, Juan. Juan Shapiro. Hey, maybe we could go out for a beer sometime or something, you know?" Brautigan started to get out of the car to give the guy a hug. He liked him.

"Juan?" Raised eyebrows of disbelief. "Hey, whatever you say. Okay, yeah, a beer. And don't forget the immortal words of the great Mannfred Mann, 'They got a name for the winners in the world. But I wanna name when I lose.'"

"But that's Steely ..." But by then, Denton was already walking into the bar, his guitar case swinging haphazardly at his side.

Brautigan popped open the cooler, sprayed himself with his redneck AC, and pulled back out onto the highway. It wasn't until Brautigan had made his way up Queen Creek and topped out on Oak Flat that he realized how he knew Denton: He was that damned alt-weekly reporter, the one from the *Outcast* who had written the exposé of Brautigan's vaguely fabricated exposé of Chad Trudeau. Brautigan shouted out a string of epithets, followed by the inexplicable phrase: "They call me Deacon Blues, motherfucker!"

Regressive Agency

After losing his job at the *Tribune*, Brautigan couldn't afford to sit around and wallow in his misery or even take some time off to map out the rest of his life. He was a member of the non-trust-fund working class, after all, and a missed paycheck would knock him right out onto the street, looking for his own piece of cardboard under which to bake. He had to find new work, quickly, yet journalism outlets wouldn't touch him.

He'd done a stint as a baker once. He liked the sensuality of it, enjoyed kneading the fleshy dough, relished in the smell of a healthy levain and the crust as it caramelized in the oven. It was relaxing to just follow the recipe and the ingredients and the routine, rather than having to create something new from scratch every day. And he especially liked the fact that a baker's number one job is to make people happy, the exact opposite of what a journalist is supposed to do.

Brautigan wanted once again to make folks happy, so when he saw the ad for a baker at a busy joint downtown, he printed up a resume, put on his old flour-caked clogs, and headed that way. As soon as he walked in, and looked back through the big glass window to the work area, he knew it wasn't going to work. Every one of the bakers was far younger than Brautigan, and far more equipped to heft the big bags of flour, stand on their feet all day, and tolerate the heat blast from the oven. He walked out without applying.

After another day of fruitlessly scanning the want ads, he typed "How to get a job" into the Google. He was amazed to find a vapid article with that exact headline, and after some clicking around discovered that it originated at an outfit called Copy Studios 101. It's a content-mill, a sweatshop for assembling words, if you will, and they were seeking word proletarians. He signed up, using a pseudonym to ease the regret. They paid him twenty bucks a pop for rearranging web search results into short articles telling readers how to replace the starter on their old Celica. It was cheap, embarrassing, maybe even a bit tawdry. If fluff pieces for style and health magazines were "whore work," as a writer friend of Brautigan's used to say, then churning out words for Copy Studios 101 was like doling out hand-jobs in a Walmart parking lot for five bucks a pop. But with economies of scale it could pay the rent and then some.

If he really focused, he could send ten stories a day to his supervisor, someone named Eve, whom he'd only met via e-mail and who scolded him regularly for not adequately optimizing his stories for search engines. He'd wake up at four in the morning and write or edit articles until he couldn't see anymore — thirteen, maybe sixteen hours each day in his stuffy apartment, the curtains all closed so he wouldn't know what time it was. His goal was to get to thirty articles per day, at which point he'd write a self-help book: *How to become a millionaire with nothing more than a laptop and Google.*

He didn't make millions, he didn't write the book, but he did stave off eviction, and his ambition during those months kept him away from alcohol until he finished writing for the day, so you could say Copy Studios 101 saved his liver, too.

He yearned to get back into journalism, sure, but it wasn't the "legit" stuff he missed. It was that final big story, the one that was a little exaggerated, and the feeling that came with his words actually reaching people. Just as he grew bored of Copy Studios 101 a new genre of news — call it fake news, if you'd like — emerged. Brautigan came up with a pen name, Michael Baines, and started pitching listicles. He remembered what Laurel, his former editor, had said about the philistines and "meme-ability," and he finally started following her advice, which paid off.

As he embarked upon his new career as an alt-journalist, he realized that maybe he had been wrong about the happiness thing. Maybe journalism *is* kind of like baking, or should be. You *can* just follow a recipe and, if it's got enough butter and sugar in it, and validates readers' preconceived notions, it can make them happy. Brautigan wrote pieces for *PatriotReport* and then *Rightbart*, and built up thousands of Twitter and Facebook followers over the course of just a few months. After spending most of his adult life earnestly writing story after story about really important things for a dwindling readership, now he was able to throw together an article in a day that would literally draw millions of eyeballs, clicks, likes, heart-icons, and automated positive reviews. Truth — that old god of Brautigan's, that merciless dictator — had been deposed.

Then Brautigan got an email from someone named Stan Hatch. The "think tank" that Hatch ran, the Utah-based GGF (God, Guns, Freedom) Foundation, was looking to start up a news outlet. They wanted Brautigan —

Michael Baines, actually — to be its star reporter and to help guide the editorial direction of the site. At first, Brautigan scoffed. No self-respecting journalist would work for a think tank, particularly one so ideologically oriented. But by then Brautigan had shed most of his self respect, and the pay Hatch dangled in front of him made his old *Tucson Tribune* gig look like a joke. For the first time in his life he wouldn't have to worry about paying the rent or have a panic attack when he had to buy new tires for his car. So Malcolm Brautigan, a.k.a. Michael Baines, signed up to be the Senior Editor for *Alt-News*.

In the beginning, as much to assert his independence as anything else, Brautigan targeted the establishment of every color and stripe — Democrats, Republicans, liberals, libertarians. He came up with a number of different pen names, so that it looked like he had a big staff that spanned the political spectrum. Michael Baines might rip into Mitt Romney for his sanctimonious bullshit, or pen a missive on the evils of the raw milk ban, while Brad Melcher would write up an investigative piece on Drumpf I and the Russians, and Juan Lopez-Shapiro would scrawl something about George Soros-funded terrorists spiking Sen. Mike Lee's Jell-o socials with LSD. To Brautigan's surprise, Stan Hatch didn't protest, even when Brautigan's pseudonymous journalists went after Romney or the Mormon church or the Republican Party as a whole. It wouldn't be until much later that Brautigan understood that even when he was doing left-wing alt-journalism he was furthering Hatch's agenda, which reached far beyond party lines.

At first, Brautigan worked under a pall of remorse. After a few payments, he got over it. He didn't need to subscribe to his clients' beliefs or ideologies. Like a doctor or a defense lawyer, his job, as he saw it, was to heal or protect his readers and validate their biases, no matter how horrid they were. He was good at what he did, and proud of it. He saw himself as a problem solver, taking a broken reality and tweaking it in such a way that made his readers happy, assuaged their guilt, or vindicated their anger. And in that way, he believed, he was doing a public service.

Keeping track of all of his so-called staff had become perplexing, so he got rid of them. Michael Baines, while giving a speech with Trad-Wife leader Tammi Shanigan on the conspiracy to silence "the male, pale, and stale" among us, was charbroiled by a Molotov cocktail thrown by a vegan Antifa protester. War-on-Christmas correspondent Brad Melcher, while embedded in a special forces platoon fighting against the Happy Holidays Militia, took a grapefruit-sized chunk of shrapnel to the skull during a melee in a lower Manhattan Starbucks. The mainstream media cabal covered up the tragedies. Brautigan couldn't bring himself to write about the fictional deaths of fictional journalists, so instead he sent an anonymous tip to Rush Jonson over at *PatriotBlast*, who picked up the ball and bombastically ran with it, devoting a spittle-filled, hour-long episode to the dual tragedies.

That left only Juan Lopez-Shapiro. He killed it on every social media platform, with the exception of Tinder, a phenomenon around which he never really could wrap his mind (nor could he figure out how to re-create the younger, better looking Juan in the flesh).

He had never imagined making this much money, particularly from writing. He felt appreciated. He felt liberated. He no longer fretted about getting the facts straight or offending anyone. Ironically he didn't worry about being exposed as a fraud now that he had become a full-on impostor. And though it sounds strange, he also had never had more meaning in his life, either. Journalism was a trade. Alt-journalism was more of a craft, or even an Orwellian art. And deep down, Brautigan had always considered himself more of an artist than a reporter or journalist. He had found his true vocation at last.

Standing on a Corner

Brautigan rolled into Winslow, an old railroad-turned-interstate town up on the high desert of the Colorado Plateau in late afternoon. He pulled into the parking lot of the hotel, a sprawling compound that had been designed by Mary Colter in the thirties to look like a Spanish colonial hacienda. The room was expensive, but worth it, and as Eliza said, he deserved it. Had he still been on Facebook he would have posted a picture and "checked-in" at the place, in hopes that Melissa would see him living the revenge life in real-time.

Brautigan took a cool shower and, resisting the temptation to just plop down on the bed and blast the air conditioning and watch television, put on the only linen pants and shirt that he owned. He mussed his shaggy mane in hopes of giving himself an unkempt, sexy look and meandered down to the hotel bar, stopping along the way to admire the bold, colorful, and somewhat frightening paintings that adorned every wall of the sprawling complex.

Brautigan had to wait for the bartender, who stood nearly seven feet tall and weighed at least 300 pounds, to finish chatting with a woman at the far corner of the bar. When the bartender finally acknowledged him, Brautigan ordered a gin martini. The barkeep measured out a hefty portion of Bombay Sapphire and a splash of vermouth and something else that Brautigan took to be homemade bitters, shook the metal container, and deftly poured the liquid into a chilled glass and slid it across the dark wood of the bar to Brautigan. It took all of Brautigan's motor skills to carry the drink with shaky hands to a corner table without spilling any.

Before opening his laptop he lifted the glass to his lips impatiently, took one big cold gulp, and then settled in for two more sips, during which he closed his eyes as the juniper-berry bitterness slid across his tongue. No sooner had the cold liquid touched his lips than a shudder ran though his whole body, and he stopped, intent upon the visceral images that filled his mind, a whole collage of memories, from visions of he and Joshua riding across the reservation in the back of that shitty ass International Harvester pickup truck, to a slow-motion reprise of the moments before his father's death.

Brautigan opened his eyes with a start, only to find the bartender staring at him from across the room. Malcolm gave him a nod of approval, despite the pounding in his chest: That was one hell of a drink, man. He took another big gulp in an attempt to soothe the adrenalin, and just like that, more than half of the drink had gone missing, along with the quivering in his hands.

He opened his laptop. In his inbox was another email from Stan Hatch: "I'm just making sure that you're working on the story about our Interior Secretary and that it will be posted soon." Brautigan sighed, rolled his eyes, and then went to work researching Albert Fallon.

Before he was appointed to head up the Interior Department and oversee a bulk of America's public lands, Fallon was a Republican Utah congressman, serving conservative causes in Washington for twenty-two years and carrying the ideological torch of Hatch's GGF Foundation. With a deep-orange canned tan and a silver bouffant, he resembled a cruise ship crooner or a television evangelist. He acted like the latter, whipping up his followers to give it up at the altar of the extractive industries. His campaign contributors' list was identical to the attendance roster for a global oil and gas conference — BP, Chevron, Exxon Mobil — tossed together with gun rights organizations, auto dealers, uranium mining corporations, and real estate agents. Near the top was something called RosaBit. Brautigan didn't recognize the name, but figured it was either a tech company or a nutritional supplement supplier, since Utah was rife with both. While in Congress, Fallon had served his donors' interests well, leading efforts to eviscerate environmental laws that stood in industry's way and waging a career-long war on the Interior Department. That Fallon was chosen to lead the same fit perfectly within the tragic logic of the current era.

As a cabinet member, Fallon waged all-out war on environmental regulations, reduced royalty rates for oil and gas and coal companies, and slashed national monuments down to a sliver of their original size in order to "restore access" for "locals" and "traditional industries." When hundreds of emails and other documents relating to the monument shrinkage were made public, enterprising journalists connected the dots, making it very clear that it wasn't locals or even Fallon who drew the new monument boundaries, but uranium and oil companies that had interests in the region, and that had long contributed to Fallon's campaigns. The documents also revealed that the companies had continued to contribute to Fallon's "campaigns" even after he was a cabinet member, and was no longer running for elected office.

Although this behavior was par for the course under both Drumpf administrations, it was an open secret that Ivanya disliked Fallon, probably because of his religious beliefs. The president also wanted to replace Fallon with her brother, Ronald, Jr. Yet it was also widely understood that if she did that, she would get blasted by @DeadRonaldDrumpf, who considered his son to be an incompetent lout, and Fallon to be his most trustworthy cabinet member. If Fallon were to resign due to revelations of corruption, however, then Ivanya could replace him without incurring the wrath of the dead. That could be disastrous for Hatch and his minders, for whom Fallon was their high-ranking puppet.

Meanwhile in San Juan County, home of the most drastically shrunken monument, the power structure was shifting. The white, Mormon men who were invariably welcoming to extractive industries were being deposed, and progressive Navajo politicians who tended to be in favor of environmental protections and the national monument were taking over. They were using Fallon's foibles as a weapon in their battle to restore the monument to its original size. Brautigan's job was to disarm them and, if nothing else, to draw some of the scrutiny away from Fallon.

As he read, Brautigan sighed heavily, then sipped his drink, sighed then sipped, sighed then sipped. This wasn't going to be easy. Still, he saw it as a challenge, and started digging around in his *Alt-News* toolbox for the right instrument for the job. Obfuscation, the most common tool for muddying the waters around climate change, wouldn't work in this case. And since President Ivanya had Fallon in her sights, the old standby of admitting the wrongdoing and then taking pride in it wouldn't cut it either. So, that left what-about-ism and deflection, not the most elegant rhetorical instruments, but effective ones nonetheless.

He'd turn the lens away from Fallon's improprieties by focusing it on those of his opponents and accusers. Sure, he'd write, the oil giants are backing Fallon, but what about the big-money environmental groups and outdoor gear corporations who fund the pro-monument commissioners and the new sheriff? Isn't that just as bad?

The facts are as follows: A philanthropist named Hans Sorenson, the multi-millionaire founder of Grenadier outdoor gear, had donated money to an organization called Planet-Aid, whose sole purpose was to give grants to small conservation and cultural organizations. Planet-Aid then gave a $15,000 grant to the Bears Ears Foundation to produce a video about the connections the Pueblo, Navajo, and Ute people have to the landscape within Bears Ears National Monument. The new sheriff — a freelance photographer — was paid a small fee for some of his work to appear in the video, long before he was sheriff. None of this was a secret, and was all laid out in detail in public filings with the IRS and emails sent to the local newspaper. Anyone with a brain would know it was meaningless. Luckily for him, Juan Lopez-Shapiro's readers weren't exactly the sharpest tools in the shed.

Brautigan tweaked the facts a bit, coming up with this:

"Documents obtained by Alt-News *reveal that radical environmentalists and outdoor recreation corporations are engaged in a hostile takeover of San Juan County, thereby usurping local sovereignty and eroding rural heritage and traditional livelihoods. Leaked emails reveal that billionaire Hans Sorenson funneled dark money to two county commissioners and the county sheriff, all of them Democrats, via the Bears Ears Foundation, thus buying their support for restoring the national monument to its original boundaries."*

Brautigan paused to admire his handiwork. By simply dropping in words and phrases such as "documents obtained," "leaked emails," and "funneled dark money," he had successfully twisted a benign situation into something sinister, perhaps even criminal.

Brautigan went on to explain that Fallon had, indeed, consulted with oil and gas and uranium companies when making his recommendations, because those were the companies that had the expertise, and who were giving jobs to the locals and pouring money into the community in the form of taxes and royalties and philanthropy. Meanwhile, what were Sorenson and Grenadier giving to the community, other than overpriced clothing? He then did some searching through the *Salt Lake Sentinel* for a punchy quote to drive the thing home, finding this little zinger: *"This is tyranny," said San Juan County Commissioner Bill Stevens, after he was outvoted two-to-one to join the tribal coalition in fighting to restore the monument. "It's an egregious example of the Grenadier-funded conspiracy to kill our heritage and the beautiful uranium industry so they can turn our county into a backpacker zone."*

Brautigan added a few hashtags — #EcoTerror, #DarkGreenMoney, #LandGrab, #UraniumIsBeautiful — and then published the story, making sure to send a separate link to Stan Hatch as he did.

He closed the laptop and sat back, overcome by a sour burn inching its way up his esophagus. He had experienced it quite often during his *Dandelion Times* days, usually just after sending the files to the printer, a strain of anxiety with which every journalist is familiar. But he thought himself cured of the affliction. He figured the relapse was the result of driving in the heat, his encounter with Ted Denton, or the fact that he still didn't like penning hit pieces targeting people who weren't nationally known public figures. But he brushed the feeling away, certain that none of the subjects would read the story anyway, and anyone who did wouldn't take it seriously. The idea was not to bust Etcitty, but to take some of the heat off of Fallon.

Brautigan gulped down the last of his drink, now tepid and salty from the olive, and stood up and let the host know he had a reservation in the restaurant. The host guided him to a four-top in a corner. "Umm, it's just me," said Brautigan, suddenly self-conscious about being a solo diner in an upscale restaurant. "Do you have a smaller table?"

"Just you, huh? No, I'm afraid not."

Eating a takeout pizza in his room at the Motel 6 would have been a lot less awkward. But the wine, a sauvignon blanc from McElmo Canyon, followed by his meal, slow-cooked pork and a smoky red chili sauce and a big bowl of thick and creamy polenta, eased the discomfort, and he was able to relax and eavesdrop on fellow diners. At the next table an older couple dressed in safari gear talked loudly about their visit that day to Hopi, letting everyone in the room know how *unjust* the ban on photography was. Two guys who looked like overgrown Mormon missionaries gnawed wordlessly on giant steaks. And at the next table over, two women, probably in their late thirties, sat across from each other, chatting and occasionally stealing glances in Brautigan's direction, which both enticed Brautigan to check them out more thoroughly, and also made him even more self-conscious about his solo status. He really wanted to know what they were eating, as that might give him some insight into their personalities, but was afraid that they'd catch him staring. And before he could discern what was on their plates, they left.

Brautigan ordered the homemade piñon nut, salted-caramel gelato for desert. Eating it made him very happy, and the creamy, cold, salty sweetness washed away the remnants of the nausea that had afflicted him before dinner. He felt pleasantly sleepy, and welcomed the prospect of heading up to his room, lying in bed, and watching shitty television. Maybe he'd even order a Scotch to take with him.

But as he approached the bar the two women were sitting there, sipping cocktails, and they had already seen him and were looking in his direction. He would have felt strange ordering a drink and then leaving with it. So he sat down a few seats away from them and quickly whipped out his phone and stared at it, so as to avoid making eye contact and perhaps render himself invisible. When he looked up, he saw the woman with dark hair, tall and powerful, stand up from her barstool and walk away, leaving the other one, with hair the color of wheat, alone.

"Well," she said in what Brautigan took to be a Minnesota accent. "It looks like there are two lonely people sitting at this bar. Whaddaya say we sit a little closer together."

Brautigan's cheeks flushed as he looked up from his phone, and the first bead of sweat instantly pooled just below his hairline. He brushed it away as casually as possible as he walked around and sat down next to her. She wore a linen blouse that was precisely the color of lilacs on a mid-May day, with sharp features, and a large and slightly crooked nose. She seemed familiar somehow, and had an edge to her that sparked the kindling in Brautigan's belly. When the bartender finally acknowledged Brautigan, he ordered himself a Manhattan.

"Let me guess," Brautigan said. "You're from Minnesota."

"Try North Dakota."

"Like Fargo?" Brautigan said, trying his best to make prolonged eye contact, just like the article in *Masculinity Monthly* had suggested.

"Yabetcha. Just like the movie, wood-chipper and all. And you? I'd say Colorado."

"Wow, I'm impressed. I mean, I live in Tucson, but I'm from Colorado, originally."

"I knew it. I spent a lotta years up in Rangely. You know Rangely? Up there in the oil fields. Boy, I'll tell you ..." She waved at the bartender, who stood stoically in front of the backbar. "Hey, how about another drink?"

The huge bartender, in a surprisingly soft voice: "Stoli?"

"Precisely."

Brautigan timidly asked for another Manhattan, even though he sure as hell didn't need one. Before Brautigan could take a drink, the woman reached over and ran her pinky up the side of the glass, collecting the dew as she went. Then she reached over and touched Brautigan's neck with her cold, wet finger. He shuddered. She laughed, flashing a row of fetchingly crooked teeth. "Oh to be the dew on your cocktail glass," she said, her words softened by alcohol.

Brautigan was left speechless, but tried to maintain eye contact nevertheless, just like the listicle in *Masculine Monthly* advised.

"Yeah, Rangely," she said, her elbow on the bar and her head resting on her arm. "Nothing but red red, neck neck, fuck fuck."

"Ahh, okay," Brautigan laughed nervously, took a gulp. "So, was your husband ... Do you work in the oil industry or something?"

"Because that's the only reason any one would live in Rangely? You got it. Petroleum engineer. Me, not my husband, thank you very much."

"Hmm. You working around here?"

"I'm up in Fuckhell Nowhere for work," she replied. "That's in Utah. They fly us in and out of Phoenix."

"Whereabouts? I mean, to what specific region of Fuckhell do you refer? It's a big place."

"Right in the middle."

"I see." He rubbed the side of his glass nervously. "And, what kind of project are you working on? Some new oil field or something?" He wanted to ask her whether she felt guilty about her role in killing the planet, but more than that, he wanted to ask her how she managed her guilt. But he figured that might disrupt the mood.

She smiled and reached out and touched Brautigan's nose. "That, my friend, is classified."

Brautigan chuckled, waiting for her to say she was just kidding. But the look on her face told him otherwise. She was serious and wouldn't say more.

"What are you doing here in Winslow," she asked. "Let me guess: standing on the corner and waiting for a girl in a flatbed Ford?"

"I actually tried that once. I got a sunburn waiting, and the girl never showed up."

"Okay?"

"I'm just stopping through on my way up to Durango. My hometown."

North Dakota looked away. "My grandparents lived there for a while."

"Really? What were their names? Maybe I know them."

"I doubt it. They weren't there for long. It was a long time ago. Why are you going there?"

"To find an old friend. It's complicated."

"An old lover, you mean?"

"Like I said, it's complicated."

"Humor me."

"An old lover called me up out of the blue to ask me to help her find her husband, who's an old friend of mine."

She raised her eyebrows at this. "Where is he?"

"He disappeared. Somewhere in the middle of Fuckhell Nowhere, in fact. Anyway, he's probably back home by now. Most likely I'll just end up going back to Tucson tomorrow."

"But what if your friend doesn't come back?"

Brautigan sighed. It was a good question, and one to which he did not have an answer. "I suppose I'll go look for him. Or not. I don't really know."

"Where? I mean, like you said, it's a big place."

"Behind the Slickrock Curtain, as Peter and I like to say. But that's a big place, too. It's all big around here. Too big to wrap your mind around, too big to find someone who's gone missing. Anyway, I guess I'd probably start in some of the places we used to go together. There's a couple of secret canyons that we considered our own, you know?"

"Which canyons? Maybe I could be of some help, since I do work up there."

"I said that they're secret. But sure, if he's still missing in the morning, maybe so."

Silence, somewhat awkward. Brautigan didn't know what he was doing, never really understood the mechanics of picking up someone in a bar or, for that matter, the casual sex that was supposed to follow. For him, sex was never casual, which was probably why he was so terrible at playing this game. Hell, he couldn't even figure out how to use Tinder, nor muster up the courage to follow through when someone else swiped left. Or right. Or whatever it is. He took another swig of the drink, dug around in his memory for some of the tips he had read in *Male Weekly*, worked on channeling Juan Lopez-Shapiro, who was surely more suave than he. "Hey," he blurted. "Has anyone ever told you that you look like a movie star?"

"Depends. Which movie star did you have in mind?"

Oh, great. Now what? He said the first name that came to his mind: "Sharon Stone?"

North Dakota squinted suspiciously.

"No, I mean, you know, you look like she did back when she was younger. Like your age." This may or may not have been true. Brautigan wasn't sure what Sharon Stone looked like, but it's the name that popped into his head when he thought of dangerous and sexy. It was a stupid pick up line, but probably not the worst he could imagine. The woman's eyes seemed to grow soft, or maybe the whiskey coursing through Brautigan's veins just blurred all the sharp edges.

"Sharon Stone? Hmmm, I think I would prefer Chloë Sevigny. But it'll do."

This seemed to be going well, Brautigan thought. And for the first time that night, he let the anticipation of human touch take hold. He allowed himself to imagine how her skin would feel under his fingertips, the resistance of her taut nipple between chapped lips, stubborn bones submerged beneath liquid flesh, the flavor of the sea on the tip of his tongue.

"Maybe you could draw me a map, now," North Dakota said a bit impatiently. "Just in case we miss each other in the morning."

Maybe it wasn't going so well, after all. Brautigan let the anticipation of late-night television take hold. He allowed himself to imagine lying in his hotel bed, alone, watching walk-in bathtub infomercials, enigmatic pharmaceutical jingles, and some blathering idiot make cute jokes about the downfall of the Empire. "I don't even know where to begin," Brautigan said, feeling his words slur, but unable to do anything about it. "There are so many canyons, so many lovely, dark, cool canyons."

North Dakota didn't press Brautigan. After a silence, they resumed the small talk, mouthed words that were lost in the alcoholic haze and the clinking of silverware from the last few diners in the restaurant. She let her fingers brush against his leg, leaned onto the bar in his general direction. He stared at the way the skin around her eyes crinkled up sexily when she laughed. They ordered another round.

"How about we finish these up in your room," she said, nearly causing Brautigan to spill his drink.

His room had a couch, which left Brautigan a place to go besides straight to the bed when they got there. He plopped down, and tried to figure out what he was supposed to do next. Didn't people sign consent forms these days? And where does one find one? Are you supposed to carry them with you? Did hotels offer them in the nightstand in place of Gideon Bibles?

North Dakota sat down beside Malcolm, sidling up close. He began babbling uncontrollably, probably due to nervous energy colliding with alcohol-dulled inhibition. He'd remember it later, and cringe at the sensation of simply losing control. "One thing you should know about me," he said, "is that I have an unusually large heart. Irregular, too." It was true. An actual doctor, not the internet, had given him the diagnosis. "After I told Melissa about what the doctor said, she told me she wanted a second opinion. Not about the surgery, but about the size of my heart."

The woman laughed. Brautigan wanted to sob. He started to stand up, just to escape his own emotional storm, a combination of arousal and embarrassment and longing and loss, maybe to pace away the nervous energy, but she put her hand on his chest and pushed him back into the couch, all the while looking him in the eyes. His giant heart thumped irregularly, his sternum reverberating against her open palm. She kept the pressure on him, holding him down as if he would float up to the ceiling if she let go. It was the most intimate gesture he'd experienced in a long, long time, and in that moment he believed that if the evening ended right then and there, he'd be satisfied.

But the evening did not end, and it was his turn to do something. Hesitantly, he moved his hand toward her and lightly touched her clavicle, circling a freckle with his finger as arousal's warmth crept into his flesh. He longed to wrap himself up inside of her, to submerge himself in oblivion, but as he leaned in to kiss her she turned her head away. In that moment of disappointment, Brautigan noticed that North Dakota's skirt had ridden up to expose her thigh and a tattoo there, the letter C.

She saw him looking and pulled her skirt down to cover it, then turned back to him, and reached over and dexterously unbuttoned his shirt. She ran her hand through the hair on his chest, her fingers across his quivering belly. He tried again to touch her, but just as his hand alighted on her breast she turned her body toward him, breaking contact. She bent down, gently sucked his nipple, mirroring what he wanted to do to her, and then moved downward from there, undoing his pants as she went. She looked up at him with alcohol-bleared sad eyes and a wan smile, and slowly took him into her mouth. He was drunker than he'd been in a long time, but the alcohol did nothing to diminish his ability to perceive the virtuosity with which she utilized lips, tongue, and even teeth to elicit pleasure from his otherwise numbed corpus.

As his body floated free of itself, he remembered that he had been to Rangely once. Just passing through on his way somewhere. And he remembered the sign outside a beaten down old building that said rooms for rent, free showers, thirty-five bucks, and how he asked the checkout girl in the little grocery store what people do around Rangely for fun and she gave him a look that smoldered of bitterness and Coors Light and the scratchy dried out vinyl of a rusty car's squeaky old bench seat. And he remembered stopping on the way out of town and just watching those pumpjacks all covered with rust and looking like they were a century old but never ever ever giving up on their relentless grind, that steady rhythm, pounding into a prehistoric era when this barren land was covered by a sea, and teeming with strange creatures, volcanoes, world-obliterating comets.

And then he was back, in that room, on the couch beneath the portrait of some old movie star that time had forgotten, North Dakota's straw-colored hair brushing against his thighs and stomach as her head bobbed in lazy rhythm. A loosening of the limbs, the unbearable tremble, the irrepressible coming. Waves rippled from his belly upward, flooding him with sweet loss. Maybe he gurgled. Maybe he yelled. When he finally unclenched his eyelids he found himself looking right into the eyes of the Sharon Stone doppelgänger from North Dakota, wearing a smile and him all over her swollen lips. Brautigan blearily plotted his reciprocation, mapped the path his mouth would take from rib to rib and downward, sketching out the silent and frenzied prayer his tongue would perform between her thighs. But first he just had to close his eyes for a few minutes and rest a bit.

"Thank you," Brautigan said, his eyes brimming with tears. "I think I love you North Dakota."

And then he passed out.

Regret

Brautigan woke up in the hotel room bed, though he had no idea how he had gotten there. His laptop was sitting on the desk, instead of in the briefcase he normally stored it in. His head hurt, his tongue felt like a desiccated marshmallow, and he was alone. The sun shone through the slats of the window shade. "Shit, shit, shit, shit, shit," he muttered. He struggled out from under the covers, put on the clothes he had been wearing the night before, and, despite the acrid smell coming from his own body, jogged down to the restaurant, hoping she — did he ever catch her name? — was there. He looked in the bar, in the lobby, out on the lawn. Nothing.

The sun and the heat inflamed his hangover. His stomach burned and churned, and he had a throbbing ache behind his ear, tender to the touch, as if he'd been bitten by a spider. He promised once again to drink less. Then he went back to the restaurant, huddled into a corner booth, and ordered coffee and the meatiest, eggiest, cheesiest thing on the menu. Not even that could sop up the guilt that gnawed at his gut, and the regret at being unable to return even a crumb of the pleasure she had given him. He wanted a do-over. But he also wanted to crawl into a corner and die.

Along with all of the other physical and emotional ailments, the hangover also plagued him with something like nostalgia, a stream of disjointed memories and an accompanying sad ache. He was able to remember every scene from the night before, up to the moment that he blacked out, as if the alcohol had enhanced his sense of perception rather than diminished it. Details in his flashbacks — the little flecks of gold in North Dakota's grey-blue eyes, her scent as she leaned in and stroked his cocktail glass — seemed far more vivid in replay than they had when they occurred. It made him doubt the veracity of both the experience and the memory. Perhaps it had all been a dream.

He cut into a fried egg, and watched the glossy yellow yolk pool on the plate before sopping it up with an over-buttered piece of toast.

The waitress must have refilled his coffee cup six or seven times. He felt jittery and hollowed out when he finally hauled himself away from the table and staggered out into the parking lot to look for a car that might belong to her. There were at least six vehicles — rentals, he supposed — with Arizona plates in the lot, along with a couple of Suburbans with government plates, and a giant pickup truck with CLEARWATER emblazoned on the door. Brautigan would have bet money that Clearwater was an oil and gas company, probably in the fracking fluids business, meaning the universe had, indeed, reached peak irony. He thought it highly unlikely that North Dakota was piloting one of those beasts, though. Maybe she had already left to catch her flight. He stared down Route 66, weighted by the realization that he would never see her again, and also the realization that maybe he loved her.

Of course it wasn't really love. But of course it was.

He skulked back to his room, took a shower, packed up his clothes, and headed back down to the lobby to check out. As he waited behind a young couple getting directions to the Painted Desert, he flipped through a complimentary copy of *Newsday*: Los Alamos remained under evacuation after the wildfire, and security agents were still searching for the missing material. Investigators determined that lightning had sparked the fire, that somehow a single thunderhead had formed in the otherwise cloudless sky and a spark of static electricity had jumped from cloud to earth. Meteorologists had no explanation.

Most of Southern Utah had been without power for more than twenty-four hours for unknown reasons.

All flights from the Phoenix airport were suspended, again, because it was too hot for planes to take off. Officials announced they would close the airport altogether from June through August, and replace it with a brand new airport near Payson, some eighty miles away, 4,000 feet higher, and much cooler — for now.

House Democrats had launched an investigation into yet another quid pro quo incident involving the current administration: A National Security Agency no-bid contract was given to IntelliCore to provide cybersecurity for multiple federal agencies after Kredit-Schweiz had bailed out Jared Kuckner — the first man, aka FMOTUS — with a high-risk, $600-million-dollar loan. IntelliCore and Kredit-Schweiz shared a parent company: OmnySyde Holdings.

Surely, the pundits opined, this would be the final straw that would sink the Drumpf dynasty, at last. Brautigan chuckled: As if. All he knew was that it was good for Juan Lopez-Shapiro, since it provided more opportunity for him to "uncover" the shady workings of the Deep State.

On page four was a shorter article about the president's proclamation that welfare and social safety nets were bad for people because people wanted to work for a living, they wanted to pull themselves up by the straps of their bootstraps or, in her case, their Christian Louboutin pumps. It was accompanied by a photo of Ms. Bootstraps herself wearing diamond-encrusted earrings.

"Excuse me, sir? Can I help you?"

"Oh, yeah, sorry. I just need to check out. Room one-o-four." Brautigan handed the key to the receptionist, she handed him the receipt, and then he stood and looked expectantly at her. "No one left me a message or anything, did they?"

"No, I'm sorry. I don't believe so."

"Oh. Hey, does this photo look weird to you?" he said, holding up the photo of the president. "Look how long her neck is. She looks like a giraffe."

"It looks to me like she was custom-made for the guillotine." She said it without inflection, irony, or humor, a blank look on her face. "Please come back and stay again."

"I will," he said. He put the paper down on the desk and hurried toward the door.

He climbed into his car, which was already oven-hot. He checked his email on his phone — no note from Eliza telling him that Peter had come home. He slid the key into the ignition and cranked the engine and pulled out of the parking lot, heading east on old Route 66, humming some forgotten song.

Given his late start, Brautigan knew he should take the most direct route, following the freeway to Gallup. But he had begun to feel apprehensive about this mission, about traveling back to his childhood home to help his ex find her husband — even if said husband was Brautigan's oldest, closest friend.

What was the point, anyway? Peter's disappearance was not a case of some kid from Connecticut wandering away from his hiking group, getting lost, and then getting found the next morning. Peter was not lost. He might be injured, pinned under a rock in some slot canyon, buzzards floating eagerly overhead. If so, Brautigan sure as hell didn't want to be the one to find him. Or he had vanished on purpose, meaning he wouldn't be found until he wanted to be found.

Which brought up the question: What the fuck was Brautigan's role in all of this? It was too much to ponder while also driving, so Malcolm pulled over just before reaching the junction of the turnoff to Highway 87 and the I-40 on-ramp, killed the engine, and considered his plight. Forty-eight hours earlier his life had been moving along fairly smoothly. He woke up, did his job, rewarded himself with a drink or two and maybe a pint of Ben & Jerry's, then went to bed and started it all over again. Maybe it wasn't the most fulfilling life, but it worked. Now his daily rituals had been blown to smithereens, the catalyst being Eliza's first phone call.

Redemption was still at hand. If he just drove south, instead of north, he'd be back in Tucson in a few hours, and could slip back into his routine — with a new coffee shop, of course — by the next day. He could make a few changes. Maybe he'd try to meet someone. He could take an Arabic class over at the community college, go to the tango lessons he'd seen, or start volunteering again with the group that puts out water and food for the people crossing the border. As disastrous as the previous night's encounter with North Dakota may have been, it had rekindled his confidence and his desire for a romantic partner and hunger for a life.

He fired up the car. He'd flip a u-turn, leisurely head back down Route 66, maybe stop for another cup of coffee, and then turn left and go back home. Eliza could find someone else to help. Before he shifted into gear, however, he noticed the gigantic billboard up ahead, next to the interstate. It was a photo of a woman's face — blonde hair, blue eyes, gleaming teeth — and below it an enigmatic slogan: "If you could go back and change just one thing, what would it be?" Brautigan let up on the clutch and let the car idle as he studied the ad, looking for some indication of what pharmaceutical product was being peddled here, and what ailment it might treat. There was no explicative fine print. It was as if he had encountered an analog meme.

It reminded him of one of Peter's aphorisms: "You only regret what you don't do." Brautigan had scoffed at this one. After all, whenever you *do* something, you're *not doing* an infinite number of other things — Brautigan's incessant logic was annoying, even to him. Still, he admired Peter for walking the talk, envied him, really. Peter was always saying yes to everything, whether it was that time he somehow figured out how to shut off that oil pipeline out of the Aneth Field, or when he skied down the Durango uranium tailings pile just before they started removing it. He was always flying right into the flame while Malcolm sat back and watched, cringing, which is probably why Peter was a semi-famous artist and Malcolm wasn't, and why Peter was married to Eliza and Malcolm wasn't.

Malcolm could turn around, return to the comfort of habit. Or he could actually do something. It was not a simple choice. Still, Brautigan knew he couldn't sit there and hold his breath forever. So he pulled the car out onto the highway and he headed north, toward the Hopi mesas. After his little car finally reached cruising speed, he was barreling along at sixty miles an hour towards the Slickrock Curtain, and home.

Let Them Eat Blakes

He accelerated until the front-end shimmy of his car settled down and sat back and enjoyed the view. He didn't need the map anymore. From here he could feel his way from one lonely road to the next. Just keep the San Francisco peaks on the left, Mount Taylor on the right. Head for the dark band of the Chuskas and keep the eyes peeled for Ute Mountain and the Bears Ears, those little lumps on the horizon in the north. They were there, always there, waypoints for finding home, the place where he felt most comfortable and also the most haunted.

He noticed the hulking vehicle of the type that might be used as an unmarked patrol car behind him somewhere near the turnoff for the Little Painted Desert. When it was still the same distance back ten miles later, he began to worry. Brautigan checked his speed, which was below the limit, his plates were current, and he had tested taillights, brake lights, and all of that before leaving. Maybe it was the sex cops, coming to arrest him for being a selfish pig the night before or, perhaps, for letting his mind drift to pumpjacks and Rangely while he had melted into ecstasy.

He relaxed a bit, tried to keep his eyes on the road ahead, but when he did glance back up at the rearview mirror, it was filled up with the Chevy logo coming at his rear bumper so fast and suddenly that he peered at the speedometer to make sure he was actually moving. The Chevy swung smoothly to the left and sped by, going at least ninety-five, tinted windows obscuring those within. Brautigan's left arm reflexively flew out the window, his hand waving wildly as he flipped the bird in the car's general direction.

The car's brake lights lit up blindingly red and the SUV swung off the pavement onto a turnout and skidded to a gravel-spraying stop. Brautigan's perspiration kicked into high gear, his heart fluttered, and his accelerator foot became rather indecisive, causing his car to jerk forward erratically. Finally his brain took control of his leg and he drifted past the SUV at fifty-three miles an hour, eyes on the road, both hands upon the wheel. The big car remained static, its bright headlights lit up. Brautigan topped a rise and dipped back down and the car was no longer in sight. After a good fifteen minutes had passed without the vehicle reappearing, he allowed himself to relax, and ease back into the rhythm of the road. He didn't see the vehicle again, and surmised that it had been some local kids screwing around, or maybe someone test-driving the vehicle, oblivious to the angry guy in the little car.

Maybe, he thought, with a nugget of terror lodging in his esophagus, the vehicle hadn't been there at all.

Outside Greasewood he slowed to get a gander at a herd of skinny cows that had converged around a dented stock tank, its side graffitied with "ZOMBIELAND" and "Water is Life." He thought about love, and relationships, and his friend Peter while the cattle looked dumbly at the tank as if it were a god, about to deliver them from their bovinity. He rolled down the window and, echoing the mystifying billboard slogan he had seen earlier, yelled: "If you could go back and change anything, what would it be?"

The cows all turned and looked at him as if *he* were the idiot.

A couple hours later, the ragged silhouette of Shiprock, or Tsé Bit'a'í, rose up ahead of Brautigan, obscured by the brown-yellow gauze of smog and dust and wildfire smoke. He turned eastward toward Farmington and followed the San Juan River through the borderland, where the northeastern edge of the Navajo Nation melds with the non-Indian world in an economic and cultural mishmash. Brautigan passed by a little stand selling tamales and kneel down bread; a strip mall with an OmnyEZLoan, a pawn shop, and a liquor store; a sprawling automobile graveyard; a slaughterhouse selling mutton; and a bright pink SEX SUPERSTORE shadowed by a huge billboard warning the superstore patrons: JESUS IS WATCHING YOU.

And in the spaces between were junk stores, big and small, from the salvage yard where Brautigan had once coveted a commercial airliner fuselage, to Hal Fox's little shack, located just feet from the highway, piled floor to ceiling with hoarded treasures. Malcolm and Peter used to come down here on the weekends to go shopping, Peter for objects to use in his artworks, Malcolm for old bikes that he could fix up and sell at a profit to Durango yuppies. The ritual usually concluded with a visit to Mister Fox, a small, weathered, energetic, overall-wearing man of indeterminate age who specialized in bicycle parts. Invariably Malcolm would try to lowball Mister Fox on a wheel, a sprocket, or a pair of handlebars, and Mister Fox would respond with an indignant tirade:

"Golly blarmit! I was on an aircraft carrier in World War Two! If it weren't for me, you'd all be speaking Deutsch! And you're gonna sit here and shyster me out of my livelihood!?" Despite the hostility, the encounter always ended genially, more or less, with Malcolm giving Mister Fox his asking price and then some.

As he approached Mister Fox's place, Brautigan slowed down. He needed to stretch his legs, and he had long hankered for an old typewriter. Fox was surely dead, but maybe one of his heirs had kept the family business going, and had an old Olivetti lying under a pile of Cabbage Patch Kids, View Masters, and Walkmen. Brautigan pulled the car onto the side of the road beside a row of old oil barrels and a couch and tentatively walked toward the shop. A man sat in a tattered La-Z Boy just outside the front door, taking sips out of a large, plastic cup. He looked remarkably like Mister Fox, was even wearing what looked like the same pair of overalls, only now the grooves cut into his tan face were deeper, the age spots bigger, and his wiry frame was stooped and shrunken.

"Uh, hi," Brautigan said. "I was wondering if you had any old typewriters?"

The man peered back as if measuring Brautigan's worthiness to own an old typewriter. "What the hell you want an old typewriter for? Is that what the hipsters up in Durango are buying these days?"

"No, I just thought, maybe … Hey, I used to come in here a lot to buy bike parts. From Mister Fox. Are you his son?"

"Son? I *am* Mister Hal Fox, and I ain't got no sons."

"Oh, jeez. I'm sorry. It's just that when we used to come here, you said you were in World War II, and so, you know, that was like eighty years ago or something? And so…"

"And so what? Spit it out."

"Uhhh, nothing. I'll just go in and look around, if that's okay?"

"Suit yourself."

Brautigan walked tentatively into the little structure, which was less antique store than a museum of obsolescence and entropy. In one corner several reel-to-reel tape machines leaned against a wall, collecting dust. An oil barrel was filled with old film cameras: Nikons, Canons, Pentax, and a bunch of Kodak Hawkeye Instamatic R4s — the same model Brautigan's grandmother had given him on his seventh birthday. Even then, the photos had seemed aged as soon as they came back from the developers, as if the smudged lens looked back in time.

"I *had* a real nice typewriter in here," said Mister Fox, who somehow had managed to extract himself from the recliner and position himself directly behind Brautigan. The old man exuded a sour odor, and his cataract-clouded, bloodshot eyes had the strangest golden color, as if they'd been fashioned out of pine pitch. "A Hermes 3000. A sixty-four. I got it new for my eighteenth birthday."

"A sixty-four? Like 1964?"

"Precisely."

"But wait. If you were eighteen …?"

"How could I have been on an aircraft carrier in the Second World War? I wasn't, you dumbass. How old do you think I am?" His guffaw turned into a juicy cough. He chased the phlegm down with whatever was in the plastic cup. "Hell, I remember you and your buddy, the tall one. I told you that story because if I told you I was in 'Nam you'd just give me the finger and spit on me."

"You were in Vietnam?"

"No. What makes you think that?"

"You just said," Brautigan blurted, his frustration building. "Wait. So that whole World War II thing was made up? Just to make us pay more for bike parts?"

"I don't make shit up. My pop was in the war. On an aircraft carrier. He was a conscientious objector so they made him be a barber even though he couldn't cut hair worth shit. After the war he opened his own barber shop in Tulsa, where I was born. But then my momma died, and my pop signed on to help build the El Paso gas pipeline and moved us out here and stayed on working as a foreman on the rigs. It's been one hell of a ride." Another round of succulent coughs erupted from the old man's chest and throat.

Brautigan held his breath and sidled as far away as the tight quarters would allow, feigning interest in the contents of a box on top of another stack of boxes. The boxes were coated with thick, greasy dust. Absentmindedly, Brautigan opened the one on top. It was filled with little white objects that, in the dim light, looked like irregularly shaped pearls, or perhaps deformed marbles or even sugar candies of some sort. He picked one up, held it up to the light. "Oh Jesus!" Brautigan said, tossing it to the ground. "What the hell? Are those human teeth?"

"Ha. Damned right they are. All those boxes. The ones that say AEC? They're all full of teeth. Hundreds of 'em."

Brautigan wanted to get away from the teeth, and this place, and Mister Fox and his tuberculosis and creepy dental fetish, but Fox stood in the only pathway between Brautigan and the front door, and there was no back door.

"Yup, those are the fruits of my labor. My first ever job, that is. When I was eighteen they moved the Atomic Energy Commission offices out of what is now the hospital, and they hired me and my buddy Norm to clean out all the crap that had piled up there, those boxes of teeth included. I used the proceeds to buy that typewriter for my own birthday."

Brautigan relaxed, a little. "So, was the atomic energy guy some sort of freak or pervert or what?"

"I'm sure he was. But that's not why he had the teeth. See, back in the late fifties and early sixties the AEC went from school to school around here and collected the kids' baby teeth — after they'd fallen out, of course — and gave them a little sticker in return. They were supposed to test the teeth to see if they had been affected by the uranium in the water, or by the nuclear testing over in Nevada."

"From Durango, I guess."

"Sure. Everyone in Farmington and Aztec and Shiprock got their drinking water out of the Animas River, and all during the war and for years afterward the uranium mill up in Durango was dumping tailings into the river. They were watering their crops with that stuff, their cows were drinking it. Hell, our whole food supply was radioactive. Anyway, the public health folks caught wind of it and decided to do a bunch of tests. Teeth remember these things."

"Remember?"

"Sure, uranium's daughters —radium, polonium, thorium. They seek out the bones and teeth and get stuck in there, zapping the blood and marrow and flesh with radiation."

"Shit."

"Oddly enough, they didn't bother doing the same tests for all the Navajos that lived further downstream, or the ones working in the mines."

"And?"

"And a couple of years later they came out with the results of the study. Made a big hoedown out of it, in fact. Said the studies definitively showed that the uranium tailings had done no harm, whatsoever."

"Well, that had to be a relief."

"A relief? What the hell is wrong with you? Look in the boxes. Obviously they never tested the teeth. They just collected them and threw them in boxes and hid them in a closet in the office. It was all a sham. A coverup! And who paid the price? We all did, Goddamnit. I knew that as soon as I found the teeth, even though I was a dumbass kid."

"You reported it to someone, I hope."

"Who was I supposed to tell? The government? A lotta good that woulda done. Look, I was saving up to go to college and get a chemistry degree so I could get a good government job. There's no damned way I was gonna throw it all away. No one woulda believed me anyway."

"But what about the truth?"

"Truth? *Truth? You're* gonna lecture me about truth? What does that even mean? If I woulda exposed this stuff today, it would be fine. The president would just dismiss it as fake news and everyone would forget about it. But back then I'd be put on a blacklist — or worse — for trying to undermine national security. So, no, I didn't tell anyone. But I held onto the Geiger counter I found in the office. And the teeth ..."

"... because you never know who might want to buy them, right?"

"Laugh all you want, kid, but I sold a box of 'em a few weeks ago. Same folks bought the Hermes and the Geiger counter. I made five-hundred clams on that sale. You wanna box of teeth? I'll give you a deal."

"No thanks. I got all I need," Brautigan said, backing away. "Well, it looks like you don't have any more typewriters, and I need an eight-track tape deck like I need a box of radioactive teeth, so I'd better be heading down the road."

Mister Fox stepped aside and Brautigan shimmied past him and walked out the door. As he was climbing into the car, he turned back to see Hal Fox looking at him in the same way that he would two decades prior when Brautigan offered him five bucks for a pair of handlebars. "Hey, Mister Fox. Do you mind me asking what kind of person buys a box of baby teeth?"

Fox looked back at him, his eyes glassy, cloudy, bloodshot, and yellow: "I couldn't tell you what kind of people they were, but I can tell you that it was a really pretty lady. Didn't catch her name, but the guy with her was Peter. Peter Simmons? Simons. That's it. Odd name."

Brautigan sat down on the blazing hot seat, slammed the door shut, cranked the ignition, and sped out onto the busy highway, all the while thinking about his friends Peter and Eliza, and the peculiar proclivities that they had developed over the years.

Fifteen minutes later he rolled into Farmington, a city oft-maligned for its strip malls and chain restaurants and bland mid-century energy boom architecture, and for being no more than a sprawling desert suburb with the gas field as its urban core. Brautigan, though, had a certain contrarian fondness for the place. Sure, its economy was built upon the extraction of fossilized sea creatures and sixty-million-year-old peat bogs. But then, the rest of society was built on the combustion of the same. This place was just more open about it, not bothering to hide the pumpjacks or the benzene-oozing wells cozied up against ballfields, or the mountains of coal ash that leak arsenic and selenium and other toxic crap into the water.

Farmington was simply more brazen about the tradeoffs that are made daily by every participant in the combustion culture. For every pound of mercury spewed from the coal-plant smokestacks that gets lodged in folks' flesh and brains, Farmington gets another high-wage job. For every billion tons of carbon spewed into the atmosphere, the place gets a spiffed up library, a nice river trail, and relatively high teacher pay. And for every year that the river is reduced to a trickle and the ozone levels shoot up and the forests burn, the place gets a Starbucks, a Fuddruckers, a Captain D's, and not one, but five, *five* Blake's Lotaburgers. And Malcolm Brautigan was going to take advantage of the Blake's bounty by steering his fossil fuel-burning machine toward the nearest such establishment.

When he saw the little white building surrounded by a sea of asphalt, he swerved out of traffic, parked, pulled his shirt onto his sweat-sticky torso, strolled into the brightly lit store, reveling in the blast of cold air redolent with that characteristic fast-food scent of cleaning chemicals and grease and ketchup, and sauntered up to the counter. Standing there against the white tiled wall, in the glow of a battery of fluorescent lights, wearing a red Blake's polo shirt with astounding panache, stood the most beautiful person Brautigan had ever seen. He tried to decipher whether the person was a he or a she, and then remembered Melissa berating him for his binary view of gender, and decided it really didn't matter. They had shiny black hair, umber skin, dark eyes, full lips, a little feather dangling from one ear. After regaining his composure, Brautigan ordered a green-chile cheeseburger, a milkshake, and fries.

No more than three minutes later they called out his number and plopped the tray down in front of him, the burger wrapped in red, white, and blue paper, the fries sprawling enticingly hot and salty from their container. He reached into his pocket and pulled out the only bill he had and looked around for the appropriate receptacle for his cash. "Tips aren't allowed here, mister," they said, in a soft voice. Brautigan stood dumbly for a moment, then dropped the bill on the counter, took his food, and sat down in the window seat. The air-conditioning chilled his sweaty skin as he meditated on the world outside, which was all pavement, concrete, and cars.

Escalades and Camrys and Navigators and Cayennes passed by at a rate of about a million bucks per minute, he figured. And then, in the slim space between the curb and the cars, a man on an old clunker bike mucked up the flow. He wore a blue work shirt and dark blue or black pants, like a janitor's or a mechanic's uniform. His bike appeared to be on the edge of disintegration, but the man with brown, furrowed skin powered up the little hill anyway, turning way too big a gear. Splotches of sweat darkened the fabric of his shirt, as cars passed far too closely, some of them honking loudly, causing the man to jerk a bit but not falter.

Brautigan saw the street as a riverbed, and all the cars on were the river — of wealth, pouring out of the oil wells and coal mines and flowing through the city before being siphoned out to Houston, Denver, London. The fancy car drivers, the chosen few, had managed to harness the current, and divert it into their bank accounts and their multitude of belongings. Meanwhile, the guy on the bike or the person flipping the burgers back there in the incessant heat, were able to catch just a few drops. And still others missed out on the bounty entirely, and instead were pummeled by it. The current picked them up, emptied their pockets and their souls, then tossed them back where they fell prey to the undertow, only finding relief when they ended up dead in the gutter after a long February night, or shot down by a frightened cop in one of the poor neighborhoods. They were the ones who go missing, really go missing, until they are accidentally found, bruised and battered and buried in a shallow grave out at the end of a gas patch service road.

"Let them eat Blake's," Brautigan said a little too loudly as his fist clenched around his burger, squeezing a blob of mayonnaise-grease-mustard juice onto the red plastic tray.

He felt people looking at him. He had overstayed the ten minutes or so it takes to choke down a burger, talking to himself all the while, thereby morphing from paying customer into a vagrant or a squatter or a maniac who would soon start screaming about the mind-reading powers of microwave ovens. He tried to ignore it by checking his email for the first time since leaving Winslow. Stan Hatch had loved his article about Fallon, and said that it was going viral, and he had some more "tips" for Brautigan. And Bill Stevens, the outnumbered county commissioner, personally wrote Juan Lopez-Shapiro to thank him for standing up to the "green deep state." It's not the type of compliment he was hoping for; even a recycled boob pic from a bot based in Serbia would be better. He sighed and turned his phone face down, not bothering to read the rest.

Reluctantly he got up and headed back out into the blast-furnace parking lot and the stagnant air of his car and settled himself gingerly onto the searing seat and pulled out onto the busy boulevard. He took the next right turn, not knowing where it would lead, then turned again, passing through residential neighborhoods, meandering along curvy streets, checking out cul-de-sacs, ignoring the looks his old car drew. He passed a woman smoothly pedaling a nice road bike, decked out in lycra and a pollution mask, her tanned skin shimmering with perspiration. He passed kids playing in sprinklers in green yards and slowed down almost to a stop as he drifted by a front-yard get-together. Three women sat in lawn chairs, drinking cocktails or wine. The men gathered conspiratorially around the grill, taking long draws off of beers and talking and laughing. The smell of charred meat wafted through the hot air. A Kenny Chesney country song about getting along played loud. Brautigan felt a stab of covetousness, a sudden longing for the comfort of domesticity, for financial and emotional security, for the carefree air they all wore so loosely.

Of course it was a lie. There is no security anymore, maybe there never was. Brautigan's envy turned to exasperation. He wanted to warn them, wanted to shake them out of their serenity. "Don't you see?" he said, under his breath. "You should be the anxious ones. You have so much to lose." Less than a mile away fish lay rotting upon dry and dusty rocks where once ran a river. The sprinklers would sputter out soon, too, the lush lawns becoming brittle and hard and lifeless. The hydrocarbon reservoirs were waning. The big oil companies that once lorded over the community, sponsoring everything from the symphony to the school of energy, had collapsed under their own weight, the executives scurrying off quietly, taking the high-paying jobs, the workers' pensions, the health benefits with them, following the old cycles of colonization, exploitation, and abandonment. The foreclosures and financial instruments would soon descend like a swarm of locusts, laying waste to the suburban scene. Even the Applebees would one day deliquesce to dust.

As the planet dies, as the insects and the birds and the beasts give way to extinction, perhaps a new species of scavenger will rise up in their wake. A terrible conglomeration of the detritus of the extraction society — pumpjacks and distillation towers and mud pumps and suction lines — a monster that emerges from the ruins of the refineries, resides in the abandoned shells of big box stores, that stomps across the charred landscape respiring hydrogen sulfide, guzzling fracking fluid, and gobbling up pipelines and transmission lines as it goes.

"I guess we will all get what we deserve," Brautigan told his dirty windshield, knowing it wasn't true, that a mass comeuppance would never come.

As the waxy blob of the sun dipped below the horizon, Brautigan pulled onto the highway, joining the flow of traffic heading northward. Suburban sprawl gave way to rural sprawl and he turned onto an undulating back road, his little car passed dusty yards and late-model modulars, their vinyl siding already warping from the recalcitrant heat, and dropped down into a miniature valley shaded by river-bank cottonwoods that were just then dropping their fluffy seeds. For a brief moment Brautigan sped through a summer whiteout, the cotton swirling chaotically in his car's slipstream. Off to his right, the Animas, the River of Lost Souls, was little more than a warm and stagnant trickle, its once abundant flows pilfered by the heat and the meagre winters and the ditches that spilled onto fields.

He cursed the irrigators for pilfering the waters. Then he praised them for creating this little oasis, this reminder of what once was. He inhaled the aroma of verdant alfalfa, of fresh-cut hay, baled and stacked in grid-like rows. The ephemeral fragrance of early summer wafted through the car, triggering, as always, a sad kind of hope that the long days to come will somehow heal all the wounds, will lift us up and carry us back to that one, brief, fugacious moment in our lives when we were whole, when everything was possible, when we ran heedlessly through fields on dusky lavender-hued evenings, when we kissed under the whispering leaves of the old weeping willow, the nighttime grass cool against our skin, and we lay on our backs in the warm dirt between corn rows at dusk, marveling at the tassels blowing against the star-studded bowl of the June sky.

Meshuga

"Hey, I'm going out," Adriana, sixteen-going-on-twenty-six, frizzy, dark hair erupting from her head, said as she strode toward the front door without showing any signs of slowing.

"Woah, woah there, young lady," said Eliza, adopting her stern-mother voice. "Just hold on a minute."

"'Lady? Really? That's a bit antiquated, no?"

"Where are you going?"

"I'm going over to Emma's and then we're going on location to work on our film."

"Dressed like that? What kind of film are we talking about? A porno?"

"Seriously, mom? Slut-shaming your own daughter?"

"It's not slut-shaming. It's called parenting. Yeah, I know, my bad. Parenting is antiquated, too, as obsolete as typewriters."

"Oh, here we go. Hey, if you're gonna give me the rotary-dial-phone lecture can you hold onto that thought? Emma and I would love to get that on film. It's hilarious."

"You don't even know what film is."

"Actually, dad gave me his old sixteen-millimeter camera a month ago. He told me he'd find film for it, and figure out how to develop it. So there. When's he gonna be back, anyway?"

"You know that I don't know where your dad is. He's missing, honey. It's serious."

"He's having a midlife crisis, mom. It's fine. He's probably driving a convertible Beemer with some young thing with fake tits, making him feel young and manly again. It's what guys do when they reach a certain age, no?"

Eliza rolled her eyes and attempted her mean-mom glare, but Adriana wasn't fazed. "Your dad can't afford a Beemer. Even an old one. We're going to have a guest tonight, so when you come home, be quiet."

"Oh, yeah, that's right. You mean your old boyfriend is coming to visit. It looks like maybe you're the one having a mid-life crisis fling."

Eliza blushed and turned away from her daughter. "He's not my boyfriend. He's your dad's oldest friend. You remember uncle Malcolm."

"Calling some guy uncle who's not related to me is awkward and pervy."

"He's not a perv. At least not like that."

"Anyway, Ann told me that you and 'uncle' Malcolm were pretty hot and heavy back in the day."

"Ann's memory gets a little cloudy. Besides, that was a long time ago. You can leave now, Adriana. Malcolm's going to sleep on the couch. Don't scare him. Try not to be too late."

"Linear time is a patriarchal construct, mom. I'll see you when I see you. Love you. Ciao!"

"Your buttcheeks are showing!" Eliza yelled, but by then, the door had shut, and she was alone.

It felt good. Felt good to be alone, at last, even for a moment. Adriana's expansive personality filled up the house, even when she was ensconced in her room. Peter, meanwhile, was either on full-blast, or wallowing in a melancholic soup, with the latter dominating over the last few months. Either way, it left little space for Eliza and her feelings or thoughts. So to have the place to herself was a rare luxury.

In the months following their move back to Durango, things had gone relatively well. Eliza had her new job, Peter had gotten back into landscape painting, and Adriana made friends quickly at her new school. Peter knew that returning home would conjure up unpleasant childhood memories, and that trips to the grocery store would be fraught with the peril of running into someone from high school whom he'd rather forget. He did not at all anticipate the emotional blow he would suffer, however, from observing the world around him, and finding that home was no longer the place that he had left so long ago.

It wasn't the growth of the town, or the gentrification, or all the boutiquey businesses in place of the old hardware stores and such that bothered him. It was the way everything else had changed — the trees, the fields, the streams, the weather. He was pushed into despair by the visible manifestations of a climate gone haywire. So much of what had made the place home was vanishing: snowstorms so big they shut down the whole town, sledding on the hills above his house, skiing the face of Smelter Mountain. Even north-facing high-mountain slopes were bare in January, and except for a few weeks it was too warm for the ski areas to make snow. The evergreens that blanketed mountainsides were ravaged by beetles, the air thick with smoke from late May to late September, the water in Hermosa Creek — if there was any — thick with ash and mud. That spring, during what should have been peak flow for the river, Peter took Adriana tubing, so that she could experience what he and Malcolm used to do all the time when they were her age. He bought a six-pack of cheap beer, she made some bologna sandwiches, and they headed out for a daylong adventure. An hour later they were back. Adriana walked into the house despondent, silently shrugging her shoulders, while Peter sat in the car and sobbed for two hours straight. Eliza figured they'd had an argument. But Adriana later explained that Peter had broken down shortly after they'd started their journey, when the water got too shallow to float on, and they were forced to walk down the nearly desiccated stream-bed, the stench of rotting fish in the air, their calves coated with thick and slimy algae that clung to every boulder.

Peter's overblown reaction appeared to be the result of a deeper depression. In fact, the changes he saw were the very cause of his sadness. As Peter descended into desolation his capacity to function in the material world deteriorated. He gave up on painting — his only reliable revenue stream — and instead toyed around with ideas for conceptual art that could provide a better outlet for his melancholia.

Believing that the philistines would wake up to climate change if they could see it — as they had briefly done when they saw the acid mine drainage blasting from the Gold King Mine — Peter set out to color the molecules in the Four Corners Methane Hot Spot bright purple by projecting infrared light through the methane clouds. But after several researchers he had contacted scoffed at the idea, he gave it up. Later he was able to pull off an interpretive dance performance on the uranium tailings repository outside of Durango, though the grant he had hoped to get for it fell through, and he had almost been arrested. A similar performance on the vast tomb-like repository in Shiprock had gone awry when a security guard interrupted and took a bottle rocket to the eyeball. Generally, though, he couldn't stick with any one of a litany of ideas for long enough to execute it.

Finally Peter seemed to have a breakthrough. He had been going up to Fort Lewis College and looking through the archives in the Center for Southwest Studies when he'd come across a couple of boxes of documents, letters, postcards, and photos that had been found in the attic of a long-dead uranium tycoon's house and donated to the center, but that remained uncatalogued due to lack of funds. Peter had come home that evening in a feverish state, talking more than he had in ages, about these incredible letters that someone had written back in the sixties about some discovery that could save the planet.

He didn't just commit to his newfound concept, but became obsessed. He started going to Utah, looking for a site for his project. He purchased odd antique trinkets on eBay — art supplies, he said. Over the months that followed he became visibly anxious, didn't eat much, lost weight. Sex? Forget it. It was as if he were transferring not only his mental being into his work, but also his physical being, as though the ailment that had infected his psyche had metastasized, reaching its malignant roots into his blood, his bones, his guts, his brain. He rarely spoke, and when he did it came out either as mundanity or fragmentary esoterica: *It was a hundred and twenty in Phoenix yesterday. Shade has become a luxury item. A star falls in a distant lung. The daughter is worse than the monster.*

Eliza had tried to be patient, picked up some shifts down at Maria's Bookshop in the evenings to cover bills, drawn up a strict budget, stopped buying organic, bought wine by the box, nixed the weekend trips to Santa Fe. Peter, meanwhile, was oblivious to it. Money had no meaning for him, which might have been charming once, but it had grown old. She finally summoned up the courage to give him the come-to-Jesus talk: "Don't you think it's time for you to take a little break from the conceptual stuff, and get back to painting? You're so good, and that gallery downtown said they could sell anything you painted, especially the landscapes. They say your work reminds people of Yvonne Martin's."

Peter had visibly bristled at the comparison with the late painter, but remained quiet.

"We *need* the money. Adriana's health insurance is going up and she'll be going to college soon. I can't keep carrying this thing on my own."

"I know, Eliza, I know. I'm on the edge of something big. *Really* big. I need a little more time, and then it will be over."

"You keep saying that. But I've been working two jobs, and I've actually finished a few pieces of art. Whereas you, well, you know."

"Then sell your art if you need money so bad." He was getting frustrated, lashing out like a cornered cat.

She responded in kind: "Yeah, right. I can see the announcement, now: 'Soccer mom-librarian art show! Will trade arts and crafts for Zumba lessons!' Come on, Peter, you know that no one's going to take my art seriously, let alone pay for it. All I am to the art world is your muse, your protector, your appendage."

"That's not true."

"But if we slapped *your* name on *my* work? We could pull in ten grand, at least."

Peter stood up then, anger, fear, hatred in his eyes: "Don't go there, Eliza. I am *not* a fraud!"

Eliza didn't mention it again.

In early June she snapped awake at three in the morning, as she often did, to find Peter sitting up in bed, staring straight ahead, as if he had awoken from a bad dream. "It's okay, honey," she said, reaching for him. But her fingers fell on clammy, unresponsive flesh.

"There's something I need to tell you," he said. A long silence followed, giving Eliza a chance to gird herself against the worst possible revelation. "I'm scared. Time is slipping."

She almost giggled with relief: "Of course you are. We all are. And we're all getting older, too. Believe me." She tried again to soothe him with her touch, but it was futile. When she awoke the next morning, she found him in the garage, packing his gear for an outing.

"I need to go," he said. "Before time runs out. You'll see me again. Call Malcolm. I think he could use some help." She didn't ask what he meant by that. They hadn't talked to or about Malcolm in months. And then he drove away. He still hadn't come back, nearly a week later.

Eliza contemplated cleaning the house, again. Instead, she went to the kitchen and poured herself a glass of white wine, panicked a little when she saw the bottle was already half empty, then returned to the table. "Buy box wine," she wrote on a little tab of paper. She considered calling Malcolm, asking him to pick up a bottle, but part of her still did not want to acknowledge that her ex-lover was actually coming to her house and to her aid, so she decided to let it go. She looked over at Peter's office door. Closed, as always. Closed like the Peter of late. An enigma.

She stood up and walked across the living room, looking over her shoulder as she did so. Peter didn't like Eliza coming into his office, not just because he was a private person, but also because he knew that she wouldn't be able to control her compulsion to clean, to rearrange, to organize. She opened the door, and the musty smell of decaying paper wafted out.

"Holy frijole," she said. It looked as if a library had exploded in the small room. Papers, books, folders covered every flat surface. His desk was an old door perched on two sawhorses. On one side was his laptop, on the other the typewriter, so that if someone sat at each of them they'd face one another as if in some battle of technologies. The space immediately surrounding the two devices was cleared, and neat. Beyond that was disaster.

She picked up a pile and thumbed through it, not sure what she was looking for. Here was an ancient bulletin from the Atomic Energy Commission about a study of kids' baby teeth, there a toxicology document about something called bone seekers, here a typewritten letter from Frank Oppenheimer to someone named Hildebrandt about uranium enrichment and nuclear cloud-seeding. A stick-it note was scrawled with "TASHA" and a string of numbers that might have been a foreign phone number, or a bank account number, or something else entirely. Another pile included an old advertisement for Doromad radioactive toothpaste, one for Tho-Radia lipstick infused with thorium and radium, and another for radium condoms. An envelope addressed to Dr. Alfred P. Nussbaum at a post office box in Los Alamos sat beside the typewriter, stamped and ready to be sent. It was on top of a worn cardboard box, of the kind that you'd put manuscripts in back in the pre-digital age, with a faded doodle of a mushroom cloud surrounded by intricate, indecipherable figures, the initials MBP in the lower right hand corner.

"Jesus, Peter, you are a fucking slob," she said. She put books on the bookshelf, arranged by size and color, not content, along with the manuscript box. She stacked the loose papers together and, as she was putting them into the old metal filing cabinet, noticed what looked like a cigarette case, ornately decorated with gold paisley patterns. On it's face it said:

RADIENDOCRINATOR

She snapped open the case to find a small, rectangular, gold-colored object, encased like a jewel in purple felt. She unfolded the piece of paper that was contained in it and read: *"MALE—Place Radiendocrinator in the pocket of this adaptor with the window upward toward the body. Wear adaptor like any 'athletic strap'. This puts the instrument under the scrotum as it should be. Wear at night. Radiate as directed."*

She put the object back in its case and returned it to the drawer. She sorted through books: one about Downwinders, Volume II of the lectures of Richard Feynman, the collected works of Borges, and a thick and musty tome on something called "Project Skywater." A collated pile of papers caught her eye: UNCLASSIFIED *The Los Alamos Primer.* She idly thumbed through the pages, reading disjointed phrases that came together sounding like fragments from Sappho, if the ancient Greek poet had been a demented maniac:

When neutrons are in uranium they are caused to disappear…
… our aim is simply to get as much energy from the explosion as we can.
Several kinds of damage will be caused by the bomb,
and since the materials we use are very precious,
we are constrained to do this with as high an efficiency as is possible.

She sorted through a few more things, including a scientific paper by Augustus C. Lavender about using targeted geo-engineering and geographically limited weather modification to save the monarch butterfly from climate change-induced extinction, and found the folder containing all of Peter's grant proposals, and just as many rejection letters. She read a few sentences. They were part gobbledygook, part Unabomber-style ravings, part equations.

"No wonder Homeland Security is sniffing around here."

She started to leave, but considered what Ann and what Adriana had said about Peter having a midlife-crisis affair with some nubile, young, adoring thing — a new muse, perhaps. She half-dreaded such a scenario and half-hoped it were true. It would be the easy way out of this morass, for him, and for her. She sat down at Peter's desk, flipped open the laptop, its glare sharp in the dark room.

"It's for his own good," she said quietly as she typed in his password.

Unheimlich

Brautigan rolled into the outskirts of his hometown along with the evening's dusk. He marveled at all the changes that had occurred since his last visit and, still in no hurry to arrive, he piloted his car slowly into his childhood neighborhood, where he was rapidly swept into a déja vu state of mind by the familiarity and the alienness of it all: There was the tree that served as the "base" for twilit hide-and-seek games, there the alley in which they'd hold running races, there the apple tree which provided ammunition for Joshua's homemade projectile launchers. Everywhere the undercurrent of violence and cruelty that growing up in America entails. It was all just as it had been, yet smaller. Both more tangible and less real.

The house in which Brautigan had spent the first sixteen years of his life still stood against the alley. It hadn't been scraped to make way for a McMansion. Yet someone had gutted it, stripped it down to its bones, and rebuilt it, virtually from scratch. Surely gone were the shitty formica countertops, the grimy linoleum floors, the cigarette smoke-infused carpet. Gone were the shingles that remembered the last moment of Frank Hildebrandt's life. Perhaps Brautigan's formative memories were gone, too, ripped out along with the old wood paneling and floorboards. And what of the residue of Brautigan's recurring, childhood dreams? Had they — and the mannequin family that populated them — escaped into the warm night air, or were they still trapped within the old joists and pillars that remained?

It was all uncanny, but in the German sense of the word: unheimlich. Un-homelike.

The sensation continued as he meandered through the streets, checking out real estate prices on his phone as he went. It was a baffling experience. The rundown place where Rick Gonzalez had lived so long ago was on the market for $849,000, and the Smith's old house was going for even more. He felt unwelcome, rejected by his own hometown's market value. He rounded a few more corners, coveted a few more homes and other people's lives, and finally pulled up in front of Peter's childhood home, where Peter and Eliza currently lived. He shut off the engine and the radio and sat while the engine gurgled and ticked, then got out of the car, stepped onto the still-hot blacktop, and walked up the driveway toward the screen door, where Eliza stood waiting, her figure silhouetted by the warm light behind her. She looked tired, her brown eyes glassy, her short black hair unkempt, but then she smiled, sending a twinge of electricity through Brautigan's belly, and she embraced him with such ardor that he immediately pulled away for fear of becoming perceptibly aroused. She beckoned him inside, and Brautigan was overcome with the same eery sense of vertigo as in his own former neighborhood.

Like almost all of the homes in this part of town — now known as Tupperware Heights — it had been a boxy affair, a rectangle divided up into too-small rooms, built in the fifties during the postwar energy boom, when the masses were migrating in a westerly direction. Brautigan's house had been much older, with outdated furniture and appliances. He had been envious of Peter and his other friends who lived over here. He coveted their dishwashers, big refrigerators stocked with pop and cold cuts and American cheese, the lush carpet and shiny linoleum, their color televisions and push-button telephones. Some even had finished basements with pool tables, air hockey, ping pong. Mostly he envied the newness of these places, the freshness, the fact that his friends didn't have to cohabitate with ghosts.

Peter's childhood house was radically different from the way it had been, but also the same. Eliza and Peter had remodeled, tearing out most of the old walls, putting down tile, hardwood floors, and a line of large windows facing the backyard. Nevertheless, the shadows of Peter's and Malcolm's youth lingered. Here is where they had sat in the dark little box of a room and played Space Invaders on the Atari. There is where they'd all gather around and roll the dice, for Dungeons & Dragons, Gangbusters, Risk, or the role-playing game that they had created themselves, Mutant Wars, set in a post-nuclear holocaust Four Corners. And right here must have been where Peter's room was, and where they pored over X-Men comics while making mixtapes from Peter's eclectic record collection: whiplash-inducing collections of the Clash, Dire Straits, REM, Brian Eno, Suicidal Tendencies. Brautigan could feel the long-gone shag green carpet under his feet, the slightly musty smell, the way the winter-afternoon light fell through dirty windowpanes. He heard the crinkly rustle made when peeling the plastic foil from a brand new Maxell XL II blank cassette tape, and the soft whisper of opening the crystal clear case.

It occurred to him, with a melancholy pang, that Peter's daughter would never know that sound.

An entire wall was now covered with a massive bookshelf, which was reassuring to Brautigan. He had half expected to walk into a more stereotypical Durango abode, with bikes, kayaks, skis, and paddle-boards hanging from walls and ceilings, and Eliza regaling him with a play-by-play account, supplemented by Instagram posts, of her latest trail-running exploit while they swigged craft beers and sucked on marijuana lollipops.

Something was missing, though, namely Peter's paintings. The walls that weren't bookshelves were bare.

In the far corner of the room, Brautigan noticed something on a small end-table. He got closer and inspected it in the dim light. It looked like a diorama of some sort, or a post-earthquake dollhouse, perhaps: A miniature structure with a peaked roof, open on one side to reveal three ceramic figures inside. There was something immediately familiar about it for Brautigan, but he couldn't place what it was. The roof was covered with what looked like miniature shingles in a way that made it look as if the artist had run out of one color midway, and had to switch to another. The walls were made of adobe or stone, with the outline of feathers and other small objects embedded in them. In some places the plaster had worn off, apparently, and the bones of the walls — made up of pages and covers of books — were apparent. Brautigan looked closer at one of these worn away areas and saw a fragment of indecipherable text that he recognized as Greek.

"This is amazing," he said to Eliza when he realized she had been standing behind him, watching silently, two glasses of white wine in her hands. "It's like Anselm Kiefer and Melissa Zink came together to build a little world of their own, you know?"

Eliza grinned.

"Yeah, wow, I mean, Peter's art has really evolved since I last saw it. So much more, I dunno, depth?"

"Peter's art?" Eliza stopped smiling. "That's not Peter's. It's mine."

"Oh. Sorry, yeah, I, I should have known that. I'm just. Driving all day. I'm a little bleary eyed. Still, though. I meant what I said. I mean, I want to look at it more closely when there's more light, but it really does have a nice mix of trauma and cerebral whimsy. It's called Time Machine IV? What's that mean?"

"I'll explain it to you sometime," she said, a heat rushing into her cheeks. "Thanks."

She handed him one of the glasses of wine. He took a big sip, and headed for the couch, but she nudged him with an elbow toward Peter's office, instead.

"Come on. I've got to show you something," Eliza said, her hands visibly shaking. "Look, I just want you to know that I would never snoop around in Peter's stuff or anything. It's just that, well, tonight, while I was waiting for you, I thought maybe I'd find something useful."

"Tonight? You waited, what, three days to poke into Peter's stuff? Four days? Sheesh. That's self control. I woulda been digging around in here the minute he walked out the door. You found something? He ran off with a barista, didn't he?"

"No. Okay, he did have a crush on this woman down at the Black Cat. But no. What is it with you two and baristas, anyway?"

"Chemical dependency?"

"I found this weird shit. Probably nothing, but maybe you can figure it out?" She opened up the laptop to reveal a screen scattered with folders and files of various names, and clicked on one called "FOIA." Inside were more than a dozen additional folders, with names such as, "White_Canyon_TS," "Bears_Ears_NM," "Daneros_U," "Happy_Bonanza_U" and so on. Brautigan moused over and clicked on the "White_Canyon_TS" folder. It contained a bunch of separate folders, with indecipherable file names, each of which contained dozens, maybe hundreds, of documents. He opened one at random. It was a multi-page email chain, apparently between several people with government email addresses. Brautigan glanced at a couple of them, catching phrases like "tar sands" and "strategic metals," things that had little meaning without context, and much of the context was blacked out.

"Do you know what any of this is?" Eliza asked, peering at the screen. "What's FOIA?"

"Freedom of Information Act. If you want to acquire government documents or correspondence you file a FOIA. Usually the agency in question will try to give you the run around, charge you outrageous fees, and delay. If and when they finally do cough up the stuff, there is so much material, with so many redactions, that it is rendered useless. I mean, there are probably a thousand pages here, and it's only marginally searchable. It could take years to find what you're looking for. And we don't know what we're looking for. Do we?"

Brautigan felt a twinge of jealousy. Why hadn't Peter called him for help on this stuff? Malcolm would have given anything to collaborate with his oldest friend on a project, to be the anchor that Peter's talent needed.

"Must be for Peter's big project he's been working on," Eliza said. "Don't even ask me what it's all about, because I haven't a clue."

"All of this for a painting? Come on!"

"He's not painting," Eliza said. "He says he's evolved, but I'm not so sure."

"Evolved into what?"

"He doesn't talk about it much, at least not with me. It's some sort of conceptual project, I think. He had plans for a series of dance performances on the uranium tailings depositories of the West, and pulled one of them off, and tried to get grant funding to create a Gold King-orange breed of corn that he could plant in a field down near Shiprock. That sort of thing. But this is bigger, or so he says."

"They give grants for that kind of stuff?"

"I said he *tried* to get funding. It hasn't worked out so well. I'm his only real funder, aside from a pile of maxed out credit cards, and he still sells an old painting every once in a while, though that stream is running dry."

"If you need money or anything, you know, just ask. I'm doing okay."

"Yeah, I bet you are," she said. "So?"

"So what?"

"Is there anything there that will help?"

"Hell if I know. Maybe. I'm too tired to dig through it now. Can we do it tomorrow?"

"Sure. I'd like to get an early start tomorrow anyway, get over to Blanding by mid-afternoon, so I'm gonna crash. I hope you don't mind sleeping on the couch. Use the shower in there. There's coffee and food in the kitchen. Make yourself at home. And if a psychotic teenager comes in, don't freak out."

"Adriana? She was pretty darned sweet last time I saw her. Granted, that was years ago, but still."

"Yeah? Well, she was suspended for three weeks from school, if that says anything, for making a sculpture of Ted Cruz for art class."

"The senator? What's wrong with that? It's because he's a Republican, isn't it. These damned political correctness police—"

"It was constructed entirely of dildos," she said, nonchalantly. "Cost a fucking fortune. And she missed finals. Now she's out smashing the patriarchy and exposing her ass to the masses and may be coming in late."

"Oh. Uhh, well, good for her. I guess. Thanks."

Brautigan closed the laptop and got up to leave the office. He froze in the doorway. Just a few feet away, hanging on the office wall, was the painting. *The* painting, the one of the woman and the stones and the eyeball and the web. The one that Peter Simons had sacrificed on the winter solstice two decades earlier.

"That damned, creepy painting," Eliza said, when she saw him looking. "He's turned down so many offers on it. I wish he'd just sell it, or burn it, or whatever he has to do to get it out of his head. It's driving him nuts."

"But Peter…"

"What?"

"Oh nothing. I'm just tired, that's all."

Used-to-be

*M*alcolm Brautigan's third grade teacher *stared at him expectantly. He was supposed to recite* The Ballad of Sam McGee *to the class, most of whom were snickering at his silence. He looked down at the faded blue type of the mimeograph in his hand for help. Instead of the verses, it was a menu from a local restaurant featuring chicken-fried chicken.*

"There are strange things done in the midnight sun," the nine-year-old Brautigan finally said. But no one could hear him, because a jet engine had fired up right outside the window, and someone was yelling, yelling, yelling…

He woke up.

His eyes felt like they were filled with sawdust. The side of his face was damp with drool. He was hungry and thirsty. His teacher and the menu were gone, but the jet engine and the yelling were not.

A voice: "Are you friggin' kidding me!? It's seven in the morning. I told you never to do this. I hate you!"

He opened his eyes with a start and sat up, his clammy skin peeling away from the couch like fruit leather from its plastic sheath. Eliza vacuumed the floor in a frantic fashion, yanking the machine back and forth. She wore orange knit shorts that were a tad too short for Brautigan's comfort, and an old, clingy, not-quite-opaque t-shirt, no bra. A willowy teenager with frizzy brown hair stood across the room, visibly angry.

"Look," the teenager said, "First you woke me up, now you woke up your guest! Smooth move, Ex Lax! You are literally the worst!"

"Don't talk to me like that," Eliza growled back, ignoring Brautigan. "And *stop* using 'literally' like that. You are, about, to see, my anger."

Hoping to break the tension, Brautigan jumped in: "Hey, Adriana. I hardly recognized you. Remember me? It's your uncle Malcolm." Adriana peered back at him, and for a brief moment he could see himself through her eyes — a hairy, smelly, middle-aged man wearing nothing but tattered underwear who called himself her "uncle." He might as well have "PEDOPHILE" tattooed on his forehead.

"Sure. Hi," she said, as she retreated to her bedroom and closed the door. Meanwhile, Eliza kept vacuuming the same three-foot-long section of floor, over and over.

"What's going on?" Brautigan said, rubbing the grit from his eyes and trying not to stare at Eliza's figure.

Eliza turned off the vacuum, closed her eyes, took a deep breath, counted to sixty, then opened her eyes. "The joys of parenting, that's what. Coffee's in the kitchen. Are you staring at my breasts?"

"Yeah, yeah, I'd like your breasts— No, no! I'd like some coffee! I'd like a cup of coffee, thank you. I'll get it myself." At which point Brautigan fled into the kitchen and hid there in the darkness.

Santos double parked her Subaru on Main Avenue in downtown Durango, half a block up from the Black Cat coffee shop.

"I'm not paying for parking," said Eliza. "I'll wait here."

Brautigan hopped out and walked briskly down the familiar sidewalk, where he had often strolled as a child, and soon became distracted again by the same uncanny sensation of being lost in time that he'd felt the night before. He peered through the window of what used to be a Woolworths, where he'd get floppy, greasy grilled cheeses as a kid. Now it was a high-end restaurant that peddled thirty-dollar slabs of chicken breast. Just as he was about to spit on the window, Eliza's honking prodded him away from his burgeoning rage. He hurried along, slowing to toss a couple of quarters to a scruffy white woman with dreads and two dogs standing — sitting on the sidewalks is illegal — with a sign asking for money or food or anything, then ducked into the coffee shop, its screen door slamming behind him.

"Hey, cowboy, what'll you have," the barista — a woman who resembled a young Salma Hayek — said, as if he had been coming in here every morning for years. He looked her in the eyes, and then forgot what he was going to say.

"Hello, there?" She said, very slowly and loudly. "What would you like to order?"

"A cappuccino?"

"Sure thing."

"Hey, do you know a guy named Peter Simons? An artist. Comes in here a lot?"

"Tall, pale, older guy? Sure. I know Peter."

"Oh, no, he's not older. He's my age."

She looked at him flatly. "Ooooh-kay. What about him?"

"He's missing."

"Still? Damnit. Yeah, Eliza told me. I'm sure he's okay. He probably just forgot to go home."

Brautigan, taken aback at this response, sat down at the bar and watched her make the coffee then hand it to him in a to-go cup. Instead of hurrying back out he lingered for a moment, trying to think of something to say. Then another customer came in, a woman with short black hair and icy blue eyes, and stomped back behind the counter and kissed the barista on the mouth, hard. Brautigan stared, his eyes wide, until they finally separated and saw him looking. He turned away and scurried out the door.

Eliza's car was gone, so he stood and waited and looked down at his coffee. On the smooth coating of milk was the perfect shape of a heart. Brautigan smiled.

"Wow," said Brautigan as he eased himself into the car. "That coffee girl in there is super cute, but Peter did not run off with her."

"Yeah, I know."

"She's a lesbian."

"I know."

"Hey," he said, "did you know that that t-shirt shop over there used to be Richey's candy shop? This ancient old lady ran the place, and they had this amazing bar and she sold pop that she mixed herself. Like syrup and the soda water. And these comic books from the fifties and sixties."

"Uggh, here we go," Eliza groaned. "It's the ol' used-to-be game. Now, why don't you tell me that that real estate office used to be a movie theater and that place used to be Parson's Drug? And you and Peter and the guys would go there and drink phosphates and eat burgers and gosh it sure has changed and wouldn't it be nice if we could go back and live those days over and over again. Make Durango Great Again! That's it. Right?"

"Jeez, Eliza, I—"

"You sound like some old dude lamenting about how his wife of fifty years is no longer young and nubile and beautiful. It's gross. People change. Places change. You need to change. Deal with it," Eliza said.

"What if it's like someone lamenting the fact that their wife no longer loves him?"

She squinted at him, trying to parse the meaning behind that statement. "What? That makes no sense." She refrained from saying any more when she saw Malcolm sinking into the seat the way he did when they were together and she'd try to get him to talk about their relationship. She really was bored of hearing the same old stories about Peter's and Malcolm's childhoods, but she knew that she was also envious, in a way. Envious of their memories, which, even if they were embellished, were far more interesting than her reminiscences of coming of age in Santa Fe, which mostly consisted of ingesting far too many mind-altering substances, of playing hacky sack in the Plaza with sullen, stinky boys, and of having drunken, stoned, and lackadaisical sex with the same.

She abruptly pulled out into traffic, eliciting a loud honk from a pickup, and drove down Main Avenue, passing by Farquahrts, a long-time watering hole for aging ski bums. Both Malcolm and Eliza were too lost in their thoughts to notice what was written on the diminutive, sign-code-compliant marquee: *Live Music Saturday: Ralph Dinosaur, with special guest, Mannfred Mannia*

They drove past the site of the old uranium mill and Malcolm started to tell Eliza about the time Peter had goaded him into climbing the fence and how they slinked around in the old buildings, poking around in the machinery that was still intact, as if it had been grinding up the ore and mixing it up with acidic chemicals and kicking out yellowcake just a week or so before. He refrained. He interpreted Eliza's silence as anger, which in turn sparked defensiveness within him. It did not dissipate as they made their way past a line of brand new hotels and then a so-called green development, and it didn't go away as they drifted further west.

"Look, Eliza," Malcolm said after they had been on the road for twenty minutes or so, "I don't know if I said something wrong, or if it's that time of the month, but — " His words were lost in the squealing of the tires as Eliza steered into a gravel pullout and slammed on the brakes for no apparent reason. Eliza's cheeks and neck were scarlet. She stared straight ahead.

"Get out, you sexist fucking pig!" she hissed.

"Sexist? I don't understand." He was almost whimpering. "Oh. I'm sorry. Let me rephrase: What did I do to make you so angry and what can I do to make it better?"

"Now you're just being a facetious dick."

"No, I'm not. I'm truly sorry. That was a dumb thing to say."

"I'm not angry. I'm disappointed. In you."

"I won't do it anymore. No more nostalgia, no more sexism. Okay?"

"Are you really capable of quitting either of those things? I don't really care about that. I just can't get over your recent choice of career. What the hell?"

Nausea flooded Brautigan. "My career? How do you know about that?"

"You told me, that's how. I can't believe that you work for OmnyBank."

Brautigan exhaled raggedly with relief. "Oh, yeah, yeah, that. The newsletters. OmnyBank. I mean, I don't really *work* for OmnyBank. I think I did one job for one of their contractors once."

"That's not the point. I don't give a shit if it's OmnyBank or DynaDikk or what have you, the point is, you're wasting your talent on this crap."

"Wasting my talent?"

"Yeah. This country's crumbling. We need everyone fighting for the cause."

"You don't understand the situation, Eliza."

"I don't understand? Why would that be? Because I'm a woman and it's 'that time of the month?' Because I'm not going through a midlife man-crisis? I may not understand that, but I know that you're helping out the oligarchs just when you should be fighting them."

"Actually, I'm just doing a job. Is that so bad?"

She shot him a look that made him want to open the door and crawl out into the highway.

"It's not like I have a choice," he said. "What was I going to do? No one would hire me after, well, you know."

"You made a mistake. Admit it and move on and others will, too."

"What's it to you, anyway?"

"I care about the world, that's what. You had a voice, a way of reaching a lot of people, and you walked away from it for a little more money, right when journalism was facing its darkest days. That's sad to me."

"Journalism isn't dying because reporters are leaving the trade, reporters are leaving the trade because journalism's dying. And it's dying because no one wants to hear what journalists have to say unless it confirms their own biases. Journalists are leaving because they're realizing that their words are inconsequential, and that it doesn't really matter whether they're spewing out words for the *Tucson Tribune*, for *PatriotBlast*, or for SynerGen's newsletter. Ask Ted Denton, he'll tell you."

"Wow. That is some dark and cynical shit. *PatriotBlast*? Really? And who's Ted Denton?"

"Prove me wrong. Go ahead. Tell me about all of the change some newspaper article has effected. I'll give you time to think. And while you're doing that, why don't you just back off, Eliza. You sit here and judge me after I drove all the way up here to help you? Come on."

"Who's helping whom here? I asked you to help me find Peter because I felt sorry for you, all alone and friendless down there in the desert, sitting around drinking cheap booze and masturbating and watching your ear hair grow and maybe writing some midlife-crisis novel. But Jesus, I didn't know you had sunk this low."

"I don't drink cheap booze." He stared out the window defiantly.

Eliza closed her eyes and rested her forehead on the steering wheel for a good four or five minutes. "Okay, never mind," she said. "I'm sorry. I still need your help. I still want your help. So, maybe we can pick up this discussion later and focus on Peter. Okay? I'm sorry for yelling."

Eliza fired up the ignition, waited for a break in the seemingly endless stream of cars whipping by at seventy miles an hour, and eased out onto the highway. Neither she nor Brautigan paid any mind to the black SUV sitting in a pullout a quarter mile up the road, nor did they notice when it pulled out behind them, following them west.

Blanding

Brautigan's indignation gave way to relief, as he slowly came to the realization that Eliza's disappointment in him was far preferable to her reaction if she found out what he *really* did for a living. He'd tell her, eventually, but there really was no rush. The pair was mostly silent as the car floated along the highway over the foothills of the La Plata Mountains, down through the old cow and sawmill town of Mancos, past the foot of Mesa Verde and through Cortez. When they passed a marijuana dispensary called The Doobie Sisters, Brautigan spoke up: "Do you think we could listen to some tunes? I've got a great playlist."

"No."

"Why not?"

"Because I am relatively certain that this playlist of yours is at least thirty percent Steely Dan."

He scrolled through the playlist. She was correct. He put his phone away.

Eliza turned on the radio and flipped through the stations until she landed on KTNN, the Voice of the Navajo Nation. Merle Haggard sang about working to buy his kids new shoes and drinking a little bit of beer in the evening. Then the DJ, speaking rapid-fire Navajo, hailed the weekly specials at the Chat 'n' Chew down in Shiprock. As Eliza steered her way around the sharp corners on the McElmo Canyon road, and as they passed the dry-ice plant and dropped into the irrigated part of the canyon, where verdant cottonwoods and alfalfa fields collided with rosy-colored stone, Buffy Sainte-Marie's *Fancy Dancer* came on.

Then Eliza swerved to the right and slammed on the brakes. Brautigan screamed as the car careened and skidded to a halt in a little turnout next to the narrow road, gravel clinking against the undercarriage. Eliza, laughing, pointed to a small, hand-drawn sign: "Asparagus Squash Lettuce $1."

As they got out of the air conditioned vessel, they saw that the pullout was actually the beginning of a two-track driveway that led through a dark tunnel of leaves and vines to a little house that moldered into the loamy earth. Two boys — a couple of barefoot, messy-haired, dirty-faced asparagus gatherers — stood in the driveway, staring mutely at the couple and their car.

"Can we buy some asparagus?"

Silence, followed by the creak of a screen door, and a woman walking tentatively out of the house and down the drive. She wore a long skirt, and a scarf covering all of her hair like a hijab. She wiped her hands off on her apron and approached.

"Can I help you?" she said, softly.

"Umm, yeah, we just wanted some asparagus, if you've got it. Maybe a pound? And are those zucchinis? How about several of those?"

"And a handful of the blossoms," Brautigan added. The woman looked back emptily. "Squash blossoms?"

She motioned to the boys, and they ran off into the garden and filled up a bag with squash, the younger one tenderly pulling the young fruit, their blossoms still attached, from the vines. As they returned with the bounty, the woman reached into a styrofoam cooler and pulled out a big bundle of asparagus, the green stalks thick, lascivious.

"We picked it ourselves," the older boy said, looking at the ground, "along the ditch."

"I used to do the same when I was a kid," Brautigan responded. "Wait, is that fresh cheese?"

"It's chèvre," the woman said, motioning to some goats in a pen at the back of the yard.

"We'll take one of those, too. How much?"

"Six dollars?"

Eliza and Brautigan looked at the pile of produce, then at the woman, then back to the produce, both calculating how much this haul would set them back if it was from Whole Foods or the Durango farmer's market. Eliza handed the woman a five, and then another one.

"Keep the change," she said. "A tip for the asparagus rustlers."

At that, the boys scurried behind the woman, gripping her long skirt. Malcolm thanked them, and they started back for the car. Eliza stopped and turned. "Excuse me," she said to the woman, who was still watching her customers. "This is a weird question, but I'm wondering if maybe my husband stopped by here about a week ago? Tall, middle aged, not bad looking, drives an old red Toyota truck?"

Without pause the woman answered: "Yes, yes he did. He paid for a bunch of asparagus then left without taking it. He's ill?"

"Ill? No, no, just a little absent-minded is all. Okay, well, thank you."

They put the produce in the cooler in the back, then got back in the car and drove along the windy, narrow road. Neither of them would mention the woman, or her cryptic assessment of Peter, again.

The Slickrock Curtain does not appear on any maps, and its location varies depending on the season, the quality of light, and even the time of day. Only those who pay close attention, or don't pay any attention at all, know about it. And on that day, Eliza Santos and Malcolm Brautigan passed through it just as they rounded a bend near a ramp of sandstone, pale and pink like a corpulent thigh, rising up from a big field of alfalfa, emerald-green and thick despite the drought. Several minutes later, they crossed the Utah-Colorado line, drawn on a map some 160 years prior by politicians sitting on the other side of the continent, men who had never set foot on this land.

Brautigan silently cursed the line for its arbitrariness, its cruel straightness, and the way people ascribed it with so much meaning. He had always been amused, and disgusted, at the way people flocked to the Four Corners monument as if it were a unique natural phenomenon rather than just the intersection of some lines drawn on a goddamned map — a point on the artificial grid that ruled over land-use in the Western US. He despised the way so-called locals had weaponized the line to take away the rights of the Hopi or Zuni or other Pueblo nations or anyone else living outside their particular lines to have any kind of say over the land where their ancestors had lived for dozens of generations. Call it Cartesian colonialism, this sadistic and misguided attempt to bind boundless, sinuous space with theodolite, plumb, and level, this murder of the old understanding, this fracturing of the cosmic cycles.

"They should put up a warning sign here at the border," Santos said as she yanked the steering wheel to dodge a pothole, causing everything in the car, including Malcolm, to shift violently to one side.

"Jeezo, slow down, wouldya?" Malcolm hissed, his hand gripping the dashboard. "Warning about what?"

"That this place is a backwards-ass theocracy."

"Like the rest of America, you mean?"

"That's a stretch."

"Seriously? What about Alabama or Georgia or whoever it was that banned abortion?"

"Okay, Utah *is* kinda like the South. But the South has barbecue and

103

bourbon and the blues and Utah has what? Jell-O? Sodas? Fry sauce?"

"First you're dissing on Steely Dan and now fry sauce? What's wrong with you?"

"Mormons baptize dead Holocaust victims. My ancestors. That's screwed up."

"Well, yeah, okay," Brautigan said, "but ..."

"But nothing." Eliza was on a roll. "They are waging culture war against Indigenous people and the landscape. That term, Sagebrush Rebels? They're not rebels. They're crusaders, trying to spread their ideology across the world in whatever way they can. Over in Africa they deploy those shiny, clean-cut, tie-wearing white boy elders; over here they just use ATVs."

"Come on, Eliza, it's not a religious thing. It's a rural thing. People feel like they're under attack from rich New Westerners and New Yorkers. Their home is being invaded and their traditional livelihoods are being stolen from them. And maybe they have a point."

"Traditional livelihoods? You mean like being a pawn to Exxon or Shell or BP or Energy Fuels? Like riding your four-wheeler all over archaeological sites? Is that what you mean?"

"They don't want Blanding to become just another Patagonia outlet store, like Durango, or Moab. And I don't blame them." They sped past a singlewide on cinderblocks tilted uncannily to one side next to a rusted out old pump jack that resembled a T-Rex doing calisthenics. A hand-written sign on a fencepost advertised a revival down a rocky two-track.

"How long has it been since you've been to Moab?"

"I don't know. Why?"

"Because there's a hell of a lot more Polaris now than Patagonia."

"Polaris?"

"Yeah, and Suzuki, Yamaha, and whoever else makes those damned side-by-side ATV things that crawl all over the streets and the slickrock. Forget spandex-wearing mountain bikers, the streets are swarming with chubby, pasty fossil-fuel junkies who think they're on spring break in Mazatlan. It's the same in Silverton. Everyone worried about gentrification, about becoming the next Aspen, and instead they got invaded by the motor heads."

"It's the same thing."

"Yeah, it is, and it's called capitalism. There are no traditional livelihoods. There is no New West versus Old West. There are just different answers to the same question: How are they gonna make money off the landscape? Is it from drilling into the earth and sucking out dead dinosaurs? Putting thousands of cows out onto dirt that can't handle it? Cutting every mesa top into lots and ranchettes and building houses? Or renting it out as a playground for people who have too much money and time on their hands?"

"Okay, sure. But all I'm saying is that a playground isn't necessarily better than a pumpjack. They both screw the place up, just in different ways. I know that miners and ranchers aren't always that kind to the land, but at least they have a connection to it. Not like some t-shirt peddler or developer. Plus those old industries pay more, and keep housing costs down, build a middle class."

"Connection to the land? Connection? Bullcrap. It's all corporate now. A guy working on an oil rig out here is probably from some Texas roustabout crew and he'll leave after a few weeks, moving on to Wyoming or New Mexico or wherever the next boom pops up. There's no connection there. Meanwhile, the corporate goons go to energynet.com to buy the rights to trample cryptobiotic soil, kill birds and bugs and coyotes, and stick their fucking drills into the earth. It's like eBay for land-rapers."

"Or like Tinder."

"Tinder's consensual. This isn't. And your salt-of-the-earth pragmatists? Hell, they've been gone for years, replaced by ideologues who use your traditional livelihoods and heritage bullshit to advance their colonial urges."

They floated past a worn out old church with weathered wood siding and a plastic steeple jutting out of the top and a crooked "JESUS" sign on the side. "I'm hungry," said Brautigan. "When we get to Blanding can we stop at that little drive-in? My stomach is digesting itself."

"Food can wait," said Eliza. "We gotta go check out the truck, first. We're gonna meet the sheriff there."

"Maybe you could just drop me off at the burger joint?"

"I need you to check out the truck with me. And talk to the sheriff. That's why I haven't kicked you out by the side of the road. Remember?"

They continued in silence across a sere land further desiccated by chronic drought, Eliza swerving around axle-breaking potholes and slowing only when they came upon mini-herds of feral horses standing near the road, their haunches a line of ribcage ripples, foraging for whatever weeds might be growing in the beer can-filled barrow ditches. Santos kept a close watch for cops. The two fit the profile, after all — an unkempt couple in a Subaru with Colorado plates. Local law enforcement had been known to gin up fake crimes to retaliate against Durango environmentalists. Close a corral gate out of common courtesy? Get thrown in jail for "wanton destruction of livestock." Hell, based on his burger craving, Brautigan was probably guilty of the very same crime. Culture war, indeed.

On the main highway Eliza floored it, cops be damned, blasting through the small Ute Mountain Ute community of White Mesa and past the metal buildings and tailings piles of the White Mesa uranium mill before finally slowing down on the outskirts of Blanding, the county's biggest town with fewer than four-thousand people. Blanding was originally named Grayson. But like most towns in the region, it wore its identity loosely, and when some rich guy came along and offered cash for a library in exchange for naming the burg after his wife, the community jumped at the offer. The town's newer name fits the overall ambience quite well, except on those rare occasions when the local girls get frisky after downing too many root beer floats at the combined bowling alley and gas station.

Peter's truck was sitting where he had left it, near Parley Redd's hardware store, the doors unlocked, some Sonic wrappers and a paper cup on the floor of the passenger side. His backpack and other gear was notably absent, meaning presumably that he had set off hiking from Blanding, which would be odd, or he had hitchhiked his way deeper into Canyon Country.

"That's not like him," Eliza said, worry in her voice. "He wouldn't want to rely on someone else like that. Unless he was purposely trying to cover his tracks by not leaving a vehicle somewhere that could lead people to him."

"And why," came a voice from behind them, "would someone want to do that?"

Santos and Brautigan wheeled around to see a man regaled in the uniform of the San Juan County Sheriff, a sizable sidearm strapped to his belt, which was cinched with a turquoise bedecked buckle as big as a dinner plate. It took Brautigan a moment to adjust. For it was Kenneth Etcitty, a longtime Navajo politician and activist from the Montezuma Creek area south of Blanding — and the subject of Brautigan's most recent "exposé." He was tall and lean with broad shoulders, and built more like an Olympic swimmer than the rodeo champ he once was.

"Hello. I'm Sheriff Etcitty," the man said. He looked at Brautigan, a spark of recognition alighting in his dark brown eyes. "Hey, aren't you that reporter? You interviewed me about Bears Ears once. That was a nice story you wrote. What's your name? Brad, right? Brian?"

"Brautigan. Malcolm Brautigan. But yeah, I did interview you once a while back."

"Oh, okay. Sorry. Your names all sound the same to me. Are you here to write a story about this missing fella?"

"No. I'm here because Peter was, is, my friend, and Eliza here wanted me to help look for him. Ya ta hey."

"Yá'át'ééh," he said, correcting Brautigan's pronunciation, "but I usually just use 'hello'. Or 'howdy' if I'm in a good mood." He held his hand out to Eliza. "I'm Sheriff Etcitty, but people call me Kenneth. It's nice to meet you."

"Eliza. Eliza Santos. The missing guy is my husband."

Etcitty waited silently for Eliza to say more. He projected an aura that Brautigan had seen often in sheriffs in rural counties: Droll, competent, understated, and fatigued, the result of having to cover a lot of ground and an oddball variety of crimes and other situations, all while being chronically underfunded, under-appreciated, and overworked.

"I called a couple days back and asked you to hold off on looking," Eliza said. "I guess it's time now to send out the search and rescue team?"

"Once you officially file a missing person's report, I'll put out a bulletin. Our deputies have already been keeping an eye on the big trailheads. We need a better idea of where he is before we can send Hank and search and rescue out there. We need to know where to start. This county's as big as a whole state out east, and as wrinkled as my uncle Herman's face. Most likely he's just wandering around out there, a little lost, but otherwise fine."

"Well?" said Santos, looking at Brautigan.

"Well what?"

"Where do you think he is? That's why you're here, remember?"

"How am I supposed to know?"

"You grew up around here. You and Peter used to come out here together all the time. You should know."

Etcitty quietly watched the verbal volley without expression.

"Okay, okay," Brautigan said. "You're right. Let's see, I would say he could be on Cedar Mesa, maybe Slickhorn Canyon, could be Grand Gulch, but I doubt it, because there are too many people down there, so you should try Arch Canyon, oh, and we used to like to go up to the Causeway and explore those canyons, and Dark Canyon, and ..."

"So, what you're saying," Etcitty said, "is that we should really narrow our search down to, oh, I don't know, two million acres? Thanks but no thanks. We need just one of those places to start with. Didn't he say anything about where he was going?"

"He doesn't say much, in general," Eliza said.

"I can probably come up with somewhere to start," Malcolm said. "But I gotta have some time to think it through, look at some maps. And I need some food. I'm really, really hungry."

Santos rolled her eyes and sighed dramatically. "I can't believe I'm being reduced to carrying snacks around for you when you get hangry, like with my daughter. When she was twelve."

"Sheesh," Etcitty said, chuckling a little, his voice deep and soft and soothing. "You two really are something."

"Sorry about my friend, here. I'm gonna take Malcolm to get some food, and then we'll sit down tonight and come up with some ideas of where he might be. Can we meet you tomorrow and talk again?"

"That sounds like a good idea, and I'll bring Hank along," Etcitty said. "And, ahhh, one other thing. Over the last few days, starting right about the time your husband went missing, we've had a few incidents in the county."

"What kind of incidents?"

"Vandalism. Theft. You probably heard about the Monticello substation. Took out the lights all the way from Red Mesa over to Hanksville and up to Green River. A bunch of copper wire and other equipment was taken from there, too. I'd say they were selling it to buy meth or something, but it looked too professional. Like they knew what they were doing. And someone vandalized equipment at the construction site on Comb Ridge."

"You're not saying Peter did that, are you?"

"I'm not saying anything. I'm asking questions. It's my job."

"Peter's an artist. He's not a monkeywrencher or a meth-head or whatever."
Etcitty nodded silently.

"What are they building on Comb Ridge? Fixing the highway?"

"No, they're building the Bears Ears resort on that old state land parcel."

"Who is?"

"Call themselves Sutherland Land and Cattle, but they sure as heck ain't running cows down there. It's all rock." Etcitty stopped talking when a gargantuan, pearly white Ford F-450 pickup truck pulled up next to them. The driver's side door opened and a man piled out. He had a youthful face, salt-and-pepper hair cut in a frat boy style, and in his broad-shouldered, meaty build one could detect a paunchy echo of his days as the star of the San Juan High football team, days that he will forever consider the apex of his existence. He approached the trio with the impatience of those who are accustomed to getting what they want, and who feel persecuted when they don't. Etcitty locked his thumbs in his belt and bit his lip.

"What you got, Sheriff? Are these the ones who parked this truck illegally here," the man said. He looked at Brautigan then and squinted. Brautigan recognized him: Bill Stevens, county commissioner, the same person who had recently praised Juan Lopez-Shapiro's work. He spoke at, not to Etcitty, irritation in his voice: "You need to do something about these people. Take them in for questioning. They could be the eco-terrorists who've been messing with cattle in the backcountry, or wrecking our vehicles at the resort."

"Thank you for your opinion, Commissioner Stevens," Etcitty said, curtly, not even bothering to look Stevens in the eye, "but this is law enforcement business, not yours."

Stevens' face flushed. After a long pause he sputtered a string of words under his breath, something about despots and Thomas Jefferson and who had won the Indian Wars, and then spun around, climbed into the pickup, slammed the door, and accelerated away, his tires kicking up a spray of gravel and the exhaust pipe blowing out a cloud of black smoke.

"I always heard this was one of the poorest counties in Utah," Eliza said.

"It is," Etcitty replied, "and it gets poorer every day, thanks to guys like that racking up the legal bills on lawsuits just to keep some roads open to ATVs."

"Then how is it that a local public servant like Stevens drives around in a brand new truck like that?" Eliza asked. "Did you see that thing? An F-450 dually? It'll put you back ninety-k, easy."

Brautigan and Etcitty both looked at Santos curiously.

"What? I'm a librarian. My mind is a catalog of esoteric tidbits of knowledge."

Nighthawks

After eating a burger and fries at the Kayelli Drive-In, Brautigan suggested that they spend the night at the Bears Ears National Monument campground. Santos was skeptical at first, but as they sat at their site's shaded picnic table with maps, Peter's laptop, and plastic wineglasses filled with cold sauvignon blanc, the only sounds those of a warm breeze and the chatter of a couple of ravens perched on a piñon nearby, she was grateful for the suggestion. They'd be able to get a lot more done in the comfort of the campground and, besides, they had the place to themselves.

"So, where do we start? You're the reporter."

"It would help if I knew what Peter was looking for when he requested all these documents. I'm going in blind. Don't you have anything?"

"When I was looking for clues in his office I found all kinds of crap about nuclear energy, uranium, that sort of thing."

"Okay, well, that's something, I guess." Brautigan thought about the teeth and the Geiger counter, but decided not to mention it. "Let's see, we can do a quick search for 'uranium' and ... oh shit."

"What is it?"

"These aren't searchable documents. We're gonna have to do this manually. Why don't you start with one folder and I'll start with another, and we'll just skim whatever's in there, watching for anything that jumps out. We'll mark any mentions of places on the map."

It was tedious work, but also soothing. They kept the laptop going with a solar charger that had come with one of the survival kits Brautigan had gotten from an advertiser, and were able to get spotty internet by tethering to Eliza's phone. They started on the premise that Peter was somewhere within the original boundaries of Bears Ears National Monument, the un-shrunken version, a two-thousand-square-mile swath of land sliced through by hundreds of miles of varicose canyons and nooks and crannies and alcoves in which a human or their body could remain for decades before being found.

By the time dusk had given way to darkness a pattern had begun to emerge from the chaos, with a bunch of the marks clustered around White Canyon, which gets its start just below the Bears Ears buttes and runs west, through Natural Bridges National Monument, before continuing on its windy path to the Colorado River and the body of stagnant water and deep silt known as Lake Powell. White Canyon was once a uranium mining hotspot, and the area is dotted with dozens of long-abandoned mines — several of which were marked on the pair's map.

"What's RosaBit?" Eliza asked, rousing Brautigan from his reverie. "I just keep noticing it in these email addresses."

"Beats me," said Brautigan. "Oh wait, I've heard of that. It's a vitamin company, maybe? Or no, one of those weird digital money things, like bitcoin? Google it."

"I tried. I just got the spinning wheel of death. The cell signal's pretty spotty."

On Eliza's screen was a long, back and forth email-exchange between at least a dozen different people. It was difficult to understand what the dialogue was about because the whole email chain was included on every reply. But it appeared as if Ivanova.Tasha@RosaBit.com was impatient with Hyde.Bill@blm.gov for botching the public relations around something they referred to as "Fry Canyon."

"Can I take a look?" Brautigan sat down at the laptop and started scrolling, scanning the names. Most of the addresses had government appendages, either from the Bureau of Land Management or Department of Interior, along with one or two from the Department of Energy. Brautigan didn't recognize many of the names, which was not surprising, given that it had been a while since he'd been on that beat, and because a lot of long-time BLM officials had quit when the national offices had been moved from Washington to Grand Junction. But one email address caught his eye. He scrolled back to it, and stared. The address belonged to Stan Hatch, his main benefactor.

A tickle of sweat slid down his temple as the connections clicked together in his brain. He shouldn't have been surprised. Hatch was, after all, the director of the GGF Foundation, one of the loudest voices opposing the designation of the Bears Ears National Monument. Still, it made him queasy to see his name here, like this. He scrolled some more, and found more emails, including one from Hatch to a long list of people touting an article supporting Drumpf's shrinkage of Bears Ears National Monument. The article was written by Juan

Lopez-Shapiro.

"Shit," Brautigan said, snapping the laptop shut.

"Problem?"

"Sorry about that. I was just, ummm, never mind."

"You look pale. Like you're gonna puke. Maybe it was the fry sauce at the burger joint."

Brautigan stared at his wineglass and, after a long pause, said, "Eliza, I need to tell you something, a confession."

"Hey, if it's about your corporate gig, I'm sorry I got so upset and yelled. I mean, I'm just disappointed. It seems so unlike you, the old you."

"I suppose it would be better if I was still with the *Tucson Tribune*, writing about stubborn belly fat?"

"At least then you'd be writing what you know."

"Very funny. I'm good at what I do. I like it."

"Good at what? Editing corporate newsletters about synergy or profit margins or workplace culture?"

"Something like that."

"Okay, fine. I'm relieved that you're not working for *PatriotBlast* or something. But what I was trying to say and, no, this isn't easy for me, but what I was trying to say is that I'm disappointed and sad that you didn't reach out to us."

"Reach out?"

"When Melissa left. When things got hard with your marriage. And your job. Just in general. I wish you'd ask for help or just talk to Peter and me. Or talk to someone? Randy or Ann or your brother or a therapist, even, now that you can afford it — you do get health insurance with these gigs, I hope."

"That was a long time ago. It doesn't matter anymore. I'm fine"

"It does matter, Malcolm. You matter."

"I don't need no stinking therapist. You spent too long in New York." Malcolm stepped away, his body tense, and Eliza followed. The sun was finally finishing its long day's journey across the cloudless sky, and simmered just near the horizon, a red-orange fireball dimmed by the atmosphere and by the smoke from the wildfires. The steep, dark slopes of Ute Mountain captured the sun's fading effulgence so as to make light seem tangible, touchable — something to inhale, ingest, or blanket oneself with. Soon the bats would come out, and maybe the coyotes, too.

Eliza began to ask a question, then stopped. She reached out and touched Malcolm's moist cheek, causing him to flinch and back away.

"I'm fine, Eliza. What do you know about me or about who I'm talking to?"

"I don't know. I don't know anything because you just dropped off the face of the earth, just like Peter. What is it with you guys, anyway? If you don't want to talk to me, fine, I get it. But talk to each other. Talk to someone."

Brautigan fell back against the camp-site's shade structure and said nothing, his bottom lip trembling. Eliza approached him cautiously, then took him in her arms, holding on as tight as she could. She felt his sobs convulse through his body before she heard them. They stayed like that for five minutes, then ten. Malcolm's body unclenched in the warmth of her embrace. She pulled him to her, pressing her body against his. They stayed like that until the nighthawks boomed against the plum-colored sky, swooping after the gnats and mosquitoes and wasps. *Voom, Voom, Voom.* Finally, she slowly let go.

"You okay, Malcolm?"

"I'm okay. Thanks."

"We should get some sleep. We've got a big day tomorrow."

"But we never decided where to tell Etcitty to start looking."

"Maybe we shouldn't tell him anything. We should just start searching ourselves."

"That's crazy, Eliza. We'll never find him on our own."

"Yeah, it's just that…"

"What?"

"Nothing. What do you suggest?"

"I think White Canyon is a good place to start. It's a huge drainage, maybe still too broad for Etcitty, but it's the best we've got."

"Okay. We'll talk about it again in the morning. I'm tired."

They cleaned up camp and Brautigan crawled into the little tent, stripped down to his underwear, and lay down on his unzipped sleeping bag and looked up at the stars through the mesh roof. He strained to keep his eyes open while Eliza went up to the bathroom. As he lay there he heard her voice and then, after what seemed like forever, the crunch of her shoes on the tent pad gravel and the sound of the zipper as she crawled in next to him.

Scorpion

Brautigan's eyes snapped open and then shut again in reaction to the glaring light someone shone in his face. No, no, it was just the moon, only half-full but still bright enough to illuminate his surroundings. His heart beat wildly, a burning dread filled his belly. Night sounds blended discordantly: The vexatious drone of the cricket chirp, the foreboding hum of the moon, a mysterious soft scratching sound from somewhere to his right, surely a scorpion trying to get into the tent. And the deep and even rhythm of Eliza's breathing.

None of it calmed the storm within Brautigan.

He had almost slipped, almost came out and revealed to Eliza what he really did to make a living. That was stupid, careless, and potentially disastrous. He could deal with Eliza's wrath, maybe even with losing her friendship. But she wouldn't be able to keep Brautigan's double identity to herself, and eventually word would get out. His family would disown him. Stan Hatch, learning that Juan Lopez-Shapiro was actually Malcolm Brautigan, would cut him off, maybe even worse.

Anyway, Eliza didn't need to know. It would only distract from the real mission, which was to find Peter.

Or *was* that the mission? Something had felt off since the moment Brautigan answered the phone back in Tucson to hear Eliza's voice on the other end of the line. Something about it all had felt staged, like it was a setup. And here was Eliza, who should be frantic, but instead was rather aloof about Peter's disappearance, and behaved almost as if she didn't *want* to find him.

Perhaps she was simply afraid Peter was dead, and wanted to delay that realization for as long as possible, much as Brautigan postponed going to the doctor when a weird-looking mole popped up on his arm, or a persistent pain nagged at his guts, because he really didn't want to know that he was dying of an incurable disease.

But then again, maybe Eliza had killed Peter. A crime of passion. Eliza didn't seem homicidal, but she did have a mean temper. Had he seen a sort of glimmer in her eye when he mentioned the lesbian barista in the coffee shop? Was Eliza, not Peter, the one having an affair? And did they conspire to dose Peter's coffee with a slow-acting drug that kicked in right about when he got to Blanding, so he parked his truck, ripped off his clothes, and walked out into the desert until he dried up and died? Malcolm made a mental note to quiz Eliza the next morning, and maybe also find out if there was a life insurance policy involved. Then, armed with this evidence, he'd pull Etcitty aside and let him in on the scheme, and Brautigan would emerge as a hero and Eliza would go to jail, where she obviously belonged.

An owl's plaintive call blew through the glowing blue light. And that damned scratching had started up again from underneath the tent — definitely a scorpion, and a big one at that. He made another mental note: Have Eliza dismantle the tent in the morning.

With a plan in mind, Brautigan closed his eyes, relaxed, and fell back to sleep.

Eliza wasn't really sleeping. The heavy breathing, quasi-snore was just an act. She had learned in life that sometimes, particularly when dealing with men, it's best just to fake it. Even as Brautigan rustled around with short-lived nocturnal neurosis, she was suffering a bout of full blown insomnia.

Looking through the documents on Peter's computer had left her severely discomfited. She had been led to believe that her husband had been working tirelessly on a big art project, and maybe he was, but he was also spending a lot of time chasing down emails between bureaucrats and executives and reading atom-bomb-building primers. Something about what he was doing had attracted the attention of those musclebound mercenaries that had shown up on her doorstep. And to top it off there was Etcitty's suspicion about the substation crime and vandalism.

It was becoming clear that Peter was in some sort of trouble, most likely with the law. He was not dead at the bottom of some canyon, nor was he running away from his wife and daughter, nor was he on a beach in Belize with a hot bi-sexual barista. Rather, he was on the lam, a fugitive hiding out in the canyons. The realization provided some relief, but it also frustrated Eliza. She couldn't afford this shit right now. It was hard enough to be married to Peter the artist. It would be far, far worse to be married to Peter the Unabomber, the terrorist, or the convict.

It meant that she couldn't lead Etcitty and his search and rescue team to Peter. If Peter saw the law coming it would scare him off, push him deeper into the canyons, or worse. He was not the kind to pull some Waco-like standoff with the cops, but he would also not go gently. He would rather perish than be incarcerated, rather die quickly than endure the slow death of a jail cell. She had to figure out how to put Etcitty off, or maybe sick him on a false scent, to ensure that she'd find Peter, first. Then she could talk him down, maybe get him to turn himself in, to agree to try his luck before a jury. Whatever crimes he may have committed, he did not do so maliciously. He did it in the name of art. Maybe that would sway a judge, but probably not.

Brautigan's jerky breathing told Eliza that he had fallen back to sleep. She reached over and gently touched his long brown, grey-streaked hair, spilled across the grimy backpacking pillow like a stain, noticing as she did what appeared to be a tiny puncture wound behind his ear. She'd ask him about it in the morning. In the meantime she would not tell Brautigan about her worries, would not let him in on her suspicions about her husband. He was the type who would bail at the first whiff of trouble, who would hightail it right out of there if he thought he might end up as an accomplice to a crime. Her challenge would be to keep Brautigan from leading Etcitty to Peter.

When Brautigan awoke again, the sun was still deep below the eastern horizon, but the sky glowed pale blue, the stars all gone with the exception of Venus, which sat coquettishly above the jagged silhouette of the La Plata Mountains. A family of coyotes yipped away in the distance. He was groggy from having fallen back asleep, but the angst and all the questions, neuroses, and harebrained suspicions from just a couple of hours earlier had vanished along with the stars.

Eliza's sleeping bag was empty, but the sound of her footsteps crunched their way into camp. He sat up, took a look around. Much to Brautigan's consternation, Eliza was wearing those same orange shorts, the ones that revealed so much of her strong legs, the ones that unearthed memories from when they were together so long ago, and the way she was so adept at extracting from him and his body exactly what she needed.

"Hey, sleepyhead," she said. "Stop staring and get your fat ass out of bed."

Reflexively, he looked down at his hairy belly, the chub hanging over the elastic band on his underwear. Fat ass is right, he thought, self-consciously putting on a long-sleeved linen shirt, despite the fact that it was warm enough to go sans clothes. Eliza walked over to the picnic table and lit the campstove and put the espresso maker on one burner and a pot of water for oatmeal on the other. Brautigan pulled on some shorts and climbed out of the tent and tried futilely to stretch the ache of age from his bones.

They walked down to the small canyon's rim and sat on the cool, lichen-laced sandstone and ate their oatmeal and drank their coffee without speaking as the sun's first light splashed across the landscape, the temperature climbing. They strolled back up to camp and quickly cleaned and packed, interrupting the slumber of a beige-colored scorpion, its almost-transparent stinger twitching about aggressively as Eliza folded up the tent.

Bears Ears Resort

Brautigan and Santos pulled into the Blue Bird Cafe parking lot in Bluff seven minutes ahead of schedule. Sheriff Etcitty was already there, leaning against his Ford F-150 patrol vehicle, his straw cowboy hat in hand, chatting with an older white woman. She was nearly as tall as Etcitty and carried with her a palpable gravitas offset by an unkempt shock of white hair. She vaguely resembled Emmylou Harris.

"Good morning," Etcitty said. He looked cool and comfortable despite the heat.

"Ya ta — Hello," said Eliza.

"This is Hank Love," Etcitty said, motioning to his companion. "She runs search and rescue. She's also a smart woman, but has some crazy ideas. Hank, this is Eliza Santos and Malcolm Brautigan."

"Hank? Oh. Okay. Nice to meet you."

"Henrietta, if you must know, which is apparently too many syllables for folks around here."

For a minute or so, silence. Brautigan fidgeted, and Santos looked up at the cliffs that stood sentinel over the tiny town. The cafe was busy, its parking lot crowded with late model cars, many with Nevada plates, surely rentals. Some people on the cafe's patio were speaking French, while another group spoke German.

Finally, Etcitty spoke, "What do you have for us? Where should we start looking?"

Brautigan answered, "We're not really sure, but we were thinking maybe — ouch!" He was stopped short by a sharp pain in his back, as if the morning's scorpion has made it into his shirt and was now stinging him. But it was just Eliza pinching and squeezing an especially thick piece of his back fat. Etcitty and Love looked at him with bemusement.

118

"What he was saying is that we don't know," Eliza said. "We worked at it for hours last night and came up with possibilities that are all over the map. Didn't narrow it down at all. We were thinking we'd go check out obvious places on our own today and cross them off the list, maybe get you a more targeted area in the next few days?"

Love raised an eyebrow.

"Huh? I suppose that will be fine," said Etcitty, hesitantly. "It's not like we don't have enough going on to keep us busy, right Hank? Last night someone stole an ATV off a trailer over at Hole in the Rock trail, and I've got another missing persons report — an old guy wandered away from his camp up at Muley Point and never came back. A drunk wrecked his car over there in Eastland, and some roughneck plowed into a herd of sheep down in the oil field."

"Gives new meaning to mutton chops," said Hank. "Meanwhile I've got my SAR guys and deputies scattered all over this damned county. Hopefully no one will decide to rob the bank in Monticello today."

"What was that all about?" Brautigan demanded of Eliza after they had gotten back into the car. "Don't you want his help? What's going on?"

"I don't trust them. One's a cop. The other's a Mormon."

"How do you even know she's a Mormon? And if she is, so what? Her name's Hank, for chrissakes! What are you gonna do, import a search and rescue team from Manhattan? You gotta get over this thing with Mormons. It's not healthy. Did you know that Brigham Young was a Marxist?"

"So was Jesus. Your point?"

"What's this really about? You took a chunk of flesh out of me back there and you won't tell me why." The dormant suspicion from the night before was re-awakening.

"Sorry. I just think it's better for now to look by ourselves. Those guys are stretched pretty thin anyway, so they probably can't do too much, and like you said last night, we haven't narrowed the search zone down enough yet. Besides, it feels messed up to put all these resources into looking for my husband when there are people who are really missing out there, and are probably in far greater danger. Let's wait for a day or two."

"And then what? They're the cops. The professionals. This is what they do. We're just two people trying to find that needle-dick husband of yours in a two-thousand-square-mile haystack."

"Wow, impressive wordplay."

"I've been working on that one for a couple of days. But hey, he's *your* husband. I just follow orders."

"Exactly. Why don't we go up to White Canyon and just take a look around, get the lay of the land. Okay?"

As they passed by the little convenience store and gas station, a shiny black Suburban next to the pumps caught Brautigan's eye. A woman walked out of the store and toward the Suburban. He only caught a glimpse, but Brautigan could have sworn that it was her: The woman from North Dakota. He craned his neck to get a better look, but just as he did the Suburban blocked his view.

"Woah, there mister," said Eliza. "You want me to go back so you can ask for her number?"

"Uh, no, no, I just thought maybe I knew her."

"Really?"

"Really. But I don't. Know her. We good on food and stuff? Ice?"

"Yeah, we're good. If you want me to go back…"

"I *said* I don't know her."

They drove on in silence across the open landscape, Brautigan growing increasingly uneasy. The car dipped down into Butler Wash, then lifted back up. As they emerged from the road cut, up onto the lower slope of Comb Ridge, the imposing structure perched just below the apex of the formation came into view. It had a wall of gleaming glass windows beneath a large sign reading "Bears Ears Adventure Resort and Guides." Etcitty had warned them, but it was shocking nonetheless. A sign on the gate said: "A project of Sutherland Farms with funding from the GGF Foundation." Bill Stevens' giant truck sat near the gate.

"You've got to be kidding," Malcolm murmured.

"That is horrific," Eliza said. "Sutherland Farms? Really? Wasn't the GGF Foundation trying to stop Bears Ears National Monument? And now they're capitalizing off of it? Ridiculous."

The car and its passengers continued through the Valley of the Gods, where red rock spires jutted up from red gravelly earth. A small herd of gangly cows stood around a steel water tank, looking terribly out of place, and hungry. Eliza broke the silence to explain that they were driving right along the border between the Pennsylvanian and the Permian geologic periods, that all the spires and the deceptively small-looking south face of Cedar Mesa in the distance were once giant sand dunes, while everything below them was deposited millions of years earlier, when this was all under a sea and the climate was sultry and dragonflies the size of small airplanes plied the humid air.

Malcolm peered out the window, trying to imagine the sea, the sand dunes, the rivers dumping their silty loads onto swampy plains. It didn't work.

The wheels left the pavement behind, and Eliza drove far too quickly on the loose gravel of the sinuous, washboarded Moqui Dugway road, occasionally removing not just one, but both hands from the wheel in order to gesture toward the scenery. Malcolm gripped the door handle, peering out at the remains of a tractor trailer lying munched and rusting on a shelf of stone below one switchback, and thought about how, several years back, a Japanese businessman intentionally drove himself and his much younger lover, a classical pianist, off the cliffs here in a bizarre murder-suicide. It is a scenic place to die, if nothing else.

"Out there?" Eliza pointed toward a place far below where the land folded upward in dramatic fashion, the sloping face decorated with zig-zag patterns that resembled those on some Navajo rugs. "That's the Raplee Anticline."

"Yeah, I've always been fond of that thing, and a little scared of it."

"Scared?"

"Sure. Just look at it. It's kind of ominous. I think the Navajo story is that it's a giant serpent that burst from the earth and looks over the land and the people. Scary."

"Actually, it was formed by the Laramide Orogeny, when two plates crashed together about sixty-million years ago," Eliza said. "Also scary, I guess."

"And no more believable than the snake story, honestly."

Atop the mesa cell service returned, and Brautigan checked his messages. Three were from Stan Hatch, urging Lopez-Shapiro to get cracking. No longer was Hatch just offering friendly "tips." He had taken on a more assertive tone. He wanted Brautigan to write a piece talking up the Drumpf II administration's plans to build more nuclear weapons, an escalation in the arms race with China, framing it as a way to revive the uranium industry in the Four Corners Country. And he "suggested" another exposé of San Juan County Sheriff Kenneth Etcitty and his numerous "conflicts of interest," whatever that means.

"Shit," said Brautigan, slamming the phone onto the dashboard.

"Hey! You're gonna crack my dash! Bad news?"

"Ohhh, just work stuff. A client. I missed a deadline."

"Uh huh. See, if you were still doing real journalism you could be writing about what's going on out here. That resort, for example, or the bullshit monument shrinkage act that our former president pulled and that the current one is sticking with, all so they can drill and mine the shit out of everything around here."

"The oil and gas and uranium are all tapped out here, so I wouldn't worry too much. Whatever happened with the lawsuit on that, anyway?"

"The administration keeps managing to delay it. Meanwhile, they're stocking the courts with fascist judges. It's not looking good, Malcolm."

Santos made time on the straight road across the mesa top. "Jesus, it's already eighty-eight degrees," said Eliza, looking at the digital temperature readout on the dash. "We gotta get some searching done before it gets worse. Hey, last night you said you had something to confess? You know, before I interrupted."

"Uhhh, I don't remember," said Brautigan as a litany of confession-worthy acts, feelings, and desires piled up in his consciousness. "Must not have been that important."

She shook her head silently. They turned onto Highway 95 heading west, and soon were able to see the sea of pale sandstone that rimmed White Canyon, another place that had been protected by national monument designation, and then, with a flick of a pen, was left relatively unprotected.

"Hey," said Brautigan, "can we pull over here. Scope things out a bit? Also, I'm starving."

"You're always starving. I'd think you had worms if it wasn't for, well," she said, motioning toward his chunky midsection. She pulled over in a clearing where yet another two-track road made its way into the piñon and juniper forest, crawled out, stretched, and opened the back of the car and started working on lunch. Brautigan stepped into the trees to take a leak. He came back with a yellow pin flag and held it up to Eliza. It was printed with black lettering that said, "Fry Canyon Energy."

"Holy shit," said Eliza. "What's that mean? Someone's looking for oil? Uranium?"

"Looks like it. There's a line of these things, spaced about fifty feet apart, parallel to the canyon."

"Didn't you just say that there's no uranium or oil left here?" Eliza opened a bag of pita bread and pulled one out, ripped it in half, and opened it up. She then poured the contents of a can of sardines into the pita bread, topped it off with some sunflower seeds and garlic powder, and handed it to Malcolm.

"Probably just local yokels playing prospector or trying to bring back the good ol' days." He sniffed the food item. "What *is* this?"

"Lunch. You said you were hungry. Eat up."

He took a big bite, his face scrunching up as his palate recoiled. "Fish coated in sawdust? What?"

"You cook next time."

As they choked down lunch, a high pitched wail tore through the silence:

Sirens, getting closer. A San Juan County sheriff's vehicle zoomed past on the highway, headed west, its lights a-flashing and sirens blaring. A minute or so later another one passed moving more slowly and without all the racket. It looked like Etcitty's truck. Eliza and Malcolm cleaned up the lunch mess, Brautigan surreptitiously tossing the remainder of his meal into a tree for the camp jays, and hopped back in the car and followed the cops.

Fry Canyon Energy

Fry Canyon Lodge, a bustling place back in the uranium days, shut down years ago. But as Brautigan and Santos approached, it buzzed with activity. Big white pickup trucks with orange flags on them, a couple of black Suburbans, and three monstrous vehicles with huge balloon-like tires sat haphazardly in the parking lot. A billboard stuck up from the gravel beside the road, announcing to passersby that Fry Canyon Energy was hiring workers for a new project. It was illustrated by a photo of a smiling young man in a hard hat above blue, sans-serif text that read: "Responsibly Fueling America's Future!" The sheriff's vehicle was there, too.

Santos slowed enough to get a look, but didn't stop, continuing on for a half-mile more before pulling into the dirt road to the old Fry Canyon runway, which was no more than a graded clearing, built back in the fifties or sixties so that the uranium mine owners could land their planes and check out their properties. Like the lodge, the runway was once again in use: A single-engine plane was sitting at its edge, and near it a black truck with "CLEARWATER" emblazoned on the side. A woman stood next to it, wearing dark pants, dark jacket, dark sunglasses, and lovingly cradling what appeared to be an assault rifle.

"Mmmm, maybe we should turn around. Find another place."

"Public land," said Santos. "We have every right."

She drove across the runway and continued down the road, passing more yellow flags and pink flags and tracks and crushed sagebrush and mangled trees, until they came to a parked white pickup. They pulled over and got out. Two men with hard hats stood at the canyon rim, looking down into the abyss.

Two vehicles came down the road behind them, one of the black Suburbans, the occupants obscured by the dark tinted windows, followed by Etcitty in his own vehicle. Etcitty slowed to a stop and climbed out, looking fatigued.

"Fancy meeting you two here," he said.

"We were just looking for a place to camp is all," said Brautigan.

"Is that right? Well, you better find someplace else. Everything around here is leased by the oil company."

"Oh, okay, we'll be on our way then."

"It's still public land, though, isn't it?" Eliza said. "I mean, we still have the right to be here. What's going on, anyway? You finally arresting these criminals for desecrating the earth?"

"Don't I wish," Etcitty muttered, under his breath. "One of their thumper trucks took a dive into the canyon up here. They think maybe someone sabotaged it. Seems the self-driving mechanism messed up and the guy inside couldn't override it. He jumped out right before it went over. Lucky man."

"Self-driving?" Eliza said. "So much for all those mining jobs for locals, right? If it drives itself why was someone in there?"

"The guy's in there to keep an eye on the robot, and to work the seismic instrumentation. It's like a sonar for finding oil deposits."

"They're gonna drill for oil here?"

"More like mine for oil. Tar sands, actually. Just this morning my friend Hank was telling me that a national monument designation would have killed this place. Smart lady, but sometimes she doesn't always see very well." He was looking off into the distance, and seemed in no hurry to deal with the wrecked thumper truck. "See the yellow dirt streaming down the slope over there? It's a uranium mine waste dump. My father worked in one of them."

The Acme Queen it was called. Chester Etcitty stayed out here for ten days in a row, then came home for three, his clothes and hair and skin coated with the fine yellow-gray dust each time. He earned enough to raise five kids, send them all off to college. The work was hard and dangerous — guys getting buried in cave-ins or yanked into the crusher or inhaling the acids they used to extract the yellowcake — but Chester was attentive and safe and lucky. Or so it seemed. Yet every day that he escaped injury, more particles took up residence in his lungs, his blood, and his bones, each one sending out wave-like signals, propaganda encouraging his cells to revolt against the body.

And so they did. Chester's kidneys went bad, then his eyes, then his knees. When Kenneth came home after graduating from college down in Flagstaff, he found a diminished man and a bloody handkerchief. Each wheezy breath Chester took sounded like piñon shells rattling around in his chest, his eyes were yellow and glassy, his cheeks sunken. Kenneth drove him over to Shiprock and the doctor there diagnosed him with advanced lung cancer. Said he smoked too much. Chester'd never smoked a damned day in his life. His teeth fell out, his skin wrapped loosely around his bones like plastic wrap, his mind launched itself on journeys across space and time as he lay in the hogan that his mother and father had built and where he and his children had been born.

Before his final breath, when Bits'iis Doo ninit'i'i was silty and swollen with San Juan Mountain rainfall, Etcitty and his brothers and sister lifted the blanket on which Chester lay, the blanket that his great-great-grandmother had woven and had carried with her on the Long Walk. And they carried what was left of their father, curled up and skeletal like a baby bird, a barely breathing husk of a man, out of the hogan, and placed him and the blanket under the spreading branches of the giant cottonwood that Chester had planted as a boy, there within earshot of the gurgling river, there where he could watch the leaves dance in sunlight against the dark grey thunderheads overhead, and later that evening, just as the first stars made their way into the turquoise-colored sky, his ghost flitted off into the space between light and darkness.

"You okay, sheriff?"

"I'm fine, fine," he shook his head sadly. "I just don't get it. All we ask is to give the land a little rest, you know? Give us all a little rest."

"I'm sorry, Sheriff. So sorry," Eliza muttered, keying into words that went unsaid. The pungent aroma of sagebrush drifted on the warm breeze and the falling cadence of a canyon wren echoed up from the gorge nearby. Brautigan looked at the line of yellow survey flags and the newly bladed road and imagined what it would all look like in a year or two. Reflexively, he began to rationalize the project, mentally jotting down the positives: jobs, energy dominance, tax revenues. But it wasn't working.

"Come on, Eliza," Brautigan implored. "Let's go find another place to camp."

"I don't think so, Malcolm. We're gonna stay right here. I pay taxes so this is my land as much as theirs."

Etcitty sighed deeply: "Have it your way. But don't come crying to me when those thumpers shoot their pulse into the ground." He motioned for the two to follow, using his lips to point toward the canyon. "As long as you're sticking around, you might as well see the carnage."

The trio walked in the huge tracks of a thumper truck, which looked as if they'd been left by two gargantuan caterpillars. Brautigan cringed at each crushed sagebrush or cactus, at the smashed cryptobiotic soil. Santos just muttered expletives under her breath. The tracks led to the pale rimrock then disappeared. The canyon here was narrow, without the benches that might have caught the truck during its tumble, and the beast had crashed and bounced all the way to the gravelly streambed down below. It looked crumpled and insignificant and small, but hauling it back up surely would be a nightmare.

One of the oil company people walked toward them with a swift gait, catching Brautigan's eye. He froze. Hot pinpricks poked at the inside of his cheeks, and the current of sweat dripping from his body intensified. For there, standing not ten feet away, on the inner-ear-pink rimrock of White Canyon, was the petroleum engineer from North Dakota, her honey-blonde hair up in a tight bun, aviator glasses hiding the look in her eyes, canvas Carhartt pants and a white, button-up shirt not doing nearly enough to obscure her figure.

"Well, well, if it isn't Malcolm," she said, her face indecipherable.

Color drained from Brautigan's face. "What are you doing here?"

"I told you I was working in Fuckhell Nowhere, and here I am. It seems that someone hacked into the mainframe of my very expensive toy. You wouldn't happen to know anything about this, would you?"

Etcitty detached himself from the conversation and started walking in a spiral, looking intently at the ground. He squatted, picked something up, then stood up straight again and walked back to the group.

"You know her?" Santos said to Brautigan.

He didn't answer. The woman from North Dakota winked at Brautigan in a disconcerting way, then turned and walked toward the Suburban, motioning to Etcitty to follow, as if he were her subordinate. Instead, Etcitty turned his back to North Dakota and opened his hand. In his large palm was a miniature bear, carved from stone, with a red eye and a turquoise spiral on its torso. "Looks like a Zuni fetish to me, but an unusual one," Etcitty said, softly, so that the oil people couldn't hear. "Or like a calling card. We found another like it over at that resort on Comb Ridge, after it was vandalized. Look familiar?" They both shook their heads. Etcitty looked from Eliza to Brautigan and back again, then closed his hand, put the fetish in his pocket, turned, and walked back toward North Dakota.

"Can we please leave now," Brautigan said to Eliza, almost whimpering.

"Yeah," she replied. "That might be a good idea."

They walked back to the Subaru without saying goodbye. Eliza turned the car around and slowly drove them out to the highway and back in the direction from which they'd come. At the bottom of the billboard was small print that they hadn't seen before: "A division of RosaBit Americas, Inc."

"Hey, wait. Isn't that...?"

"Yeah. From the emails."

Five minutes later Santos pulled off onto a little two-track that took them to the canyon rim, parking so the car was not visible from the highway. She got out and opened the hatchback and dug a couple of cans of Coke out of the cooler, handing one to Brautigan. He popped the top, relished the sound of the release of carbon dioxide, and immediately took a big, bubbles-burning gulp. "There is nothing better than the first drink of a Coca-Cola from a can.

Nothing. Better than sex. Almost."

"Speaking of sex, who was that woman?"

"I don't know."

"Umm, yes, you do."

"I don't know her … name. I, um, we, um…"

"You slept with her?"

"Not quite. She, ahhh, well, she, kinda oral sexed me."

Eliza's eyes bulged as Coke erupted from her nostrils. "Arrrggh, oh, god, that hurt, ow. Oral sexed?! Whuuut? Where do you get this stuff? It's golden. And then?"

"I passed out."

"Oh dear. Oh Malcolm. When did this happen?"

"A few nights ago. In Winslow. At the fancy hotel. She was there in the bar and, you know, I guess I kind of seduced her."

"Yeah. Likely story. So, what's her name?"

"…"

"You don't even know her name?! No way! But wait, she knows your name. How'd you manage that?"

"It wasn't like, intentional or anything. We just never introduced ourselves. It was very organic in that way. And she doesn't know my name, either."

"She called you by your name today, when she first saw you."

"Oh?"

Eliza left it at that. Wordlessly, she headed off into the trees, presumably to go pee. Brautigan opened the car door and sat down in the passenger seat and waited, each sip a slightly warmer, flatter, and coyly sweet shadow of that first, bubbly, ice-cold, divine taste. He was contemplating the way a can of Coke is like life, or maybe love, when Eliza came dancing up in front of the car, a broad smile on her face, a bundle of the yellow Fry Canyon Energy pin flags in each hand.

"Woah, woah, woah," Brautigan jumped out of the car. "What are you doing? That's illegal. What if someone saw you?"

She tossed them on the ground, picked up a big boulder, and put it on top of them.

"All better," said Eliza as she got in the car and fired up the engine and the A/C. "You coming, or what?"

As she drove to the highway, Santos hummed a familiar Leonard Cohen tune, only with altered lyrics:

"I remember you well, in the Winslow hotel, you were talking so drunk and so sweet. Giving Malcolm head, on the unmade bed, while your flatbed Ford waited in the street…"

Comb Ridge

"S o," said Brautigan, as the car sped east along Highway 95. "That was a pretty cut and dry case. Mystery solved. Now we just have to wait for Peter to come home. I know a place we can camp tonight and celebrate."

"What are you talking about?"

"We figured it out. Peter was working on some art thing, stumbled upon the Fry Canyon deal, researched it, and decided to expose it. A normal person would have just gone to a journalist, but this is Peter we're talking about. So he planted all those docs where you would find them, and then went missing. We went searching for him, which led us to uncovering the tar sands operation. It's performance art. My role now is to write up an exposé of the RosaBit project while we wait for Peter to emerge, which might take a while, since he's going to want to get as far away from that wrecked thumper truck as possible."

Eliza shook her head: "Interesting theory, but I don't think so. There's nothing artistic about driving a truck off a cliff."

"That part was a mistake. He was trying to do something else more creative and it went awry. But the Zuni bear fetish? A very nice touch. It's like the revenge of the Bears Ears, right? I love it."

"Hm."

"So we can stop searching. We'll have a nice meal tonight out on the slickrock then go back to Durango tomorrow, and I can get back to my life. And when Peter gets back I'm going to rip him a new one for not looping me in earlier in the process. I would have loved to collaborate with him on something like this." Brautigan was almost giddy. He hadn't felt this way in a long time. "Woah, slow down, take this left up here. And now I get why you've been so weird, too."

"Me?"

"Yeah, you know. You didn't want Etcitty and Love out there looking for

Peter because you knew Peter wasn't really missing. And if they would have found him too soon, it would have wrecked the whole performance. Besides, you'd probably have to pay for the rescue."

"That's not why…"

"Right up here, take that little two-track off to the right. Jeez, slow down, would ya? Okay, there's not a lot of shade at this campsite, but the views. Wow. Anyway, that was a good move on your part. Well played."

Eliza had almost been convinced by Brautigan's theory, probably out of desperation more than anything else. But it didn't hold up in so many ways. "Malcolm, it sounds like you've figured it all out, but you're wrong. I didn't want the sheriff looking for Peter because I think Peter may be in trouble. With the law."

"He is in trouble with the law, for driving the thumper truck off the cliff. And so are you, for stealing the survey flags."

"No, not for that. These meatheads from Clearwater showed up at my house the other day. They said they were working for the Department of Homeland Security. Contractors, I guess. They asked if I knew where Peter was, where he might be, whether he mentioned any specific mines? That sort of thing. And then they left. But this morning before you woke up Adriana called. She told me that they were still around, parked across the street, like they were keeping an eye on her."

"Jesus, that is creepy. You should call the cops."

"They are the cops, Malcolm. Aren't you listening? Homeland Security. And today, at Fry Canyon, one of the trucks had 'Clearwater' on the door."

"Clearwater?" The name was familiar to him, but he couldn't place it. "It's just a coincidence. But let's just say that you're right, that the Clearwater folks that questioned you are somehow working for RosaBit. If that's the case, then they're just trying to intimidate you, and me, and Peter, so that we don't expose their tar sands racket."

"Expose? They're conducting this project right out in the open a few feet from a major highway. What's there to expose?"

"Whatever kind of backroom deals went down that allowed these people to sneak this thing under the radar. Tar sands mining is major shit, but it's getting less attention and environmental analysis than a single oil well would. Someone's getting paid off somewhere, and Peter's leaving us to figure that one out. It's part of the performance, obviously. The nice thing is, he compiled all the documents on his laptop. We just have to sift through them and find the smoking gun."

Eliza shrugged and threw up her hands. "You've got an explanation for everything, don't you?"

"But it makes sense, doesn't it?"

"Let's set up camp." Eliza got out of the car into the searing sun and pondered the campsite, a flat clearing on the slickrock. She walked around it in a circle, squinting in that way that she has when she gets lost in thought. "I've been here. You brought me here. The first time we went camping together."

Brautigan smiled sheepishly, remembering. They had driven down in early June from Silverton, where it was still winter, and arrived late, after dark, and had lain their sleeping bags right out on the stone and slept under the stars. They awoke at dawn and sat in their bags and watched first sun spill across stone as they drank coffee. Then they made love, ravenously, until the sun climbed high into the sky and the stone heated up and their bodies shone with sweat. "I remember it well. I got quite the sunburn in some, ah, interesting places."

But Eliza wasn't even listening. She was in her own place, treating herself to her own reminiscences of that day and that time, her thighs growing weak. "Do you ever wonder if the landscape has a memory? Like this stone here, if it remembers our little, umm, liaison."

"I sure as hell remember it," he said, turning away from Eliza to cloak his arousal, "quite vividly."

Eliza smiled broadly, her cheeks flushing. Surprised by her own reaction, she turned away, as well, quivering. For a long moment, neither spoke. But the frisson eventually melted away and they could once again function normally.

They set up the tent then retreated into the shade of a nearby alcove to resume their search through the digital pile of papers on Peter's laptop. But the battery was dead. "I guess we have no choice but to take a nap," Brautigan said, laying back in the sand, relishing the imminent end of their fruitless adventure. He was ready to get back to work — and not on Peter's crusade, but on taking *Alt News* to the next level. "There's no hurry, anyway. This can wait until we get back to Durango tomorrow."

Within a few minutes, he was snoring. Eliza tried to sleep, too, but she was restless, thoughts and doubts swirling around her brain.

Brautigan woke up face down in the sand, a clump of drool and dirt stuck to his cheek, grit in his teeth, fogginess on the brain. He staggered out of the alcove and up to camp, somewhat alarmed to find that time had passed, that the sun had slid its way across the sky and was now lingering in the cloudless blue directly above the Bears Ears. Eliza had spread a tarp from a juniper tree to her car, and sat under it on a lawn chair, sipping a glass of wine and mousing

132

furiously on Peter's laptop.

"There you are," she said. "You've got to see this."

On the screen was a photo of the North Dakota petroleum engineer, wearing a hardhat and business suit, standing on the edge of a canyon. "Tasha Ivanova," the accompanying text said, "VP of Operations, RosaBit Americas."

"Huh? Does it have any contact info for her?"

"Yeah, it does, and guess what, it's the same email address that was on that thread we were looking at the other night in the FOIA docs. And check this. RosaBit Americas is a subsidiary of RosaBit International, which is a Russian company. Bit stands for bitumen, the other name for tar sands. I Googled around a bunch and found that the owner, or big investor, or something, is Ivan Ivanov, a Russian or maybe Bulgarian oligarch and arms dealer, who also seems to be tied up in uranium and aluminum companies."

"Wow. So the Russians are about to mangle White Canyon to get at the tar sands? I still don't get how they were able to stay under the regulatory radar."

"I figured that out, too. Interior Secretary, um … What's his name?"

"Albert Fallon."

"Yeah, he removed a bunch of so-called burdens from the energy industry to achieve so-called energy dominance. That included creating a sort of loophole in the Mineral Leasing Act so you can lease land for exploratory purposes without going through any kind of environmental review. A categorical exclusion, I think they call it. Officially, they're just doing exploration, and that billboard with the hunky dude and the promise of jobs makes locals so dewy-eyed that they don't even think about how horrific tar sands mining is."

"How did you figure all this out?"

"I've been staring at this damned screen for hours while you snored away in that cave. I'm losing battery, and I've already lost my patience with some dumbass named Juan Lopez-Shapiro, who has been writing all kinds of bullshit maligning the tribes and trying to make Fallon look less corrupt. Some outlet called *Alt-News*."

Brautigan was silent, his face pale.

"I know, right? It's totally nauseating crap. And that name? Fake. Has to be. I mean, look at the picture. It's some weird stock photo. I think I can still see where he tried to get rid of the watermark."

"Fake?"

"Yes, fake. Who has a name like Juan Lopez-Shapiro? I'll tell you who: some washed up, resentful, doughy white guy pretending to be Jewish so people won't compare him to Goebbels."

"That sounds vaguely anti-semitic to me, Eliza."

"May I remind you that my mother's Jewish? And my dad is, well, something."

"I thought he was Hispanic?"

"I prefer New Mexican. But his sisters freak if I say that. They insist that they are pure Spanish, whatever that means. My dad, meanwhile, was a crypto-Jew, or so he claimed, once he met my mom, then he was Mayan, then he was Tewa — says his great-grandfather was from Santa Clara Pueblo."

"So your dad can appropriate another ethnicity, but this Juan character can't?"

"My dad's a dick, Malcolm. I love him, but he's a horny old bastard who will do anything to get laid, even still. He's currently writing a Shaman's guide to investing or some such bullshit."

"I kinda like him."

"Figures. Whoever this Juan guy is he's spewing some insidious shit out there. It's bad."

"Sounds to me like he's just trying to offer an alternative to the corporate mainstream media viewpoint. Is that so bad?"

"Seriously? Your devil's advocate shtick won't work on this one. Anyway, these people — the ones on the email threads with Ms. Ivanova and this Hatch guy and Fallon's staff — are using Juan's so-called journalism to justify monument shrinkage and regulation rollbacks. It's almost as if he works for them."

"Uh, okay. Well, good job on all of that. Now who does a guy have to oral sex to get a glass of wine around here?"

Brautigan did a quick inventory of foodstuffs. Eliza's cooking was generally inedible, but she had compiled an impressive pantry, nonetheless, with fresh pasta, basil, garlic, salad greens, bread from the bakery in Durango, and, of course, the produce and goat cheese they had picked up at the farm-stand in McElmo Canyon. Brautigan pulled out an armful of ingredients, organized them on the roll-out river table, and went to work, while Eliza sat in her makeshift shade structure, drank another chilled glass of wine, and watched him.

"Isn't there something you could be doing?"

"No. Am I making you nervous?"

"It's fine. Maybe you could tell me a story or something."

"I'm not much of a storyteller."

"Okay, then, tell me about that artwork in your house. Why did you call it a time machine?"

"Funny, I was just thinking about that. And about the memory of landscape."

"That craziness you were talking about earlier? Aren't we the ones who contain the memories, and the landscape just evokes them, like Proust's cookie or my aunt Clara's Jell-O, carrot, and cream cheese salad?" He handed Eliza a loaded plate and sat down with his own.

Eliza gazed down at the plate and a pile of pasta, enrobed in green pesto, orange cherry tomatoes, and torn up yellow squash blossoms, with some asparagus on the side. "This is gorgeous, Malcolm. Not your aunt's Jell-O, I guess, but it'll do."

"I call it the Slickrock Sooprize. Go on."

"Well, it is kind of like the madeleines and Jell-O, it's just extending the phenomenon to a place. Just like you're the accumulation of all that you've experienced, so too is a house, or a rock, or this particular part of the ridge. Like a tree with its rings. A tree vividly remembers everything that it's lived through."

"A tree remembers, eh? Anthropomorphize much?"

"And just like in a tree, time goes in circles. Concentric circles, reaching outward. Or maybe a spiral. Anyway, at moments like this afternoon when we got here, the spiral compresses and you actually touch the past. It's like the landscape has a memory, or rather, like the landscape *is* the memory. I mean, what is Place, with a capital P, if not memories, collective memories?"

"Interesting."

"So it's no wonder the tribes fought so hard to get some protection on this land. The memories of all the people who lived here and their descendants actually live in this landscape, and if you start messing with it, you erase the memories, you tear chapters out of the book. Landforms aren't just symbols of history, they *are* history, the sky, this place, they are the gods, inextricably linked to the people who call it home. And when you stick your drill bits in it or burrow into it to get at the uranium the land remembers, as do the people, and their bones and bodies and cells."

"And climate change? How does that play into this?"

"I suppose it throws it all into disarray." Eliza paused to look at the smoke-obscured sun dipping towards the horizon. "Think about a lake that is part of a people's creation story, the place where they emerged from the previous world eons ago, and where people continue to go to pay their respects, dozens of generations later. And now the lake is dried up. Is it still the emergence place? What about the stories about the lake, do they still have meaning? I don't really know. It's like the whole world is being afflicted with Alzheimers. The memories all erased."

The sun dipped behind Elk Ridge and the Earth's shadow stretched across the land, enveloping White Mesa and the Great Sage Plain and the distant bean fields and the slopes of Ute Mountain and Mesa Verde and the La Plata Mountains beyond that — space and light and beauty of the kind that you yearn to take into your mouth and swallow.

Contrails sliced the sky jaggedly overhead, and a passenger jet glimmered in the fading light, an aluminum tube stuffed with cramped humans chugging their expensive booze and tomato juice and those salty pretzels, zipping along at six-hundred miles per hour, oblivious to the wonders — and all the fading memories — down below.

Bonanza

"**M**alcolm, wake up. Wake up."

Brautigan emerged from a dream and opened his eyes. Outside the tent it was still dark. Santos was looking expectantly at Brautigan, her face lit up by the glow from Peter's laptop.

"What are you doing? What time is it?"

"It's five-thirty. Time to wake up. I've been doing some research. This is nuts. Look."

"No, it is not time to wake up. It is time to sleep for another two hours. Now leave me alone."

"We've got to keep searching."

"For what?"

"For Peter. We can't give up."

"Oh for crying out loud, Eliza. I thought we settled this. Peter's fine. He's coming out on his own."

"Your theory doesn't add up."

"It absolutely does!"

"Why the hell did some hot oil executive choose you to, um, you know, back in Winslow?"

"What does that have to do with anything? Why are you asking me about my virtually nonexistent sex life when I should be sleeping?"

"Has it not struck you as odd that this beautiful, successful, smart woman picked you up in a bar and took you up to her room."

"*My* room. And who says *I* didn't pick *her* up? What are you insinuating, anyway?"

"I'm just saying that it's one hell of a coincidence that you two hooked up and then she ends up being at the center of this ... of whatever it is that Peter's investigating."

"You really do wonders for my self esteem, did you know that? I need some coffee."

"Here, I made some rocket fuel. Drink up."

He took a swig. "What is this? Bitumen? Damn."

"Just drink it and shut up."

He took another big gulp, the tar-like substance coating his tongue with grit. He rubbed the chunks out of his eyes, blew his nose, rubbed his teeth with his fingertip, and took another drink. The caffeine kicked in. "Okay, let's have it your way. North Dakota — er, Tasha — somehow got wind of Peter's plans, and somehow knew I was going to come up and write the major exposé of her corrupt project, and somehow found out I was staying at La Posada, and seduced me in order to blackmail me and keep me from writing my Pulitzer-winning article that no one will run because I blew my credibility a long time ago. Yeah, right. And even if it were true, it reinforces my theory, not weakens it."

"I don't think so. I don't think they give a damn about anyone exposing their tar sands project. Why would they? And the backroom deals? No one would care about it anyway. This is post-Drumpf America. It's what people expect from corporations and bureaucrats and politicians. Most of the public would be disappointed if Tasha *weren't* bribing Fallon."

"And why did Tasha seduce me? I mean, besides to get a little taste of that Malcolm Mojo?"

"Oh, gross. I don't know, to be honest. But what I do know is that these people are up to something beyond the tar sands, and I think Peter's on to them, and their methods are sophisticated. Here's something else: All of these folders are full of documents, right? Hundreds and hundreds of pages of just the most boring shit. But this one? The 'Happy Bonanza' folder? It's empty."

"So?"

"Don't you think that's odd?"

"What's a Happy Bonanza? A Latvian porn site?"

"No clue. Have the rest of the coffee. It's awful."

"There is a Bonanza Canyon, I guess. Maybe there's a connection?"

"Well, duh, where?"

"It runs into White Canyon near Fry Canyon. Peter and I used to go there a lot. It's got some sweet slot sections that no one knows about."

"Why haven't I ever heard of it?"

"Because it's Leetso Canyon on the maps, which is a Navajo word. White locals call it Bonanza Canyon. Just like they call the Abajo Mountains the Blue Mountains."

"So the Mormons are weaponizing names to perpetuate colonialism?"

"I guess so." The red-orange fireball of the sun emerged over a low mesa to the east. "Or maybe they just have a hard time pronouncing non-English words."

"I say we start the search there. It's still a pretty big piece of ground," Eliza said, studying the map on her phone. "Leetso Canyon is a large drainage, with several branches. But I guess it's all we got."

"Agreed. Let's call Etcitty and get this search started. And we can get out of their way and go back to Durango where we can really dig into this stuff. We'll make your house incident command."

"Malcolm, didn't we talk about this? We can't send the law after Peter. What if Etcitty's in on this? Or Hank? Or what if Peter really did steal the wire from that substation or vandalize the equipment at the resort or even crashed the thumper truck? These days that stuff qualifies as terrorism. We'd be sending him straight to prison. Maybe even Guantanamo. We have to do this on our own."

"So which is it? Is Peter a good guy or a criminal? I'm getting confused."

"Maybe he's both. What if he's being framed?"

"Oy. This is getting ridiculous. Okay, we can go search today. But you have to promise me that if we don't find any more clues supporting any of your harebrained scenarios, we call it off and go home and wait for Peter to come out on his own. Deal?"

"Deal."

"Oh, and hey, wear something you can swim in. Bonanza is what I call a wet canyon."

They broke camp, then drove westward again, passing the Fry Canyon Energy complex and continuing along the highway to a place where White Canyon widened and shallowed enough to allow some long-gone uranium miner to build a road across it. Eliza slowly maneuvered the Subaru around a few big boulders, and up some ledges, and continued northward. That's when she saw the truck in her rearview mirror.

"Someone's following us, Malcolm." Brautigan looked in his side mirror. A big white pickup was about a quarter mile back. Could be coincidence. Probably not.

"Are they cops? Should we stop?"

"They're not cops." Eliza let off on the gas a little, anyway, just to see how the other driver reacted. He slowed, too. She threw it into second then and punched it, hard, the engine revving loudly as the RPMs kicked up. The car lurched forward. Brautigan gripped the handle over the door with one hand, his other clinging to the dashboard. The car careened on the soft dirt and gravel, gaining speed, but the truck didn't back off.

"He's still there! Drive, woman! Drive!"

"If you call me that one more time I'm ejecting your ass!" The car was bouncing erratically now, rocks thunking against the exposed innards underneath. "Fuck Jesus! The road is getting bad. I can't go any faster. Plan B. Plan B!"

"Okay, okay, okay. Let's pull over. We'll confront the motherfucker. Do you have any weapons?" Eliza skidded to a halt, throwing Brautigan forward into his shoulder harness.

"Weapons? Of course not!"

"Wait! I do!" Brautigan undid his seatbelt and reached back for his backpack and rooted frantically until he found what he was looking for: the flare gun from one of the survival packets he had brought. He held it up, realized he didn't know how it worked, and threw it at Eliza, who juggled the bright-orange, toy-like device as if it were a steaming hot potato. He dug in the pack and pulled out a fat canister of bear spray. He clicked off the safety and pointed it at the windshield.

The truck had slowed way down, and by the time it was even with the Subaru it was creeping along. The occupants had close-cut hair, dark sunglasses, and black shirts or jackets. The man in the passenger seat had a phone camera pointed at the Subaru as they passed. Brautigan wiggled the bear spray in what he hoped was an intimidating way, while Eliza dangled the unloaded flare gun out at her side. "CLEARWATER" was printed on the door and tailgate of the pickup. It sped up again, and disappeared around the next bend.

"They kept going."

"We scared the crap outta them, that's why."

Eliza looked over at Brautigan holding the aerosol can. "Yeah, no."

"We shouldn't park here out in the open." Brautigan pulled out his phone, on which he had downloaded the Bonanza drainage map so that he could look at it without a cell signal. "There's a little road up ahead. It looks like we can get the car out of sight and hike from there."

Eliza pulled the car behind a big juniper. They loaded their packs with water, food, power bars, M&Ms, and electrolyte drink. Then they dropped into Leetso a.k.a. Bonanza Canyon.

Eliza and Malcolm forced themselves to move slowly because of the heat, which beat down not only from above, but also radiated upward from the sandstone on which they walked. Each step was carefully considered, since the consequences of a slip or a trip could be fatal. When they reached the bottom of the canyon, they did not find the respite for which they yearned. The sand was just as hot and dry as the rock up above. Despite the heat, the canyon bottom allowed for a brisk pace, and Eliza took advantage of it, much to Brautigan's consternation. After fifteen minutes or so her impatience overcame her and, without consulting her traveling companion, started jogging.

"Hey, where are you going?"

"Come on. I won't go too fast."

Brautigan hadn't run in weeks. Okay, months. So, with back- and belly-fat jiggling uncomfortably, and latent knee-pain kicking in like an old friend coming to visit, Brautigan struggled after Eliza, who bounded lightly from boulder to boulder. He finally caught up to her when she stopped where a tributary ran into the canyon.

"Which way?"

"Let's stay in the main stem, for now," he said, gasping for air. "We should probably move more slowly so we can keep an eye on things above us. I'm guessing we're looking for either Peter, who would be down here somewhere" — in which case he would be dead, bloated, and stinky, something he left unsaid — "or the Happy Bonanza, which sounds like a mine to me, and would be up high."

"You are drenched in sweat, Malcolm. Are you okay? |

"No, I'm not okay. I have an enlarged heart, diaphoresis, and hyperhydrosis, not to mention psoriasis of my nether regions—. Oh. I didn't mean to say that part."

"Ewww. You've been internet-diagnosing again, haven't you?"

"Yes. And it could be fatal."

"Life is fatal, Brautigan." Reluctantly, Eliza slowed her pace. Brautigan followed, peering up through sweat-blurred eyes at the cliffs above, trying to catch sight not only of their quarry, but also of hungry predators that might be stalking them. He'd seen mountain lion tracks around here before and surely the drought had taken a toll on the big cat's usual prey. Two big walking hunks of meat would look quite appetizing right about now, and Brautigan was surely the weaker, slower quarry. Judging by Eliza's cooking, Brautigan was also probably the tastier of the two, his wine, garlic, and ice cream-infused perspiration marinating his marbled flesh.

"What are we even doing down here?" Eliza blurted into the silence. She turned around and looked imploringly at Malcolm, her eyes welling up with tears. "Why would anyone want to just vanish, to leave it all behind? I mean, I know I can be a difficult person to live with, but Jesus, this is taking it to the extreme."

Brautigan could think of all kinds of reasons a person might want to vanish, disappear, escape. He silently stared up at the sky, as if waiting for rain. When it became apparent to Eliza that no answer was forthcoming, she threw her hands up in frustration, then turned and continued up-canyon. Malcolm followed. What else was he going to do?

They rounded another bend, and the canyon narrowed, as if its stone walls were giant mandibles, and the monster's mouth was slowly snapping shut. The path was blocked by a wall, streaked with desert varnish. Beneath it was a vague memory of water, a brittle shell of cracked, desiccated mud, the tracks of birds, packrats, coyotes, and other sundry critters quasi-fossilized within. Brautigan found himself playing a particularly disheartening version of the used-to-be game: The last time he was here was years ago in early July, and he and Peter had stripped off their clothes and jumped into the chill waters of this very pool and swam across it, barely able to touch bottom.

Eliza and Malcolm had to backtrack for fifty yards or so to a pile of boulders that afforded access to the next level of the canyon, where the gorge narrowed, the shade grew deeper, and the temperature was a good twenty degrees cooler than the sun-blasted lower portion. The sky was a skinny strip of blue embraced by black-streaked waves of stone.

Desert water has a particular redolence to it, akin to the feel of a smooth river stone in the mouth: cool, dark-green, metallic, moldy. The miasma reached them first, then the water itself, a stagnant pool topped with grey-green pond scum. Malcolm got a running start through the cool sand, leapt onto the steeply angled sandstone wall above the water, and using friction and momentum made his way across the stone, managing to stay dry, but banging his shin on a chockstone at the far end of the pool.

Eliza refrained from such antics, and walked straight into the pool like a sandstone Venus de Milo, oblivious to the scum coating her skin. Nor did it bother her when the little black tadpoles, with their bulbous bodies and lance-thin tails, tickled her toes.

At the second pool, the carcass of a bird floated on the surface, gray-green dross coating its luminous blue feathers.

At the third pool, a dead snake, its body almost torn in half.

If this were Ancient Greece, these would be seen as omens, prophesying the emergence and downfall of a great leader, or the drowning of truth and beauty by evil. But here behind the Slickrock Curtain, they were merely mundane reminders that the great circle of life and death goes on, usually unnoticed, even in these cool depths. Malcolm followed Eliza's lead and waded into the water this time, sucking in breath as it reached his crotch, maneuvering as far from the snake-corpse as he could, shivering but reveling in the coolness, wishing he could store it up as if he were a battery, and release it later when he needed it most. He searched the mud for human tracks. Found none.

They reached another pool. This one was devoid of carcasses, but the bottom was almost solid black with wiggling little tadpoles. They trod gingerly in the muck so as to avoid committing mass larvaecide. At the far end, the stone slanted upward with increasing steepness, topping out with an overhang. The opening at the top was narrow, a big chockstone and a bunch of driftwood lodged into it. A ragged piece of red webbing was attached to the chock, a leftover from someone's long-ago rappel down the pour-over. They both looked at the pool, then at the water-stained spout that they'd have to climb, then at the rock above.

If Peter were dead, his body might be in a place like this. He wouldn't have hesitated to climb up or down this, unassisted, and he would have fallen, broken a leg, or his back, or gotten pinned under rock or debris, where no one would have heard his cries for help. He would have lain within the sensuous curves of the canyon walls, rueing the knowledge that the Facebook notification of his demise would be plastered with comments meant to console: "At least he died doing what he loved!"

The dark cove grew ever slightly darker, a sign that a cloud had passed before the sun. Brautigan flinched, calculating routes of a rapid escape. An upstream cloudburst would send a roiling torrent down this narrow passage, filling it up nearly to the brim within minutes. But the cloud vanished within seconds. The forecast was achingly dry, with nothing but thirst on the horizon.

Brautigan walked through the pool and eased himself into the lower, less steep portion of the spout. He then jammed his body, somewhat painfully, between the slick opposing walls, and awkwardly chimneyed his way up, fueled by the knowledge that a fall would result in a twisted or broken ankle, at the least. He grunted awkwardly, straining until he could grab onto the webbing. With limited leverage, he yanked on it as hard as he could. It felt solid enough. The chockstone had been jammed into the narrow passage with such force that it had almost melded itself to the opposing walls, or so Brautigan hoped. He grabbed the webbing with both hands, lifting up his feet, so that his whole weight hung from it. It held. He wouldn't be able to hold on for long, though. So he kicked his feet up and got a heel lock in the debris and dragged himself up, holding onto the top of the chock stone while using the webbing as a foothold from which to power his way up. He hugged the chock stone at the top, gasping for breath, sweating profusely, and silently gloating over his climbing acumen.

"I think you can do it, Eliza. It's tough, but you've just got to…"

But she was already holding a long piece of webbing that had a bunch of loops in it. She clipped two carabiners on one end, then tossed the whole thing up to Brautigan. It was a rope ladder and it was the perfect length. He clipped the carabiners into the webbing, and Eliza climbed up gracefully, looking like a trapeze artist in a circus. She wasn't winded at all when she got up.

"Thanks a lot for, um, letting me in on that," he said, still out of breath.

"You looked like you were having fun. I didn't want to interrupt."

After that, the canyon was shallower, the going far easier, almost meditative. Eliza moved quickly ahead while Brautigan settled into a steady gait behind her, just fast enough to keep her in view. The extra mind space allowed him to contemplate the last week of his life, which seemed to have spanned many years, and which, with each passing hour, seemed less and less real. He couldn't shake the feeling that he was merely an actor in some elaborate play, that there was an architect out there who had been intent on shaking the foundations of Brautigan's life, intent on ripping him out of the solitary but stable routine into which he had settled. He stopped walking, let Eliza wander out of sight. "Oh, fuck," he muttered under his breath. "Peter, you motherfucker."

That was it. He had solved the mystery. This wasn't just Peter's way of getting him to expose an environmental catastrophe, it was a far more encompassing piece of performance art, engineered by Peter, with Brautigan playing the leading role. It was the only explanation. How did Eliza know to bring the perfect piece of webbing to get up over that pour over? It was in the script, that's how. Why were Tasha Ivanova and Malcolm at the hotel in Winslow at the same time? Because the script said so. Why didn't Eliza want to get search and rescue involved? Because they weren't written into the script.

Brautigan had to hand it to Peter — and Eliza, who was clearly in on it. They had done a great job of fabricating all of the FOIA documents and the RosaBit website with the photo of "Tasha Ivanova." The Fry Canyon Energy set would have been a bigger undertaking, sure, but with some fat government or foundation grant they could have hired actors, rented equipment, the whole deal.

He mentally knit the pieces together. There was no Bulgarian oligarch, no RosaBit, no conspiracy to lease tar sand land. Tasha Ivanova was an actor, after all — who knows, maybe she *was* Sharon Stone. Hidden cameras placed throughout the canyon and drones hovering high overhead captured his every movement. Tasha had implanted cameras and body-function sensors all over Malcolm's body — maybe even his brain, explaining the wound behind his ear — so that viewers would be able to track his heart rate, his gallons per minute of perspiration, the intensity of electrical vibrations shimmering through his nerves so that, in essence, they could read his thoughts. Perhaps the spectators watched all of this in real time in a Los Angeles screening room while drinking their bullet-proof coffees. Some day in the future a very select group would pay five-grand a pop to take a boat from Moab, down the Colorado River, to some hidden alcove, where they'd watch Malcolm's life, the incident in Winslow, his arguments with Eliza, and his copious perspiration play out in a projection on a canyon wall while sipping artisan sagebrush liqueur and slurping zebra mussels harvested from the murky waters of the Colorado: A New West spectacle if there ever was one.

"Malcolm!" Eliza's voice echoed against the canyon walls, followed by the sound of her hurried footsteps in the gravel. "Hey, what the hell are you doing? I thought you had gone missing, too. Jesus, you scared me. Woah, you don't look so good. Let's eat. Have you had any water lately? Dehydrated?"

Brautigan was hungry. And thirsty. And angry. He gobbled down two energy bars and another of Eliza's sandwiches, this time with peanut butter, honey, and bananas instead of sardines, as Eliza looked on. He didn't say anything. He was at a loss for words. They began walking again, and he felt lighter, almost giddy with his epiphany. He stealthily scanned the canyon walls for hidden cameras, rued the fact that he hadn't bothered to fix his hair that morning, and tried to decipher where Eliza was hiding her own body cam.

"So, what now?" Eliza asked when they got to the fork in the canyon.

"What's the script say?"

"Script?"

He looked at her knowingly. She looked confused. "Sure, I get it. How about we just keep going until we see a way out, then circle back to the car up above."

"That works," Eliza said as she started walking with Malcolm right behind, following her cues.

Dirtbag Ditty

U **p on the rim of Bonanza Canyon** the going was somewhat slower than they expected, not because the terrain was rugged, but because they were determined not to step on the cryptobiotic crust — a symbiotic melding of lichen, moss, and bacteria that keeps a good portion of Utah from becoming a giant dust cloud. For Eliza and Malcolm, that meant making huge ballet-dancer-like leaps, minus the grace, from slickrock patch to slickrock patch. Malcolm imagined that whoever was watching the drone footage was getting quite the show.

Brautigan was no longer so sure of his own conspiracy theory, though. If Ivanova was Peter's invention, then so were Stan Hatch and the GGF Foundation and all the rest. And if that was true, then where did real life end and art begin? Were Melissa and Chad Trudeau in on it? What about the Bears Ears Resort? Did Malcolm Brautigan even exist, or was he actually Juan Lopez-Shapiro, pretending to be Malcolm Brautigan pretending to be Juan Lopez-Shapiro? He felt dizzy. "Hey, Eliza, I'm just curious, how did you know to bring that webbing ladder thing into the canyon? Had you been there before?"

"No, silly, of course not. I looked it up this morning on ropewiki."

"Rope-what??"

"Malcolm, this isn't 1989. Get a clue. Canyoneering is a thing now, a sport, and like all sports it doesn't mean anything to the fanatics unless the journey is documented on Instagram and Strava and everywhere else. The bros go to every canyon with even a hint of a slot, GPS the whole goddamned thing, then put 'reports' up on canyoneering sites, which draws more people to the canyons, who then just have to post their adventure reports, and so on."

"On the internet?"

"Yes, on the internet. Where else?"

Brautigan stopped, a baffled look on his face. "Goddamnit. Fuck that shit!" Brautigan yelled, relishing the echo off of a nearby cliff.

"So that's how I knew how much webbing to throw in this morning. Why does it matter anyway?"

"Oh, nothing, I just ... Let's go." He looked up into the sky and scanned from horizon to horizon. No drones in sight.

They were able to follow an old two-track, most likely left over from the uranium years, up and around the other branch of Bonanza Canyon, until they joined the road they had come in on. Again, they chose to run, because they were eager to get back to the car for an ice-cold soda-pop and some food. Brautigan was feeling a bit confused, and irked, but also triumphant. They hadn't found any clues, meaning Eliza had no choice but to call things off. Brautigan struggled to keep up, but couldn't help admiring Eliza's new haircut from behind and the way sweat glistened on her tan, muscular shoulders. He was about to comment on her hair when she stopped abruptly, causing Brautigan to crash into her. It was a rather pleasing collision, at least for him.

"Damnit. Damnit. Damnit," Eliza muttered, turning around.

"I know. We didn't find anything. I'm sorry."

"It's not that. I did find something. And I kept it. That's the problem. Back there in the canyon? When you were lallygagging? I picked something up. I was doing the thing that Peter and I do, where we sort through the gravel in the stream bed and just feel the cool, smooth rocks, looking at the designs on them. And I found something that wasn't a rock, and I kept it. I'm cursed for life. What was I thinking?"

"What is it, Eliza? What did you take?"

"A tooth. A human tooth. It probably washed down from some burial site where it's been for hundreds of years and now it's in my pocket. I'm no better than Earl Shumway."

"A tooth? Can I see it?"

She reached into her pocket and pulled out a smooth, white object.

"Yeah, it's a tooth, alright." Brautigan inspected it tentatively, holding it away from himself so as not to get any of the bad juju on him.

"It was impulse. I wasn't thinking. Now I'm just another grave robber. I feel sick."

"I wouldn't worry too much. Look. That dark spot? It's a filling made of amalgam. It's a baby tooth. Probably some kid was out here camping and lost it and put it underneath his pillow and his parents gave him a nickel and threw the tooth into the canyon. Heck, it could be mine."

"You think so?"

"I know so. Look at it. That's not ancient."

"Oh. Then it's okay, right? That I took it? That's a relief." She pulled another three teeth from her pocket. "Especially since I picked up all of these, too."

"All in the same place?"

"Of course. Odd, huh? You think this is like the Tooth Fairy's dump?"

"Yeah, something like that," Brautigan said as far more grisly possibilities crowded into his brain.

Another quarter mile down the road, a beige-colored van approached, a full-on adventure-mobile equipped with a solar panel up top, gas and water cans on the bumper, and three mountain bikes on a trailer-hitch rack. The beast of a vehicle slowed down and the passenger window rolled down. A guy with mirrored sunglasses stuck his head out, giving Eliza the twice-over. He was handsome, muscular, tanned — a classic outdoor-head "dirtbag." The skin on his hands was covered with chalk and red dust, his face with a layer of scruff. With a shower and a shave, however, he could be cast in Hollywood as a heartthrob, a frat boy, gang rapist, or hedge fund manager. The man in the passenger seat looked about the same.

"Hey there," he said, flashing a set of perfect teeth at Eliza, while ignoring Malcolm. "Does this road go up to the head of Leetso?"

Eliza looked up the road, as if searching for an answer. Malcolm silently calculated the value of the vehicle and gear, putting it at a hundred-grand or more. Was this part of Peter's performance, paid for by the government grant? Had Eliza handpicked the guy with the smile and the pecs to play her love interest? On the dashboard, as if placed there by the movie set designers, was a beat up copy of *Desert Solitaire*. Brautigan was getting agitated, and was only slightly soothed when the side door opened and a blonde woman, probably in her late twenties, scantily clothed and lean and wiry, hopped out and started doing yoga moves on a boulder by the road. He was able to get a quick glance into the van, catching sight of a computer monitor and some sort of control panel.

"Sure, you can get to the head of Leetso," Eliza finally said. "But it's not that great. Water's low, and stinky. You'd be better off going to Lake Powell or something."

"Stinky?" the guy said, snickering and looking at the yoga woman. "Sounds right up your alley, Gaia."

"Shut up, Kale. Y'all want a beer?"

"Sure," Eliza said.

Brautigan grudgingly took one, too, now convinced that only Hollywood — or Peter — could come up with names like Kale and Gaia for these two. The beer was cold, the bitterness of the hops nice.

"Have you guys been out here for a while? I mean out in this area?" Eliza asked the woman.

"We *live* out here, girl," she said. "We're doing research for the most comprehensive guidebook of the area ever. One percent of the profit will go toward enviro groups trying to save this place from the drill rigs and the bovines!"

"And who's going to save the place from the likes of you?" Brautigan muttered inaudibly.

"We're kind of looking for someone," Eliza said. "A tall guy. He would have been backpacking, probably."

"Sure," Gaia said, turning toward her friends. "Yeah, when was it that we picked that pasty dude up in Blanding? Monday? Tuesday? Something like that. He didn't look too healthy. What was his name?"

"Frank," Kale said, still ogling Eliza.

Eliza's face fell.

Gaia: "That's right. Frank was his name. Frank Hill-de-something. Hildebrand? Cool name. It was funny, because when we dropped him off, he looked me in the eye and he said, 'If anyone asks, tell them you saw Frank Hildebrand.' He was very mysterious."

Brautigan chuckled a bit too loudly. "Do any of you have any fucking idea who Frank Hildebrandt is?"

"Uh, yeah, he's the dude we picked up."

"No, seriously. Does the name sound familiar at all?"

"??"

"That's what I thought," Brautigan continued. "Here's a little hint. When you write your guidebook, learn a little bit about the place before you unleash the masses on it, okay? And I don't mean just figure out where the coolest trails are, or the best slot canyons, or the sickest drops to capture an insta on your mountain bike. I mean learn about the place, the history, the people who were here before, and the people who came later, and made it their home and who then fucked it all up with their greed. Do that before *you* and your guidebook fuck it all up all over again, okay? Please?"

"You need to mellow out, man. You're gonna burst an artery or something," Gaia said, as she climbed back into the van.

"Oh, oh, oh, and also? That Ed Abbey guy that you idolize? He's a racist, xenophobic, misogynistic pig!"

"No, shit, Sherlock," Gaia said. "But he can write. That's a hell of a lot more than I can say for you."

"And one other thing," Brautigan said. "If you douchebags or dirtbags or whatever you are put up a slack line between the Bears Ears, I'm gonna—"

"Okay, Malcolm, calm down," Eliza said. "Sorry about him. His psoriasis-of-the-buttcrack has spread to his brain. Makes him testy. Where did you drop this Frank off, anyway, if you don't mind my asking?"

"Up by the Bears Ears. Said he was an artist, and that if we stuck around here, we'd see something that would blow our socks off. I asked if he had a permit for his artwork and he just laughed. Kind of a strange dude."

"Well, cool. Thanks. And thanks for the beer. Good luck in Leetso."

The driver fired up the engine. Gaia closed the door, giving the stink eye to Brautigan. As they pulled away, Brautigan threw the half-full can of beer at the departing vehicle, managing to spray himself with about three dollars' worth of IPA in the process. He reached down and grabbed a rock to throw, but Eliza grabbed his arm and squeezed, hard.

"Dude, chill. Seriously. You're acting idiotic."

He took a deep breath. "That was Peter they were talking about. Had to be. You know that, right?"

"Yeah, I know."

"Frank Hildebrandt was only the most famous uranium miner in the state, maybe anywhere. It's unbelievable that …"

"I know, Malcolm, I know." She was shaking her head in disbelief or maybe disappointment. "Did you see what was hanging from their rearview mirror?"

"No, I was trying to avoid looking at those sleazeballs. What?"

"A bear fetish. Exactly like the one Etcitty showed us back there with the thumper truck."

Frank Hildebrandt

Eliza said nothing as they walked the rest of the way to the car, and when Brautigan started rooting around in the cooler for a cold pop, she brusquely ordered him to get in the car, fired up the ignition, and tore out of the parking place, sending up a thick cloud of orange dust. She should have been gloating, Brautigan thought. After all, they'd found the clue that they needed to continue the search. Instead, she was angry, and was taking it out on the car. She opened her window and pushed the accelerator further to the floor, gravity pulling and combustion pushing the pod-on-wheels faster and faster and faster as they descended the long ramp of Cedar Mesa.

"Eliza? Could you maybe slow down?"

"Shut up. You never got anywhere by being safe, did you?"

As they approached the apex of the inverted parabola, or the point where the highway crosses Comb Wash, the vehicle began shuddering violently, causing the fuzzy dice hanging from the mirror to dance an obscene jig. Brautigan, by then, had pressed his body up against the corner of the car seat and the door, like a cartoon cat in a crashing space ship, trying not to look at the speedometer, but unable to help himself. The needle approached 101, the wind-roar was deafening, and pieces of paper and clothing whipped around the back of the car. Eliza leaned back on her seat, her hands gripped on the steering wheel, her jaw muscles clenching and unclenching in rapid fire.

Malcolm: "Ohhhhh shiiiiiit, we're gonna die!!!!"

They did not. Die, that is. Instead, the car started climbing the other side of the wash, slowing considerably, so that by the time they went through the road cut the car was again moving at a reasonable speed, even if Malcolm Brautigan's heart rate was not.

Eliza grinned so hard it looked like her cheeks might pop. She giggled at Brautigan, whose greasy hair had been sculpted by the road wind to give him a

Flock of Seagulls bouffant. "Just look at that road cut. That's like ten million years right there."

"Great. And you just took, like, thirty-million years off of my life."

"So what. Time slows down when you go faster, so that makes up for it. We're even."

"No, no, time goes faster. Like with the guy on the Vespa."

"Vespa?"

"Yeah, from that one episode of *Cosmos*. Remember? Paolo, this Italian kid, gets on a Vespa and takes a quick ride — at the speed of light — to grab an espresso. When he returns his buddies are all gone, or dead, except for his younger brother, Vincenzo, who is an ancient man sitting there on the park bench. And Carl Sagan says they experienced the dilation of time."

"Exactly. Time slowed down for the guy on the Vespa. He didn't age but the other people did."

"Oh? I guess you're right. Anyway, what always struck me about that episode, besides the fact that they went all the way to Italy to film it, was that Paolo's brother waited around for sixty, seventy years for him to come back, sitting there on that damned park bench, his life on perpetual hold. Meanwhile Paolo was out having a great time, oblivious to his little brother's silent suffering."

"What does that have to do with anything?"

"So is Peter actually Paolo? Am I Vincenzo? Peter took off to New York on his Vespa way back when, and here I am, still sitting on that park bench, holding my breath, waiting for my life to really begin, but just getting older and older while he's out there doing what Peter does, not thinking about me at all."

"Wow, Malcolm."

"I'm serious, Eliza. I love the guy and all, but what the hell? It's pretty obvious that he's not dead. He's not pinned under a rock in a canyon chewing his arm off. He's not in a Page hotel room with an underaged carhop from Sonic. He's just out there doing Peter shit, riding around in a dirtbag van with Gaia, doing some performance art thing in which you and I may or may not be unwitting players, while we run around worrying ourselves to death and aimlessly looking for him. Frank Hildebrandt? Why—?"

"What is it? What's wrong?"

"Frank Hildebrandt. The riddle."

"You're talking gibberish."

Brautigan undid his seatbelt and reached back for his briefcase and dug around in it until he found the envelope with the riddle on it that had come in the mail back in Tucson. He pulled it out, and slowly unfolded it. He read it to himself, then aloud to Eliza as she turned down the gravel road that led to their Comb Ridge campsite. After the first few words, Eliza cut him off: "Okay, okay. That's enough. I get the picture. It's awful. Is that your idea of postmodern poetry?"

"It's from Peter. It's got to be."

"From Peter? I don't understand."

"I got this in the mail a few days ago."

"Peter sent you something? Why the hell didn't you tell me?"

"I didn't know! I thought it was from Josh, my brother. I mean it still could be, but ..."

"Who's this Frank dude? Besides being a dead uranium miner."

"Tonight you cook, I'll tell you about Frank Hildebrandt."

Back at camp, Eliza fired up the stove and opened some cans as Brautigan found himself a pool of shade under a stunted juniper tree, popped out the laptop, and tethered it to his phone. He was almost afraid to check his email, but being a cyber-addict, he really had no choice. And, just as he feared, there was a scolding message from Stan Hatch, not-so-gently prodding him to get on the ball and write something for *Alt-News*. He reiterated his previous assignments, and added one: "We need a piece about a wave of job-killing ecoterrorism in the Bears Ears area." Brautigan fidgeted nervously, reflexively turning the computer screen away from Eliza's line of sight, even though she was a good fifty feet away.

On a whim, Brautigan typed "Stan Hatch" into the search bar. He had no trouble finding Hatch's basic and utterly predictable bio, accompanied by a similarly predictable photo, on the GGF Foundation website. He'd graduated from BYU with a business degree, did his LDS mission in Bulgaria shortly after the dissolution of the Soviet Union, and worked as a mid-level executive in the oil and gas business, in Russia, Kazakhstan, and Rangely, Colorado, before joining the Foundation. Now he was married with six kids, loved to waterski, snowmobile, and read Ayn Rand and the Constitution.

"Hey, Eliza, what was that RosaBit oligarch's name?"

"Ivan Ivanov. Easy to remember."

Brautigan typed something then skimmed the search results. Nothing too interesting, except for the fact that the Drumpf II administration had recently lifted sanctions on the guy, much to congressional Democrats' dismay. But as he was about to shut down his laptop so he could eat some dinner, one of the "images" results caught his eye. He clicked on it.

"Holeeee shit," he said, staring dumbly at the screen.

Eliza stopped chopping and walked over to see what Brautigan's fuss was about. Tasha Ivanova, wearing a curve-hugging, sparkly evening gown, looked sultrily back from the screen. She stood next to Stan Hatch, in a grey suit with blue tie. Also with them was a boxy guy whose suit had a metallic sheen. The caption read: *"Ivan Ivanov and his wife Tasha were the guests of honor at the GGF Foundation's annual gala at the LDS Conference Center in Salt Lake City. Here they pose with their longtime associate, GGF Executive Director Stan Hatch."* Brautigan clicked on the photo and was taken to a gallery of images from the event. Another of Hatch's special guests was Interior Secretary Albert B. Fallon.

"Woah," said Eliza. "Talk about crony capitalism. That Ivanov guy looks like he could crush you with his pinky. You might wanna avoid further liaisons with his wife."

She was right. Of even greater concern to Brautigan was the fact that Juan Lopez-Shapiro's patron was undoubtedly getting his cash, directly or indirectly, from Ivan Ivanov and his wife, Tasha, which meant that Brautigan was indirectly working for them — and a Russian tar sands company intent on destroying the canyons. His hands grew clammy, and the perspiration kicked in. He'd have to come clean with Eliza, somehow.

"We'll look more later. Now it's time to eat. And for you to tell me all about Frank Hildebrandt."

Brautigan barely touched his food. His constant hunger had been displaced by a big knot in his gut. Besides, he wasn't entirely sure what it was that Eliza had cooked.

"When I was a baby, my family moved into an old house in a quiet Durango neighborhood." The two-story house had a big yard, fruit trees, including an achy and prolific old apricot that left a cloying layer of orange mush on the yard every summer. "My parents paid Joshua and me a nickel apiece to slop them up. We could buy a lot of Fun Dip with all that cash. There was a strange line on the roof, where the shingles changed color. On one side of the line, the roof was red and tidy-looking. On the other, it was green and black and ratty looking. It clearly marked the spot where someone, while re-shingling the roof, had decided to stop. That wouldn't have been very important, except that there were also ghosts in the house."

Sometimes, at night, after the lights were turned off, the sound of knocks came from the attic or the roof, as if someone was walking around up there. A terrified young Malcolm would curl up under his blankets, trembling himself to sleep. Then he would answer the call, crawl out of bed, and slip through a knothole in the wall's wood paneling and enter another world. Inside the wall was another house, like theirs, but newer, cleaner, where a bunch of children lived. They were nice kids. Normal kids. They were cruel at times, but not in ways that left any permanent scars, and like all children they liked to laugh and create imaginary worlds in which they could spend their days or, in this case, nights.

But they were mannequins. Some had heads with vacant eyes and others had only a neck-stump. Others had arms and legs made of that strangely colored plastic material, but others — like many mannequins — were simply torsos without any appendages at all. They were latchkey mannequins, and spent a good part of the day alone. The mother, who had legs and feet, arms and hands, and a head topped with plastic yellow and wavy hair, worked at the Montgomery Wards store downtown, modeling plaid bellbottoms and frilly blouses and such. At the end of her day, which was the middle of Malcolm's night, she would come home and unpack groceries and make a snack for the children. Malcolm liked her, and the snacks were always just right, and often involved Ritz crackers and Cheez Whiz. But he couldn't stick around and savor it because the father would be home soon, too, and Malcolm didn't want to be around when that happened.

Sometimes, later, the father came out of the wall to visit Malcolm. He had no head, no legs, and no arms. He wore a gold lamé vest overlain with a velvet paisley pattern. The father never hurt the boy, just hovered silently and ominously above his bed, while Malcolm cowered under the blankets, searching insistently for his scream. Once he found it, his parents came rushing in to comfort him.

"I thought you were telling me about Frank Hildebrandt? Come on."

"I am. By the time I was around six or seven, maybe, I became convinced that the nightmares and the knocking weren't in my head, but in the house itself. That they were all just memories swirling around in the house's consciousness. That the house was a sort of time machine, a place where the past and present came together for occasional rendezvous, and I had happened to stumble upon these meetings randomly, or maybe because I was younger I was able to see them more clearly than everyone else."

"Hello! My time-place theory in action."

"One day I presented my suspicions to my parents. I intended to unearth the complete history of the house, and acquaint myself with everyone who had ever lived there. So my mother took me to the county courthouse and the local historical society to look up old records, and to the public library where I pored through decades of newspapers on microfilm. My mother was very patient, as long as she got to step outside to smoke an occasional cigarette or drink a Pepsi. And this is when I learned that Frank Hildebrandt had lived in our house. And died there."

Frank Hildebrandt was a legendary uranium tycoon who had immigrated from Germany as a young man, landing in Thompson Springs, Utah, after World War II. Like a lot of folks during that time, he got caught up in the uranium craze, and after a lot of false starts finally struck it rich with a vein south of Moab. He's often considered the father of the Utah uranium boom, and immortalized himself by building a mansion up on the slopes of the La Sal Mountains, looking out over the Lisbon Valley. But he overextended himself, and in order to keep expanding his empire, he had to broaden his mining portfolio, which required him to take on partners and East Coast investors. He and his main partner, Ian McClintock, started a company — a conglomerate, really — called Acme Uranium. Hildebrandt, though, was a loner by nature, and his constant conflicts with his financiers eventually led to Hildebrandt getting ousted from his own company. Broke and broken, he and his wife Mary Jean and daughter Ruthie moved to Durango, where Frank worked as a manager at the uranium mill that was perched on the banks of the Animas River.

The roof of the house, built in the early 1890s, was getting pretty shabby, so one summer Frank started re-shingling it. On a Saturday in late June 1964, Frank tied off a safety rope — he didn't survive years of prospecting without taking precautions — and climbed up the ladder to the roof.

It so happens that at the same time, the cherry tree in the yard was weighted down with fruit, and cherry pie was Frank's favorite, so Mary Jean decided to bake one as Frank worked. She soon discovered she was out of Crisco, and you can't bake a pie without Crisco. So she went out, started up the big Ford Fairlane, pulled out of the parking spot next to the house, and drove down to Safeway. When she came back out of the store she noticed a frayed hemp rope tied to the bumper. Thinking it was a gag, she coiled it up and put it in the trunk and drove home. It wasn't until she was half a block away from their house that she saw Frank — or rather his mangled and lifeless body — lying in the Royce's flower garden, crumpled up against the birdbath. He had anchored his safety rope to the car's bumper and Mary Jean, unwittingly, had yanked him off the roof and dragged his broken body for a block or so before it had broken loose.

Eliza's eyes widened at this. "Are you kidding me?"

"True story."

Hildebrandt had been developing a new mining project in Utah when he died, and had struck up a friendship with Frank Oppenheimer — Robert's lesser-known brother, who had also worked on the Manhattan Project and, after getting blacklisted for his political views, had been relegated to teaching high school in Pagosa Springs, about an hour east of Durango. But the newspaper articles said no more about the mining project, and Brautigan could find no other mention of it or Hildebrandt after his obituary ran. Mary Jean Hildebrandt and their daughter, Ruthie, promptly sold the house and moved far away, to Minnesota, maybe, or one of the Dakotas. Six years later, Brautigan's parents bought the house, complete with a half-shingled roof, Frank Hildebrandt's ghost, and the family of mannequins living inside the walls that visited Brautigan in his dreams.

Young Brautigan's research did little to ease the nightmares, but it did serve to inject Frank Hildebrandt into Brautigan family lore. One spring Brautigan's parents took the boys out to canyon country during a raging March blizzard, while Brautigan had a nasty case of strep throat. The family took shelter from the storm in a modest stone miner's cabin, and Brautigan's dad fixed his ailing child some Mormon tea. As they sat around the tiny fire, Malcolm's dad told a story about how the cabin was Hildebrandt's hideout, and how he had lost his arm, got a gold-plated prosthetic, and after he died some kids from Massachusetts dug up the arm and got rich and were forever haunted by Hildebrandt's ghost. "And then, the really scary one was where Frank ran an orphanage in Farmington that got swept away in the 1911 flood. The drowned orphans came back from the dead in the form of milky-eyed Waterbabies that slither from the silt of the San Juan River and snatch young children who disobey their parents."

"Woah, there. Wait a minute. Stop right there." Eliza looked furious.

"What is it?"

"*You* are the originator of the Waterbabies?"

"Not really me, actually."

"You son-of-a-bitch. Do you have any idea how many nights our daughter refused to take a bath because she was convinced these Waterbabies of yours would slither up through the drain and kidnap her?"

"Now, I don't think that ..."

"Oh, yes, I think that you did. It was on that river trip on the San Juan, when Adriana was five. I went to bed early and you stayed up and told ghost stories. Ann was there with her kids, too. She's spent thousands of dollars on therapy and anti-anxiety medication for Erich. I should kill you."

"I happen to think it's healthy to give children something real to fear, to give form to their anxieties."

"Can I just say that it's a damned good thing you never had kids."

"Yet. Haven't had kids yet, thank you. Anyway, the cabin also played a role in the stories and, eventually, in the novel I wrote when I was, like, twenty."

"I didn't know you wrote a novel. Can I read it?"

"Good luck with that. It's gone. Peter and I sacrificed it to the solstice gods, along with ..."

"With what?"

"A painting of his. Anyway, Peter's alive and well, which is a relief. And he's trying to send us some clues with this riddle, so let's figure this thing out. He says 'Hildebrandt knows'...."

"What if I don't give a shit about his little scavenger hunt?"

"Huh?"

"Don't you get it, Malcolm? He's playing games with us. We're pawns in his stupid performance. I'm worried sick, Adriana's wondering whether her dad's dead or screwing some CrossFit bitch, and he's out there riding his metaphorical Vespa around, dangling us along and laughing at us, just like you said. You're riding around on a Vespa too. I'm the stupid one whose sitting around on a park bench waiting for you two to get your shit together."

"I'm on a Vespa?"

"Sure, your corporate news job and your bachelorhood are your Vespa. It's your way of escaping from reality and accountability and anything with meaning. Where's my Vespa? Huh? When do I get to escape? I don't. I never do. It's always you guys."

"Oh, yeah, like you never ran away. You never escaped? I seem to remember differently." Anger, blended with defensiveness, gurgled in Brautigan's esophagus. "Anyway, I don't do corporate newsletters, Eliza."

"And what do you do? You're actually writing a novel and you're broke? You're a prostitute? What is it?"

"I have my own news organization."

"Really?" Her face relaxed, her voice dropping an octave and several decibels. "That's so awesome, Malcolm. Thank God. When are you going to launch it?"

"I already have," Brautigan hissed through clenched teeth. "It's called *Alt-News*."

"But ... ?"

"I'm Juan Lopez-Shapiro. And I write fake news. If you've got a problem with it, fuck off."

All expression drained from Eliza's face and her body slumped, rag-doll-like. She looked away from Malcolm, trembling. "You racist fascist dickwad. Oh my God, Malcolm. How could you even—. Wait until your mother finds out. Wait until Peter finds out. Holy shit."

"You're going to tattle on me? Come on, Eliza. Grow up. We can't all be perfect, virtuous idealists. Some of us have to pay the rent."

"Oh, boy, Malcolm. So who pays your rent? Who signs the checks?"

"Advertisers, sponsors. You know. And I get a little help from a foundation." Malcolm's righteous indignation was leaking out of him as he spoke, and he felt like vomiting, or like curling up in a ball under a rock and not coming out for a year. "Stan Hatch pays the bills. Okay? Are you happy?"

While Eliza stared into the emptiness in stunned silence, Malcolm told her the whole story, about the divorce, leaving the *Tribune*, his inability to find a real job, and how Hatch had come to him, about how he had funded the whole endeavor, about the payments, the GGF Foundation, the tips they'd given him, and the stories he'd written at their bidding. Eliza said nothing, but visibly grew more tense, her lips twitching.

"Do you realize that means you're also working for that woman? Tasha what's-her-name? And Russian tar sands oligarchs?"

"Technically I'm an independent contractor. I'm working for myself."

"Technically you're a fucking whore, facilitating their whole operation." She didn't say anything for several seconds and the silence terrified Brautigan far more than shouts or screams. "Un-fucking-believable."

"I'm sorry. I should have told you earlier. But you know what? It's just a job. They're only words. They don't really matter. It's not like anything I write changes minds, or influences their vote, or anything like that. It just makes my readers, who are already batshit crazy, happy. And besides, I do liberal stuff sometimes, too."

"And you think that makes a difference? Are you completely blind? Hatch and whoever his minders are don't care about Republican or Democrat or conservative or liberal. They don't. You are their tool. Their wrecking ball. And you know what you're wrecking? The Truth. The whole idea that there even is such a thing. That's the real objective here. Don't tell me you're too dumb to know that."

"Oh, come on. You're being melodramatic. What was I supposed to do? I was desperate, okay? And this guy came along and offered me a ton of cash. I couldn't get a real job. Do you know why Melissa left me? She left because I couldn't make enough money for her to feel secure enough to have kids. Now I do."

"Am I supposed to be impressed? I'm sure there were other reasons she left you, but that's neither here nor there. Women are not all interchangeable, you know?"

"I know that. Anyway, I'm done with it now. I've already decided to cut myself off from Hatch's payments. He doesn't own the website, I do. And I get about half my revenues from ads and donations, so it will be fine. I can even put up a paywall, maybe do a Patreon."

"Oh, I see. How ethical of you. Maybe you can get RosaBit to advertise. How about that?" Eliza wore a thin, menacing smile as she looked out toward the horizon and shook her head. "I've got to go back to Durango tomorrow. I need to see Adriana, run some errands, restock our food and ice, that sort of thing. Believe it or not, I actually have responsibilities other than chasing my missing husband and his juvenile friend around the desert."

"Great. Okay. I could use a shower and stuff anyway."

"Oh no, you're not coming with me. You will stay out here and keep looking for your buddy Peter. Maybe you can come up with a real plan, one that doesn't involve aimlessly hiking up and down canyons. Or is that part of the job description?"

"Job?"

"Do I have to spell it out for you? You were clearly sent here to mislead me or, worse, to guide your friends Hatch and Tasha to Peter so that they can stop whatever it is he has planned."

"You don't think I …?"

"I don't know what to think anymore. I don't know who you are or what you're doing here. And I sure as hell don't believe your porn-flic fantasy about Ivanka Natalyatta or whatever the fuck her name is. I don't know if this whole thing is just some plan that you and Peter came up with, or if you kidnapped Peter because he was about to expose your Russian friends' tar sands operation, or what. I feel like I'm in a low-budget postmodern suspense thriller."

"*You* called *me*." Malcolm got to his feet, one fist clenched into a little ball, the other clutching his half-empty wineglass, his voice rising in volume and sharpness. "I had a pretty good thing going in Tucson, and then you called, and I dropped it all, and jeopardized everything I've built. For what? To come up here and help you. Why? Because I care about you. I care about Peter. I'm here to help. And what do I get? Abuse. Nothing but abuse and your constant judging and criticism. And now you're gonna go off and abandon me?"

Eliza stood up, looking away from Malcolm, a tremor in her voice: "You have no idea, Malcolm, no idea. I'm going to bed. Goodnight."

Green spots of rage appeared in Malcolm's vision. He took a last swig from his wineglass, a hefty amount of the liquid dribbling down his chin, joining his salty tears, and then hurled the goblet with all of his strength at the back of Eliza's head. Time slowed and he cringed in horror as he realized that for the first time in his life his aim was spot on. The glass hurtled through space and crashed into the back of Eliza's skull. Neither head nor glass shattered, however, in part because the glass wasn't actually glass. It fell to the ground, bouncing flaccidly with a plastic clatter before rolling to a stop on the pale sandstone. Eliza didn't even look back.

Brautigan picked up the plastic wineglass, threw it as hard as he could at the ground. It still didn't break. Defeated, he reached down and picked it up and refilled it and sat down on the warm sandstone and gazed out across the darkening land. A billow of clouds sat above the La Plata Mountains in the distance, as if it had sprouted from the diorite peaks. The clouds vaguely resembled an angel, standing all alone in a sky of blue, an angel promising relief in the form of rain, an early summer storm cycle that might soothe the thirsty earth, give a little water back to the rivers, dampen the sand at the bottom of the canyons. How odd, though, that the clouds were only *there*, in that one little spot on the horizon, and that the rest of the sky was empty. The clouds' color was off, too, a charcoal gray rather than puffy white, and they seemed to be growing, reaching higher and higher into the otherwise glassy dusk-sky.

"Oh no," he whispered. He fetched his phone and walked up to a high point for a signal. The *Durango Herald* website confirmed what he already suspected: A fire had broken out in the forests north of Durango, and was tearing through the trees at a horrifying speed, sending up a mushroom of smoke and ash, an angel of terror. The pyrocumulonimbus plume piled higher and higher until darkness fell and the stars emerged and flickering orange lined the horizon. It looked like the end of the world. It was terrifying, and it was beautiful.

PART TWO

Oblividrine Blues

Even before Brautigan had groggily made his way out of the tent, Eliza was pulling up the stakes. She had been awake for at least an hour, had cooked breakfast, cleaned, and packed. The coffee was now cold, the oatmeal congealed into a slithery mass. Brautigan ate it anyway.

"Come on," Eliza said. "Let's go. I want to get back to Durango a-sap. I just need to make sure everything's okay, what with the fire and all."

Still bleary-eyed, hungover, his hair a tangled mess, Brautigan slumped into the passenger seat of the Subaru. Eliza drove silently and a little too fast down the two-track, then the dirt road, and then out onto the highway.

"Where should I drop you off? Blanding? Bluff?"

"I don't care. Wherever."

"There's a nice library in Monticello. How about there? That hotel on the north side of town's not bad."

"You're not coming back?"

"Not today. Maybe in a day or two depending on how things go."

"What things?"

"The stuff I have to do."

"Yeah, okay, fine, the library's fine."

Eliza left Monticello and Malcolm behind, minding the speed limit until the state line, then she gunned it up to eighty-five, which felt like the natural velocity for traveling through the rolling bean and sunflower fields, past the long-abandoned drive-in theater and the house littered with automobiles and storage containers. JESUS SAVES was written on the side of a barn, along with a mingling of Biblical passages and NRA rhetoric, because Jesus, as everyone knows, was a gun nut.

She pulled over outside the rundown town of Dove Creek, across from the burg's most distinctive feature: a phallus-shaped bean elevator. Once the "Pinto Bean Capital of the World," Dove Creek's glory had faded as farmers replaced pintos with sunflowers, hoping to cash in on a biodiesel craze that had flourished briefly before busting dramatically. Eliza never understood why someone didn't try to turn pinto beans into fuel, instead.

On her phone, she pulled up the number for Vin. He preferred Vincent, but Eliza thought the name unsuitable to the person, a twenty-something part-time employee at the library, semi-pro kayaker and mountain biker, and aspiring poet. Vin, with his square jaw and easy smile could have been an LL Bean model. And his crush on Eliza was readily apparent, not only to her but to just about everyone who worked at or regularly patronized the library, including her friend Ann. Eliza had brushed it off as just another young man with an older woman fetish, a lost boy looking for his mother. She didn't return his affection, though she found it endearing, and she allowed herself to bask in his flirtation and indulge his gift for gab, something that Peter once had, but had lost in recent years, along with his libido.

Vin was just what Santos needed at that moment.

"Hey, Vin. It's Eliza."

"Hey, I was just wondering if you're up. Or, I mean, if you're around. I thought maybe I could swing by and you know, uh, chill?"

"Yeah? Awesome. Okay, cool. I'll be there in like an hour or so?"

"Hey," said Vin, as he threw open the door of the tiny, backyard guesthouse rental. He grinned in a welcoming way, teeth white and just crooked enough to be charming, his eyes pale blue, a fetching contrast to his nearly black, curly, unkempt hair. Vin was shirtless, but without an iota of self-consciousness, wearing only a pair of running shorts that left very little to the imagination. His skin was smooth, a line of black fuzz leading downward from his belly button. "I'm glad you're here. I've got a couple new poems I want to show you." But she wasn't here for his shitty poetry. She was here because Eliza was the one who balanced the checkbook, who worried about Adriana's grades, who anchored Peter's artistic temperament, who would never veer off of the road of responsibility, who would never wander into the fucking desert without telling anyone just because of art or midlife crisis or whatever the hell Peter was after, who would never assume a new identity in order to evade accountability, who would never disengage, who would never take off on a Vespa at the speed of light.

Today, and today only, Vin would be her Vespa.

"Maybe later," Eliza said. She reached out and touched his small, wine-colored nipple, and gently tugged at it, rubbing as she did so. His eyes went glassy and a little vacant as she ran the fingernails of her other hand down his chest, through the little valley of his abs, circling his belly button. She watched his shorts come to life, his erection straining to be free of the light, clingy material. She liberated it, pulling the elastic waistband out, pushing it down around his ass. As his sex sprung free she had to stifle a laugh because all she could think about was a porpoise leaping from the sea, and in that moment she understood the look in men's eyes when she lifted her shirt over her head, unclipped her bra, slipped her underwear down over her thighs. That look of unbridled hunger.

She wrapped her fingers around his sex, relishing in the heat it exuded, in the contradiction of its hardness and its pliability, in its weight. She imagined that she could feel it throbbing. Maybe she could.

She simply held onto him like that until finally Vin seemed to snap out of a trance and reached down and clumsily pulled off Eliza's shirt. He reached for her breasts but she gently pushed his hands away.

That's not what she came here for.

He tried to kiss her, but she turned her head.

That's not what she came here for.

She pulled the condom from her pocket, the condom she had picked up at the convenience store in Mancos on her way here — she wasn't totally irresponsible, after all — and tore the packet open and pulled it out and handed it to him. She pulled her shorts and underwear off and guided him to the futon in the corner of the room, thinking he could have at least made the damned bed for her, but then forgetting when she looked into his eyes and saw the submissiveness and eagerness to follow her lead. So she led. She pushed him back onto the bed. He looked at her. "I find stretch marks so sexy," he said, as if he'd rehearsed it in the mirror many times.

"Please just shut the hell up." She crawled onto the bed, lowered herself onto him, taking him inside of her.

She watched his face as she rode him, grinding her pubis into his, trying to match his erratic rhythm. She watched as his visage transformed from admiration to the emptiness of desire to the clenched teeth of climax. She watched his eyes roll back in his head, watched his fingers dig into her back, and finally, at long last, she was no longer watching anything but the splashes of color inside her own mind as she had her own little moment of disengagement, of unreasonable detachment, as she escaped into her own pleasure, which rolled up her belly in sharp waves. And for a very brief moment, Eliza Santos went missing, too.

Afterwards, she didn't even bother laying down, and certainly didn't cuddle. She just hopped up and out of bed and hurriedly put on her clothes. Vin looked on with something like disbelief.

"So, I gotta go, Vincent. Maybe we can do the poetry thing later," she said, as she hurried out the door.

As Brautigan was walking into Sheriff Etcitty's office in downtown Monticello, a young woman — younger than Brautigan, that is — was walking out. She had on dark-framed glasses, those sixties-style things that have made a comeback as of late, a tank-top, shorts, beaded earrings, silver bracelets. She smiled at Brautigan, and Brautigan couldn't help but smile back.

"Who was that?" He asked, as Etcitty motioned him to sit down next to Hank Love, who lounged in a plush office chair next to Etcitty's expansive desk.

"That's Lisa Yazzie. She's been fighting against drilling down there by Chaco and somehow caught wind of the tar sands stuff over in White Canyon and now she thinks she's going to stop that. Told me I should go arrest them since they're violating the Fundamental Law of the Diné."

"And ...?"

"She was joking, kind of. But she is convinced they're skirting federal environmental laws, and the BLM folks won't give her the time of day, so she figured she'd see if I could do anything. I can't. She'll figure something out, though. She's smart as a whip and ambitious. She's already a software engineer and is getting her PhD in settler colonialism and environmental justice."

"That's quite the combo."

"So, are you here to tell Hank where to start looking for your friend?"

"We haven't quite figured that out yet. He could be just about anywhere, I guess. We wouldn't want to waste your time or anything."

"I *do* appreciate that," Hank said in a way that might have been facetious, as she leaned back and made a triangle shape with her hands. "Not everyone is so considerate. Especially the dead ones."

"Well, then, what *can* I do for you today, Mr. Brautigan?" Etcitty said, giving a bit of a stink eye to Love.

"Actually, it's kind of about the tar sands folks. I was just wondering whether you had ever heard of the GGF Foundation."

"Sure, I know them. That think tank out of Salt Lake. They made a bunch of slick videos during the Bears Ears debate. Said that a national monument would somehow keep local kids from realizing their dreams to become astronauts or teachers."

Love guffawed, her laugh echoing through the hallways.

"Ha. See, even Hank gets a kick out of that one and she's LDS *and* anti-monument."

"Oh, come on, Kenneth. I'm not anti-monument. I just worry that drawing a line around a place and slapping a name on it will rob it of something. Commodify it so that the marketing people can brand it and bring the masses in, and meanwhile the folks in Washington are cutting all the funding, so there's no one to keep an eye on things."

"And tar sands are better?"

"Let's not do this now, darling. You know that my feelings are evolving."

"Sutherland butted into the elections, too. Put together a bunch of ads for my competitor. Tried to get me kicked off the ballot. They said I didn't live in the state, that my real residence was down in Kayenta. It didn't work but it wasn't so much fun either."

"Sorry about that," Brautigan said, sheepishly. "I heard that maybe GGF and Sutherland Farms might be connected. And maybe even tangled up with those tar sands folks."

Etcitty raised an eyebrow. He stood up and closed the office door, then sat down again. "How so?"

"I'm not really sure. Peter, my friend who is missing out there, was working on some project and did a big Freedom of Information Act request with the BLM, maybe the Department of Energy. I looked at some of the files and it appears that Stan Hatch, the GGF guy, is also the Sutherland guy, and is buddies with Tasha — that tar sands woman out there at Fry Canyon."

"And ...?"

"I don't know. It's interesting, I guess?"

Etcitty sat silently for at least a minute or two, looking at Brautigan, then at Hank Love, who continued to grin mischievously. Finally, he sighed deeply, and spoke. "Are you here as a news reporter? Or as a concerned citizen?"

"Oh, no, I'm not even a real journalist anymore. I'm just looking for my friend."

Another silence, another sigh. "Look," said Etcitty, "I don't see what difference any of it makes, but the county did give tax breaks to that resort that Sutherland is building. And they did the same for the tar sands people. It's a little bit crazy. The county commissioners want them to come to the county so they can get more tax money, so in order to lure them here they exempt them from taxes."

"Then what does the county get out of it if not taxes?"

"My point, exactly. A few jobs here and there, maybe a fat contribution to their campaigns or special interest groups. Rumor has it Bill Stevens has a stake in the resort. Maybe they just like the idea of harvesting God's bounty. These folks are mostly holy rollers, LDS — no offense, Hank. Around here that usually means they're Republicans and bowing down to the oil companies and uranium outfits."

"With some notable exceptions, thank you very much," Love said, the lines on her face bunching up in an even bigger smile. "I do sometimes wonder what Brigham Young would think of all his disciples tearing up his promised land with their drill rigs and draglines."

"Ah, hell, I bet they never go after the tar sands, anyway," Etcitty said. "They'll just drive those thumper trucks around and around, fleece their investors, and call it good. They're probably getting some kind of federal funding for those experiments they're doing, and funneling half of it off to their Swiss bank accounts. "

"Experiments?"

"The way I figure it, tar sands ain't worth it, even with oil above a hundred. They're just cashing in on some sort of r-and-d subsidy for experimental fuels or whatnot. Anyway, it's none of my business until another piece of equipment falls off the edge. I got other things to do, like not looking for your friend. You mind telling me why you don't want to find the guy?"

This time it was Brautigan's turn to be silent.

"Okay, then, I'll guess. *He* doesn't want to be found, for one reason or another. Maybe he's running away from that lady you were with? Or from the tax man? Or what?"

"Could be." Brautigan had promised Eliza not to say anything that might lead Etcitty and Love to Peter. It was a promise he really didn't want to break. "I don't think he's really running from anything. He's an artist. He's not a criminal or whatever. He's just looking for … something."

"I'm not sure what that means," Hank said. "But since my guys have their hands full looking for that old guy who wandered off from Muley Point a few days ago, that's fine by me. Like I said, not everyone is as considerate of my time as you and your friends."

"Feds are breathing down my neck to find him, yesterday," said Etcitty. "Turns out he was some major dude down at Los Alamos labs."

"Shouldn't be too hard to find him with this heat. Just follow the smell, and the vultures. Hey, do you happen to know if Frank Hildebrandt had any mining claims out in the White Canyon area?"

"Hildebrandt? *The* Frank Hildebrandt? I doubt it. I think all his holdings were up toward Moab, in the Lisbon Valley. Hank?"

"I heard he was poking around over there, but I don't think he made any claims. Chester Tsosie might know. He worked with Hildebrandt back in the day. Elizabeth Turin sells his jewelry at her trading post in Bluff. She might be able to track him down for you."

"You could also ask Judy in the assessor's office. She knows the ownership history behind every private parcel in the county, not to mention every juicy detail about every marriage in southeastern Utah." Etcitty pointed the way to the assessor with his lips. "And if she says anything about me, it's a lie. Now get out of here. I've got to file a report about the last report I filed."

Eliza stepped into the front door of her own home. It felt foreign. Maybe because for the first time since she moved there she needed the keys to get in. Maybe it had something to do with marriage, and symbolism, and everything that had happened over the last week — and the last hour. Maybe it was because there were still two goons in a black SUV a few houses down.

She was supposed to meet Adriana here to check in, see how things were going, but Eliza was a little early, and Adriana surely would be a little late. Eliza opened up Peter's office door, looked around. It was tidy, just as she'd left it. The painting on the office wall caught her eye.

The painting had a curious meaning for Peter. Eliza had never seen it until they moved back to Durango, and within days Peter had dug it out of storage and hung it in the office. Peter had told her no fewer than three different stories about what inspired the painting and what it meant. The explanations were insipid enough to make Eliza understand why Peter hated to talk about his art. Once, when Peter's mother came to visit, he took the painting down and turned it against the wall behind his desk, as if he were ashamed of it. He never told Eliza why.

She studied the figure, the woman made of stone, and the eerie eyeball that dismembered her with its gaze.

"Hey, mom."

Eliza jumped back. "Oh! Adriana."

"Are you okay?"

"Yes. You just startled me."

"Sorry."

"It's okay. You're early."

"I'm right on time."

"On time is early for you."

"Real funny. I guess you didn't find him yet?"

"Not yet, but we're pretty sure he's okay. He's just doing his art. He'll be back."

"I'm really sorry, by the way, for saying those things about his midlife crisis and all. It was just my lame attempt to lighten things up."

"It's okay. I know this must be hard for you."

"It's just that dad's, like, been acting kind of funny lately. Did you know he took me to Farmington and bought me an old typewriter? He said I could write my first novel on it. As if."

"He took you to Farmington? I didn't know that."

"Yeah, we went and checked out junk shops. And then a few weeks ago, he started coming into my room at night and singing me to sleep just like he did when I was little."

"Singing?"

"Singing. Dad. The night before he left he did it and then just sat there crying."

"What did he sing? On that last night?"

"That Simon and Garfunkel tune. The one that starts out 'Many a time I've been mistaken, many times confused,' and goes on about dying and flying and stuff. It's the same chord progression as St. Matthew's Passion, by the way."

"I'm sorry. Your father ..."

"No, no, it's okay. It was sweet. And sad."

"Hey, come over here and look at this painting."

"What about it?"

"What do you think about it? What's that yellow line? Has that always been there?"

Adriana got close to the painting, so close that her nose touched the glass and left an oily mark, and scrunched up her face. The line — perfectly straight and sharp — came up from the bottom of the canvas, through the stone, and into the torso of the woman, at which point it branched out into capillary-like threads that faded into dark red. It was the only straight line in a painting full of curves. "I dunno. I've never looked that closely. It's a weird painting, a bit eldritch, in fact."

"What's eldritch?"

"Oh, come on, mom, Google it. I think the yellow thing is a needle. And it's injecting poison into the woman. Yellow poison. Do you think it's supposed to be heroin? Is dad a junkie? Is that why he ran away?"

"Not quite."

"It could be a *Breaking Bad* thing, you know? He's probably building a giant meth lab out in the desert. Which would be sorta cool. We'd be rich, at least. Right?"

"The only person who's breaking bad is your so-called uncle, Malcolm."

"He's dealing drugs? What kind?"

"In a way, yes," she said, absentmindedly, as she took the painting off the wall, unclipped the clasps on the back of the frame, removed the artwork, rolled it up, and placed it gently on Peter's desk. "He's selling lies."

"Nope, Frank Hildebrandt never patented any mining claims over in the White Canyon district," Judy, the county assessor, said matter-of-factly, after punching some things into the keyboard on her computer.

"How about the Happy Bonanza? Is there any claim anywhere with that name or anything like it?"

"Doesn't look like it. There's a Happy Jack. No Bonanza, though."

"Huh? Thanks, anyway." He turned and started for the door.

"But Hildebrandt's company, Acme Uranium, did have one claim out there. But it's not happy or a bonanza, as far as I can tell."

Brautigan stopped, turned. Funny name, Acme. Like the company that made all the contraptions Wile E. Coyote used in his chronic pursuit of the Roadrunner. He smiled. She was still looking at him with a dry expression.

"The Acme Queen claim. Filed by Hildebrandt's partner Ian McClintock in 1959, patented in 1964, went to tax sale in 1984. Let's see …" More keyboard punching. "Hmmm, okay, it was picked up by Cal Black at tax sale, and then he sold to EnergyUnited in the mid-nineties and finally, in January 2018 the title was transferred to Natasha Ivanova, who gets her tax bill at PO box 32 in Williston, North Dakota."

"Natasha?" said Brautigan, a lump growing in his throat.

"Yep. Sounds Russian. Sandy Shumway's kid ran off with a Russian woman when he was on mission over in Lithuania. He still hasn't come back." She still had the exact same non-expression on her face, coupled with the dry, monotone delivery. "I can't blame him. I saw her picture on Facebook. She's quite the looker. Legs up to here. Those Eastern European women are supposed to be firecrackers in bed, too."

"Where is the Acme Queen located?"

Judy — he never did catch her last name — turned the computer around so that it was facing Brautigan. There was a map on the screen, aerial photo view, with a tiny rectangle on it near the head of an unnamed tributary of Leetso, or Bonanza Canyon. "Give me your email address," she said, "and I'll send the map to you. Oh, now, wait a minute. Here's another claim in the White Canyon

District made by Ruthie Steen. She would have been pretty darned young back then."

"I don't understand. Who's Ruthie Steen?"

"Well she's Frank Hildebrandt's daughter, of course, from wife number two, Mary Jean. Steen was Mary Jean's maiden name. My mother went to high school with Mary Jean down in Blanding. I guess she always wanted to be a fashion designer. Mary Jean, I mean, not my mother. Had a bunch of those big dolls — mannequins? — for the dresses she designed. Wanted to go to Paris and make clothes but Frank — he was still loaded then — came in and swooped her off her feet when she was just seventeen. So much for her dreams."

"But why Steen?"

"Frank probably put 'Steen' on the claim so no one would know it was him. He had creditors after him, the tax man, you name it. It's called the HB235. Odd name, but you never know, do you?"

"I guess not. Where is it?"

"There's no location here in my confuser. That's what I call computers, by the way. Let's check the book." Judy walked to a giant shelf in the back of the room and pulled out what looked like a giant's story book from *Alice in Wonderland* and brought it back over to the counter. As she opened the tome, an aroma of must filled the air. Judy was far more adroit in moving through the big pages than she was on the keyboard. "Here it is, the HB235 claim. Ten acres. Staked in 1961. Patented in 1965. But look …"

The basic information was there, written in the same old-school handwriting that always seems to be on documents like this, but the place where the location — township, range, section — was supposed to be was empty, except for the words "Code 4455."

"Oh, well, darnit," said Judy.

"What's that mean?"

"It means the location was never entered due to national security reasons. It would have been kept on file over at the Atomic Energy Commission. It's not uncommon for these Cold War-era uranium claims, but usually someone comes in and enters it later on. A claim's not much good if you don't know where it is, now, is it?"

"If it was national security shouldn't the government own it?"

"Oh, no. The whole uranium boom was one big public-private scam. The feds subsidized everything, guaranteed a price for uranium, built roads all over the place, paid ten-grand bonuses to prospectors, and cleaned up the mess afterwards. They didn't pay for my mom's cancer treatment, though, or my sister's, God rest her soul."

"I don't understand."

"As you drive out of town slow down and check out that area near the golf course. Used to be a uranium mill. We kids swam in the raffinate pond, and everyone put the tailings in their gardens. Loosened up the clay soil around here. My sister had to take out a second mortgage and do one of them go-fund things to pay for her treatment. Didn't have any insurance."

"The teeth." Brautigan hadn't meant to say it out loud, but Judy's look of confusion told him he had. "Oh, I'm sorry. It's just … I grew up in Durango. We had a mill, too, right beside the river. We played there. We ate the fish. And it's just … I'm really sorry about your sister." He staggered out of the office, forgetting to ask about where the county sent the tax bill for the HB235.

Brautigan texted Eliza frantically, then called her, then texted again, then called: "Pick up, damnit. Eliza. Call me back, please. It's important." She did not respond.

He tried again, this time with another text: "How are you, Eliza? I just wanted to say again how sorry I am, and that I'm going to change. I'm going to get help for my condition. Please don't out me. And please come back to help search for Peter. I found some important info." Brautigan wasn't entirely sure what condition he was going to get help with. Was it his drinking? His tendency to throw plastic wine glasses at Eliza? His low emotional IQ? His fake news habit?

Eliza did not respond.

Eliza Santos floated through the darkness. That's what it felt like, anyway, as she pedaled the cruiser along the bike path, sans headlight, beside the dwindling waters of the Animas River, her daughter close behind. They'd eaten a nice, lingering meal with Ann at the conglomeration of food trucks down on Main, and were grateful for the northerly winds that kept the wildfire smoke away from town.

They'd sipped wine, chatted with acquaintances as they passed by their table, ate good food, relished in the way the warm evening light set their faces aglow, and gossiped about old friends. Randy had taken a tenure-track position in Boulder, and he and Leeann would be moving up there by the end of the summer. Scott was in Denver dealing with his sick mom. Cam and Jolene were 'decoupling' because their life-visions simply didn't meld anymore.

"Are you fucking kidding me?" Eliza had blurted, far too loudly, after snorting wine out of her nose, not just because of the New Age euphemism for divorce, but because of the idea that incongruence of life-vision was cause for the end of a twelve-year-old marriage with two kids, a house, and various other entanglements. "Here, hold my beer. I'll give you a fucking reason for *decoupling*."

"My life vision is just to get through the day without killing anyone in my household," Ann said. "As long as Scott feels the same about me, I think we'll stay coupled. What about you, Adriana? What's your life vision?"

"I'm just looking forward to season two of *Russian Doll*," she said in a perfectly timed deadpan.

Having Ann along did not interfere with the mother-daughter get together. Quite to the contrary. Like her father, Adriana — as brash and loud and opinionated as she could be — became awkward and taciturn in one-on-one dialogue with any sort of emotional weight. With Ann, however, she opened up and matured: She was no longer Eliza's teenaged daughter, but a thoughtful, feeling, adult friend. It was with small groups of friends that Eliza learned the most about her daughter's inclinations, her love life, her artistic ambitions.

And having Adriana along allowed Eliza to skirt telling Ann about her rendezvous with Vin, or about how fucked up Malcolm was these days.

"So, how's things with Malcolm?" Ann said, "How's the search going?"

"Malcolm's got some issues. And he's gonna need a new job soon."

"Yeah?"

"Yeah. So, with that in mind, business idea: Malcolm makes his famous cookies, and you and I sell them to clubbers in Berlin. We call them, 'Better than Keks.'"

"Better than *what*? I don't get it."

"'Keks' means 'cookies' in German. And it rhymes with …"

"Oh, clever. So Malcolm would be in a bakery all day and we'd be clubbing all night dropping ecstasy. Excellent."

"It's called *Molly* you old farts," said Adriana, smiling. "And what about me?"

"You're the one who will get us into the clubs."

Now, with a couple of glasses of wine in her, Eliza was riding home in a state of bliss, the day's post-coital tingle still clinging to her skin. She was able to forget about her missing husband, forget about the ex-lover and fascist-propagandist that she had invited back into her life, and forget about the financial struggles that nagged at her with every waking moment. If she concentrated on the feeling of riding a bike in the dark, of speeding into the emptiness, she could even rid herself of the niggling concern over the first line of the poem that Peter had sent to Malcolm. She had found her Vespa, after all, and it wasn't Vin, it was a squeaky old cruiser bike that Malcolm and Peter had rescued years ago from some old dude's junk shop down near Farmington,

Eliza had plenty of gripes about living in Durango. It was filling up with trust-funders and wealthy retirees and equity refugees. The art and culture scene was lousy. Tourists and traffic clogged the streets and sidewalks year-round. Teachers were underpaid. Rent was too damned high. And yet, in that moment, with the cool breeze blowing through her hair, the odor of freshly cut grass wafting in the air, the streetlight-reflections sparkling off the river, she could forget all of that, and relish just being in this Place, with her job, her talented and intelligent daughter, and even her husband, who may have been driving them into bankruptcy and perhaps insanity, but at least he wasn't a corporate executive or, for that matter, some fake news hack. She had no life-vision, but if she did, it might look something like this. If she had a notion of being at home in the world, it might feel like this.

"Hey, Adriana, let's go to the park."

"But mom, it's after ten!"

"So what? You gotta hot date or something?"

Ten minutes later, the two were gleeful pendulums on the swings in the little park down by the bridge over the river, and exactly five minutes after that, just as Eliza had anticipated, the automated sprinklers kicked in with a hiss and a pffft, soaking the two instantly. Maybe it was the cold water, or maybe it was the fact that she was reveling in one of Peter and Malcolm's favorite adolescent summertime activities, but something triggered an epiphany in her. And then she knew that she had to find Peter. And she also sensed that he wouldn't be coming back. She let the swing slow to a stop, and sat silently, the spray of water mingling with her salty tears.

Brautigan had planned to hike up onto the lower slopes of the Abajos and camp, but the blistering heat and smoky air dissuaded him. He resigned himself instead to staying in one of the hotels on the north end of town.

Once in the room, Brautigan opened the window in hopes of dissipating the aroma — a combo of cigarette smoke and chemical air freshener — and cranked the AC up to full blast, the climate be damned. After a long hot shower he sat down at the desk and searched around the internet for mentions of the Happy Bonanza, Ruthie Steen Hildebrandt, Frank Hildebrandt, Acme Uranium, and the like. The only thing of interest was a Latvian porn site, where oil-glazed, hairless bodies slapped together repetitively until the paywall popped up and he was kicked out.

He put on some clothes and walked across the street to the Burger Hut and got a burger and fries and a milkshake, his back fat and enlarged heart be damned, and headed back to his room, sat down, and stared at the laptop's screen. He was jonesing, for alcohol, for a cyber-fix. Finally, he put in the url for *Alt-News* and checked the stats.

As he expected, and to his relief, the piece about the county commissioners had not received many clicks for the first couple of days it was out there. It was far too local to get a lot of traction outside of the general vicinity, and too complicated. But something had set it afire that day, and the page views were skyrocketing. Not good, he thought. The last thing he needed was for that particular post to go viral while he was right in the middle of it all. He had been careful to conceal his real identity from his *Alt-News* audience and even Stan Hatch. But surely some hacker could track him down through cyberspace and make the necessary connections. He needed to post something new in order to distract readers from the older post. He started searching for fodder.

The fire north of Durango had started near the railroad tracks the previous day, blowing up to more than sixteen-thousand acres by nightfall, sweeping through one of the last trailer parks in La Plata County and reducing it to ash, leaving many of its former residents to camp out in their cars in the Walmart parking lot for an indefinite period of time. "Miraculously," the *Durango Herald* story read, "several multi-million dollar homes on the tinder-dry face of Hermosa Mountain had been saved."

The "miracle" had come in the form of the United Corporations of America Wildland Urban Interface Firefighting Force, colloquially known as Woofer, which was created by State Farm, Allstate, IntellInsure, Prudential, AIG, and several other large homeowner insurance companies in reaction to the Four Mile Fire in Boulder and other similar conflagrations that had torn through upscale residential areas. The insurance companies realized that climate change was rendering a good portion of the West's most valuable real estate uninsurable. Clearly these corporations couldn't stop selling insurance. So instead they came together and created their own firefighting force, complete with a Reno-based national command center, a private, enhanced version of the National Interagency Fire Center in Boise.

Brautigan had visited Woofer's headquarters for a story when he was with the *Tribune*. It was like NORAD: whole walls covered with video monitors, their screens splashed with data and maps showing every fire start in the nation. Herds of analysts — scientists, financial experts, and traders — tracked each fire, crunching data on weather, soil moisture indices, vegetation, humidity, and, most importantly, the value of the insured real estate that was in the flames' paths. It was a real-time, cost-benefit risk analysis, and when the cost of not fighting the fire reached a trigger point, teams of elite firefighters were dispatched from the nearest regional satellite office via plane, chopper, and vehicle. Quite often the Woofer crews were on scene hours before the wildland hotshot teams arrived, building fire lines around upscale subdivisions while their private aircraft dropped red clouds of retardant. Woofer's existence explains how, a few years back, devastating California fires burned the relatively low-income community of Paradise to the ground, while billionaire celebrities' Malibu mansions were saved from a similarly destructive wall of fire. Saving Paradise simply didn't pencil out.

Brautigan found the dynamic fascinating: Even fire had become another one of Wall Street's financial instruments. But the story probably wouldn't fly on *Alt-News*. An easier sell would be an article citing studies — funded, of course, by the National Timber Association — attributing the increasing frequency and intensity of wildfires not to global warming, but to heavy-handed environmental regulations. Or maybe he'd just write a piece revealing that the fire was started by Antifa eco-anarchists, the same ones who snuck into the country via the hole in the border wall.

He opened a blank page and started to type: "Even as the flames tear through timber north of Durango, Colorado, threatening lives and homes, the greens are politicizing the suffering ..." He stopped. Deleted it. Tried again. Stopped. He just couldn't do it. The words wouldn't come. He resumed his scrolling.

Drought had so diminished the West's reservoirs that hydropower generation had taken a dive, forcing utilities to burn more natural gas and coal to keep the air conditioners running, in order to keep buildings habitable during the chronic, region-wide chronic heat wave. That would do. He listlessly wrote up a quick piece pointing out how lucky it was that the "radical greenies" hadn't been able to shut down all the fossil fuel plants because it was clear that the plants were needed during times of extreme weather, like this one. He didn't bother pointing out the inherent irony.

His work day done, Brautigan turned on the television just as the evening news from a Fox station out of Salt Lake City began. Brautigan hadn't watched television for years, and he was immediately transfixed and disoriented by it all. He couldn't keep up with the quick cuts from one scene to another. He didn't understand what the advertisements were trying to sell. And attempting simultaneously to comprehend both the chyron streaming at the bottom of the page, and the words coming from the talking heads' mouths, made him feel so dizzy that he had to lie down on the bed. Worst of all, it was that fat-necked white guy spewing his peculiar melange of hate, anger, entitlement, and victimhood. Watching the spectacle made him feel dirtier than he did while gazing at the Happy Bonanza porn site, but he also couldn't look away.

Thankfully, Tucker took a break for a commercial, and the First Man's Doppelgänger appeared, telling the camera that he's "always ready for Mrs. President with Potenza," as a zesty jingle jangled in the background. In the next ad a late-middle aged white man told viewers to ask their doctors about something called Oblividrine, "For times like these." Brautigan jotted the name down in his notebook.

Tucker came back on: "We go to a remote corner of Utah, where good folks have been building an American heritage for over a century. Now it is in peril, as the elitist environmentalist sect, Antifa-Green, invade and try to destroy the local culture and the traditional industries that have turned a desert wasteland into something useful." On a monitor behind Carlson was a screen-shot of a tweet from the president, the former one, the dead one. This time, the tweet hit close to Brautigan's home. It was a link to Juan Lopez-Shapiro's story about the county commissioners and the Interior Secretary. Brautigan had hit the *Alt-News* jackpot — a tweet from @DeadRonaldDrumpf, himself — and it made his stomach churn. "Luckily," Carlson continued, "we have real journalists like Lopez-Shapiro digging up the dirt on these hateful eco-terrorists." He went on and on like that, citing "the authoritative reporting of *Alt-News* that uncovered a major scandal and triggered an investigation by the Utah attorney general."

"Fuck, fuck, fuck, fuck," Brautigan muttered. He yelled at the giant screen: "It was a goddamned joke! You weren't supposed to *believe* it!" But Carlson just kept blabbing on, the meaning of his words evaporating before they reached Brautigan. Was the state really investigating? Or had that been fake news, as well? And how the hell was anyone supposed to know the difference, anyway?

He sat on the bed, unmoving. He stared at the little refrigerator in the corner, willing it to contain a bottle of booze, and knowing that, of course, it did not. He rifled through his first aid kit in search of a substitute: some cough syrup, a Percocet, anything to soothe the clacking in his head, and the self-loathing in his gut. Maybe if he went to the emergency room they'd prescribe Oblividrine or, better yet, a bottle of gin.

Brautigan picked up the remote and flipped through the channels to make sure that this wasn't some kind of closed circuit feed, piped into his television by Peter Simons — yet another piece of his all-encompassing performance art. But it was real — or at least as real as anything else on the screen. Brautigan grew dizzy, and sat back down on the bed to keep from collapsing onto the floor. And then he sobbed, uncontrollably, deep into the night.

Yellow Devil

Brautigan **woke up in the hotel room feeling oddly refreshed,** a sensation that instantly was wrecked by the message from Eliza on his phone: "not coming back today."

No "sorry," no "I miss you," no heart-face emoji. Just four words that left Malcolm Brautigan in Monticello with nothing to do and nowhere to go. He had little desire to keep following Peter's performance-art breadcrumbs without Eliza. He wanted nothing to do with *Alt-News*, Juan Lopez-Shapiro, or Stan Hatch, which meant he had to escape from the internet altogether. He didn't even check his Twitter feed, even though he knew it would be on fire.

So, with no real alternative, he chose to walk. He filled his pack with water and energy bars, slapped sunscreen on his face, shouldered the pack, and hiked south on Monticello's main drag, not bothering to stick out his thumb. The last thing he needed was a ride and the stilted conversation that would entail. When he got to the old uranium mill site he veered to the east, down the nature trail, and then beyond it, following a little draw. He made it through a couple of patches of private land without being seen, bushwhacked through a shallow canyon, then met up with Montezuma Creek, a deep, broad canyon that cuts through the Great Sage Plain.

This part of the canyon doesn't show up on the internet or in the guidebooks. And that's why Brautigan liked it. The landscape here asks very little of you. There's no need to climb a sphincter-clenching cliff or swim through icy waters or race to get to your favorite campsite before the masses. You just walk, keeping eyes open for cacti or snakes or the mariposa lilies that gather around lichen-covered stone. You sit, watching the light congeal as it fades, attentive to the way stone glows from within as darkness falls. You listen to the soft coo of the mourning dove or the descending song of the canyon wren.

No one would bother Brautigan today. Of that he was sure. He wandered slowly, stopping to marvel at the random arrangement of broken stone, or to smell the umber-hued bark of every single towering ponderosa that he passed, asking of each the age-old question: Is the scent vanilla? Or butterscotch? Here the bleached bones of a long-dead cow, there a sagebrush bigger than a tree, on the gentle slope a cliffrose smothered in white, as if it had snowed the night before. His shirt was heavy with sweat, but a steady breeze cooled him. He stopped, closed his eyes, and listened: The wind sings one song as it runs its hands through piñon's bristly hair, another as it caresses soft stone.

In a side canyon to a side canyon, just below a wall of lichen-smeared sandstone blocks, a magnificent old juniper grew illogically out of the center of the wash, its gnarled roots clinging to giant stones, its upstream side scoured of furry bark, wearing a half-necklace of driftwood and debris. Old Man Juniper's substantial girth told Brautigan that he was close to a thousand years old, maybe older.

Brautigan leaned his tired body up against Juniper's curved, shaded trunk, and pondered infinity, the cool, water-smoothed gravel on which his thighs rested, a single cloud in the blue. He asked Juniper why it is that the desert always smells so clean. And why the hard light of September makes him feel lonely, and why the wind in August crackles ecstatically. He asked the old tree about his memories, about how his world had changed over the years.

And Juniper, that crotchety old man, launched into a whispery monologue: I've endured flash floods and droughts, icy winters and scorching summers. I've eavesdropped on the chatter of a million ravens, and God the things they have to say. I was a spindly youngster when the men and women carved the blocks and built those structures over there, while children tended to me, watered me, loved me. I've watched two-dozen generations of humanity come and go. I've seen those who take, and those who give, those who destroy, and those who create.

Brautigan pressed his back into Juniper, as if they were lovers on a cold night, and listened. He was about to nod off when he noticed it, the odd coloring at the tips of tree's scaly leaves. He stood and looked more closely: The deep green was slowly turning brown. Juniper had endured so much, avoided being chopped down or burned up in a fire or bulldozed to make way for cows or condos, but this drought — this grand aridification — was proving too much.

Brautigan stood up stiffly, opened the cap on his Camelbak, and poured some water on the ground at the tree's base. The earth was so parched that the moisture was gone in an instant. He took one more sip for himself, then gave the rest of his water to the tree, even though he knew it was futile, knew that the water would never reach the vast network of roots that reached twenty, thirty feet down into the Underworld, where they mingled with the worms and the grubs and the dead, and where they'd continue to do so long after Juniper had perished, when all that remained in the Upperworld was a stump. He touched the tree then, bid farewell and begged forgiveness before turning to go.

As always, the temptation to continue walking down canyon tugged at him. To walk until worry disappeared, until his name vanished, until time slipped away, and walk and walk until all that remained was an idea. He'd go until he found a little overhang that would accommodate his body, and he'd wait quietly there for death, or for coyote to come, or perhaps both. But his humanity tugged at him, urged him to return to society.

Besides, he was craving a cheeseburger.

He hated to backtrack, so he headed up the nearest side canyon and was soon walking along a fence between two bean fields. As he strolled he formulated his next move. He would go back to Tucson and take advantage of Juan Lopez-Shapiro's newfound notoriety — the dead president had tweeted out his story!

If and when he saw Eliza again he'd tell her he was done with the whole charade, that he wasn't interested in being a pawn in Peter's — and Eliza's — performance. Yes, he now had evidence that she had been in on it all along. That they both were toying with him, for reasons that eluded him. Perhaps they had grown bored of their lives and wanted to screw up his in order to score a hit of Schadenfreude. Or maybe they really were trying to help Malcolm by jerking him out of his routine and getting him to see the errors of his ways.

His phone beeped. It was a message from Eliza. She was on her way back to the Slickrock Curtain, after all. Instantly, all of his plans crumbled.

To avoid the crazed, shirtless, unkempt man who burst from the bushes into the road, Eliza Santos swerved into the path of an eighteen-wheeler. But quick reflexes and deft steering-wheel work saved her from getting pummeled, and she was soon safely pulled over and waiting for Brautigan to gather his stuff and get in.

"Eliza, I have something to say ..." But the look on her face silenced him.

"I don't know if I can ever forgive you for what you've done, Malcolm. You've hurt so many people. Do you realize that? You're sick, and you need help, like from a professional. But right now I need you to help me find Peter."

Brautigan had fortified himself to push back against Eliza's anger. She came at him, instead, with a combination of sadness and frantic concern, befuddling him. "But, I …"

"He sent that riddle poem to you. Why? I don't know. But it means he wants *you* to find him. We have to find him."

The defiant speech Brautigan had prepared eroded away into tenderness. He couldn't bail. No matter how frustrated he was with her, no matter how angry he was that she and Peter were toying with him like this, he just couldn't do it. Playing along and continuing with the search was the only way to stay within Eliza's good graces. If he quit now, she'd toss him out by the side of the road and be done with him, killing any chances of his redemption. Reflexively, Malcolm reached over and lay his hand on Eliza's thigh in hopes of offering a bit of comfort. She did not resist.

"I'm worried, Malcolm. Really worried. Didn't you say you had found something? What is it?"

"I did, but I haven't eaten anything but energy gels today, and my stomach's imploding. So can we maybe stop at the A&W in Blanding? I'll tell you everything." Well, maybe not *everything*.

"I'd rather not spend my money in Blanding. They don't like my kind, anyway."

"This again?" But as Brautigan mentally prepared his argument in favor of tater tots and root beer floats, he reconsidered. "Actually, let's go to Bluff. I need to talk to someone down there, anyway."

As they drove, Brautigan explained how he had found the Acme Queen, and that it apparently belonged to Tasha Ivanova, whose real name was Natasha, and who was, indeed, from North Dakota, and that Hildebrandt also had filed a claim called the HB235, but that its location was unknown.

"Meanwhile, the Happy Bonanza does not exist, I'm afraid. Nor does the Sad Bonanza, the Gay Bonanza, or the plain old Bonanza. That was just some decoy that Peter threw in there to mess with us."

Eliza looked at him as if waiting for the punchline. When none came, she spoke: "You are so daft, Malcolm."

"Huh?"

"HB? Happy Bonanza? Get it?"

"Oh." He could just unclip his seatbelt, open the door, and roll out onto the highway and be done with it. "Very clever."

Blue Bird Cafe was, once again, hopping. It looked as if everyone visiting Canyon Country had been scared away from sightseeing or hiking or mountain biking by the heat, and decided instead to hang out in the air-conditioning or on the shaded deck and have a beer or iced tea. The predominant attire — calf-socks with sandals — indicated a strong foreign presence, most likely European, as one would expect. Eliza ordered some fries to keep Brautigan's blood sugar levels from crashing and then the two of them went across the road to ask the owner of the Magpie Trading Post, Elizabeth Turin, if she knew how to find Chester Tsosie.

"Today's your lucky day," Turin said from behind a glass display case after Brautigan had explained what he was after. "Chester should be coming in soon."

Turin was busy with customers, so Eliza and Malcolm went out on the front porch to sit in the shade and wait.

"The last time I was here, on this porch, was on your wedding day," said Brautigan. "Best party ever."

"Mmm hmmm," said Eliza, remembering.

It had been a progressively raucous fete on a September's eve following a dust-filled tempest. The weather had driven Eliza into a state of hysteria. Dark clouds roiled across the sky that day, pushed by a steady gale that carried with it eye-stinging sand, dirt, gravel, sticks, and anything else that wasn't battened down. The dinner portion of the celebration had to be moved indoors, the long tables crammed into a series of rooms on the back of the trading post. But as the party got under way, the threat of a downpour passed, the wind subsided to a pleasant, warm breeze, and the dust lingered in the air in such a way that it captured the day's last light, giving everything a soft glow, and making the bride and the groom and all the guests look and feel even more beautiful than they already were.

Brautigan had been terribly jealous. After all, he was, and always would be, in love with Eliza. But he was also happy for his best friends, for he had always considered Eliza a friend as much as a lover, and he was grateful that they had invited him, had chosen to keep him in their lives. Besides, he had found his own new love, Melissa, which tempered any hard feelings he might have had. The ceremony itself was held in the alfalfa field behind the trading post, presided over by their buddy from Silverton, Randy Glaxson, who was not a priest but sometimes acted like one.

They had feasted on fresh food of all sorts — corn, squash, basil, tomatoes, and lamb cooked over a wood fire by a crew of Navajo women. Wine freely flowed, along with gin, beer, and vodka. A Gypsy band played deep into the night. And as the party raged, Melissa and Brautigan snuck away to the alfalfa field and lay down in the cool grass and talked about the stars and about what their wedding would be like and all of the places they would live. Brimming with dreams and wine and food and love, they kissed, and their clothes came off. The grass was cool, her thighs were warm, and they made love out there in the dark green damp, their cries rising up and lingering with the sound of the music, the dancing, the revelry.

Brautigan was torn from his memories by the sound of tires on gravel. A Dodge pickup truck pulled into the parking lot a little too fast, kicking up a cloud of dust and rocks as the driver braked just in time to avoid crashing into the iconic old car and trading post mascot. It was only then that Brautigan noticed that Eliza had gotten up and walked out into the alfalfa field where her marriage ceremony had taken place years before.

Brautigan followed Chester Tsosie inside, preferring to let Turin make introductions. First, he had to wait for them to conduct their business. Tsosie had a new batch of jewelry — silver rings, earrings, bracelets, all with polished, inlaid stones. Brautigan, not normally a jewelry kind of guy, was dazzled by the craftsmanship and the clean aesthetic.

Finally, Turin introduced the two, and explained what Brautigan was looking for.

"Sure, I worked up in White Canyon, way back, did some reports for the USGS ..." He talked about how Navajo people had been in the White Canyon area for at least six-hundred years, about how they had sought refuge there when the Mexican general Vizcarra came through in the 1820s, slaughtering everyone in his path, about how Kayelli and his people hid out there during Kit Carson's scorched earth campaign against the Navajo, about how they had held out for the whole Long Walk, never surrendering. Finally, he got to the uranium. After World War II, when the AEC started its policy of buying up all uranium ore produced domestically, things went nuts in White Canyon and most of the rest of the region. Roads were bulldozed across every mesa, and jeeps full of Geiger counter-toting prospectors swarmed like flies. They staked dozens of claims up and down White Canyon.

Hildebrandt didn't start poking around in White Canyon until around the time he moved to Durango. That's when he found it, or said he found it — a naturally-occurring deposit of high grade U-235.

"A what?"

"The ore you take out of a mine is mostly rock, with just a tiny bit of uranium, and only a minute percentage of the uranium is the good, fissionable stuff, uranium-235. So you gotta mill the ore, convert the yellowcake, then enrich it. It's energy-intensive and costly and you need specialized facilities. That's why you don't have nuclear bombs all over the place, because it's so hard to enrich uranium. If you could just pull the 235 isotope right out of the ground at five or even ten percent it would be huge, and a little scary, since it's that much closer to being weapon and reactor ready."

"I guess that explains the name."

"What's that?"

"Hildebrandt's claim. Or his daughter's claim, technically. The HB235."

"Nahhh. He filed a claim? I dunno. Seems risky, considering … "

"Wait a minute. Are you saying that mine is a natural bomb factory?"

"Could be, if Hildebrandt was right. But he was a little wacky by then. Talked a lot about opening up some hole in the time-space continuum, about tinkering with the clouds and the weather, that sort of thing. So, I wouldn't bank on it."

"Time-space what?"

"Hell, I don't know. Atomic fission is some really intense stuff. It destroys mass, you know? Converts it into energy. E equals m-c squared and such. They say he and Frank Oppenheimer were working on a theory that brought electrons into the equation, in the form of electricity, which travels at the speed of light. If fission destroys mass, why couldn't it do the same for time?"

"Time travel?"

"Something like that. More like … It doesn't matter. He was crazy. No one would listen to him, no investors would give him any money for his project, and the feds started getting worried, harassing Frank and his family. The only guy that would listen was Oppenheimer, and he had his own problems. That's about when Frank's wife went out for groceries and yanked Frank off the roof."

"You wouldn't know where his claim is, would you? The HB235? Maybe there's a cabin with it?"

"Naaah. Frank and his partner had the Acme Queen, sure, and they pulled ore out of there, but it wasn't anything special. This other thing, it ain't real. There's no claim. And if there were you'd be better off staying away. There's a reason it's called Leetso Ch'įįdii Canyon, you know."

"What did you say?"

"Nothing, nothing, I'm messing with you. Look, it was nice talking to you. I've got to head home now. The wife's gonna get suspicious. She gets jealous when I come see Elizabeth."

Tsosie went back into the store to say goodbye to Turin. Brautigan followed, and before the geologist-turned-jeweler ambled out the door, Brautigan reached for one of the bracelets that Tsosie had brought in. "I'd like to buy this one," he said to Turin.

Tsosie, instead of smiling in gratitude, frowned. "No, no, you don't want that one. You say you're going to look for the ghost of Frank Hildebrandt? You need this one."

Brautigan had never been very good at picking out jewelry. When he would find something that seemed perfect for Melissa, she would thank him, wear it for a day or two, then put it away in a drawer from which it would never again emerge. Besides, he didn't even know why he was buying this bracelet or for whom, so one was as good as another. Brautigan asked him what the stone — a melange of deep red, black, and green — was.

Tsosie looked at him for a moment, as if sizing him up. "I call it the Monster Slayer stone," he said, in a dramatic whisper. "Anyone who wears it will have the power to ward off the monsters that survived the Hero Twins: Hunger, poverty, but more importantly old age and winter. These are the monsters that keep us humble. Problem is, people are slowly killing winter. That's one monster we need to save."

Brautigan looked at him skeptically.

"I'm kidding, man. It's just petrified wood! Pretty, innit?"

Brautigan caressed the smooth stone with his thumb. Eliza had once informed him that petrified wood wasn't wood at all, but the minerals that had gathered within the wood, taking on its texture. It wasn't the tree, but the minerals' memory of the tree. He followed Tsosie outside, thanked him, and waved goodbye, then went back into the trading post to pay for the bracelet. "Hey, Elizabeth, do you happen to know what Leetso Chindi means?"

She looked up, but not at him, and seemed intent on not making eye contact. "Leetso is yellow dirt, it's the Navajo word for uranium."

"And Chindi?"

"That's a bastardization of the word that usually means ghost, or demon. Sometimes it means hell. It's not a word you want to use in mixed company, if you know what I mean."

He had no idea what she meant, actually, but didn't have time to ask because just then Eliza walked in the door, her eyes red and puffy. "Sorry I wandered off. Did he tell you where the Happy Bonanza is?"

"No. He doesn't think it really exists."

"Did he tell you anything?"

"Yeah, yeah, I think so. But I sure as hell don't know what any of it means."

Dr. Nussbaum

"**S**o, I guess Hildebrandt thought he had found some bomb-ready uranium deposit," Malcolm said as they drove out of Bluff, rising up onto a pallid plateau of sand and stone. "And he was hoping to use it to travel through time."

"Really? So your buddy Frank was a nut job, eh?"

"Apparently."

"Oh, Jesus Christ! Fuck. The bomb manual. In Peter's office. Before you got to Durango I found this thing. *The Los Alamos Primer.* It seemed to be a manual for building an atomic bomb. You don't think …?"

Brautigan chuckled. "Seriously? Now *that* would be art. I wouldn't worry too much, though. Peter has the mechanical skills of a slug. I used to have to fix his bike for him all the time. I doubt that he could build a bomb."

"Good point."

"But the time travel thing? He *would* try that. But with his luck he'd punch a hole through the time space continuum, transporting himself back to 1987, where he'd be condemned to listen to U2's *Joshua Tree* on infinite loop."

Eliza was so busy laughing that she didn't notice the San Juan County Sheriff's Department vehicle riding her bumper. She didn't even notice when its lights started flashing. Then the siren blared, causing both of the Subaru's occupants to jump in alarm.

"What the fuck?"

"I told you not to drive so fast!"

"I was going fifty-two in a fifty-five zone," said Eliza, looking in her side mirror. "But it's cool. It's just the sheriff friend of yours. Seems like a nice guy. I bet he'll let us off."

Brautigan looked in his side mirror, too, and what he saw was not nearly as reassuring: A burly, buzzcut man in riot-cop gear stepping cautiously out of the passenger side of Etcitty's vehicle. He carried what looked like a military rifle, his finger on the trigger.

"Hey, Sheriff," said Eliza, opening the door to step out before Malcolm could stop her.

Everything unfurled in stop-action motion after that. Someone yelling at them: "Keep your hands where I can see them!" Buzzcut man swinging his rifle, the muzzle pointed at Eliza then at Malcolm. Etcitty, his sidearm at the ready, circling wide out into the highway.

Slowly, Malcolm and Eliza got out of the car, as instructed, keeping their hands in the air, and then placing them on the roof of the car. Etcitty and the other cop approached cautiously, and frisked the two. Finding no weapons, Etcitty signaled for the other man to stand down.

"A little piece of advice," Etcitty said. "When you get pulled over, stay in the damned car, both hands on the wheel. Got it?"

"Sure," said Eliza, clearly trembling. "Is this really necessary? I wasn't speeding."

"I don't care how fast you were going. I care about the fact that I've got a deputy missing out here. I've got an eighty-year-old scientist missing. I've got thousands of dollars worth of equipment gone from a substation and a construction site. I've got thumper trucks driving off cliffs ..."

"A deputy's missing?" Brautigan asked in a whimper.

"Disappeared this morning. Someone reported a possible sighting of your friend, Simons, over near Fry Canyon, and Deputy Nielsen went out to look into it early this morning. He sent a distress signal and then his radio went quiet."

"..."

"Thing is," he continued, "all of this stuff started happening at about the same time your friend went missing. And then this morning, I get a dispatch from DHS saying that they've had their eye on him for a while, and that we need to bring him in."

"Come on, Sheriff, Peter's an artist, not a terrorist. This is crazy."

"Let me see if I can remember," said Etcitty. "Trespassing on federal property, trespassing on federal property with intent to destroy property, destroying federal property, and then last March he nearly blinded a federal employee."

"That's all false," said Brautigan. "Lies. Or they got the wrong Peter Simons, or ..." He stopped when he saw Eliza giving him one of those looks.

"So, what? You're going to arrest us for something my husband allegedly did," said Santos.

"We're not arresting anyone. We just need to ask you some questions. I'll need you to drive over to the command post in Blanding. We'll follow."

"What kind of bullshit are they spewing, anyway?" Malcolm said when they were back in the car.

"It's not complete bullshit, I'm afraid. Trespassing? Yeah, he went up to the Animas-La Plata project grounds while it was still a 'construction area.' He climbed onto the Durango uranium depository to cover it with neon green sheets of cloth, kind of like Christo. That's the intent to destroy federal property charge."

"And?"

"And last spring he decided to do a fireworks display on top of the Shiprock uranium depository and some knucklehead security guard ran up there to put a stop to things and got hit in the face by one of the fireworks. He's not blind, he just got some minor burns."

"Sounds like Peter, actually. Why's he not in jail?"

"He got probation for the first two and had to pay a fat fine. On the Shiprock thing they couldn't prove it was him, so he got off, but it still went on his record. Due process is dead."

"Thanks a lot for telling me about all of this before I put my life on hold to look for your felon husband. Jesus. I guess I see why you didn't want law enforcement looking for him."

"Look, I know it's a lot to ask, and I know Peter's an ass. But whatever they do to you, please don't tell them anything about Peter. Don't tell them about the Acme Queen or atom bombs or time travel."

"The feds are involved, now, Eliza. I don't know what's going on, or what part Peter is playing in all of this, but we're way over our heads here. This is starting to get dangerous, and probably illegal. We've gotta come clean with these guys and then just turn this thing over to them. Let the cards fall where they will as far as Peter's concerned. He dug his own nest."

Eliza looked straight ahead, her mouth closed, her jaw muscles flexing. "Malcolm, listen to me. The meathead with the gun back there? The one with the sheriff? He was one of the Clearwater people who came to my house asking about Peter, and who's been stalking my daughter. The same Clearwater goons who are in cahoots with your friend Tasha. Something super shady is going on here, and I think Peter may have gotten tangled up in it. He may be in danger."

Centennial Park, a sprawling complex of a few baseball diamonds surrounded by emerald green grass that gulps up oodles of water, resembled a zoo for burly law enforcement agents. A dozen black SUVs with darkly tinted windows and government plates sat in the parking lot, and a dispersed herd of men, and two or three women, all of them wearing flak jackets emblazoned with "DHS" or "CLEARWATER," with various forms of weaponry hanging from their belts, ambled around like bored teenagers looking for something to do. "Jesus," said Eliza. "It's like a goddamned police state barbecue around here."

The Buzzcut from Etcitty's truck escorted Santos and Brautigan to a table in the shade and told them to wait. Lisa Yazzie, the woman Brautigan had seen in the courthouse the day before, sat a couple tables away, texting fervidly. She looked up at the two newcomers. Brautigan quietly told Eliza what Etcitty had told him about Yazzie, about how she was an activist fired up about the tar sands.

"So she's on our side," said Santos. Then she stood up, walked over, and sat down across from Yazzie. Though the latter initially seemed to resent the intrusion, the two were soon smiling and talking animatedly, leaving Brautigan to feel like a socially inhibited doofus. Finally, he stood up and slinked over to the table and joined the conversation.

Yazzie had been picked up by sheriff's deputies a couple hours earlier out at the Fry Canyon Energy site. She was just wandering around checking things out, taking pictures of the survey flags and the damage done by the thumper trucks, and when she got back to her car the cops were waiting. They said they needed to bring her in for questioning about a missing person, and that if she didn't cooperate, they'd press charges for trespassing and stealing survey flags — which she didn't do, of course.

"This is messed up," said Eliza. "Why do they need all these Homeland Security mercenaries to find some deputy who just got lost? Didn't he just wander away this morning?"

"They must know something we don't," said Brautigan. "Maybe the deputy was taken hostage. And these are the negotiators?"

Etcitty slowly ambled in their direction. He looked tired. "Agent Harrison here is going to question each of you individually, at that tent over there," he said, pointing with his lips toward a white cabin tent set up in the grass. "You're not under arrest or anything, so you don't have to cooperate, but it would be better if you did."

Harrison was a tall, muscular man, with dark sunglasses and a long, but meticulously groomed black beard. Like all the other agents in the park, he was dressed for combat. Santos was in the tent for about fifteen minutes, and she was led out as Brautigan was being taken in. Brautigan couldn't see any bruises on her, so there was that.

The odor blasted Brautigan's olfactory department as soon as he opened the flap-door of the tent. He recognized the particular mingling of musk and fermented mare's milk immediately. It was the same pungent aroma that had wafted out of his mailbox where he found the poem-slash-riddle, and that he had worn with pride as a scrawny and desperately horny fifteen-year-old, virtually guaranteeing that he remain in a state of un-sated desire indefinitely. Agent Harrison offered Brautigan a glass of ice water. He accepted it. Agent Harrison then launched into the interrogation: When did you last see Peter Simons? Where was he headed? Do you have any idea where he might be? Does the word "Boradine" mean anything to you?

Brautigan heard "Oblividrine" rather than "Boradine" and he proceeded to tell the agent that, yes, of course he'd heard of it and he planned on asking his doctor about it during his next check-up, thanks so much for asking. That kicked up a bit of confusion, but they quickly untangled things, and Agent Harrison, with a raised eyebrow, wrote something down in his notebook.

"Are you acquainted with Dr. Alfred Nussbaum and his work?"

"No. Never heard of him."

"How about Peter. Has he ever mentioned Nussbaum to you?"

"No. Honestly, I haven't spoken with Peter in years."

"What about geo-engineering? Or uranium enrichment? Project Petrichor? Or Los Alamos labs?"

"What about them?"

"Did Peter ever talk about these things?"

"Not that I remember, no."

Harrison appeared to ponder that answer, as if it contained some hidden meaning. Then he put his finger up to his black earpiece and pressed on it, paused, then sat down in a chair. He pulled a pair of glasses — goggles almost — out of his pocket and put them on, then looked Brautigan in the eye. "Tell me about your memories of the Happy Bonanza."

Brautigan flinched, and looked away. "I don't remember anything about it." And yet, just then, something appeared to Brautigan at the very edge of his consciousness, a fleeting image of a window in a stone wall. He closed his eyes, tried to think about baseball. "Nope. Nothing."

"And Hildebrandt's Hideout? What do you remember about it?"

"I don't know what you're talking about."

Harrison smiled faintly, put his finger back up to his earpiece and nodded. "You may go."

Yazzie and Santos looked expectantly at Brautigan as he emerged from the tent.

"Pretty strange questions. They seem mostly to be interested in this Nussbaum character, not Peter. And did you smell that guy's cologne?"

While Brautigan was being interrogated, Eliza had filled Lisa in on what they had found. In return, after some hesitation, Lisa told Eliza and Malcolm what she knew about RosaBit, about how the company had sprung onto the scene rather quickly over the past couple of years. Even though it was clearly a large corporation that touted projects all over the world, their major focus — maybe their only real project — was tar sands at Fry Canyon. "Their website says they are doing tar sands mining in Canada, Venezuela, and in northern Utah, but we checked it all out, and there's nothing happening in those places. RosaBit has an office in each community, but it usually turns out to be just a PO box or a little hole in the wall with a RosaBit sign and no one inside. With the exception of Grand Junction, that is."

"Why Grand Junction?"

"RosaBit now shares an office building with the Bureau of Land Management's national headquarters in Grand Junction. When Drumpf relocated the agency from DC they moved into a building owned by, wait for it, RosaBit's parent company's real estate arm."

Brautigan and Santos stared at Yazzie in stunned silence as they tried to work that one out in their heads.

"Jesus," said Malcolm. "That is whacked. And what about White Canyon? It seems like it's the worst place to do tar sands."

"I've wondered about that, too. Maybe it's to provide cover for whatever's going on at this Acme Queen that you found. And then there's Fallon, the Interior Secretary, and his role in all of this. He was a real bad dude when he was a senator. Screwing over the Utes and the Diné, trying to roll back environmental protections. And since he got on the cabinet, he's been up to all kinds of no good, including shrinking Bears Ears, energy dominance, you name it. Guess how he got out here when he came to visit Bears Ears to shrink the national monument?"

"Drove?"

"Private jet, owned by one of Ivanov's companies. Right after Fallon was appointed, his wife got hired doing graphic design for the GGF Foundation, and rumor has it she's getting three-hundred-grand a year for it. Who ever heard of anything like that? And this is even crazier. A few months ago, Fry Canyon Energy 'donated' nearly a million bucks to the Utah State BLM office so they could hire more people to streamline energy permits."

"A Russian company bribed the feds?"

"Pretty much, but this sort of thing isn't even against the law. It's an 'innovative public-private partnership.' Happens all the time," Yazzie said, motioning her lips toward the row of black SUVs. "And these Clearwater guys? That's the scariest part."

She popped open the laptop, opened one of twenty tabs on her browser, and turned the screen so Brautigan and Eliza could read it: *Clearwater Incorporated is a private security and para-military contractor founded in 2003 that provides security services to a variety of corporate clients, particularly oil companies working in hostile regions. In 2019 and 2020 Clearwater received at least six contracts, together totaling more than $700 million, from various agencies and departments within the United States government. Clearwater troops have been spotted on the southern border, guarding construction sites for the new border wall; acting as security guards at federal laboratories where biological, chemical, and nuclear weapons are developed; and patrolling public lands as part of the administration's War on Eco-terror. Clearwater was founded by Sonny DeVos, but was acquired by IntelliCore, a wholly owned subsidiary of OmnySyde Holdings, in January 2017.*

"Oh. That's nice, isn't it?" Brautigan said. "Really comforting to have so many of those 'troops' running around out here."

"Running around looking for Peter," said Eliza, looking warily at the heavily armed agents milling around the park.

"Or this Nussbaum character," said Lisa. "And we don't even know who they're working for. It could be the tar sands folks, the feds, Tasha Ivanova, or all of them at the same time."

"I can tell you this," said Brautigan. "If Obama were still president and these government goons were invading like this, the locals would be going nuts. They'd probably even call in their militia buddies and prepare for war, like the whole Bundy debacle, or Malheur."

"So maybe we need to get the word out, get people riled up," said Yazzie. "If nothing else, the commotion would distract these guys. I've got some cousins over in Aneth, all LDS, and they've got guns, too. They could get their buddies to help out."

"Uh, no offense, Lisa, but I don't think right-wing rednecks are going to listen to you, or Eliza, or me, or even your cousins, for that matter. We could show them evidence that the government's working with Russian oligarchs to turn their county into a radioactive playground and they wouldn't care. They'd just cover their eyes and ears and start yelling, 'Fake news!' It's an epidemic in this country."

Lisa sneered at Brautigan. "That's the problem with people like you. You assume that just because someone works in the oilfield they're automatically right-wing corporate stooges. It's not true, man. My cousins organized all the workers over there and formed a damned union. Their parents were part of the Navajo Liberation crew that occupied the Texaco pumping plant and shut down the whole oilfield. These Aneth people are badass."

Brautigan looked at his feet with both shame and consternation.

"My cousin's buddies from Blanding, on the other hand? The ones they played football with back in high school? Yeah, they're meatheads. And those guys sure as hell won't take up arms against an oil company, unless the Church told them to."

"They won't listen to me," said Eliza. "And they might not listen to Lisa. But there is someone whom they respect. A media outlet that has their ear. And he owes me one — owes the world one."

"And who's that?"

"I believe his name is Juan."

Bone and Shadow

L anguid light. The murmur of stone. Shadows stretching across sage. The wind, part of an unseasonable storm front, had blown a lot of the smoke and dust and smog away, to menace another land somewhere else, leaving the Four Corners Country air unusually clean and clear — aside from the plume lifting up from the fire near Durango. From his perch upon a swath of Comb Ridge sandstone, Brautigan felt like he could reach out and touch Ute Mountain. In the dying light, a virga — a curtain of rain that probably would never reach the parched earth — hung over the ominously dark Carrizo Mountains.

After the interrogation, Eliza and Malcolm had returned to their previous camp spot on Comb Ridge, the spine of the world, and cooked up a nice dinner with all of the fresh ingredients Eliza had brought. Eliza carried a bottle of wine and two glasses up from the car, along with a box, which she set down in front of Brautigan. "A present, for you, from Peter's office."

He looked at her quizzically, then at the box. It had drawings on top, a mushroom cloud, strange doodles, squares, triangles, an abstract form of a woman's body. Hesitantly, his hand trembling violently, he opened it. He literally jumped to his feet when he saw what was inside.

"What is this, Eliza? What kind of shit are you playing now?"

"Calm down. I just found it in Peter's office and opened it and saw your name on the first page. I didn't read it or anything. I thought you'd appreciate it. What is it?"

"It's something I wrote. A long time ago. A novel. But it shouldn't be here. It doesn't exist."

"I'm confused."

"I sacrificed it. On the solstice, like we do, Peter and me. On the same solstice that Peter sacrificed that painting hanging on his office wall. That painting doesn't exist. I watched him burn it. And this—" He flipped through some pages, confirming that it was real. "What's going on, Eliza?"

"Maybe there was some mistake. Or there was a copy."

"There was no copy. I wrote this on a typewriter. Do you know how much it would have cost to get this many pages copied? I was a starving college student." It was an IBM Selectric. Brautigan's mom had picked it up for him used down at Peterson's Office Supply as a high school graduation present. It was a top-of-the-line machine, but by that time was sliding rapidly into obsolescence. Most people his age had computers — Apple IIs or even Macintoshes. It probably weighed thirty pounds, hummed like a distant swarm of bees, and every word he pounded out on the keyboard let out a satisfying staccato as the little ball spun and hammered at the page. So many goddamned words. It was his manifesto, his stand against the injustice of the world, his piece de resistance. Until he read it, then let his dad read it, then Peter blew his publishing dreams all to hell. And then it went off the cliff, where it belonged.

"So you burned this thing?"

"No. Peter's lighter didn't work. We were up on Muley Point. It was winter, colder than hell, windy. I tossed it off the cliff."

"Are you sure?"

"Sure? Yes. No. I'm not *sure*. I'm not sure of anything anymore."

Eliza lifted the lid from the box and read the title aloud: "*Hildebrandt's Hideout*, by M.P. Brautigan."

"Yup."

"Hildebrandt again. Like in the riddle poem that Peter supposedly sent to you."

"Supposedly?"

Eliza looked out into the darkness. "Tell me the truth, Malcolm. Did you write that poem? It sounds like you more than like Peter."

Brautigan threw up his hands, shaking his head with exasperation. "Why would I write that?"

"To distract me. Throw me off the scent, maybe. I'm not sure, but I am pretty sure that you're not telling me everything. That you're involved in this thing, whatever it is. Did you write it?"

"No!"

"Okay, then why did Peter send it to you, of all people? Why not to me?"

"I don't know, Eliza, maybe for the same reason that *you* called *me* for help. What are you insinuating?"

"You know why I called you? Because Peter told me to do it."

"Huh?"

"Before he came out here. Right as he was leaving. He said, 'Call Malcolm. I think he needs help.' Can you explain that shit to me?"

Brautigan sat silently, shaking his head. "I know what you're doing here, Eliza. And it won't work. You're the one who has some explaining to do. It's time to stop. Time to call Peter and let him know he can come out now. Game over. This is getting dangerous, and scary. It's not funny anymore and it sure as hell ain't art."

"What are you talking about?"

"Stop it, Eliza! Stop. This is a game, and you're in on it. I have proof. And it's gone too far."

"It's not a game, Malcolm."

"Okay, then what about the goddamned teeth? That was some act you put on, what with the grave robbing and all of that. You know perfectly well where those teeth came from, because you and Peter bought them from Mister Fox. He told me."

"Peter told you *what?*"

"No, not Peter. Mister Fox told me."

"Mister Fox? Farmington Mister Fox? He's dead, Malcolm."

"Dead?"

"Yes, dead. Years ago, right after we moved to Durango, Peter and I went down there to try to find a bike for Adriana. The place was gone, replaced by a payday loan store. Peter looked it up in the Farmington paper and found the obituary. He was an old dude. He'd probably be about a hundred now. It was crazy to think that he'd still be around in the first place."

"Stop. Please. Just shut up." Brautigan's fingers worried nervously at the hem of his shorts, his eyes darting erratically. "Is this part of the script? Is that what's going on here? You're trying to make me believe that I'm insane because you don't like my career path? I know what I know. You and Peter bought a typewriter, a Geiger counter, and a box of radioactive baby teeth from some guy a few weeks ago. You paid five-hundred bucks. Those are verifiable facts. I'm not making this up!"

"I haven't been to Farmington in years, and I sure as hell haven't bought any of that stuff. Teeth? What kind of sicko …? Did Peter put you up to this? That's it, isn't it?"

"Mister Fox told me. Maybe it was Mister Fox's son, or nephew. I don't know. But I was there, just a few days ago. He said that Peter bought that stuff from him, and that he was with you — with a 'pretty lady,' he said. Obviously that was …"

"It wasn't me, Malcolm." Her voice had become little more than a whisper, barely audible over the hum of the night. "It wasn't me."

The two were silent, each lost in their own thoughts. Brautigan stood up. Pacing, he circled a perfect little zen garden, a depression in the sandstone where, over the years, dirt had gathered and grown into cryptobiotic soil. Where a yucca, a prickly pear, a manzanita, and a few stands of rice grass had taken root.

Brautigan thought about memory.

Santos thought about loss and trust.

Both had lost hold of the thread. The narrative was tangled.

"Let's focus, Eliza. I'm sure there's a rational explanation for the whole thing with Mr. Fox. But we've got to find Peter and unravel this mystery. I've been thinking about the riddle, and it's kind of making sense. The stuff about dire diagnosis and planet on fire is, obviously, about climate change. The monster? That's the Chindi that Tsosie was talking about. Hildebrandt's Hideout is the cabin I went to as a kid, which is at the Happy Bonanza, which, as you kindly pointed out, is the HB235. Pretty good so far, eh?"

"Malcolm, I'm too tired. I can't do it anymore." Eliza held her head in her hands listlessly.

"Can't do what?"

"This morning when I left Durango everything was so clear to me. And now?"

"Clear?"

"I was going to let this thing play out. Let you and Peter finish your performance. I'd go along with it. And then ... I'm just tired." Night fell and clusters of humanity revealed themselves as distant sparkles of flickering light — houses, cars, towns, industrial sites, the White Mesa uranium mill.

"Then what?"

"I don't know, Malcolm. Maybe I was going to leave Peter. Or give him an ultimatum. I really don't know."

"I would think that since he's, ummm, collaborating with a 'pretty lady,' you might ahhh, well. You know, it might make it easier to leave."

"Maybe."

"Don't you think we should find him so we can figure out what's really going on?"

"I don't think I want to find him anymore."

"Yeah, I get it. Believe me, I do. You'll feel better in the morning. Let's go to bed."

"Malcolm! Malcolm! Wake up. You gotta see this."

He had just closed his eyes, or so it had seemed, and now Eliza was badgering him yet again.

"What's wrong?" Then he saw the blast of light, illuminating everything around them. Lightning. The low rumble came about twenty-seconds later. Brautigan tried to remember whether that meant that the lightning was four miles away, or ten. He crawled out of bed, wearing just his underwear, put his headlamp on, and got out of the tent and dug the rain fly out of the bag. He threw it over the tent and motioned to Eliza to batten down her side. It probably wouldn't rain, but it's better to be safe than sorry. Then he started climbing back into the tent.

"What are you doing? You can't go back to bed. We gotta watch the show. Why do you think I woke you up, anyway?" She had a frantic look in her eyes. She appeared to be wearing lipstick.

"Oh. Okay."

Eliza led Brautigan to a belly shaped sandstone bump, complete with its own navel. She had a bottle of gin in her hand.

"That's lightning," he said. "And we just climbed up to the highest place around. I don't think you're supposed to do that."

"Relax. If it gets scary, we'll get into this pothole." She sat down and pulled a hand-rolled cigarette out of her pocket and lit it up. Eliza didn't smoke, not usually. She was in one of those moods, which Brautigan recognized all too well: Restless. Frantic. Dissatisfied. Manic. Disappointed. One of those moods where she slaps on lipstick even though she's got nowhere to go, where she roots through the drawer in the kitchen and finds the tobacco and rolling paper from last time she felt like this, where she pours herself a half-tumbler of vodka and doesn't even bother to put an ice cube in because that would dull the burn, where she moves erratically, as if a murder of crows fighting over a pile of chicken bones resides just beneath her skin.

Brautigan's response was also familiar, a leftover from long ago. His diaphragm tightened, his intestines felt like they were tying themselves into knots. He took a swig of gin, then another, to try to push back the defensiveness that rose up in his esophagus like bile. "You know, Malcolm, when I met you I was on my way to Paris or Rome or somewhere. And now look where I've ended up, as a mother and wife in suburban Durango married to your errant buddy, Peter. Nice, eh? So much for dreams. And Peter, Peter, he dreams only about his art. That's it. He is his art, nothing else."

It was just like before, when her dreams, her wanderlust, her restlessness threatened to subsume him. He took another drink. "Can we not talk about your husband, for once?"

"Okay, then say something, Malcolm. Anything. What's your dream?" She sucked hard on the cigarette, leaving a wet, red stain on its end. "Do you have any dreams? Did you ever have any dreams?"

"Sure, everyone has dreams, right? I just ..."

"Don't be so fucking afraid. Just say it."

"It's just an image I guess. A vision. Of sitting on a terrace in a dry, rocky place. Maybe Utah, or New Mexico, or Italy, or Greece. Eating sardines and sipping a glass of wine after a long day of writing in a dark room, kept cool by thick stone walls, with a view across the desert or the sea or both."

She looked at him, her face softening a bit, maybe because of what he said, or because the gin and nicotine were taking hold. "Tell me more," she said. And he did. And she talked, too. About what, who knows? Their bodies slowly unclenched, they leaned into one another, fingertips brushing thighs, toes touching.

He turned to her, admired her profile in the light reflected from the clouds. He ran his hand idly along her clavicle, she brushed a hair away from his eye and tucked it behind his ear.

"And you," Malcolm said. "You were always there, too. In my dreams."

She turned to him and their lips touched lightly and then they collided into one another and her mouth tasted just as it had twenty years earlier, the woody sour combination of lipstick and cigarette and gin, the bumps on her tongue as it did battle with his, the slippery teeth, the valley of her spine under his frantic fingers as he pulled her to him. They trembled madly.

The sky exploded with light again. The thunder grew louder and sharper, and then faded away. The rain, like those dreams, never arrived.

"Good morning, sunshine," Eliza said, when Brautigan opened his eyes. Stars still stood watch overhead, but they were fading. And he was still on the rock, still in his underwear. It hadn't rained, nor had they been struck by lightning, but an electrical current shimmered in Brautigan's bones. They walked back down to the camp. When Eliza unzipped the tent, she erupted into laughter. Brautigan looked over, curious, only to see a flurry of white feathers fluttering from the tent door.

"What the hell happened?"

"Someone's sleeping bag blew up all over the place."

Eliza knelt by the tent door, trying to gather up feathers. The rainfly was ripped. The scene did not make any sense. Sleeping bags don't just explode. Had lightning struck the tent? Eliza slowly turned to Malcolm, her face a pale green color, her hand held out toward him. In her palm, along with some feathers, were several BBs. Lightning hadn't struck the tent. Someone had shot it, with a shotgun. Brautigan instinctively crouched as if the shooter were still nearby, taking aim.

"Last night during the thunder," Eliza said. "They, they thought we were …"

Brautigan stood up again, slowly did a pirouette, scanning the surroundings for signs of another human. Nothing. He walked over to the Subaru. At first glance, it seemed fine. Then he saw the chunks of glass on the front seat, like uncut diamonds. Someone had busted out the window. Brautigan opened the car and looked around. Nothing seemed to have been disturbed, aside from the window.

"My wallet's here, in the tent," Eliza said. "Yours is too. Phones are here, too. Intact and working."

Before going to bed Malcolm had put Peter's laptop on the car's front seat so that he'd remember to plug it in first thing in the morning in order to juice up the battery. He had placed his manuscript on top of the laptop to shield it from the morning sunlight.

The novel was gone.

Etcitty, along with a young deputy, showed up at their camp about an hour after Brautigan had called his office. Though he was not the type to wear his emotions on his sleeve, his frustration was readily apparent. He had two missing persons — three if you count Peter — a host of felony-grade property damage and theft cases, and a herd of Clearwater agents poking around in the name of at least two different entities. Now this, an apparent attempted murder. He rolled his eyes when Eliza explained how it was that someone fired a shotgun into their tent without hitting either of them. While his deputy collected evidence, Etcitty walked around, looking at the ground, then at the trees, then at the sky. At one point he wandered into a stand of junipers below the camp and didn't return for twenty minutes or so. "Looks like the shooter came up from down below that little ridge, where you wouldn't have seen his vehicle, if he had one."

"If he had one?" Brautigan asked.

"Yeah, his boot prints lead back to the road down there. If he got into a car there, it's impossible to tell. The road surface is too hard for prints. Any idea why someone would want to shoot you? Or break into your car and not take anything?"

Brautigan, who hadn't told him about the manuscript, shrugged.

Etcitty: "Can I talk to Ms. Santos alone for a moment, please."

"Yeah, sure."

Brautigan walked up to the slickrock and sat in the shade of a piñon tree and watched the exchange between the two. Etcitty was almost motionless, while Eliza gestured wildly. After ten minutes or so, Etcitty waved him back over. Eliza was fuming, but she kept quiet. "We'll send this evidence in, run the prints we found, that sort of thing," Etcitty said. "In the meantime, I'd suggest you all just head back to Durango. You're not doing anyone any good around here, and you're just putting yourselves in danger. We'll find your husband. Leave it to the professionals."

"He's got nothing to do with your deputy, or the old guy, or any of this, okay," Eliza said.

"If you say so, ma'am. You have yourself a good one. And if you do keep poking your noses in things around here, don't be surprised if those Clearwater folks call you in for questioning again." Etcitty got in his truck with his deputy and drove back down the road.

"That bastard thinks Peter did this," she said, after he was out of sight. "He thinks it's some jealous husband thing or something. Can you believe that?"

Malcolm thought back to the night before, and how it might have looked to Peter, had he come wandering into their camp to surprise them, to do the big reveal, and seen his wife and one of his oldest friends tangled together in a giant stone woman's belly button.

"I don't know."

"What do you mean, you don't know? This is Peter we're talking about!"

"Yeah, but, we were —"

"Use your brain. A jealous guy walks into camp in the middle of the night, sees his wife and friend kissing on the rocks watching the storm, and he does what? Shoots the tent and steals his a manuscript that he'd had in his own office for years? Wow, that makes a lot of sense, doesn't it?"

"Then what's going on? Why did someone take the novel? Did you read any of it?"

"No. I told you. I looked at the title page and that was it. Why?"

"So it might have just been a big pile of blank pages?"

"I guess. But why ...?"

"I don't know, Eliza. I really don't know."

"You heard the sheriff," Brautigan said, once they had cleaned up all the feathers and the tattered remains of the tent. "It's over. We should skedaddle back to Durango, at least until things cool down a bit and the Homeland Security and Clearwater muscle go back to their bunkers."

"I'm not letting these people intimidate me," Eliza said, as they sat in the car at camp, motor running, air-conditioner blasting. "Who the hell do they think they are?" Eliza looked at the clock, noticed that it was already two in the afternoon. "If you want to take off, fine. Fine! I'll drop you off in Blanding and you can drive Peter's truck back to Durango. But don't hang out there. Get your car and go back to Tucson and your miserable stupid life. Maybe you can find Natalya, the barista, or Jenna, the barista, or one of the other baristas you're so smitten with and you can fake the news and they can fake their orgasms and you can live a sweet little life of fakery and fuckery."

"What's wrong with you? Last night—"

"I was upset last night. Now I'm angry. I'm angry at you, at Peter, at that sheriff, at that bitch Tasha. I'm just angry. I'm going to find my husband, and I'm going to find out what's going on here, and I'm going to stop this tar sands shit in its tracks. You can tag along, or you can run away. Your choice."

"Well, then. Okay. I'll ..."

"Great. Apology accepted," she said, her countenance brightening. "The first thing you need to do is write that story. The one that will rile folks up, maybe create some sort of diversion. Then you need to figure out where the hell Peter is."

"Wait a minute," said Brautigan, "you want me, or Juan, to spark a full-on Sagebrush Rebellion against these hired guns? How?"

"I'll leave that up to you. You seem to have it figured out."

"Who says I even have access to *Alt-News* anymore? It's not my website, you know."

"Hmm, let's see," Santos said as she pulled out her phone and punched something into the keypad with the dexterity of a fifteen-year-old. "Ah, ha, here it is. 'Coal plants keep grid going during heatwave,' by none other than JLS, yourself. You still have access, and your bullshit-spewing keyboard is fully functional, clearly."

"So, what? Throw away my livelihood just like that? For what?"

Santos looked him in the eye in a way that said far more than words ever could. Malcolm reached into the back seat and grabbed his laptop and unfolded it on his lap.

San Juan Hill

EXPOSED: FEDERAL CONSPIRACY TO DEFRAUD RURAL UTAH FAMILIES

An **Alt-News** *exclusive by Juan Lopez-Shapiro*

Blanding, Utah — Documents recently obtained by Alt-News reveal a conspiracy between federal officials, a Salt Lake City think tank, a Russian oil company, a San Juan County Commissioner, and private businessmen to profit off of Bears Ears National Monument and to deprive local citizens of access to one of the most important Church of Jesus Christ of Latter Day Saints sites in the region.

"It is disturbing to see a bishop and member of our own flock trade away our hallowed lands in the name of greed," said Monticello Stake President Harlan Smoot. "The Church does not condone this behavior and will take appropriate actions."

The conspiracy took root in 2016 when Sutherland Farms purchased a parcel of state land located on Comb Ridge. Sutherland Farms is registered out of Provo, Utah, under the name Stan Hatch. The business appears to exist solely for the purpose of purchasing state land that lies in or near national parks and monuments. Hatch is also the executive director and founder of the GGF Foundation, based out of Salt Lake City.

The land purchase occurred prior to the establishment of Bears Ears National Monument, but it was clear by then that the parcel would most likely fall within the boundaries of such a monument. Hatch indicated that under private ownership the parcel would continue to be accessible to locals, and hinted at turning it into a monument to the Hole-in-the-Rock pioneers.

County officials praised the purchase of the land.

The GGF Foundation has received millions of dollars in funding from Russian oil tycoon and oligarch Ivan Ivanov, a close associate of President Vladimir Putin. The GGF Super PAC, in turn, was the top spender on Interior Secretary Albert R. Fallon's 2014 congressional campaign, as well as the late-President Ronald Drumpf's 2016 bid and inaugural fund, and President Ivanya Drumpf's campaign.

Soon after Obama's designation, Hatch and the GGF Foundation joined efforts by Utah's congressional delegation to have President Drumpf abolish or shrink the monument. Drumpf assigned Fallon to the task. And Fallon brought in Hatch for advice. While Fallon consulted with most local officials, such as the Board of San Juan County Commissioners, via aides, he had several personal meetings with Hatch. The two also spoke on the phone and corresponded with one another directly.

Alt-News obtained copies of the correspondence between the two, and they revealed a tangled plot in which Hatch dictated where the new boundaries were drawn based purely on his own self-interest. He removed the White Canyon tar sands area and uranium district from the boundaries in order to open it up to development by RosaBit, a Russian company owned by Ivanov, Hatch's primary benefactor. RosaBit's subsidiary, Fry Canyon Energy, is currently working on a major tar sands development project near Fry Canyon and is receiving large subsidies and regulatory relief from the Drumpf II administration.

Meanwhile, Hatch intentionally kept the south end of Comb Ridge within the monument boundaries so that it would increase the value of Sutherland Farm's land. It would also heighten the desirability of the Bears Ears Adventure Resort, which is currently under construction on the parcel. Hatch had always intended to use the parcel for the resort, and was courting investors long before he purchased the property. One of the primary investors, Alt-News has learned, is Two Falls LLC, which was registered with the State of Utah by Lola Fallon, Secretary Fallon's wife. Blueprints for the resort include plans for a brewpub and bar, which reputedly would be operated by the Fallons.

In order to keep the Sutherland Farms parcel within the monument, however, San Juan Hill, one of the most important landmarks on the Hole-in-the-Rock trail, also had to be kept within the monument boundaries. That may limit access to members of the LDS Church and the descendants of Hole-in-the-Rock pioneers, who have made annual pilgrimages to San Juan Hill in order to commemorate the arduous journey their ancestors endured. Local church leaders had implored Fallon to exclude San Juan Hill from the new monument boundaries.

"Along with Salvation Knoll, San Juan Hill is the most important site in this region," said Bishop Nathan Redd. "Now they are planning on putting a bar right on top of it. We must rise up and reclaim what is ours, and Stan Hatch must be held to account."

Other documents obtained through the Freedom of Information Act show that Hatch funneled at least $200,000 to Bill Stevens' 2018 county commissioner campaign through the GGF Super PAC. In exchange, Stevens convinced his fellow county commissioners to refrain from protesting the new boundaries drawn by Hatch, which in no way resembled what the commissioners had lobbied for. He also pushed the county to rush the development approval process for Hatch's Bears Ears resort, and to offer it an economic development property tax credit.

The great Brigham Young was known to extoll against capitalism, greed, and private property, once stating: "There shall be no private ownership of the streams that come out of the canyons, nor the timber that grows on the hills. These belong to the people; all the people."

"Hatch and Stevens must have forgotten about that," said Bishop Redd, who counts both men as members of his Stake House.

DISCLOSURE: Alt-News has received funding from Stan Hatch and the GGF Foundation, and past coverage has been influenced by that funding. As a result, the Alt-News team has wittingly taken part in the mass deception of the American people, disseminating lies, disinformation, propaganda, and inaccuracies in order to forward an ideology and, mostly, to confuse our readership to allow our nation's leaders to seize power and wealth. Our recent article "exposing" San Juan County Sheriff Kenneth Etcitty, was based on false information supplied from Hatch and GGF, and was riddled with untruths, lies, and false accusations. We hereby retract the article, and apologize deeply to Mr. Etcitty and to the people of San Juan County. Alt-News Editor-in-Chief Juan Lopez-Shapiro has been dismissed in absentia, as he went missing behind the Slickrock Curtain before he could be held to account.

Brautigan read it over. It was short, and sweet, but did what it needed to do. He was proud of it. After all, it had everything: religion, greed, Russians, corruption, a quote from Brigham Young, the "American Moses" who had led the Mormons to their promised land in Utah. As problematic as Young was as a leader and a human being, he also had a few things going for him: He was anti-capitalist, believed in equal distribution of wealth, was a staunch advocate of education and science, and his writings and speeches indicate that he understood evolution. Surely he would have been alarmed at what capitalism and climate change were doing to God's creations.

Still, Brautigan had no faith in the article's power to sway the people of San Juan County to turn on Hatch or Stevens or even Fallon or RosaBit. After all, they had advocated the destruction of Indigenous religious sites for decades without a second thought. And Christians' support for the Drumpfs only grew in fervor each time Drumpf I blatantly lied or paid off a porn star with whom he'd had an adulterous affair, or when the Drumpf II organization built a gold-plated tower on the Golgotha in Jerusalem. The Drumpfs could violate every one of the Ten Commandments on live television and their Evangelical followers would prostrate themselves even more deeply, so long as it annoyed the liberals. Why would it be any different on a local level?

Yet Santos wouldn't rest until he did something, and he hoped that this might earn him a tiny bit of redemption in her eyes. Maybe it would quiet down his conscience, too, which had nagged at him with increasing intensity over the last several days.

Brautigan put the story up on *Alt-News*. He found photos of Hatch, Ivanov, Ivanova, Stevens, and Fallon online, and worked them to look like booking shots. He also embedded the most incriminating emails and documents into the story, so people could see the evidence first hand, and to fend off the inevitable charges of "fake news" that would be aimed at the least fake story he had written as Lopez-Shapiro. But he didn't publish the story. At Eliza's bidding, he scheduled it to go live the next morning. By that time, if all went according to plan, he and Eliza and Lisa Yazzie would be on their way to the Happy Bonanza mine.

Joshua

Malcolm held the phone a few inches away from his ear as the voice of Joshua, his older brother, prattled on with a coffee-fueled monologue, his agile and crowded mind one step ahead of his words. He talked for a good ten minutes about his latest raft trip on the Chama River in New Mexico — which turned out to be a paddle-board trip because the water was so low that rafts were scraping bottom — before launching into some project he was working on that had to do with tiny nuclear reactors that could be paired with renewables to run entire cities with virtually no greenhouse gas emissions. It would be ready to deploy in a decade, maybe two. Brautigan, huddled under Santos' shade structure, looked around, wondered if it wasn't getting a little late for that sort of thing.

When Joshua finally stopped to breathe, Brautigan launched into his own soliloquy, trying to sum up all he knew about Frank Hildebrandt's weird project, naturally occurring uranium-235, time travel, electromagnetism, and the Vespa-riding guy in *Cosmos*. Joshua started snickering about halfway through and was in tears by the time Brautigan finished.

"Malcolm? Are you okay?" He finally said.

"Yeah, no, I'm fine. Look, I just want to know if it's possible for there to be a natural deposit of enriched uranium."

"I'm a physicist, not a geologist."

"Sure, but, don't you guys down at Los Alamos deal with this sort of thing? Maybe you could ask a colleague?"

"I work at Sandia, not Los Alamos."

"I knew that."

"It's complicated. Theoretically, yes, you could have high-grade U-235 occurring naturally, but if it was critical, it would then start a nuclear reaction. That happened in a place called Oklo, in Africa, but it was a billion years ago.

Can't happen now. I'm not even going to try to explain."

"Okay, forget that then. But say there were a natural deposit of U-235, and you were to zap it with a massive amount of electricity, could you cause an atomic reaction that would, I don't know, allow you to time travel?"

"If vaporizing yourself and everything within a half-mile radius is time travel, then yes. Look, Malcolm, you're talking crazy here. Are you messing around with mushrooms or ayahuasca again? "

"I don't do that stuff."

"Oh, really? How about that time you checked yourself into the hospital because Carlos Castaneda was talking to you through the ceiling fan."

"That was for a story."

"The answer is no. You can't travel backwards in time because it would violate the Second Law of Thermodynamics. Entropy, you know? And we're always traveling into the future. It's how time works. So give that up. As far as the enriched uranium goes, if you find it let me know. I could use some. It would make running a reactor a lot cheaper."

"Well, thanks. Next time I see you I'll buy you a beer or a shot or something."

"Seriously, Malcolm?"

"What?"

"I'm sober. Six months, four days. Jesus."

"Oh, yeah, sorry. I mean, congratulations. I'm thinking of doing that, too. Cutting back a bit on the booze."

"It doesn't really work that way."

"Okay, well, anyway, the real reason I called is because I was wondering if you remember where Hildebrandt's Hideout is."

Silence.

"Joshua?"

"Do you have Signal?"

"Cell signal? Ah, duh. I'm talking to you aren't I?"

"No. Signal. The app. For encrypted phone calls."

Brautigan did, in fact, have it, a remnant from his days as a real journalist. Joshua told him to hang up and wait for his call. It came.

"What's up with the secrecy? Are you doing drugs?"

"Shut up, Malcolm. You're the second person to ask me about Hildebrandt in the last two weeks. They brought contractors in to do our annual security evaluation last week, which I think is crazy. And they asked about Hildebrandt, and the Happy Bonanza. Asked about my memories of it, not where it was."

"Contractor? Let me guess. It was Clearwater Security."

"How did you know?"

"I've become well acquainted with those folks, believe me." Brautigan told him about Peter and Eliza and the tar sands project and about his own interrogation at the hands of Clearwater Security.

"Nussbaum ..." Joshua finally muttered, as if to himself.

"What did you say?"

"An old colleague. Works at Los Alamos and Sandia. He went missing a few days ago out near Muley Point, right after the fires."

"Oh, the old guy? Yeah, yeah, and a deputy's missing too, now. It's like the damned Sagebrush Triangle out here. Wait, who is this Nussbaum guy, anyway?"

"He's one of the world's foremost experts on uranium enrichment. Or he was. In the past decade or so he's moved into geo-engineering."

"You mean, like, sucking carbon out of the atmosphere with giant vacuum cleaners? Or covering the earth in mirrors to deflect the sunlight?"

"Yeah, that's the idea, but the details of his project are secret. No one knows what he's working on, exactly. Anyway, you need to get the hell out of there, Malcolm. And take your girlfriend, too."

"She's not my ..."

"Just do it. Leave. You're compromising my job by being there. Okay? And it's not safe. Please stop poking around over there. It's not worth it. Bye, Malcolm, I've gotta go. I love you."

Before Malcolm could respond the call ended. Joshua had never said anything like that to him before.

"You okay?" Eliza asked when she saw the look on Malcolm's face after he had hung up.

"He said we should..."

"What?"

"He said he loved me? He said you can't travel through time because of atrophy. And he said he's a physicist not a geologist and that he'd ask around."

"It's entropy, not atrophy. What about the Hideout? Did he remember?"

"He says it's in a tributary of Bonanza, near a cliff dwelling. Not a whole lot of help. Hey, I know it's a sore subject, but where, exactly, did you find those teeth?"

Eliza described the gravel bed, located where two tributaries ran into Bonanza Canyon from either side. Brautigan ran to the car and pulled out the topo map and the printout that Judy, the county assessor, had given him. They located the confluence on the map. One of the tributaries led directly to the Acme Queen claim.

"Peter put the teeth there to guide us," Brautigan said, pointing to a place on the map. "The Happy Bonanza. It's right there. I remember now."

"So you did have something that Tasha wanted, after all."

"Yeah?"

"Yeah. Memories."

Coyote, Leetso, Changing Bear

The usual routes into Leetso Canyon would be too conspicuous. So, early the next morning Brautigan and Santos met Lisa Yazzie in Bluff, piled into Yazzie's Nissan Sentra, and headed north and west in order to circle around and drop into Leetso from the opposite side, making for a long day. They parked the car under a tree and loaded their packs with a variety of high-sugar goodies and water. As an afterthought, Brautigan tossed the bear spray into his pack, and the bright orange flare gun and two flares into Eliza's.

They moved deftly through a stand of trees before plodding into a vast, rectangular clearing, a mile across. The trees were all gone. Decades ago two bulldozers had driven side by side, a giant chain stretched between them, tearing out ancient junipers and piñons as they went, dragging the carcasses to the far side of the clearing where they were left to rot. In just a few hours they had destroyed millions of years worth of trees, of arboreal memories, in order to make way for forage for cattle in a land where cattle simply didn't belong. It had been forty years since the bulldozers growled through here, and the trees still hadn't returned, the cryptobiotic crust hadn't recovered, and instead of grass, the clearing bustled with Canada thistle, toadflax, knapweed, bindweed, medusa head, and, of course, cheat grass.

It was just another wound, one of too many: Road scars and well pads, waste dumps and ATV tracks, beetle-killed junipers and overgrazed glades, pit mines and tailings piles, poisoned waters and poisoned blood and a species conspiring to commit mass suicide and ecocide, all at once.

"Fucking assholes," Santos said. "And this is public land. *Our* land."

"Not really," Yazzie said, turning toward her companions.

"Sure it is. This is all BLM. Maybe state land, but still."

"Have you ever asked how this became 'public' land? It was stolen, first. Forcibly stolen. All of it. And it wasn't stolen to allow rich white folks to hike

213

in peace, it was stolen to make way for mining and drilling and logging and grazing. When you do that thing? That 'our land' thing, that jingoistic American exceptionalism thing, when you fetishize public lands, you're erasing the history."

"I honestly had never thought of it like that, before," Eliza said, defensiveness creeping into her voice. "You're right. But ... how are we supposed to honor that history?"

"You could start by giving the land back. You probably won't do that. So, the national monument, as we proposed it, would have been a start. To have the five tribes co-manage it. But even Obama wouldn't go that far. And now ...."

"Yeah. I'm sorry." Eliza said. "You're right. I'll try to do better."

"Just remember the history, remember whose land you're walking on, that's all." They walked past the remains of a hamlet or community that had been built and inhabited a millennium ago. The buildings had been dragged with the chain, scattering some of the rubble, and holes in the dirt indicated that someone had dug and looted it, pilfering the artifacts and maybe even human remains to sell to Santa Fe traders, or to place on their mantel in Blanding. A line of stone that had somehow survived the chain and the bulldozers pointed directly to the gap between the two Bears Ears, right where the sun would rise on the solstice two days from then. They all stopped and pondered this for a moment, knowing that they were in the right place.

The trio walked across the plateau, and dropped into Hayden Canyon. The plan was to follow it upwards to a small tributary called Scorup's Canyon, which they'd use to access a narrow ridge dividing the Hayden drainage from Leetso Canyon. From that point they should be able to see right down to the Happy Bonanza, aka the HB235, aka Hildebrandt's Hideout. No one had spoken about what they expected or hoped to find there. After a long spell of silence, Yazzie launched into a soliloquy to help pass the time:

It is said that long ago, shortly after the people emerged into this, the glittering world, there lived around here a bad-ass woman and her brothers. She was smart, sexy, and could fell a deer and dress it like no other. Men came from all over to court her. She rejected most of them out of hand.

Brautigan started to butt in. He knew this story. It was in a favorite book of his as a kid. But Yazzie's story took a turn, and Brautigan stayed silent.

If she liked one, she'd take him into her bed and ravage him for a night. If he performed to her satisfaction, and her vagina cried out with joy, she might do it again, and even another time in order to give him a chance to learn the idiosyncrasies of her pleasure. Yet after a week or so, she always sent them on their way, leaving them broken and haunted and forever changed by their short time with her.

The tales Brautigan read as a kid left out the part about joyful vaginas, unfortunately.

Then, during a great dry spell, when the trees turned brown and even the most ancient springs dried up, Coyote showed up to try his hand. She turned him down immediately. He persisted until, finally, she said that if he killed one of the giants that terrorize the people — a seemingly impossible task — she'd consider giving him a try, to see if his lovemaking skills could even come close to matching hers. Coyote may have been a skinny guy with patchy fur, but he was the Trickster, endowed with wile and cunning. Confidently, he strode off to the mesas above White Canyon, to the lair of the Orange Giant, a brutish, cruel, greedy, and ugly beast who lied to and bullied the swarm of gophers that followed him around, and beat people and animals to death with a club, sometimes in order to eat them, sometimes just for fun.

Yazzie continued the meandering tale, veering back and forth from the traditional narrative to one of her own devising.

Coyote ended up killing the giant through trickery, and the woman reluctantly allowed him into her bed, despite the fact that he stank and was a bit of a rascal. Coyote was always getting into trouble, mostly because he bided by the credo that you only regret what you don't do. In a game with beavers he lost all his fur, he got squished during a rock-sledding session with lizards, and while playing with magpies he lost his eyeballs. He had to beg Raven to fashion him new ones out of piñon sap, which could cause problems if he got too near to the fire. Still, Coyote and the woman were happy together, although she refused to marry him until the great drought ended. If he could manage to slay Drought, and to bring back the rain, the snow, the streams, and the springs, then she would devote herself to him for eternity.

Coyote knew that even he couldn't kill Drought. But in his restlessness, and his desire to impress the woman, he sought to rid the world of the second most terrible monster of all, Leetso Chindi, who had been dormant for eons until the Orange Giant's followers had roused him from his slumber, hoping to harness some of his power. Coyote ventured into the canyons until he found its lair, carrying his big black stick that he had fashioned with the monster-slayer stone. The two engaged in a spirited battle, and though Yellow Monster was by far the most powerful of the two, Coyote had his slaying stick, and got the upper hand. Just as he was about to slay Yellow Monster, however, Coyote had an idea. He stopped and spoke: "Yellow Monster, you have terrorized my people for so long, but I know that you only did it because the people disturbed you. I believe that down deep you are good, and that only you can help me slay Drought and save Old Lady Winter."

Yellow Monster pondered this for a moment and then agreed. They devised a plan to use Leetso's power to fill the clouds with rain and headed off to Drought's hideout, hoping to catch him by surprise. But on their way, Coyote was ambushed by none other than Leetso's daughters, the Bone Seekers, who were unaware of the pact between their father and Coyote. They glared at Coyote with their killer yellow eyes and he weakened, fell to his knees, and died.

When Changing Bear Woman learned of her lover's death she was filled with passionate rage, and used her magic to transform herself into a bear. She tore through the forest until she found the Bone Seekers, and attacked them viciously. But their dark magic was too strong even for Changing Bear Woman. And the Bone Seekers ripped her limb from limb and scattered the pieces to the winds, her dismembered body parts becoming rock formations or plants or animals. Her nipples became the piñon nuts that the people still harvest today; her vagina is now the porcupine. Her long spine became Comb Ridge. And the crown of her head became Shashjaa, or the Bears Ears.

The story, and Yazzie's melding of magic and the mundane, did what it was supposed to do. They were so lost in the tale that they barely noticed the mid-morning sun beating down on them, the sweat soaking their shirts, the ground-heat making its way through the thick soles of their running shoes.

Brautigan, being Brautigan, missed some of the most salient details of the story — such as if and how Drought was ultimately conquered — and instead honed in on the erotic, and he thought of another tale in which the hero is ultimately dismembered for love: Orpheus and Eurydice. Both stories seemed to be saying that if you love ardently and completely, you will be torn limb from limb, and your atoms and molecules will get scattered about, melding with the land. Love too much, it said, and you will become Juniper, or sagebrush. You will be transformed into sandstone, perpetually caressed by wind and water. You will become the towering cottonwood, leaves dancing with the sun, and monkey flower, dangling from desert varnish in defiance of gravity.

They turned up Scorup's Canyon without a word. On the maps, the canyon isn't much of a canyon at all — maybe a half mile long, branching into two forks divided by a narrow fin of white rock. When they reached the fork, they found a damp piece of sand and a welcome patch of shade in which to eat lunch. Brautigan suggested his companions take the right fork, while he went left.

Lisa and Eliza, it turned out, were happy to part ways with Malcolm. Brautigan, however, made it only a few steps up the canyon before he started feeling lonely, almost painfully so, as well as a little scared. He sensed that someone was watching him, but when he spun around, only canyon peered back.

He pushed on, the way strangely familiar. He reached a pool, which seemed odd, given the long dry spell, and he lay down on his stomach and slurped some up, careful not to swallow a tadpole. He was tempted to strip down and jump in, but didn't want to sully the clear water, so he skirted around the pool, and continued up the canyon. The slope got steeper as he went. He forced himself to move slowly, rounded a little bend, scurried up a little steep section. He shimmied up the sandstone onto the next ledge, where the rocks were noticeably warmer, and then scrambled up through the boulders to a point from which he could get his bearings. It didn't work. He was completely disoriented.

"Goddamnit!" He said, a little too loud. It was all wrong. He had thought he was climbing the ridge above Leetso Canyon. In fact, he had topped out on a false summit on the ridge between the two tributaries of Scorup's Canyon. At this point his only options were to backtrack, or to climb to the top of this ridge and see where it took him. So he scrambled upward impatiently, moving far too quickly for the desert. Just as he was levering himself over the last lip of the rim, a hummingbird-sized, orange and black arthropod collided with his forehead with a sickening thump. This was not just any bug, but a *Pepsis grossa*, otherwise known as a tarantula hawk, its name coming from its habit of stalking a tarantula, paralyzing the spider with its painful sting, dragging it back to a burrow, and laying eggs on the tarantula's abdomen. When the eggs hatch, the wasp larvae eat the immobilized but living and sentient spider. Malcolm jolted backward, slid off of the rim, and crashed butt-first into a small piñon tree. The tree managed to hold his weight, saving him from a bone-breaking plummet. He was more grateful that he was spared from the wasp's traumatic sting.

After he caught his breath and calmed his racing heart, Brautigan picked himself out of the tree and climbed back up onto the slick rock, this time far more warily. He walked over to the fin's edge, from where he could see into the canyon's other branch. There, in the narrow stream bed, stood Lisa and Eliza, talking to two other people, a blonde woman and a tall, thin man. Brautigan closed his eyes, and with the sleeve of his shirt, wiped the sweat away. When he opened his eyes again, the same tableau presented itself to him. He staggered backwards and almost fell off the cliff. Lisa and Eliza were speaking to Tasha Ivanova, and to Brautigan's old buddy and Eliza's missing husband, Peter Simons.

Holy hell, Brautigan muttered, his skin prickling with confusion as much as chagrin. He tried futilely to still the blizzard of puzzle pieces swirling around in his brain: Peter, Tasha, Eliza, and Lisa. Peter and Tasha were working together. That much was clear. Tasha was the "pretty lady" Mr. Fox had mentioned, who had bought the teeth and the Geiger counter. While researching his art, Peter had probably unwittingly stumbled upon Tasha's scheme to get the enriched uranium, and build a weapon or a time machine, and she had roped him in as a willing accomplice. Peter was like that. If he were a moth, he'd have burned up long ago. But where did Eliza and Lisa fit in? More importantly, what the hell was Malcolm's role in all of this? He'd figure that out later. Right now he just had to escape and get help. Surely he was in danger.

It was all Peter's fault. If Brautigan hadn't abided by his phony credo about regret and all, he'd still be in Tucson, writing a few fake stories a day, getting the stinky-eye from baristas, and drinking himself to sleep every night with pricey gin. He had said yes, instead of no, and now he regretted the shit out of it.

Brautigan backed away from the edge, so he was out of the line of sight of the others, and assessed his situation. Going back the way he came would be to walk right into Ivanova's web. Continuing up the drainage as originally planned would be to walk right into his so-called friends' trap. His best bet was the most counterintuitive: Hunker down somewhere up high, wait for Ivanova and the others to come after him, then drop into the other branch of Scorup's Canyon and run like hell.

Before he could even turn around, however, he was halted by a fluttering sound. A painful thud hit the base of his skull, closely followed by an intense burning that radiated from neck to brain to spine to legs. The tarantula hawk was not finished with him, and she had come back to punish him for violating her space. He tried to yell to Eliza, maybe for help, maybe as a warning, maybe just to curse her treachery, but the sound wouldn't come, his mouth wouldn't open, his tongue had become molten lead, swelling up and filling his being.

The earth rushed toward him, giving him just enough time to hope that he would die before the wasp's eggs hatched.

When Darkness Calls

The darkness was clingy and elastic, like the web of a black widow spider strung across the dim corner of a stone alcove. Malcolm Brautigan was a fly, caught in the web, wiggling about frantically, each movement only exacerbating his entanglement. It was only when he held perfectly still and no longer resisted that the light finally came in, dimly, through the crack between the closed curtains and the softly plastered wall. He felt a warmth behind him, and after the brief moment of terror that follows a nightmare, he relaxed and inspected his surroundings. He was in a bed, under a blanket, and visions of the previous night's *liaison erotique* returned. He rolled over and there was the petroleum engineer from North Dakota looking warmly at him with eyes that might have been brown, or hazel, or amber. Brautigan almost wept with joy and gratitude. He had been transported back to the hotel room in Winslow and given another chance.

"I just had the craziest dream," he said.

She smiled. "I hope I was in it."

"Oh, you were."

"And the Happy Bonanza? Did you dream about that?"

"Yes, I did, and those women. Wow they can do things with their ..."

"Not *that* Happy Bonanza."

"You're right, we don't need porn," he said. "We've got each other." Brautigan moved to unbutton her shirt, but was cut off by a distant pounding. Housekeeping, surely.

"Come back later!" Brautigan yelled.

The pounding continued, and now the housekeeper was yelling: "Malcolm! No! Malcolm, wake up!"

"I am awake! Please, do not disturb," he said, as nicely as he could muster, before noticing the look of irritation on North Dakota's face. He looked around for the first time, really looked around, and realized that they had been taken out of La Posada and plopped into a Motel 6, an especially seedy one, with reinforced doors and windows with wires through them, upon which Eliza and Lisa banged frantically.

"Oh for fuck's sake," said Tasha Ivanova, abruptly rolling off the bed, standing up, and hastily re-buttoning her shirt. "We were getting somewhere. Okay. He's awake. Let them in."

"What the hell are *they* doing in my hotel room?" Brautigan demanded, realizing that he was not in a bed at all but lying on a hospital examination table. He jumped off of the table, prepared to wrestle himself back into his dream, or punch his way out of this nightmare, or whatever was necessary for him to regain that sense of peace that had saturated his being just seconds earlier. But instead of punching or kicking Malcolm, his adversaries assaulted him only with stares at his mid-section and, from Yazzie, a barely muffled laugh. He was naked. He was also in a vivid state of arousal. He fell to the ground and wrapped himself up in a fetal position, as much to cover himself as to block out the emotional trauma of being uprooted from a pleasant dream. His head pounded and something squirmed in his skull. "Oh God, oh God," he muttered. "The wasp eggs are hatching."

"That's the tranquilizer," Ivanova said, warmly. "We haven't worked out all the kinks. But if you relax and just go with it, it's not unpleasant."

Brautigan relaxed, for a moment, before tensing up again. "What the hell's going on? Never mind. I know what's going on. This is a big set up. You can come clean. Peter can come out from wherever he's hiding. I saw you in the canyon. I know you're all working together. I don't know why, yet, but I'm sure I'll figure that one out."

"Slow down, Malcolm," Eliza said. "I don't know what they put in that tranquilizer they shot you with, but you're talking crazy right now. There's no conspiracy—"

"Okay, then why were you talking to Peter in the canyon just a minute ago? Or yesterday? Or … what day is it, anyway? How long was I out? When do I get to go back to Winslow? What the hell are these things on my head?"

"We weren't talking to Peter. We were talking to this lady" — motioning toward Ivanova — "and her doctor friend, Nutbalm."

At that, a man walked in the door, tall, thin, and looking a lot like Peter might if he were eighty years old. "Nussbaum is the name, thank you," he said in a sonorous voice. For what seemed like the first time in hours, Brautigan remembered to breathe. Eliza, Lisa, and Tasha Ivanova looked at him, expectantly. He was overcome with something like fatigue, but more like a yearning to turn the clock back to the moments before Eliza had called so that he could go throw his own telephone into a gaping pit mine just as Ted Denton had done.

"We'll leave you alone, now," Ivanova said. "Those things on your head are sensors. The tranquilizer is experimental, and we're monitoring its aftereffects. Please ignore them. We'll be eating in an hour or so."

With their captors out of the room Eliza wrapped her arms around Malcolm and forcefully hugged him, then pointed to his clothes, folded neatly on a white countertop. He put them back on, noticing that everything was intact, even his backpack and the few items he had put in there — minus the bear spray.

She filled him in on what had happened after they had parted ways at the fork in the canyon some eight hours earlier. Lisa and Eliza had walked up the canyon bottom, chatting all the while, mostly about settler-colonialism, and art, and Eliza's time-spring theory, and what the hell it was they were looking for out here, and also scanning the slopes on either side of them for signs of a mine or a cabin. So intent had they been on their conversation and their observations that they had walked right into the arms of Nutbalm and Ivanova, who somehow knew that they'd be there. Ivanova acted frantic, and told them that her people had found Peter and he was in trouble and that Eliza needed to accompany her in order to get him help. The whole thing seemed sketchy, but Eliza couldn't exactly decline, because if she did so and Peter died, she'd be complicit in his demise, a scenario that would probably lead to years of therapy for both Adriana and her, which she could not afford, since the library's insurance plan didn't cover mental health. Armed guards had then emerged from the trees, detained Lisa and Eliza, blindfolded them, and brought them here.

"Where is here? And what do they want from us?"

"We don't know, but it seems like we're underground. There are no windows."

"They want us out of the way," said Yazzie. "They know we know what they're up to, and they don't want us to tell the world. These people are not messing around. And no one knows we're out here. My aunt must be freaking out right now."

"*Do* we know what they're up to?" Santos asked.

Brautigan looked at the little camera embedded into the ceiling of the room. He pulled a pen from his pocket — he always carried one and they hadn't taken it from him — and wrote something on his hand, then opened his palm for his friends, but not the camera, to see. It said, "TIME TRAVEL."

"Oh, come on, Malcolm, seriously?"

Brautigan whispered, his face turned away from the camera. "Haven't you even looked at Nutbalm? That's not some doctor, it's Peter. The resemblance is uncanny. He went into the future and now he's like eighty years old or something."

"No, no, no, you dummies, time travel doesn't work like that," Lisa said. "You don't get older, you get younger relative to everyone else when you travel through time. If Nutbalm is Peter, then *we* traveled through time."

"In case you were wondering where you are," Ivanova said, "you're deep underground, in the Moenkopi formation. You probably know it as the Acme Queen mine."

"So that's it," said Malcolm. "You are mining uranium, and the tar sands project was just a smoke screen. But that means we're probably surrounded by uranium and radium and have radioactive rays blasting us as we speak. Thanks a lot."

"No, on both counts. We are not mining uranium, at least not here. And we are not in any danger down here thanks to Dr. Nussbaum and the Boradine he developed."

"Nussbaum's into uranium enrichment. My brother told me. And he also knows we're out here. So don't think you're going to get away with this."

"I've heard good things about your brother. We could use someone like him. And you are correct. Nussbaum is also the world's pre-eminent authority on fuels for nuclear reactors and, for that matter, bombs. But a moral man can only tolerate the horrors wrought by the uranium industry, particularly in Navajo country, for so long. So he developed Boradine, which renders uranium and its daughters impotent, which is, by far, his greatest achievement. Thus far."

Brautigan, Santos, and Yazzie stood stunned and silent. Ivanova continued: "The doctor has, essentially, stolen Prometheus's fire back from humans and returned it to the gods. As you can imagine, his colleagues are not happy about it, which is why there was all of that commotion after he went missing. They will kill him if they find him. Now, let's eat. Shall we?"

"Wait," said Yazzie. "You said 'thus far'. What did you mean?"

"I'm sorry?"

"About Nussbaum. You said it was his greatest achievement thus far."

"Ahhh, yes. Excellent question. I'm afraid I can't answer it, yet. But trust me. You'll know it when you see it." She paused. "And in anticipation of your next question: You are here because, as much as it may pain us to say so, we need you. Particularly Mr. Brautigan. No more questions, please."

Ivanova escorted them into the dining room of the complex, an elegantly set table in its center. The trio sat down and, moments later, two security goons, badly disguised as waiters, entered the room with two plates, which they set down in front of Yazzie and Santos. "For the ladies, slow cooked lamb, a fresh, heirloom cherry tomato salad, with buffalo mozzarella made in western Colorado, and bruschetta with a white bean spread. I believe it will be very familiar to Ms. Santos."

"My wedding meal," Santos said, her face going pale.

Brautigan, however, was not at all disturbed by the coincidence, and literally salivated in anticipation when the waiter returned with a third plate for him. The plate was the same as the two women's, but the stuff on it was quite different. Instead of lamb and tomatoes, Brautigan was given a can of Vienna sausages, a jiggly cube of green Jell-O with shredded carrots inside, and a biscuit that looked like it came out of a can and was cooked in margarine.

"Look familiar?"

"Ha ha. Unfortunately, yes. That's my aunt's 'salad,' and my dad's campfire biscuits, and our old camping lunch standby. It's really not funny."

"Oh, it's not meant to be. The good news is, it pairs fabulously with this." She unveiled a bottle of 1982 Montrachet and poured it not into a wineglass, but a coffee mug. Malcolm had tasted this wine once before. He took a sip and swirled it around on his tongue. He would have liked to say that he tasted the terroir, but instead all he tasted was that solstice night so long ago. Ivanova looked down at a computer tablet she was holding, then back at Brautigan, smiling in a way that made his loins tingle.

"I get it," Eliza said, pushing her plate away. "She's trying to Proust us. Trying to spark memories with food. Well, well, well. Tasha here doesn't know where the Happy Bonanza is, and she thinks Malcolm's going to lead her to it."

Ivanova smiled. "Something like that, yes."

"Forget it. He won't do it. And what's with serving me my wedding meal? Is this some kind of last supper deal?"

"Hey, ahh, Eliza?" Brautigan said, interrupting. "Are you gonna eat all of that? Because …"

"Perhaps it's to stir up some warm feelings for your husband, with whom you will be reunited soon. As soon as we get to the HB235, that is."

"*You* know where Peter is?"

"As I said …"

"And why are you so interested in the mine, anyway? I thought you said Nussbaum's Boradine rendered uranium impotent?"

"You are a feisty one, aren't you. I do see why Malcolm is so smitten. I'm interested in the HB235 because it belonged to my grandfather. I had expected Malcolm to make the connection by now."

Brautigan's eyes grew wide. "You're Hildebrandt's granddaughter?"

"That is correct. My mother was Ruthie Hildebrandt-Hendricks. She spent a rather tragic portion of her childhood in the same house in which you grew up, Malcolm. She died two years ago, and I inherited the claim. My grandfather was on the brink of developing that claim, and getting at the richest deposit of uranium on the planet. He could have changed the course of history, and perhaps saved the planet, with that. Unfortunately his dream was cut short by his untimely murder. Now I'm picking up where he left off."

"Murder? But I thought ..."

"You don't really think that an intelligent man would tie his safety rope to the bumper of his car and then toss the keys down to his wife so she could drive it to the grocery store, do you?"

"But why?"

"This deposit alone would have been able to fuel all the nation's nuclear reactors and its warheads for years and years, and all without milling or enrichment. People were willing to kill for it then, just as they are now." Ivanova walked over to a cabinet, opened it, pulled out an e-book reader, and put it on the table in front of Brautigan. He picked it up and turned it on, and the title page of his novel, back from oblivion once again, shone back at him.

"Where the hell did you get this? Are you the one who —" He was cut off by an under-the-table kick and silencing glare from Eliza. He paused, scooted his chair so he was out of Eliza's range, and continued. "You Prousted me already. You've been Prousting me all along, haven't you? The martini in Winslow, the riddle. You sent it, didn't you? Admit it."

"It doesn't matter who sent it," Tasha said, her composure crinkling for the first time. "I suggest you read the novel tonight, particularly pages thirty-six and four-fifty-two. And next time you write a novel? Make it shorter. Now, we all need some rest. We have a big day ahead of us tomorrow. And as a show of good faith, we're going to go ahead and send Ms. Yazzie home tonight. She is smart enough, I presume, not to bother going to the sheriff or any other law enforcement. Not that they'd believe her, anyway, considering most of them work for us."

Two men walked in and led Yazzie out of the room. She didn't resist, but at the doorway she turned and looked Eliza in the eyes. "Beware of the Bone Seekers," she said. Then she was gone.

Project Petrichor

Full-spectrum lights, embedded in every wall, the floor, and the ceiling, gradually illuminated to full power, mimicking the rising sun. Simulated sounds of a southeastern Utah morning filled the air, easing Eliza and Malcolm from their slumber. During the night, Malcolm's recurring childhood dreams had returned for the first time in decades, and were so vivid and potent that waking was a relief, for it meant he could finally rest. Their clothes were waiting on a side table, freshly laundered, and a hunky guy came in with coffee and oatmeal, prompting snide remarks from Eliza. They were then led through what seemed like miles of gleaming white hallways. Occasionally windows broke up the otherwise seamless walls, giving a glance into control rooms, with people in white lab coats turning chunky dials, reading analog meters, pushing big lit up buttons. In one, Brautigan glimpsed a large, red button that said "SCRAM" below it. A door had the words "SILVER IODIDE" on it.

"What the hell *is* this place?" Eliza asked. "Are we in an old James Bond movie set?"

Their meaty minder wore the same tactical clothing as the security contractors on the outside, but instead of saying "CLEARWATER," theirs read "СНЯГ," which Brautigan tried to decipher by reading from right to left, to no avail. The minder instructed them to board a squat but wide, enclosed, and windowless vehicle. It rumbled along for an indeterminate amount of time, during which Eliza took it upon herself to remind Malcolm about their previous night's conversation. She forbade him from even looking at the novel. He was to clear his memory of any thoughts of the Happy Bonanza, or Frank Hildebrandt, or anything else, for that matter, so that he would not inadvertently lead their captors to their destination and, apparently, Eliza's husband.

"I don't understand what the problem is, Eliza," Malcolm had pleaded. "We want to find Peter. And Tasha's motives are obviously not that sinister. This whole Boradine thing sounds alright to me. And besides, I think she kinda liked my novel, though I do wonder why she didn't just give me back the hard copy. I don't much like e-books."

"Don't be daft. That's all some sort of ruse. Why would someone go through all the trouble to find this uranium deposit if it's only to render it impotent? It makes no sense. You heard what she said: People will kill for this. They'll kill us. As soon as we find the Happy Bonanza, we will become liabilities, and they'll get rid of us. They have no choice."

"You've been watching too many damned movies, Eliza."

"Oh really? Then what about the other night? Someone tried to kill us, remember? And it had to be Tasha. Where else would she have gotten your novel?"

"She doesn't seem like a murderer, but okay, I get your point," Brautigan said, listlessly. "How the hell am I supposed to clear my mind?"

"For you, it shouldn't take much."

The vehicle came to an abrupt halt. The back door swung open, and blinding morning sunlight splashed the two in the eyes. There was no sign of the Acme Queen, or whatever it was in which they had spent the night. Ivanova and Nussbaum waited along with a woman — the same one who had been with Tasha back at Winslow — her dark brown hair pulled back tightly into a ponytail. She wore tactical gear, also emblazoned with "СНЯГ," and rose-tinted aviator sunglasses. She carried a long, minimalist rifle that resembled those used by biathletes. Her name-badge said, "Ace."

"Good morning," Ivanova said, holding up her phone so that the screen was only about six inches from Brautigan's still-unadjusted eyes. A video showed Lisa Yazzie being dropped off at her car, getting inside, starting it, and driving off. "Your friend is safe and sound, just like we said. Now, let's go."

"Fine," said Brautigan. "But first can you take these damned sensor things off of my head? I'm pretty sure the tranquilizer has worn off by now."

Tasha Ivanova smiled back at him wanly. "I'm afraid not, Malcolm. Take us to the Happy Bonanza. Please."

Brautigan smiled back at her. Memories were coming hard and fast into his brain, but he didn't need to meditate or perform any mind erasure, because none of them had anything to do with the Happy Bonanza. So he chose a direction randomly and walked, aiming vaguely for the head of Bonanza Canyon, which is where the dirtbag crew had been headed a few days earlier. If Brautigan could get their attention, maybe they'd get help or provide a diversion that would allow Brautigan and Santos to escape.

The going was slow, mainly because everyone in the quintet — even the steely-eyed para-military guard — was intent on not stepping on the cryptobiotic soil. That allowed Brautigan to focus on the stream of recollections storming his mind. Whatever Tasha had Prousted him with, it was effective. Nearly everything he saw or smelled conjured up something new: The scent of piñon took him back to that time he and Peter had sat on a rock and ate a whole pound of piñon nuts they had bought from a booth beside the road, and the sight of a cholla cactus brought him painfully back to that time he'd collided with one while running through the desert in New Mexico.

"I'm a little disoriented," Malcolm said. "Can I go climb up on those rocks over there and get my bearings? I won't run."

"I know you won't," she said, glancing toward Ace.

A bit of a breeze cooled him as he stood up on the outcrop, and he took a long draw of water from the tube dangling obscenely from his backpack. He took the backpack off and rifled around inside of it, taking inventory of the energy bars and drinks the folks back at the Acme Queen had provided. He was relieved to find, in an interior pocket, the bracelet he had bought a couple days earlier from Chester Tsosie. He still didn't know what he was going to do with it, but it seemed somehow important that he have it with him, particularly now, particularly with the trials that surely lay ahead of Eliza and him.

As he put his pack back on, a familiar and horrifying sound, a fluttering buzz, rippled through the air: a tarantula hawk. Reflexively, he ducked and started slapping the back of his neck, which only made his dart-wound hurt more, before realizing his buzzy tormentor wasn't a tarantula hawk at all, but a quadcopter drone, hovering before him at eye level.

He looked back to see if his companions had noticed. They hadn't. And with the cicadas screeching at high volume, they wouldn't hear it, either. The camera swiveled up and down, as if signaling him. Then the copter tilted back and forth and spun around. He waved awkwardly, not knowing what else to do, which the drone seemed to take as a signal to depart, and it zoomed off in the same direction from which it came.

"Well?" said Ivanova, when he had rejoined the others.

"It looks right to me," Brautigan said. "Let's go."

Big, chunky clouds had been gathering above them all morning. Now they were really piling up, getting darker and gathering a violence-portending texture, wisps of smoky-white mist roiling around against a slate-grey, curdling background of cloud upon cloud upon cloud. Winds kicked up, too, gusty, swirling winds that turned everyone's hair into the tubular air-dancers that grace every roadside jerky and chainsaw-carving stand in the West. It was a good day to stay low, so as not to make oneself a lightning rod, but not down-in-the-canyons low, where a well-targeted cloudburst could send thousands of cubic feet of water between the sandstone walls, pummeling all in its path. "We've got to hurry," Ivanova said, rushing ahead but smiling broadly, reveling in the drama playing out above, "before the electricity begins."

Brautigan laughed out loud, not only at her stilted choice of words, but also at the storm itself, at the way the warm wind caressed his face and his thighs, at the energy in the air, at the vaguely electric smell, and at the premonition that something magnificent and threatening awaited just over the next rise or around the next bend. The first flicker of lightning somewhere over the Abajos lit up the landscape, revealing a giant medtal needle emerging from a juniper tree atop a nearby ridge. The flash of electricity also revealed people or ghosts or spirits lurking all around the group.

Brautigan tried to walk close to Eliza, so that they could make a plan, but she and Nussbaum leaned into one another, conversing. So Malcolm ended up walking next to Ivanova, instead. He tried to ease the discomfort with small talk.

"So, um, how'd you meet your husband, anyway?"

"We worked together. He liked me. I liked his money. We got married."

"Any kids?"

She turned and squinted at him, as if calculating something, and the skin bunched up around her eyes in that sexy way again. She glanced at the screen of her phone and the sides of her mouth turned up subtly. "A son. He's twelve."

"Must be hard to raise a kid these days. The earth is going to be uninhabitable by the time he's ready for his midlife crisis, if he doesn't get gunned down in the meantime by some gun-toting maniac."

"He's in Switzerland. In boarding school. They don't have to worry about guns over there. Besides, it was scary when we were that age, too. We had AIDS, the looming threat of nuclear holocaust. Remember that one?"

"But that was all in the future. A possibility yet to be realized. Now the future has arrived and it's almost as bad as we'd feared. Climate change isn't just a looming possibility, it's already upon us. The diagnosis is in and the planet has cancer and there is no cure, just a slow descent into the fire."

"If you weren't so grim you might have more luck with the ladies, you know? Besides, who said there isn't a cure?"

Malcolm tried to come up with a rejoinder, but failed. He was too caught up in his own musings to realize that she was leading the way, rather than him. "So, what's the deal with Stan Hatch? Is he your boss, or what?"

"Not exactly. Stan Hatch, and his buddy Albert Fallon still believe they've been clearing the way for Fry Canyon Energy's big project."

"What *are* they clearing the way for?"

"Don't be stupid."

She was silent for a moment, looked Brautigan in the eye, then seemed to make up her mind about something. "Do you know what the HB235 is all about?"

"It's a big fat deposit of weapon-grade uranium. Or so your grandfather seemed to think."

"Exactly. And do you have any idea what Saudi Arabia will pay for that material? Or Iran? Or ISIS? It's like Nescafe for nuclear bombs."

"So you're going to sell this to Saudi Arabia? So they can, what? Nuke Israel?"

"Is that how you think of me? As some sort of ecocidal maniac?" She smiled as she said it. "And here I thought you fancied me. Perhaps I'm the one who's going to keep this out of the wrong hands."

"And who might that be?"

"Stan Hatch, maybe. Not that he's that capable. More worrisome is someone named Ivan Ivanov. Perhaps you've heard of him?"

"Your husband."

"Exactly."

"Trouble in Paradise, eh?"

"I prefer to think of it as diverging life visions."

"So you're trying to find the HB235 to keep it away from your own husband? You've gone rogue?"

"I suppose you could say that, yes. Only he doesn't know that. He thinks we're working together on this. And that we're actually going to mine tar sands. He can be a little dense at times, particularly when money's involved. And with him, money's always involved."

"If you don't want him getting his hands on this stuff, then why don't you just go to the feds or the cops?"

"You don't seem to understand how our system works, Malcolm. Your statement is predicated upon the delusion that there is a clear dividing line between my husband's holdings and the federal government. There is not. Perhaps you're familiar with Clearwater Incorporated and their work and their contracts with various branches of the government? What you may not know is that, via proxies, of course, my husband is the majority stockholder in

OmnySyde Holdings, Clearwater's parent company. Think of him as a cancer cell embedded in this nation's bones, slowly spreading and taking over all of its organs. Those few branches of the government that he hasn't infiltrated, he will purchase. Just as he did with Secretary Fallon and, of course, the presidents. Besides, I have my own plans for the material."

"You're going to build your own bomb?"

"Of course not. I'm going to use it to save the planet, Malcolm. And you can pat yourself and your alter-ego Juan on the back for playing a little part by writing that story about Fallon and our mutual friend Stan Hatch. They had served their purpose, and you helped push them out of the way at just the right moment. It could have gotten messy."

"Save the planet? With nuclear power, I take it? You sound like my brother. Is that why you sent your goons to question him?"

"What goons? What are you talking about?"

"My brother, Joshua. Your Clearwater people put him in a room and interrogated him about the Happy Bonanza. He's not too psyched about it, either."

Tasha smiled, as if Malcolm had told her a joke. Then her countenance grew cloudy. She grabbed Malcolm's bicep with a tight grip. "Clearwater people? Are you sure?"

"That's what Joshua said, and that guy's a stickler for details. So, yeah, I'm sure."

"No. No, no, no. That means that ... Oh my God." She motioned to the guard, Ace, who had been trailing them by about ten meters the whole time. The woman approached, and Tasha whispered something to her that Brautigan couldn't hear. Ace stepped back, swung the rifle from her shoulder, and scanned the horizon. She started to say something, but was cut off by a sharp sound, like a branch snapping, followed by a deep thud. An instant later Ace was on the ground, moaning.

"Argggh," she groaned. "I've been shot. Down, get down!"

"Down! Everyone down!" Ivanova repeated. With frightening speed, Ivanova reached out with her right arm and crossed it over Malcolm's chest and knocked his legs out from under him with her foot, causing him to plop hard onto the dirt. Then she fell on top of him.

"What's going on?" Eliza, who had taken cover behind a yucca, cried out.

"We're under fire," hissed Tasha. "Ivan's on to us. Fuck, fuck, fuck. It was one of his men who shot Ace."

"I'm good," said Ace, through gasps. "It hit my vest. Fucker's gonna leave a hell of a bruise on my boob, though. Ow."

"Snow-Five, throw us cover. We're on the move," Tasha barked into her earpiece. "Project Petrichor is a go. Engage Charlie Sierra, target three-seven-six-eight-eight-two, ionization cloud at thirty-three percent. Repeat. Project Petrichor is a go."

A haze of confusion enveloped Brautigan. He no longer knew what was real, and what his mind had fabricated. The sun still loitered overhead like a bad houseguest, but it was obscured by a thick cloud cover that cast a dusky pall over the land, broken only by flashes from lightning leaping through the clouds. Gauzy sheets of grey dangled from the clouds and brushed against the high aspen- and oak-covered slopes of Elk Ridge.

"We need to move. Now! Get up, but stay low."

"But I don't know where to go!"

"It's that way," Tasha yelled. "Over the top of that rise. Go!"

"But if you know where it is, then what am I doing here?"

"Because Peter thought it would be better this way, would help stimulate your memory. I'll explain later. Let's go. Now. There is danger everywhere."

"Peter? Did you just say Peter?"

Nussbaum powered up the side of the ridge like someone half his age, Santos followed close behind, Brautigan and Ivanova taking up the rear. At the rim, Brautigan paused and turned around, trying to process it all and failing. The drone was back, hovering just out of earshot. In the distance, a vehicle's headlights bounced in their direction, and then those of another, and another. The curtains of rain moved closer, along with the lightning. Soon, it would reach them. He turned around and followed the others to the inevitable end.

Beautiful Bones

They tore across the mesa top, pausing at the edge of the deep and narrow tributary of Leetso Canyon to marvel at the spectacle before them. Directly across the canyon, etched deeply into the shiny desert varnish, was a perfect spiral, a seemingly infinite line looping around and around and back on itself.

Below the spiral was an alcove where plaster walls with tiny, dark windows nestled, a place where a family, maybe two or three, had lived centuries prior, probably staying for a few generations at least, building on as the family grew, growing corn up on the mesa top, seeking shade in the canyon's bottom. Not a bad place to make an existence, Brautigan thought. And as good a place as any for your existence to cease, too. He turned around and saw the cabin, just as he'd remembered it. Walls made of quarried sandstone. A tiny window that mirrored those on the cliff dwelling. And a shingled roof with a jagged line down the middle where the shingles changed colors.

The sky lit up. A spaceship hovered above. Only it wasn't really a spaceship, but a hologram projected onto the low clouds. It had to be Peter's artwork, and it wasn't a nuclear bomb. Eliza almost giggled with relief.

That's not to say that she immediately recognized what the hologram depicted. A white circle, albeit not a perfect one, that contained a grayish, variegated substance, with bright white spots scattered throughout. An aerial view of a bowl of soup? A polluted lake? A sonar image of the rich uranium deposit lurking somewhere nearby? The image faded into a giant, leafless cottonwood tree, which morphed into a map of the human nervous system, which then transformed into a mushroom cloud. The projection faded again into another that resembled the first in color and tone, and that was shaped a bit like the mushroom cloud: a cross section of the MRI scan of a human neck and head. There was the skull, bright white, and inside it the brain, the sky visible through it. And within the brain a smattering of smaller, white dots, like stars, but not.

Warm dry wind wafted through the air and hair. There was no rain on the Happy Bonanza, but they could see and smell the downpour just a half mile up canyon. The first pulse of the flash flood far below roared, the roiling water carrying rocks and sticks and mud and carcasses and all the other detritus that had built up in the wash bed since the last rain, so long ago.

"Malcolm?" Ivanova said. "If you could go back and change just one thing, what would it be?"

"Seriously?" Brautigan said, immediately recognizing the slogan from the Winslow billboard. "My last words are going to be about regret, eh?" He had become convinced that these were his final moments among the quick. Now that they had found Hildebrandt's Hideout, Tasha would kill him. And if she didn't, then her husband's troops would. In his fatigue he didn't fear death. Yet he also wasn't ready to stop living, and this sure as hell wasn't how he wanted to go. He peered down at the raging torrent in the canyon and inched himself toward the precipice. A big log made its way toward them. If he could just time his leap right he could ride that thing down the canyon like he and Peter once had done in the icy waters of the Animas River, or like Slim Pickens astride the nuke in *Dr. Strangelove*. He'd perish, of course, but it least he'd be doing what he loved, right? "Well," he said, "since you asked, I suppose I would have jumped onto the back of Peter's Vespa way back when."

"Vespa?" replied a voice that did not belong to Tasha. "I never had a Vespa."

Malcolm spun around to find himself face to face with his old friend, Peter Simons. Peter looked terrible. His face was gaunt, his cheeks sunken, but his eyes still had that manic energy to them.

"Peter! I missed you, man. No, I just meant that I should have gone with you. To New York. You only regret what you don't do, am I right?"

Peter grinned: "I'm not so sure about that anymore. It's good to see you. I'm so glad you're here."

Brautigan, forgetting about the danger, motioned to the sky, "Is this the, uh, art piece you've been working on?"

"Not exactly," Peter said in a near-whisper. "I'd love to catch up, but we have work to do, and time's running out."

"We?"

"You, really." Peter motioned toward Hildebrandt's Hideout. "You have to go now. Please. Go to the cabin and let the memories flow. The art needs you. The planet needs you. Tasha will explain everything later."

Brautigan didn't say anything. The words were all gone. Instead, he stepped away from the cliff and reached into his pocket and pulled out the bracelet that Chester Tsosie had made and handed it to Peter. Then, trancelike, without understanding why, he walked to the cabin. From behind him Eliza called out, saying something that, inexplicably, made him laugh: "Peter. It's you, isn't it? It's your head up there in the sky."

Monster Slayers

Below the window of the cabin a voluminous sacred datura plant, its dusky viridescent leaves more suited to a jungle than a desert, grew against the stone wall. One of its concupiscent blossoms had just opened, exuding a haunting odor, and a big bumblebee wallowed around drunkenly inside, its fuzz coated with yellow dust. Brautigan plucked the flower free from the plant, folded the bee into the petals, and put the white, silky package into his mouth. He held it there, savoring the bitter and sweet, the soft and silky, the buzz against his tongue. He chewed slowly and deliberately.

He walked to the cabin's doorway. The exterior dimensions must have been about twelve-by-fifteen feet, but inside it seemed to stretch on forever. The walls of the single room were bare except for the door and small windows on each wall. Darkness had seeped into the mesas and stones outside, broken only by distant flashes of lightning. In the cabin, warm, dim light — rose-colored and blue, lavender and green — came from everywhere and nowhere all at once, flooding every surface of the interior, as if it were a James Turrell installation. The light not only was tangible, but also he could taste it, smell it, roll it around inside his eyes like a piece of hard candy.

On the far side of the room a figure sat silently in a beat up old chair, cigarette in one hand, plastic cup in the other, gazing out the window at something that Brautigan was unable to see. Brautigan walked slowly toward the man in the chair, whom he knew was his father, dead for fifteen years now.

A world sits between the one in which we operate on a daily basis, and the one that we inhabit only in our dreams. This is the world of the artists and the poets, the mentally deranged and the psychics, the moths that fly too close to the flame. Brautigan had stumbled into a waypoint in this world, a gathering place for its inhabitants, and since he is no poet nor artist, neither dancer nor musician, he simply can't express what he witnessed there with any accuracy. But he will tell you, if you ask him, that the experience that night confirmed Eliza Santos' theory of time.

Malcolm sat down in a tattered lawn chair and filled a plastic tumbler from the box of white wine from which his father drank. Even dead he still had the furnishings of a transient, and was still drinking that cheap swill. His father leaned over and whispered something in Brautigan's ear.

"I know, dad. I know. I'm sorry, too."

"Words have weight." Malcolm's father said, "Be your words. Love the world. Be the flame."

"Like Peter? Well, guess what, the world's dying …"

"… and growing more beautiful every day."

Malcolm silently cursed his father. What did he know, anyway? He who didn't have to worry about paying the rent, or the insurance premium, or student loan payments. He who would never have to figure out how Tinder works.

"I wish I knew how to do that. All of that."

"You do. You always have. It's just around the corner, kiddo. Look! Look! There it is. See it?"

Malcolm leaned back in the lawn chair, causing it to squeak under the strain, and closed his eyes. Images spilled across the darkness of his mind, memories and imaginings and the two intertwined:

He is young, cuddled up in his sleeping bag, and first he sees his breath rising up above his face. Then the stars, scattered across the big blue bowl like shards of broken glass. Then the outlines of the bare branches of the cottonwood above him, achingly reaching out for the sky in a way that makes him think of the pictures of the human circulatory system.

A few embers still glow in the campfire, but the flames died a while ago. Two lawn chairs sit empty, the pile of beer cans next to each glimmering in the light of the stars. The silence is enough to make his ears ache. He sits up. His brother is asleep beside him, but the other sleeping bags are empty. The car is gone, too.

"Papa?".

Silence.

"Paapaaa! Where are you?"

Joshua sits up sleepily and lightly punches him in the arm. "Be quiet, Malcolm. They just went out to get more beer. They'll be back soon."

"What if they crash? Or get arrested?"

"They won't! There's no one on these roads."

The dark outline of Comb Ridge. The sliver of light where the new highway slices through the giant wave of stone. Joshua climbs out of his sleeping bag and walks over to the fire, puts a few branches on the coals, and crouches down and blows on the places that glow. Smoke rises, then flame. Malcolm gets out of his bag and sits down in his dad's lawn chair and leans over the flames.

"How about a story?" Joshua says. "You know that old shack where we holed up today? That was all that's left of Frank Hildebrandt's secret uranium mine, the Happy Bonanza."

Now they are walking. The world is pink. The world is white. Giant snowflakes fall all around. Malcolm's throat hurts so bad he can barely swallow. He wants to stop.

His dad says, "Just around the next corner, kiddo, just around the next corner."

Up ahead, in a wall of rock, sits a cliff dwelling, a stone palace sitting in a bubble of stone, windows like dark eyes staring back. "C'mon," Joshua says, "let's check it out. We can start a fire there and get warm."

"No, Joshua," their dad says, not wanting to disturb the dead. "The cabin."

It's no warmer inside than out, but it's dry. Malcolm sits against a wall and shivers while his dad puts a pile of twigs on the dirt floor and lights a match. He pulls an empty Fanta can from his pack and fills it with water, and then adds the Mormon tea he had picked from a bush outside and boils the water.

The tea is bitter, but the heat feels good on Malcolm's throat. Bees buzz behind his eyeballs.

"This is a story about Coyote and the Yellow Monster, and his terrible daughters, the Bone Seekers," his dad says, but when Malcolm looks back at him he sees Peter, and Greg Whitman, and Coyote, his piñon pitch eyes liquefying in the heat of the fire. He tries to scream but is instead transported to the backyard of his home in Durango. Frank Hildebrandt's home, too. The stars are scattered all over the sky and yellow light spills out of the back door. Voices spill out, too — one loud, unrestrained, and wracked by sobs. The other calm and quiet and cold. She tells him to quiet down, he'll wake up Malcolm.

He really screams then, "I am Malcolm. I am Malcolm, and my wife is in love with another man."

Malcolm feels every word, every curse, every sob, every weep, every fist, every dish hitting a wall and shattering, the shards raining down on the dirty linoleum floor. Every sound banging on the inside of his skull.

It goes calm then, tranquil. All the noise has softened. He is no longer in the sleeping bag on the cool grass. He is floating above, looking down at the boy and the adults as if they are all a movie that don't concern him. He steps onto the roof, right at the place where the shingles go strange, and goes inside the roof to the place where the mannequins live. The mother of the mannequins is there, telling him it's better up here, far away from the earth. Then she points to a place on the wall, down near the floor. Something's written there. Numbers. Before he can read them he is back in Comb Wash, in his sleeping bag, morning sun blasting over Comb Ridge, the sound of coffee perking, and the smell of canned corned beef hash and biscuits cooking up in bubbly squeeze-margarine in a blackened pot on the campfire. The car is back, sitting near camp. There is a long scratch down its side, a prickly pear hangs from the radiator grill along with clumps of root and dirt. A piece of sagebrush dangles from one of the side mirrors.

"What happened to the car, papa?"

"The monsters got it, kiddo. We were coming down the dugway and got attacked by the Great White Coyote, the Man with the Golden Arm, and the Waterbabies, all at once. But we escaped. It's all okay now. Everything's okay. We are here."

"Are we really? Are we really ever anywhere?"

Malcolm smiles as his father hands him a mug of hot chocolate, the steam rising up from the sweet liquid almost thick enough to touch. On the side of the mug are the same numbers that were on the wall of the house. Zero six three zero one nine six four. Zero six three zero one nine six four, zero six three zero one nine six four ...

A light flashed, and Tasha Ivanova's voice echoed in his head or in the cabin or off the canyon walls outside: "That's it. Thank you, Malcolm." Then he snapped out of the trance.

Brautigan looked back at his father for some explanation, but the chair was empty, his father gone, the butt of his cigarette still smoking in the ashtray on the arm of the chair. Brautigan stood up, sat down in his father's chair, poured himself another glass of wine from the tattered box, and peered out the window. Maybe he understood, maybe he didn't.

Figures moved frantically on the slope outside the cabin and as he watched, a mine portal opened in the blank cliff face. Peter perked up and motioned to the others to move quickly.

Bone Seekers

This wasn't the entirety of the artwork. It couldn't be. It surely was merely a prelude. For the work contained nothing but despair, and Peter had been so adamant about inspiring some kind of hope with his art. Eliza began looking around frantically for the artist, who was also — she understood with a sinking feeling that threatened to collapse her — the artist's subject. He was his own canvas. She spotted him standing next to Malcolm and Tasha Ivanova, at the edge of the canyon.

"Oh, Peter," she said, walking briskly in his direction. "It's you, isn't it? It's your head up there in the sky."

He smiled sadly, barely nodding in the affirmative. "The Bone Seekers got me. Nasty little bitches." Peter's voice was hollow, like his cheeks and eyes.

"How long have you known?" Her voice had lost its softness, and had taken on the more familiar tone of disappointment, concern, and judgment.

"How long?" He talked slowly, with long pauses. "All my life, maybe. Or six months. Who can say? I kept telling myself it was nothing. A bug. Not enough coffee. But I always knew it would come to this."

"And you didn't tell me? You didn't ask me what I thought? Instead you just, just leave without telling anyone to come out here and … and do what, exactly?"

"I'm sorry, Eliza. I'm not that strong. I've never been strong enough for you. And besides, I'm terrible at goodbyes."

"You're terrible at a lot of things."

"I know I am. I'm sorry."

"That's not what I meant. I'm sorry, too, Peter. I know I'm difficult to live with. I know. I know that. I'll try to be better."

"You're not so easy to die with, either, you know." Peter laughed again, before nearly collapsing into a coughing spasm.

"That's not funny. You'll come back now, now that this is over. Whatever *this* is."

"I can't."

"Adriana?"

"I said goodbye to her already."

"You told her?"

"She knows. She's more percipient than you think."

"She thinks you're out here making meth, like that television show."

"Yes, exactly. I'll miss her so goddamned much. I tried." Peter's pallid face was shiny with tears.

"I know you did, I know."

"It's better this way."

"No Peter. No it's not. Come home."

"Your hair is standing straight up, Eliza, like in the cartoons." He snickered, and when he did it brought up a moist cough. "It means we're running out of time. Alfred and Tasha need our help."

"Help with what, Peter? And who is Tasha, anyway? What is the art? Where? Those images projected on the clouds?"

"That's the eternal question, isn't it?" Peter started moving slowly toward Ivanova and Nussbaum, who stood near a blank cliff face, as if searching for some secret message held within the desert varnish. "Look beyond the images to what's behind them. That is the art."

"The clouds? The storm? What?"

"Precisely. Malcolm has found his memories by now, and Tasha will have the code. You'll understand it all later."

As they approached the others, a dark square appeared on the cliff's face — an opening in the rock, the Happy Bonanza Mine — where there had been only a clean slate of stone moments earlier. The air crackled with electricity. Peter directed Eliza to pick up a dense block stacked neatly with several others outside the opening, and to heft it into the dark mine portal. She and Tasha dragged the ends of thick copper wires into the tunnel, and Nussbaum attached them to what looked like bowling pins sticking out of a platform. Bulbs dangled from the ceiling, dimly illuminating a machine made mostly of the black blocks, but with buttons and knobs and dials, too. It resembled something from a sci-fi flick from the fifties. Eliza went back out, grabbed the final block and carried it inside, adding it to the meticulously arranged pile. Nussbaum clipped wires to bobbins, turned dials, pushed a button. "We're ready. It was a pleasure to make your acquaintance, Eliza, I do wish I could have met you sooner. Peter? It's time."

"You have to go now, Eliza," said Peter, gently taking Eliza by the arm and leading her toward the mine opening. Tasha was already making her way down the slope. "Tell Adriana I love her, and that I'm sorry, and that all of this is for her, for her future. Tell Malcolm hey, too, and that Tasha will have the money for the collective."

"You know what Malcolm thinks that thing is?" Eliza asked, motioning toward the blocks in the darkness. "He thinks it's a time machine."

"It is, in a way," Peter laughed, coughing up more lung. "We are all time machines, Eliza. It's all just one big beautiful time machine."

Malcolm stood motionless in the doorway of the cabin and beheld the frantic scene outside. Lightning and rain and the roar of rushing water. Four figures running around, then Eliza and Peter stopping, speaking. Peter reaching out to touch Eliza's face, his own face shiny with tears as he backed into the portal.

Eliza and Tasha scrambled down the slope. Eliza stopped next to a blooming cliffrose, started back toward the mine, then froze, stuck between worlds. Tasha continued down the slope, stopping near the edge of the flooded gorge and tapped at her digital tablet, which illuminated her face. She spoke into the earpiece in a stern way, but at the same time she seemed calm, happy, as if things were going just as planned.

Brautigan gazed at her, a strange swelling feeling rising up from his belly into his chest. Maybe it was fear. Maybe desire. Maybe a little bit of both.

Tasha looked into her digital tablet again, and then turned her gaze toward Malcolm. She smiled warmly at him. He began to walk toward her but was halted by another lightning strike and eerie blue splashing across stone and trees and human figures darting about. One-one-thousand — CRACK-BOOM. Tasha, seemingly unperturbed by the violence in the sky, paused and looked up towards the mesa top as if to answer a question. Her eyes grew wide. Then her head jerked back. A rose bloomed on her cheek. She reached up slowly to caress its petals, a gesture of perplexity rather than pain. Blood trickled onto her chin and dribbled onto her white shirt, leaving a scarlet stain across her chest. She staggered backwards, fell to her knees, looked back toward Malcolm imploringly, and toppled sideways into the void and the roil and toil of the gorge. Brautigan screamed and leapt forward but was stilled by a blinding flash and a simultaneous peal of thunder that shook the depths of the stone. The light, bright like the sun, persisted. A hum, as if a hive full of bees had taken up residence inside Malcolm's skull.

Eliza was gone. Peter was gone. Nussbaum was gone. Ivanova was gone.

A hummingbird moth appeared from the darkness, and hovered over a glowing white datura flower. A whisper emanated from its blurred wings. It unfurled its proboscis and, like the final stanza of a perfect poem, pierced the flower's being, extracting sweet nectar, while leaving the blossom undisturbed.

Oh to be the moth's tropane-alkaloid dream.

Lightning Field

"Well, I'll be damned, you're alive!" Brautigan heard Sheriff Etcitty say this before he even had a chance to focus his vision enough to identify who said it. "Looked like you got struck by lightning. I was sure you were toast."

"How long have I ... ?"

"Hard to tell. Time seems a little strange around here. Come on, we gotta go check on your friend."

"Eliza? Is she okay? Is she in the mine?"

Brautigan got to his feet, his head spinning, and staggered toward the cabin door, Etcitty following close behind, ready to catch the younger man if he happened to fall. They hurried up the hill toward the mine — or rather toward the place in the side of the mesa where the mine portal had been. Now it was gone, seemingly erased. The big copper cables were blackened and frayed. The lightning-harvesting antenna up on the mesa top was busted in half, the top part dangling restlessly in the breeze.

"Oh, fuck," said Brautigan. "Eliza was in there when it blew. She's gone. Oh my god. Oh no."

"I don't think so," Etcitty said. "She should be right up ahead here, past this thicket of cliffrose, right where she was when the lightning hit."

Just behind the shrubs, Eliza Santos lay on warm sandstone, sleepily pondering a Spanish bayonet plant that was just inches from her face. She slowly sat up, looked up toward the mine, and sighed deeply when she saw nothing there. *"That* was a wild ride."

"We could have been vaporized, Eliza. And what about Peter? And Nussbaum? Where are they? We need to get a mine rescue team in here, pronto!"

"Peter's gone. He's on the other side by now. It's time to stop looking."

"The other side? Of what? This mesa? Is he dead?"

Instead of answering, Santos held her finger to her lips to shush Brautigan. The deep thud-thud of a helicopter echoed through the canyons. Brautigan and Santos looked around for places to take cover. "They're coming for us," Brautigan said. "Probably Clearwater. We've got to hide."

"No, no, it's okay," said Etcitty, looking up at the blue sky. "I called the chopper in to haul you two out of here. I'll call them off and have them shift over to looking for the tar sands lady. Or her body. Come on, let's get out of here. It's a long walk back to my vehicle."

"I guess it worked, right? Peter's project. He did it. He compressed the time spring and jumped back about thirty years. Fucking amazing. And he didn't even vaporize the rest of us. Here's what I'm thinking. The Peter of our time went back to, I don't know, the eighties, right? And then he went to Germany and changed his name to Nussbaum and studied physics. Then he got a job at Los Alamos, where he developed his Boradine, which is actually time travel juice. Then, last week, he went camping on Muley Point in order to connect with present day Peter to carry out his experiment at the HB235. I mean, this is the weird part: Nussbaum-Peter and our Peter co-existed. But it totally fits into your coil theory. I think. But it got hijacked by North Dakota, who kidnapped Nussbaum to coerce him into helping her with her bomb project."

"Peter's dead, Malcolm." Her voice was quiet, devoid of emotion. "So is Nussbaum."

"Okay, so my theory has a few holes that need filling. But it's real, Eliza." Tears welled up in his eyes, he staggered drunkenly along, moving more and more slowly with each step. "He's probably back in 1984, stuck in the Gaslight theatre, watching *Footloose* with Nikki Felcher and her mall hair and their matching Swatches. Oh, man, he didn't bargain for that one, did he?"

"Peter was dying. He had cancer."

"Bullshit. Not Peter."

"He'd been sick for a while, but finally went to the doctor a few weeks ago. By then it was too late. It was in his brain. There was nothing they could do."

"I'm not gonna listen to this. You don't believe it. I know you don't. Peter's doctor was in on it, the whole thing. North Dakota, the Russians, Hatch. It was a ploy to get—. It's FAKE NEWS, Eliza! Fake. Fake. Fake." Malcolm crumpled then, falling to his knees in the soft, dry soil, tears streaming down his face, snot oozing onto his lips. Eliza stood next to him, her hand on his head, like an ancient healer. "Dumbest fucking art project ever," Malcolm bellowed. "He calls that shit original? Suicide by mine cave in? Dime-a-fucking-dozen. It's about as authentic as an oil painting from IKEA. Goddamnit Peter. Goddamn you fucking coward."

Etcitty, who had been trying to mind his own business, stopped, bowed his head, then turned and walked back to the couple. He squatted down and gently took both of Brautigan's hands in his. Without looking Brautigan in the eyes, he stood, pulling Malcolm up with him.

Malcolm teetered limply, sobbing. "Ohhh, Eliza. I am so, so sorry."

"I know, Malcolm, I know. So am I," she said, tears streaming down her face. "But you're right. It was a stupid fucking artwork."

"It got a little messy out there," said Etcitty as he drove along the bumpy road, his windshield spider-webbed with cracks and a single bullet hole. "Hank and I got to the end of the road and no sooner had I stopped than someone named Ace comes bolting out of the trees and pretty much yanks us out of the truck. Seconds later, the shot came. She saved our lives."

Tipped off by Malcolm's brother Joshua, Etcitty and Hank Love had assembled — with the help of Lisa Yazzie — a ragtag team made up of a demographic cross-section of the county: men and women with white skin and brown, long-hair and clean-cut, old, young, ATV-riding, Toyota-driving, AR-15-toting, and one rotund old, suspender-wearing man named Ben, with a holstered, rusty six-shooter hanging off his belt. It was like a melange of *Mad Max*, the Coalition for Navajo Liberation, Burning Man, the Pecos Archaeologists' Conference, and a Monticello Stakehouse meeting of the LDS Church, all converging on a high desert battlefield. Many of them — inspired by Juan Lopez-Shapiro's article — were fresh off of running Bill Stevens and Stan Hatch out of the area, and were ready for more.

They'd gathered at the beginning of the Leetso Canyon road, and Etcitty and Love had gone on ahead, ordering the heavily armed team to hang back and proceed cautiously after a half-hour. After pulling Etcitty and Love out of the line of fire, Ace had given them her version of what was happening: Ivan Ivanov's Clearwater people were trying to reach the HB235 so that they could use the uranium within for nefarious purposes, while Tasha Ivanova, Simons, and Nussbaum were trying to get there first to stop them. Clearwater had several gunmen scattered throughout the trees, including a sniper somewhere on the mesa top who was shooting to kill. Meanwhile, Gaia — the woman posing as an adventure-capitalist — already had her drone in the air, and was able to direct the offensive. While the big crew went out in search of the Clearwater troops, Love and Etcitty targeted the sniper.

"Somehow we managed to rout the Clearwater people with only a few casualties, mostly thanks to Hank's sharpshooting skills. That woman really is something."

"Hank killed Tasha?"

"No, no. That was the Clearwater sniper. He was able to fire off the fatal shot just seconds before Hank got a clear headshot on him. She's really beating herself up about it. She's like that, you know?"

The swaying, bumping, and jiggling caused by fast speeds on the rough road lulled both Santos and Brautigan into silence. Brautigan had his novel's manuscript in his lap, cherishing and dreading its weight on his legs. Etcitty's deputy had found it in one of the Clearwater trucks. Fine moondust rose up behind the truck. Everything was still terribly dry. The previous night's downpour had been an isolated, hyperlocal event, and had done zero to alleviate the drought conditions all around them. The tips of the needles on many of the piñon trees they passed had turned brown, and the sky still had a gauzy, smoky feel.

"Sheriff, have you ever seen anything like that storm last night? Such an isolated downpour?"

"Can't say I have. But you know what the craziest thing is? There was another storm just like it, right at the same time, over near Durango, where that fire was burning. Didn't put it out, but the firefighters are finally getting a handle on it."

"I've heard that fires can create their own weather. Maybe that's it," said Brautigan, without necessarily believing the words.

As the vehicle rounded a big curve and left the shadow of Elk Ridge, Etcitty picked up his radio's mic and called dispatch to let them know he was in radio range again and was bringing the two back to their car in Bluff. The crackly voice of the dispatcher responded with news that the Fry Canyon Energy site and the Bears Ears Adventure Resort both had been vandalized. The dispatcher then switched to Navajo, and let out a string of sentences that caused Etcitty to chuckle.

After signing off, Etcitty turned to his passengers: "She says that they put up a pumpjack right in front of the Bears Ears resort, and filled up the swimming pool with oilfield wastewater. They also managed to hack into the self-driving thumper trucks at Fry Canyon and now they trucks are running loose along the highways. Melanie took it upon herself to track the trajectories, and they all seem to be headed toward Grand Junction. Any idea why?"

Santos and Brautigan looked at each other silently. It appeared as if the Bureau of Land Management and the RosaBit regional office were about to get

246

a visit from some very large vehicles.

"Whoever did it left their John Hancock in graffiti. 'Coyote was here,' at the adventure resort, and 'Beware Changing Bear Woman,' at Fry Canyon. You wouldn't happen to know who that might be, would ya?"

Santos and Brautigan both smiled. "What about the Acme Queen, Sheriff?"

"Lisa Yazzie said we should go check it out, and my deputies did. Nothing there. Portal's caved in. No sign that anything's happened there in ages. Why? Do you know something I don't?"

"No. Just curious." Eliza and Brautigan looked at each other, but said no more.

"I did get my missing deputy back," Etcitty said. "Turns out he got stung by a wasp or something and had an allergic reaction and blacked out for a good twelve hours before coming to and walking out of there."

"Tell me about it," Brautigan said.

"Strangest thing, though. They still haven't found that tar sand lady's body. Must be getting pretty ripe by now."

The vehicle rolled up to the intersection with Highway 95. Etcitty, a little groggy, rolled through the stop sign out of habit, like he had done dozens of times before, but as the vehicle eased out into the eastbound lane, directly into the path of a large truck, Eliza let out a little yelp, and Etcitty hit the brakes. It was the strangest sight: A caravan of leviathan vehicles floating eastward along the highway's heat shimmer, a whole line of ragged, dirty trucks, their trailers loaded down with odd apparatus studded with colorful lights, out here on this otherwise empty road.

"Well would you look at that," Etcitty said, as the caravan rolled past. "It's the circus!"

Indeed, it was.

Perhaps it was the datura kicking back in, but Brautigan could have sworn that all the trucks and the two buses had the same logo on the side and, written in a retro-typeface, the bold words: "Circus Borislava."

Spirals

Etcitty dropped the two off at Eliza's car, still parked in Bluff. Eliza unlocked the doors, threw her pack in the back, pointed at the cooler, then said she'd be right back. She walked across the road to Magpie Trading Post, past the old jalopy out front and the stone building, and walked through a little gate in the fence and out into the knee-high field of alfalfa, waiting for the first cutting of hay. She walked directly to the spot where, many Septembers before, she and Peter were married to one another, and collapsed into the ditch-muddied earth, her body spasming with sobs.

Brautigan stood helplessly by the car. He wanted to go to her, to do something to soothe the pain, to stem the tide of grief that washed over her. But he had nothing to give except a hollow ache that ran from his eyebrows right down to his toes.

When she finally stood back up, her knees covered in red mud, she was in exactly the same place and stance as when she and Peter had read their wedding vows.

Peter had taken it upon himself to write their vows. He agonized over them for weeks, but on the morning of the big day had only several lines of verse that resembled the riddle Peter had sent Malcolm. Finally, that morning, a hungover-Peter asked a hungover-Malcolm for help. Malcolm didn't hesitate. He ran over to the cafe, ordered an entire pot of coffee, brought it back, and the two of them sat right over there, in the shade of that old cottonwood, brainstorming, writing, rewriting, and rewriting those lines again to — as his former editor Laurel used to say — make them sing.

Malcolm had certainly put more time into stories and essays before, but never had he put more of himself into his words than he did on that tempestuous early autumn morning surrounded by stone and sky. It may have been an act of sublimation, of channeling his *eros* for Eliza into something transcendent, but it was mainly an act of love for Peter, who in his own peculiar way had always been there for Brautigan and had goaded him on to live his best life. And Malcolm had forged those lines of their vows with the knowledge that his two most intimate friends would now be together, forever.

God, did those lines ever sing. And the catch in Peter's voice as he read, and the look in Eliza's eyes as she gulped up the lines while standing in the calf-high alfalfa that glowed in the muted sunlight, against a backdrop of sandstone cliffs illuminated as if from within, brought everyone to tears, and would have convinced even the most jaded cynic, with the most battered and hardened heart, that this world may be broken but it will always be flooded with beauty, and that love really does exist and can overcome almost anything, and that, yes, words do have weight, and meaning, and power.

It wasn't until puffy-eyed Eliza had returned to find a similarly puffy-eyed Malcolm leaning against the car and smiling weakly, not until she had pulled a couple cold pops out of the cooler, tossing one to Brautigan, and not until both of them had climbed wordlessly into the car, that they noticed the manila envelope that had been pinned under the windshield wipers. It was addressed to M.P. Brautigan and E.F. Santos. Eliza got out, grabbed it, and tore it open. She held up a copy of the *Durango Herald*, dated June 21, 1978.

It was just a newspaper, yellowing with age, notable mostly for the naive-seeming ads, the retro graphics, and the bulk of the thing. Stories about the energy crisis and Jimmy Carter. A followup on the Lake Emma disaster up in Silverton. *Grease* and *Jaws 2* were showing at the relatively new Gaslight Theater. A Durango doctor was conducting a study of high incidences of lung cancer on the south side of town, which he attributed to the uranium tailings pile that sat on the banks of the river there.

Brautigan flipped through the rest of the paper, and sat up when he saw the front page of the arts and entertainment section, and a black and white picture of a gentle-looking woman with glasses and a head of unkempt hair: Yvonne Martin, the painter. She stood in the old Fort Lewis College art gallery, her paintings hanging on the walls behind her.

"Peter really admired her work. That must have been one of her early shows."

"Yeah. Her landscapes ... no one could capture the play of light and stone and sage and beauty and ... desire like she could. That woman could see. And feel. And paint."

"And everything she did was true. That's the remarkable part. She was fearless when it came to the truth."

He read the story. He studied the photo of the artist and the work hanging behind her. And that's when he finally saw it, and understood so much more about his friend Peter, about the painting Peter burned on the solstice so many years before, and about his pathological quest for authenticity. For there, hanging on the wall behind Martin, was the painting of the woman, the eyeball, the thread or web, the stormy sky. The caption said the painting's title was "The Male Gaze," which, frankly, made a hell of a lot more sense than Peter's title. And standing with their backs to their camera, gazing at the painting, were two people, a boy with a terrible haircut, wearing a striped shirt and blue jeans; and another, taller boy, with lighter hair. The old photo was faded, but Brautigan could have placed the two anywhere. It was the boy named Malcolm Brautigan and his friend Peter Simons.

"Hey, Eliza."

"Yeah?"

"Thank you."

Sacrifice for the Sun II

"How does it end? Your novel. What happens to the brothers?"
Eliza Santos' dark hair, salted with strands of grey, fluttered upward with the wind as she crouched on the sandstone at the end of the world, meticulously stacking stones, building the altar for the sacrifice. It was the summer solstice. Malcolm Brautigan sat crosslegged on the stone a few yards away, watching intently as she worked, the observation of her meditative act an act of meditation itself. From his point of view, Santos seemed to be hovering over the abyss, for she was only a few feet away from Cedar Mesa's southern edge, where it made an abrupt, thousand foot drop, and where the world unfurled before anyone fortunate enough to stand here. His manuscript from so long ago sat next to him.

"I don't really remember how it ends," he said. "I don't even remember writing it. First tell me what the hell was going on out there at the Happy Bonanza. What did Nussbaum say to you? And Peter?"

"Honestly, it didn't make much sense. The cancer was in Peter's brain already and it was clearly interfering with his thoughts. Nussbaum's words were just as confusing. They were both working with Tasha on something related to the Happy Bonanza."

"Like what? Building a bomb? Neutralizing the uranium with Boradine? Making art? I don't get it. And what the hell is Project Petrichor?"

"Project what?"

"Tasha said something about it on the radio that night."

"Beats me. Maybe that's what Peter and Tasha were talking about right before it all went to hell in a hand-basket. They got all emotional and huggy and said the project was a success, thanks to you."

"Me? What the hell did I do?"

"I think you provided the memory."

251

"But they knew where the Happy Bonanza was. They didn't need my memories."

"They didn't know how to get inside. Hildebrandt had locked it, and it was accessible only with a code that he had written in a closet in your old house. They were gambling on the possibility that you had seen the code, and that it was floating around somewhere deep in your residual memory bank."

"Why didn't they just, you know, ask me for the code?"

"And what would you have said? You wouldn't have had any idea what they were talking about. Or you would have made something up. Memories like that need to be nurtured, brought slowly to the surface, lest they get jumbled or erased or ... faked. Speaking of, where's your sacrifice?"

Brautigan pulled out his phone, and held it up for Santos to see and then, with the touch of the screen, he deleted the *Alt-News* site — and for that matter, Juan Lopez-Shapiro — forever. Then he reached back and threw the phone as hard as he could out into the emptiness, this time making sure that he cleared the bench below, and that the device made it all the way to the bottom of the cliff.

"I hope that didn't hit anyone," Eliza said. "And I also hope you know that won't undo all the damage you've done."

"I do know that. I really do. I'm sorry."

"Don't apologize to me, apologize to the truth."

Brautigan looked down and sighed. He felt as if he'd just awoken from a long and troubled dream. "I know, I know. By the way, I got an email from Matt Jaramillo, the guy who owns the *Dandelion Times*. He wants to take this winter off. Wants me to run the paper for a few months. I think I might do it."

"A whole winter in Silverton? There goes your plan to get sober."

"Yeah, let's just hope it snows a bit this year," he said, looking out at the darkening sky. "You know the riddle-poem? Do you think Peter sent it, or Tasha? And was it just to jog my memory, or did it mean something?"

"Oh, Peter sent it for sure. I think it was a weird way of saying goodbye. He loved you, you know? He loved to tell stories about your zany adventures together, and he also admired you for sticking to your guns, and standing up for your homeland."

"Admired *me*?"

"Yes. I mean, the fake news thing might have put a damper on that. Or he may have seen it as the ultimate work of art. He was a bit amoral about things like that. But deep down he regretted leaving to go to New York instead of staying and launching your nutty collective with you. He just wasn't very good at expressing this stuff, or picking up the phone and calling you."

"And why didn't I call him? What the hell is wrong with us? If I had known he was sick."

"You and me both."

"I just wish I understood what he was trying to do out there. I don't get it. And I sure as hell don't understand the artwork. I mean, it was heavy, and all, but sorta anticlimactic."

"He said something funny about the clouds. He said that they were the artwork, not the images he projected into the sky. What's that supposed to mean, Malcolm? He said that it would become clear, that Tasha would explain it, and that she'd even pay us for our troubles, and help you finance your collective."

"But Tasha's gone. They're all gone."

"I'm sorry, Malcolm. It seems as if the whole thing went wrong. Unless ..."

"Unless what?"

"Unless it all went precisely as planned."

The temperature had dropped a good twenty degrees from the day before, and dark clouds had gathered into a soft, thick comforter that reached from one horizon to the other without interruption, creating the kind of subdued light that portrait photographers dream of. The potholes on this point remained dry, however, the life that they contained still desiccated and dormant.

Eliza determined that her altar was complete, and stepped back. The wind picked up, warm and soft on their sunburnt faces.

"Isn't it weird that summer begins on the solstice?" Malcolm said. "It seems like it's been summer forever already."

"Yes, forever. As if it will never end. As if the other seasons have just vanished."

"What are you going to sacrifice?"

Santos smiled sadly. She gazed off the edge of the world, down to the Goosenecks of the San Juan River, to the spires of Monument Valley, to the dark hump of Navajo Mountain. Then she reached into a large tote bag and pulled out Peter's painting that wasn't really his, even though he had been the one to wield the brushes. "Here's hoping the seasons return," Eliza said, as she flicked the lighter and set the thick, dry paper aflame. "It's funny. These days stealing an idea from someone else and putting it into your own painting wouldn't even raise an eyebrow. And yet, this haunted Peter his whole life."

"He burned Yvonne's painting that night out here, didn't he? The original. She gave it to Peter's parents after that show when we were kids and they were too puritanical to hang such a weird painting of a naked woman on their wall.

So they hid it away in the attic. Peter must have found it, copied it, put his own name on it, and then burned it so no one would know."

"Yes, and you threw your novel off the edge, only Peter rescued it. You haven't answered my question. How does it end?"

He pulled off the brittle old rubber band and opened the box. He flipped past the title page to the dedication, hoping to refresh his memory. "For my friend, Peter," it said. On the next page, some verses of a poem by Richard Shelton. And then page one:

My old car creaked and bobbed along the two-track road over an undulating sea of stone, the wailing of an Ennio Morricone cassette slicing through the silent night. After coming to a stop, I killed the music, then the engine, then the headlights, and Peter and I sat silently and uncertainly, listening to the motor's ticks and gurgles as our eyes and ears adjusted. Starlight and silent satellites and the blinking red and white beacons of jet planes carrying their human loads from L.A. to New York or Denver or Chicago scraped away at the moonless night. I envied and pitied those aboard the cramped aluminum tubes.

Peter began to speak: "Malcolm, I ..."

"I know, it's a big leap, Peter," I said rapidly, not wanting to hear what Peter had to say. "I know we've been talking about this forever, but this is it. I've got a line on a building, an old fruit warehouse out toward Bayfield, and get this, I even found a printing press. Hand-cranked. We can print our own books. I figure we call it the Animas Art Collective. Or maybe the Durango Art and Culture Collective? Except I want it to be political, too, you know? I want to change the way people think and do things. To be a catalyst for a paradigm shift. Or is just calling it a 'collective' enough?"

Malcolm put the pages back, closed the box.

"Well?"

"It hasn't ended yet, Eliza. I think it's just beginning."

She looked back at him, her face scrunching up in that inquisitive way of hers.

"The rain's coming."

"At last."

A big drop splattered on the sandstone beside them, evaporating immediately, and then a swarm of them, pulling from the stone the metallic odor of ozone and blood. The scent triggered memories, memories from eons ago, when the sea was here and the air humid and sultry, and it triggered memories of just weeks earlier, when Malcolm sat on the stoop outside his apartment and gazed out into the smoky city night, and Natalya urged him to remember her.

Another orb of rain splashed Brautigan cold on the cheek. Thunder rumbled in the distance. He looked to the sky and the clouds and considered the sweet relief they would bring. And for just a brief moment he understood it all, and realized that Peter's artwork wasn't that stupid after all.

The raindrops grew more insistent and the two stood up, not to seek shelter but to revel in the rain. Malcolm trembled. Eliza laughed. Then she wrapped her arms around him and pressed her body into his. They anchored one another to this earth, this beautiful old earth. The raindrops sped downward from the heavens, giving in to gravity's sweet ache, at last, wetting stone and sand and sending a signal to the strange and ancient creatures slumbering in the thin lining of dust at the bottom of the potholes: It's time to wake up, to ply the warm waters, to live, if only for a flittering moment.

Malcolm Brautigan felt himself exhale deeply, and then inhale, and then again. Because you can't hold your breath forever.

Acknowledgments

Writing a novel can be quite the journey, not just for the author, but also for those who have to live with the author. And so, I owe a huge debt of gratitude to Wendy — my wife, my love, my inspiration — who has not only tolerated this process, but also supported it emotionally and financially and creatively. She also read the awful early drafts and didn't throw them — or me — out the window. I appreciate that.

Thanks also to Kirsten Johanna Allen, of the wonderful Torrey House Press, Shawna Bethell, Jay Canode, and Steve List for reading the manuscript and giving candid, helpful feedback. You all made this book far better than it was before.

And a big pile of thanks to the folks who contributed to the Lost Souls Press crowdfunding campaign. You enabled me to get this venture off the ground. I couldn't have done it without you. My plans for a grand launch party were dashed by the pandemic, but I hope we can still do it, we'll just have to wait a bit.

And, as always, thank you to my parents for instilling within me a love for the written word, and for the Four Corners Country.

— Jonathan P. Thompson
September 2020

SNOWSCREEN

A Malcolm Brautigan and
Eliza Santos Novel
By
Jonathan P. Thompson

Forthcoming Autumn 2021
***

Prologue

"Powder snow skiing is not fun. It is life, fully lived, life lived in a blaze of reality. What we experience in powder is the original human self, which lies deeply inside each of us, still undamaged in spite of what our present culture tries to do to us. Once experienced, this kind of living is recognized as the only way to live — fully aware of the earth and the sky and the gods and you, the mortal playing among them.

— Dolores LaChapelle, writer, skier, scholar, mountain-lover.

"The study of slides is a science, and the study comes pretty close to getting the answers but not close enough. About the only good rule is not to go in a storm. They ask us how an accident could have been prevented in many slides. The best answer to that is — They should have stayed in bed."

— Louie Dalla, longtime road supervisor for the Silverton District of the Colorado Department of Transportation.

January 6, sometime in the not too distant future

Randy Glaxson leans his tall frame against the trunk of a spruce tree to catch his breath and looks out across the field of snow, its surface glistening as if it were crusted with diamonds. The effort- and elevation-induced hypoxia has fogged up the vocabulary portion of his brain almost as severely as his breath clouds his eyeglasses, and he can't find the right word to describe what he's looking at. "Field" doesn't cut it. Maybe tilted plane? Anyway, this particular tilted plane is the loading zone for the North Battleship, a sizable avalanche path and, when the conditions are right, an excellent ski run that plummets off of a ridge west of Silverton, Colorado.

Glaxson is a snow scientist. That is, he's a hydrologist whose focus is snow, its composition, structure, dynamics, and, particularly, the ways in which the structure of the snow on a tilted plane like this one can disintegrate

Prologue

"Powder snow skiing is not fun. It is life, fully lived, life lived in a blaze of reality. What we experience in powder is the original human self, which lies deeply inside each of us, still undamaged in spite of what our present culture tries to do to us. Once experienced, this kind of living is recognized as the only way to live — fully aware of the earth and the sky and the gods and you, the mortal playing among them.

— Dolores LaChapelle, writer, skier, scholar, mountain-lover.

"The study of slides is a science, and the study comes pretty close to getting the answers but not close enough. About the only good rule is not to go in a storm. They ask us how an accident could have been prevented in many slides. The best answer to that is — They should have stayed in bed."

— Louie Dalla, longtime road supervisor for the Silverton District of the Colorado Department of Transportation.

January 6, sometime in the not too distant future

Randy Glaxson leans his tall frame against the trunk of a spruce tree to catch his breath and looks out across the field of snow, its surface glistening as if it were crusted with diamonds. The effort- and elevation-induced hypoxia has fogged up the vocabulary portion of his brain almost as severely as his breath clouds his eyeglasses, and he can't find the right word to describe what he's looking at. "Field" doesn't cut it. Maybe tilted plane? Anyway, this particular tilted plane is the loading zone for the North Battleship, a sizable avalanche path and, when the conditions are right, an excellent ski run that plummets off of a ridge west of Silverton, Colorado.

Glaxson is a snow scientist. That is, he's a hydrologist whose focus is snow, its composition, structure, dynamics, and, particularly, the ways in which the structure of the snow on a tilted plane like this one can disintegrate

SNOWSCREEN

A Malcolm Brautigan and
Eliza Santos Novel
By
Jonathan P. Thompson

Forthcoming Autumn 2021
***

catastrophically. He's an avalanche guy, in other words. And the tiny town of Silverton, which sits at 9,318 feet in elevation, surrounded by mountains that rise up some four-thousand feet higher that are covered for several months out of the year by a notoriously unstable snowpack, has more snow scientists per capita than anywhere else on the planet. The fifty miles of highway over three mountain passes, with Silverton smack dab in the center, is the most avalanche-riddled in the lower forty-eight. Snow slides once buried miners with frightening regularity, crushed and splintered entire boarding houses, took out mining trams, killed snowplow drivers. On St. Patrick's Day 1906, two dozen died in the tiny county in a single twenty-four hour period. Back in sixty-three, a reverend and his two daughters and their car were buried so thoroughly that the bodies didn't emerge until the May thaw. These days — assuming there is snow to slide, which isn't a given anymore — the victims are more likely to be backcountry skiers, ice climbers, or snowmobilers, folks who invariably will be eulogized as having died doing what they loved.

Glaxson, standing in the relative safety of the forest, looks back out at the slide path and genuflects — he does it instinctually, out of respect for his lost comrade, despite the fact that he rebuffed Catholicism when he was a teenager. Just days earlier, the North Battleship claimed its latest victim, a snow safety professional and one of Glaxson's former students. Glaxson is here to try to understand what happened, or maybe just to come to terms with it. He's read the accident report already, and with an additional six inches of snow piled atop the accident scene he's unlikely to glean any new information by coming here. And yet something about it all bothers him, like a subtle itch that you just can't reach.

He takes off his pack and hangs it on a branch poking out from the tree and pulls a long, icy draw off of his water bottle. He removes the little shovel from the pack, and then pauses, opens the pack again, pulls out a Butterfinger, unwraps it, takes a bite, and revels in its frozen crispy sweetness. He'll save the Dr. Pepper until he's done. He peers through foggy glasses in the direction from which he came, looking for a sign that his companions are near, but sees nothing but spruce and fir boughs and a pine marten bounding across the snow.

He looks back out to the loading zone, and tries to mentally map the accident. The report said that Scott had dug a snow pit. But Glaxson sees no evidence of one. Perhaps the group had entered the slide from the opposite side — they had been brought in by chopper, after all — and dug the pit there. Scott hadn't liked what he saw, so he told his companions that he would ski a line skirting the trees while they watched him from the top of the ridge. He'd only made three or four turns before triggering the slide. The witnesses said they immediately lost sight of him, and called for help right away. It was too late.

Had Scott known what was coming? Did he feel the snow settle with the telltale *whoomph* before the entire upper layer failed? Or had his deep powder rapture wrapped him in a cocoon of oblivion as the wave of white inundated him? More importantly: What the hell had compelled him to try to ski this thing rather than just call the chopper back to pick them up or find a safer way down? What had driven the group to come out here that morning, just after a big dump had piled three feet of snow on top of a deep, rotten layer?

Glaxson steps away from the tree, just to the edge of the clear area, and starts digging, methodically removing the snow in blocks so that he has a flat cross-section of the snowpack to analyze. Layer after layer of snow, with subtle differences between each — a timeline of the winter every bit as revealing as the geological timeline that is laid bare in deep road cuts and gorges. Beneath the first several centimeters of new snow he sees what Scott must have seen: a layer about a meter thick that has bonded well, and in which major slabs could form. Admittedly, it would have been sweet to catch some freshies in that layer. But it sat atop another meter of granular, faceted depth hoar with about the same bonding power as sugar: absolutely none. Together they make up a recipe for catastrophe.

Glaxson stops digging and steps back into the trees, again looking and listening for his missing companions. "Where the hell are they?" He mutters. "I knew Malcolm was out of shape, but damn it's taking him a long time. And Mary should have been right behind me. Eliza is usually way ahead of me." A burning sensation rises from his gut to his throat. Something is wrong. Or maybe they are just lallygagging — again.

He looks back out at the North Battleship and ponders its stillness. There may be nothing so tranquil, so pure-looking, as a vast field of untracked snow, all a homogenous shade of white: A blank canvas on which an aspen tree casts a shadowy self portrait, where even a tiny mouse's tracks are visible. But to the snow scientist the virgin snow field is anything but empty or static. It is world of heterogeneous motion: multifaceted, stratified, dynamic, seething.

Even now, as Glaxson analyzes the snow, it is changing. It is flowing, thawing, freezing, gliding, creeping, settling, subliming, rotting, transpiring, trickling, diffusing. It is, as the great snow scientist Ed LaChapelle put it, "a granular disco-elastic solid close to its melting point. You can't make it much more complicated than that." It is constantly experiencing destructive metamorphism.

only made three or four turns before triggering the slide. The witnesses said they immediately lost sight of him, and called for help right away. It was too late.

Had Scott known what was coming? Did he feel the snow settle with the telltale *whoomph* before the entire upper layer failed? Or had his deep powder rapture wrapped him in a cocoon of oblivion as the wave of white inundated him? More importantly: What the hell had compelled him to try to ski this thing rather than just call the chopper back to pick them up or find a safer way down? What had driven the group to come out here that morning, just after a big dump had piled three feet of snow on top of a deep, rotten layer?

Glaxson steps away from the tree, just to the edge of the clear area, and starts digging, methodically removing the snow in blocks so that he has a flat cross-section of the snowpack to analyze. Layer after layer of snow, with subtle differences between each — a timeline of the winter every bit as revealing as the geological timeline that is laid bare in deep road cuts and gorges. Beneath the first several centimeters of new snow he sees what Scott must have seen: a layer about a meter thick that has bonded well, and in which major slabs could form. Admittedly, it would have been sweet to catch some freshies in that layer. But it sat atop another meter of granular, faceted depth hoar with about the same bonding power as sugar: absolutely none. Together they make up a recipe for catastrophe.

Glaxson stops digging and steps back into the trees, again looking and listening for his missing companions. "Where the hell are they?" He mutters. "I knew Malcolm was out of shape, but damn it's taking him a long time. And Mary should have been right behind me. Eliza is usually way ahead of me." A burning sensation rises from his gut to his throat. Something is wrong. Or maybe they are just lallygagging — again.

He looks back out at the North Battleship and ponders its stillness. There may be nothing so tranquil, so pure-looking, as a vast field of untracked snow, all a homogenous shade of white: A blank canvas on which an aspen tree casts a shadowy self portrait, where even a tiny mouse's tracks are visible. But to the snow scientist the virgin snow field is anything but empty or static. It is world of heterogeneous motion: multifaceted, stratified, dynamic, seething.

Even now, as Glaxson analyzes the snow, it is changing. It is flowing, thawing, freezing, gliding, creeping, settling, subliming, rotting, transpiring, trickling, diffusing. It is, as the great snow scientist Ed LaChapelle put it, "a granular disco-elastic solid close to its melting point. You can't make it much more complicated than that." It is constantly experiencing destructive metamorphism.

catastrophically. He's an avalanche guy, in other words. And the tiny town of Silverton, which sits at 9,318 feet in elevation, surrounded by mountains that rise up some four-thousand feet higher that are covered for several months out of the year by a notoriously unstable snowpack, has more snow scientists per capita than anywhere else on the planet. The fifty miles of highway over three mountain passes, with Silverton smack dab in the center, is the most avalanche-riddled in the lower forty-eight. Snow slides once buried miners with frightening regularity, crushed and splintered entire boarding houses, took out mining trams, killed snowplow drivers. On St. Patrick's Day 1906, two dozen died in the tiny county in a single twenty-four hour period. Back in sixty-three, a reverend and his two daughters and their car were buried so thoroughly that the bodies didn't emerge until the May thaw. These days — assuming there is snow to slide, which isn't a given anymore — the victims are more likely to be backcountry skiers, ice climbers, or snowmobilers, folks who invariably will be eulogized as having died doing what they loved.

Glaxson, standing in the relative safety of the forest, looks back out at the slide path and genuflects — he does it instinctually, out of respect for his lost comrade, despite the fact that he rebuffed Catholicism when he was a teenager. Just days earlier, the North Battleship claimed its latest victim, a snow safety professional and one of Glaxson's former students. Glaxson is here to try to understand what happened, or maybe just to come to terms with it. He's read the accident report already, and with an additional six inches of snow piled atop the accident scene he's unlikely to glean any new information by coming here. And yet something about it all bothers him, like a subtle itch that you just can't reach.

He takes off his pack and hangs it on a branch poking out from the tree and pulls a long, icy draw off of his water bottle. He removes the little shovel from the pack, and then pauses, opens the pack again, pulls out a Butterfinger, unwraps it, takes a bite, and revels in its frozen crispy sweetness. He'll save the Dr. Pepper until he's done. He peers through foggy glasses in the direction from which he came, looking for a sign that his companions are near, but sees nothing but spruce and fir boughs and a pine marten bounding across the snow.

He looks back out to the loading zone, and tries to mentally map the accident. The report said that Scott had dug a snow pit. But Glaxson sees no evidence of one. Perhaps the group had entered the slide from the opposite side — they had been brought in by chopper, after all — and dug the pit there. Scott hadn't liked what he saw, so he told his companions that he would ski a line skirting the trees while they watched him from the top of the ridge. He'd

Snow is a quasi-living organism, in other words. And like all living things, it has the power to kill.

CPSIA information can be obtained
at www.ICGtesting.com
Printed in the USA
FSHW010509081220
76701FS